Andrew Lang

was born and raised at Selkirk, a Scottish border county. His nurse told him local tales and legends, and early in his life he developed a preference for fantasy and enchantment. A prominent member of the Folk Lore Society in London, he wrote a lengthy introduction for Charles Lamb's version of "Beauty and the Beast" in 1887, but it was in 1889 that he published *The Blue Fairy Book*, which made him famous. Lang emphasized that he did not create the stories, but took them "from those told by grannies to grandchildren in many countries and in many languages—French, Italian, Spanish, Catalan, Gaelic, Icelandic, Cherokee, African, Indian, Australian, Slavonic, Eskimo, and what not." The book was an immediate success, and Lang went on to bring out twelve collections of tales in all, the last book, *The Lilac Fairy Book*, in 1910. A man out of place in the modern world, he only reluctantly rode in automobiles, refused to ride in an airplane, and didn't wish to own a phone. But Andrew Lang collected dozens of fairy and folk tales that might have otherwise vanished and preserved them for children forever.

MICHAEL PATRICK HEARN is the acclaimed editor of *The Annotated Christmas Carol*, *The Annotated Wizard of Oz*, and *The Annotated Huckleberry Finn*. He is also the author of the afterwords to the Signet Classic editions of *Tom Brown's School Days* and *The Merry Adventures of Robin Hood*.

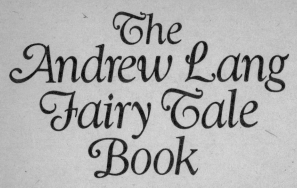

The Andrew Lang Fairy Tale Book

41 Stories from Around the World

EDITED AND
WITH AN AFTERWORD BY

MICHAEL PATRICK HEARN

A SIGNET CLASSIC

NEW AMERICAN LIBRARY

NEW YORK AND SCARBOROUGH, ONTARIO

For Margaret Coughlan
—M.P.H.

NAL BOOKS ARE AVAILABLE AT QUANTITY DISCOUNTS
WHEN USED TO PROMOTE PRODUCTS OR SERVICES.
FOR INFORMATION PLEASE WRITE TO PREMIUM MARKETING DIVISION,
NEW AMERICAN LIBRARY. 1633 BROADWAY.
NEW YORK. NEW YORK 10019.

Copyright © 1986 by Michael Patrick Hearn

C

SIGNET TRADEMARK REG. U.S. PAT. OFF. AND FOREIGN COUNTRIES
REGISTERED TRADEMARK—MARCA REGISTRADA
HECHO EN CHICAGO. U.S.A.

SIGNET, SIGNET CLASSIC, MENTOR, PLUME, MERIDIAN AND NAL BOOKS
are published *in the United States* by New American Library,
1633 Broadway, New York, New York 10019,
in Canada by The New American Library of Canada Limited,
81 Mack Avenue, Scarborough, Ontario M1L 1M8

First Signet Classic Printing, June, 1986

1 2 3 4 5 6 7 8 9

PRINTED IN THE UNITED STATES OF AMERICA

Contents

Ball-Carrier and the Bad One

AMERICAN INDIAN

———◆◆———

FAR, far in the forest there were two little huts, and in each of them lived a man who was a famous hunter, his wife, and three or four children. Now the children were forbidden to play more than a short distance from the door, as it was known that, away on the other side of the wood near the great river, there dwelt a witch who had a magic ball that she used as a means of stealing children.

Her plan was a very simple one, and had never yet failed. When she wanted a child she just flung her ball in the direction of the child's home, and however far off it might be, the ball was sure to reach it. Then, as soon as the child saw it, the ball would begin rolling slowly back to the witch, just keeping a little ahead of the child, so that he always thought that he could catch it the next minute. But he never did, and, what was more, his parents never saw him again.

Of course you must not suppose that all the fathers and mothers who had lost children made no attempts to find them, but the forest was so large, and the witch was so cunning in knowing exactly where they were going to search, that it was very easy for her to keep out of the way. Besides, there was always the chance that the children might have been eaten by wolves, of which large herds roamed about in winter.

One day the old witch happened to want a little boy, so she threw her ball in the direction of the hunters' huts. A child was standing outside, shooting at a mark with his bow and arrows, but the moment he saw the ball, which was made of glass whose blues and greens and whites, all frosted over, kept changing one into the other, he flung down his bow, and stooped to pick the ball up. But as he did so it began to roll very gently downhill. The boy could not let it roll away, when it was so close to him, so he gave chase. The ball seemed always within his grasp, yet he could never catch it; it went quicker and quicker, and the boy grew more and more excited. That time he almost touched it—no, he missed it by a hair's breadth! Now, surely, if he gave a spring he could get in front of it! He sprang forward, tripped and fell, and found himself in the witch's house!

"Welcome! welcome! grandson!" said she; "get up and rest yourself, for you have had a long walk, and I am sure you must be tired!" So the boy sat down, and ate some food which she gave him in a bowl. It was quite different from anything he had tasted before, and he thought it was delicious. When he had eaten up every bit, the witch asked him if he had ever fasted.

"No," replied the boy, "at least I have been obliged to sometimes, but never if there was any food to be had."

"You will have to fast if you want the spirits to make you strong and wise, and the sooner you begin the better."

"Very well," said the boy, "what do I do first?"

"Lie down on those buffalo skins by the door of the hut," answered she; and the boy lay down, and the squirrels and little bears and the birds came and talked to him.

At the end of ten days the old woman came to him with a bowl of the same food that he had eaten before.

"Get up, my grandson, you have fasted long enough.

Have the good spirits visited you, and granted you the strength and wisdom that you desire?"

"Some of them have come, and have given me a portion of both," answered the boy, "but many have stayed away from me."

"Then," said she, "you must fast ten days more."

So the boy lay down again on the buffalo skins, and fasted for ten days, and at the end of that time he turned his face to the wall, and fasted for twenty days longer. At length the witch called to him, and said:

"Come and eat something, my grandson." At the sound of her voice the boy got up and ate the food she gave him. When he had finished every scrap she spoke as before: "Tell me, grandson, have not the good spirits visited you all these many days that you have fasted?"

"Not all, grandmother," answered he; "there are still some who keep away from me and say that I have not fasted long enough."

"Then you must fast again," replied the old woman, "and go on fasting till you receive the gifts of *all* the good spirits. Not one must be missing."

The boy said nothing, but lay down for the third time on the buffalo skins, and fasted for twenty days more. And at the end of that time the witch thought he was dead, his face was so white and his body so still. But when she had fed him out of the bowl he grew stronger, and soon was able to sit up.

"You have fasted a long time," said she, "longer than anyone ever fasted before. Surely the good spirits must be satisfied *now*?"

"Yes, grandmother," answered the boy, "they have all come, and have given me their gifts."

This pleased the old woman so much that she brought him another basin of food, and while he was eating it she talked to him, and this is what she said: "Far away, on the other side of the great river, is the home of the Bad One. In his house is much gold, and what is more precious even than the gold, a little bridge, which lengthens out when the Bad One waves his hand, so that there is no river or sea that he cannot cross. Now I want that bridge and some of the gold for myself, and that is the reason that I have stolen so many boys by means of my ball. I have tried to teach them how to gain the gifts of the good spirits, but none of them would fast long enough, and at last I had to send them away to perform simple, easy little tasks. But you have been strong and faithful, and you can do this thing if you listen to what I tell you! When you reach the river tie this ball to your foot, and it will take you across— you cannot manage it in any other way. But do not be afraid; trust to the ball, and you will be quite safe!"

The boy took the ball and put it in a bag. Then he made himself a club and a bow, and some arrows which would fly further than anyone else's arrows, because of the strength the good spirits had given him. They had also bestowed on him the power of changing his shape, and had increased the quickness of his eyes and ears so that nothing escaped him. And in some way or other they made him understand that if he needed more help they would give it to him.

When all these things were ready the boy bade farewell to the witch and set out. He walked through the forest for several days without seeing anyone but his friends the squirrels and the bears and the birds, but though he stopped and spoke to them all, he was careful not to let them know where he was going.

At last, after many days, he came to the river, and beyond it he noticed a small hut standing on a hill which he guessed to be the home of the Bad One. But the stream flowed so quickly that he could not see how he was ever to cross it, and in order to test how swift the current really was, he broke a branch from a tree and threw it in. It seemed hardly to touch the water before it was carried away, and even his magic sight could not follow it. He could not help feeling frightened, but he hated giving up anything that he had once undertaken, and, fastening the ball on his right foot, he ventured on the river. To his surprise he was able to stand up; then a panic seized him, and he scrambled up the bank again. In a minute or two he plucked up courage to go a little further into the river, but again its width frightened him, and a second time he turned back. However, he felt rather ashamed of his cowardice, as it was quite clear that his ball *could* support him, and on his third trial he got safely to the other side.

Once there he replaced the ball in the bag, and looked carefully round him. The door of the Bad One's hut was open, and he saw that the ceiling was supported by great wooden beams, from which hung the bags of gold and the little bridge. He saw, too, the Bad One sitting in the midst of his treasures eating his dinner, and drinking something out of a horn. It was plain to the boy that he must invent some plan of getting the Bad One out of the way, or else he would never be able to steal the gold or the bridge.

What should he do? Give horrible shrieks as if he were in pain? But the Bad One would not care whether he were murdered or not! Call him by his name? But the Bad One was very cunning, and would suspect some trick. He must try something better than that! Then suddenly an idea came to him, and he gave a little jump of joy. "Oh, how stupid of me not to think of that before!" said he, and he wished with all his might that the Bad One should become very hungry—so hungry that he could not wait a moment for fresh food to be brought to him. And sure enough at that instant the Bad One called out to his servant, "You did not bring food that would satisfy a sparrow. Fetch some more at once, for I am perfectly starving." Then, without giving the woman time to go to the larder, he got up from his chair, and rolled, staggering from hunger, towards the kitchen.

Directly the door had closed on the Bad One the boy ran in, pulled down a bag of gold from the beam, and tucked it under his left arm. Next he unhooked the little bridge and put it under his right. He did not try to escape, as most boys of his age would have done, for the wisdom put into his mind by the good spirits taught him that before he could reach the river and make use of the bridge the Bad One would have tracked him by his footsteps and been upon him. So, making himself very small and thin, he hid himself behind a pile of buffalo skins in the corner, first tearing a slit through one of them, so that he could see what was going on.

He had hardly settled himself when the servant entered the room, and, as she did so, the last bag of gold on the beam fell to the ground—for they had begun to fall directly the boy had taken the first one. She cried to her master that someone had stolen both the bag and the bridge, and the Bad One rushed in, mad with anger, and bade her go and seek for footsteps outside, that they might find out where the thief had gone. In a few minutes she returned, saying that he must be in the house, as she could not see any footsteps leading to the river, and began to move all the furniture in the room, without discovering Ball-Carrier.

"But he *must* be here somewhere," she said to herself, examining for the second time the pile of buffalo skins; and Ball-Carrier, knowing that he could not possibly escape now, hastily wished that the Bad One should be unable to eat any more food at present.

"Ah, there is a slit in this one," cried the servant, shaking the skin; "and here he is." And she pulled out Ball-Carrier, looking so lean and small that he would hardly have made a mouthful for a sparrow.

"Was it you who took my gold and bridge?" asked the Bad One.

"Yes," answered Ball-Carrier, "it was I who took them."

The Bad One made a sign to the woman, who inquired where he had hidden them. He lifted his left arm where the gold was, and she picked up a knife and scraped his skin so that no gold should be left sticking to it.

"What have you done with the bridge?" said she. And he lifted his right arm, from which she took the

THE DEATH OF THE BAD ONE

bridge, while the Bad One looked on, well pleased. "Be sure that he does not run away," chuckled he. "Boil some water, and get him ready for cooking, while I go and invite my friends the water-demons to the feast."

The woman seized Ball-Carrier between her finger and thumb, and was going to carry him to the kitchen, when the boy spoke:

"I am very lean and small now," he said, "hardly worth the trouble of cooking; but if you were to keep me two days, and gave me plenty of food, I should get big and fat. As it is, your friends the water-demons would think you meant to laugh at them, when they found that *I* was the feast."

"Well, perhaps you are right," answered the Bad One; "I will keep you for two days." And he went out to visit the water-demons.

Meanwhile the servant, whose name was Lung-Woman, led him into a little shed, and chained him up to a ring in the wall. But food was given him every hour, and at the end of two days he was as fat and big as a Christmas turkey, and could hardly move his head from one side to the other.

"He will do now," said the Bad One, who came constantly to see how he was getting on. "I shall go and tell the water-demons that we expect them to dinner to-night. Put the kettle on the fire, but be sure on no account to taste the broth."

Lung-Woman lost no time in obeying her orders. She built up the fire, which had got very low, filled the kettle with water, and passing a rope which hung from the ceiling through the handle, swung it over the flames. Then she brought in Ball-Carrier, who, seeing all these preparations, wished that as long as *he* was in the kettle the water might not really boil, though it would hiss and bubble, and also, that the spirits would turn the water into fat.

The kettle soon began to sing and bubble, and Ball-Carrier was lifted in. Very soon the fat which was to make the sauce rose to the surface, and Ball-Carrier, who was bobbing about from one side to the other, called out that Lung-Woman had better taste the broth, as he thought that some salt should be added to it. The servant knew quite well that her master had forbidden her to do anything of the kind, but when once the idea was put into her head, she found the smell from the kettle so delicious that she unhooked a long ladle from the wall and plunged it into the kettle.

"You will spill it all, if you stand so far off," said the boy; "why don't you come a little nearer?" And as she did so he cried to the spirits to give him back his usual size and strength and to make the water scalding hot. Then he gave the kettle a kick, which upset all the boiling water upon her, and jumping over her body he seized once more the gold and the bridge, picked up his club and bow and arrows, and after setting fire to the Bad One's hut, ran down to the river, which he crossed safely by the help of the bridge.

The hut, which was made of wood, was burned to the ground before the Bad One came back with a large crowd of water-demons. There was not a sign of anyone or anything, so he started for the river, where he saw Ball-Carrier sitting quietly on the other side. Then the Bad One knew what had happened, and after telling the water-demons that there would be no feast after all, he called to Ball-Carrier, who was eating an apple.

"I know your name now," he said, "and as you have ruined me, and I am not rich any more, will you take me as your servant?"

"Yes, I will, though you have tried to kill me," answered Ball-Carrier, throwing the bridge across the water as he spoke. But when the Bad One was in the midst of the stream, the boy wished it to become small; and the Bad One fell into the water and was drowned, and the world was rid of him.

—*The Brown Fairy Book* (1904)

Beauty and the Beast

FRENCH

———◆◆◆———

ONCE upon a time, in a very far-off country, there lived
a merchant who had been so fortunate in all his undertakings that he was enormously rich. As he had, however, six sons and six daughters, he found that his
money was not too much to let them all have everything they fancied, as they were accustomed to do.

But one day a most unexpected misfortune befell
them. Their house caught fire and was speedily burnt
to the ground, with all the splendid furniture, the books,
pictures, gold, silver, and precious goods it contained;
and this was only the beginning of their troubles. Their
father, who had until this moment prospered in all
ways, suddenly lost every ship he had upon the sea,
either by dint of pirates, shipwreck, or fire. Then he
heard that his clerks in distant countries, whom he
trusted entirely, had proved unfaithful; and at last from
great wealth he fell into the direst poverty.

All that he had left was a little house in a desolate
place at least a hundred leagues from the town in which
he had lived, and to this he was forced to retreat with
his children, who were in despair at the idea of leading
such a different life. Indeed, the daughters at first
hoped that their friends, who had been so numerous
while they were rich, would insist on their staying in

their houses now they no longer possessed one. But they soon found that they were left alone, and that their former friends even attributed their misfortunes to their own extravagance, and showed no intention of offering them any help. So nothing was left for them but to take their departure to the cottage, which stood in the midst of a dark forest, and seemed to be the most dismal place upon the face of the earth. As they were too poor to have any servants, the girls had to work hard, like peasants, and the sons, for their part, cultivated the fields to earn their living. Roughly clothed, and living in the simplest way, the girls regretted unceasingly the luxuries and amusements of their former life; only the youngest tried to be brave and cheerful. She had been as sad as anyone when misfortune first overtook her father, but, soon recovering her natural gaiety, she set to work to make the best of things, to amuse her father and brothers as well as she could, and to try to persuade her sisters to join her in dancing and singing. But they would do nothing of the sort, and, because she was not as doleful as themselves, they declared that this miserable life was all she was fit for. But she was really far prettier and cleverer than they were; indeed, she was so lovely that she was always called Beauty. After two years, when they were all beginning to get used to their new life, something happened to disturb their tranquillity. Their father received the news that one of his ships, which he had believed to be lost, had come safely into port with a rich cargo. All the sons and daughters at once thought that their poverty was at an end, and wanted to set out directly for the town; but their father, who was more prudent, begged them to wait a little, and, though it was harvest-time, and he could ill be spared, determined to go himself first, to make inquiries. Only the youngest daughter had any doubt but that they would soon again be as rich as they were before, or at least rich enough to live comfortably in some town where they would find amusement and gay companions once more. So they all loaded their father with commissions for jewels and dresses which it would have taken a fortune to buy; only Beauty, feeling sure that it was of no use, did not ask for anything. Her father, noticing her silence, said: "And what shall I bring for you, Beauty?"

"The only thing I wish for is to see you come home safely," she answered.

But this reply vexed her sisters, who fancied she was blaming them for having asked for such costly things. Her father, however, was pleased, but as he thought that at her age she certainly ought to like pretty presents, he told her to choose something.

"Well, dear father," she said, "as you insist upon it, I beg that you will bring me a rose. I have not seen one since we came here, and I love them so much."

So the merchant set out and reached the town as quickly as possible, but only to find that his former companions, believing him to be dead, had divided between them the goods which the ship had brought; and after six months of trouble and expense he found himself as poor as when he started, having been able to recover only just enough to pay the cost of his journey. To make matters worse, he was obliged to leave the town in the most terrible weather, so that by the time he was within a few leagues of his home he was almost exhausted with cold and fatigue. Though he knew it would take some hours to get through the forest, he was so anxious to be at his journey's end that he resolved to go on; but night overtook him, and the deep snow and bitter frost made it impossible for his horse to carry him any further. Not a house was to be seen; the only shelter he could get was the hollow trunk of a great tree, and there he crouched all the night, which seemed to him the longest he had ever known. In spite of his weariness the howling of the wolves kept him awake, and even when at last the day broke he was not much better off, for the falling snow had covered up every path, and he did not know which way to turn.

At length he made out some sort of track, and though

at the beginning it was so rough and slippery that he
fell down more than once, it presently became easier,
and led him into an avenue of trees which ended in a
splendid castle. It seemed to the merchant very strange
that no snow had fallen in the avenue, which was entirely composed of orange trees, covered with flowers
and fruit. When he reached the first court of the castle
he saw before him a flight of agate steps, and went up
them, and passed through several splendidly furnished
rooms. The pleasant warmth of the air revived him, and
he felt very hungry; but there seemed to be nobody in
all this vast and splendid palace whom he could ask to
give him something to eat. Deep silence reigned everywhere, and at last, tired of roaming through empty
rooms and galleries, he stopped in a room smaller than
the rest, where a clear fire was burning and a couch was
drawn up cosily close to it. Thinking that this must be
prepared for someone who was expected, he sat down
to wait till he should come, and very soon fell into a
sweet sleep.

When his extreme hunger wakened him after several
hours, he was still alone; but a little table, upon which
was a good dinner, had been drawn up close to him,
and, as he had eaten nothing for twenty-four hours, he
lost no time in beginning his 'meal, hoping that he
might soon have an opportunity of thanking his consid-
erate entertainer, whoever it might be. But no one
appeared, and even after another long sleep, from which
he awoke completely refreshed, there was no sign of
anybody, though a fresh meal of dainty cakes and fruit
was prepared upon the little table at his elbow. Being
naturally timid, the silence began to terrify him, and he
resolved to search once more through all the rooms; but
it was of no use. Not even a servant was to be seen;
there was no sign of life in the palace! He began to
wonder what he should do, and to amuse himself by
pretending that all the treasures he saw were his own,
and considering how he would divide them among his
children. Then he went down into the garden, and

though it was winter everywhere else, here the sun shone, and the birds sang, and the flowers bloomed, and the air was soft and sweet. The merchant, in ecstacies with all he saw and heard, said to himself:

"All this must be meant for me. I will go this minute and bring my children to share all these delights."

In spite of being so cold and weary when he reached the castle, he had taken his horse to the stable and fed it. Now he thought he would saddle it for his homeward journey, and he turned down the path which led to the stable. This path had a hedge of roses on each side of it, and the merchant thought he had never seen or smelt such exquisite flowers. They reminded him of his promise to Beauty, and he stopped and had just gathered one to take to her when he was startled by a strange noise behind him. Turning round, he saw a frightful Beast, which seemed to be very angry and said, in a terrible voice:

"Who told you that you might gather my roses? Was it not enough that I allowed you to be in my palace and was kind to you? This is the way you show your gratitude, by stealing my flowers! But your insolence shall not go unpunished." The merchant, terrified by these furious words, dropped the fatal rose, and, throwing himself on his knees, cried: "Pardon me, noble sir. I am truly grateful to you for your hospitality, which was so magnificent that I could not imagine that you would be offended by my taking such a little thing as a rose." But the Beast's anger was not lessened by this speech.

"You are very ready with excuses and flattery," he cried; "but that will not save you from the death you deserve."

"Alas!" thought the merchant, "if my daughter Beauty could only know what danger her rose has brought me into!"

And in despair he began to tell the Beast all his misfortunes, and the reason of his journey, not forgetting to mention Beauty's request.

"A king's ransom would hardly have procured all that

my other daughters asked," he said; "but I thought that I might at least take Beauty her rose. I beg you to forgive me, for you see I meant no harm."

The Beast considered for a moment, and then he said, in a less furious tone:

"I will forgive you on one condition—that is, that you will give me one of your daughters."

"Ah!" cried the merchant, "if I were cruel enough to buy my own life at the expense of one of my children's, what excuse could I invent to bring her here?"

"No excuse would be necessary," answered the Beast. "If she comes at all she must come willingly. On no other condition will I have her. See if any one of them is courageous enough, and loves you well enough to come and save your life. You seem to be an honest man, so I will trust you to go home. I give you a month to see if either of your daughters will come back with you and stay here, to let you go free. If neither of them is willing, you must come alone, after bidding them good-bye for ever, for then you will belong to me. And do not imagine that you can hide from me, for if you fail to keep your word I will come and fetch you!" added the Beast grimly.

The merchant accepted this proposal, though he did not really think any of his daughters would be persuaded to come. He promised to return at the time appointed, and then, anxious to escape from the presence of the Beast, he asked permission to set off at once. But the Beast answered that he could not go until the next day.

"Then you will find a horse ready for you," he said. "Now go and eat your supper, and await my orders."

The poor merchant, more dead than alive, went back to his room, where the most delicious supper was already served on the little table which was drawn up before a blazing fire. But he was too terrified to eat, and only tasted a few of the dishes, for fear the Beast should be angry if he did not obey his orders. When he had finished he heard a great noise in the next room, which he knew meant that the Beast was coming. As he could do nothing to escape his visit, the only thing that remained was to seem as little afraid as possible; so when the Beast appeared and asked roughly if he had supped well, the merchant answered humbly that he had, thanks to his host's kindness. Then the Beast warned him to remember their agreement, and to prepare his daughter exactly for what she had to expect.

"Do not get up to-morrow," he added, "until you see the sun and hear a golden bell ring. Then you will find your breakfast waiting for you here, and the horse you are to ride will be ready in the courtyard. He will also bring you back again when you come with your daughter a month hence. Farewell. Take a rose to Beauty, and remember your promise!"

The merchant was only too glad when the Beast went away, and though he could not sleep for sadness, he lay down until the sun rose. Then, after a hasty breakfast, he went to gather Beauty's rose, and mounted his horse, which carried him off so swiftly that in an instant he had lost sight of the palace, and he was still wrapped in gloomy thoughts when it stopped before the door of the cottage.

His sons and daughters, who had been very uneasy at his long absence, rushed to meet him, eager to know the result of his journey, which, seeing him mounted upon a splendid horse and wrapped in a rich mantle, they supposed to be favourable. But he hid the truth from them at first, only saying sadly to Beauty as he gave her the rose:

"Here is what you asked me to bring you; you little know what it has cost."

But this excited their curiosity so greatly that presently he told them his adventures from beginning to end, and then they were all very unhappy. The girls lamented loudly over their lost hopes, and the sons declared that their father should not return to this terrible castle, and began to make plans for killing the Beast if it should come to fetch him. But he reminded them that he had promised to go back. Then the girls were very angry with Beauty, and said it was all her fault, and that if she had asked for something sensible this would never have happened, and complained bitterly that they should have to suffer for her folly.

Poor Beauty, much distressed, said to them:

"I have indeed caused this misfortune, but I assure you I did it innocently. Who could have guessed that to ask for a rose in the middle of summer would cause so much misery? But as I did the mischief it is only just that I should suffer for it. I will therefore go back with my father to keep his promise."

At first nobody would hear of this arrangement, and her father and brothers, who loved her dearly, declared that nothing should make them let her go; but Beauty was firm. As the time drew near she divided all her little possessions between her sisters, and said goodbye to everything she loved, and when the fatal day came she encouraged and cheered her father as they mounted together the horse which had brought him back. It seemed to fly rather than gallop, but so smoothly that Beauty was not frightened; indeed, she would have enjoyed the journey if she had not feared what might happen to her at the end of it. Her father still tried to persuade her to go back, but in vain. While they were talking the night fell, and then, to their great surprise, wonderful coloured lights began to shine in all directions, and splendid fireworks blazed out before them; all the forest was illuminated by them, and even felt pleasantly warm, though it had been bitterly cold before. This lasted until they reached the avenue of orange trees, where were statues holding flaming torches, and when they got nearer to the palace they saw that it was illuminated from the roof to the ground, and music sounded softly from the courtyard. "The Beast must be very hungry," said Beauty, trying to laugh, "if he makes all this rejoicing over the arrival of his prey."

But, in spite of her anxiety, she could not help admiring all the wonderful things she saw.

The horse stopped at the foot of the flight of steps leading to the terrace, and when they had dismounted her father led her to the little room he had been in before, where they found a splendid fire burning, and the table daintily spread with a delicious supper.

The merchant knew that this was meant for them, and Beauty, who was rather less frightened now that she had passed through so many rooms and seen nothing of the Beast, was quite willing to begin, for her long ride had made her very hungry. But they had hardly finished their meal when the noise of the Beast's footsteps was heard approaching, and Beauty clung to her father in terror, which became all the greater when she saw how frightened he was. But when the Beast really appeared, though she trembled at the sight of him, she made a great effort to hide her horror, and saluted him respectfully.

This evidently pleased the Beast. After looking at her he said, in a tone that might have struck terror into the boldest heart, though he did not seem to be angry:

"Good-evening, old man. Good-evening, Beauty."

The merchant was too terrified to reply, but Beauty answered sweetly:

"Good-evening, Beast."

"Have you come willingly?" asked the Beast. "Will you be content to stay here when your father goes away?"

Beauty answered bravely that she was quite prepared to stay.

"I am pleased with you," said the Beast. "As you have come of your own accord, you may stay. As for you, old man," he added, turning to the merchant, "at sunrise to-morrow you will take your departure. When the bell rings get up quickly and eat your breakfast, and you will find the same horse waiting to take you home;

but remember that you must never expect to see my palace again."

Then turning to Beauty, he said:

"Take your father into the next room, and help him to choose everything you think your brothers and sisters would like to have. You will find two travelling-trunks there; fill them as full as you can. It is only just that you should send them something very precious as a remembrance of yourself."

Then he went away, after saying, "Good-bye, Beauty; good-bye, old man"; and though Beauty was beginning to think with great dismay of her father's departure, she was afraid to disobey the Beast's orders; and they went into the next room, which had shelves and cupboards all round it. They were greatly surprised at the riches it contained. There were splendid dresses fit for a queen, with all the ornaments that were to be worn with them; and when Beauty opened the cupboards she was quite dazzled by the gorgeous jewels that lay in heaps upon every shelf. After choosing a vast quantity, which she divided between her sisters—for she had made a heap of the wonderful dresses for each of them—she opened the last chest, which was full of gold.

"I think, father," she said, "that, as the gold will be more useful to you, we had better take out the other things again, and fill the trunks with it." So they did this; but the more they put in, the more room there seemed to be, and at last they put back all the jewels and dresses they had taken out, and Beauty even added as many more of the jewels as she could carry at once; and then the trunks were not too full, but they were so heavy that an elephant could not have carried them!

"The Beast was mocking us," cried the merchant; "he must have pretended to give us all these things, knowing that I could not carry them away."

"Let us wait and see," answered Beauty. "I cannot believe that he meant to deceive us. All we can do is to fasten them up and leave them ready."

So they did this and returned to the little room, where, to their astonishment, they found breakfast ready. The merchant ate his with a good appetite, as the Beast's generosity made him believe that he might perhaps venture to come back soon and see Beauty. But she felt sure that her father was leaving her for ever, so she was very sad when the bell rang sharply for the second time, and warned them that the time was come for them to part. They went down into the court-yard, where two horses were waiting, one loaded with the two trunks, the other for him to ride. They were pawing the ground in their impatience to start, and the merchant was forced to bid Beauty a hasty farewell; and as soon as he was mounted he went off at such a pace that she lost sight of him in an instant. Then Beauty began to cry, and wandered sadly back to her own room. But she soon found that she was very sleepy, and as she had nothing better to do she lay down and instantly fell asleep. And then she dreamed that she was walking by a brook bordered with trees, and lamenting her sad fate, when a young prince, handsomer than anyone she had ever seen, and with a voice that went straight to her heart, came and said to her, "Ah, Beauty! you are not so unfortunate as you suppose. Here you will be rewarded for all you have suffered elsewhere. Your every wish shall be gratified. Only try to find me out, no matter how I may be disguised, as I love you dearly, and in making me happy you will find your own happiness. Be as true-hearted as you are beautiful, and we shall have nothing left to wish for."

"What can I do, Prince, to make you happy?" said Beauty.

"Only be grateful," he answered, "and do not trust too much to your eyes. And, above all, do not desert me until you have saved me from my cruel misery."

After this she thought she found herself in a room with a stately and beautiful lady, who said to her:

"Dear Beauty, try not to regret all you have left behind you, for you are destined to a better fate. Only do not let yourself be deceived by appearances."

Beauty found her dreams so interesting that she was in no hurry to awake, but presently the clock roused her by calling her name softly twelve times, and then she got up and found her dressing-table set out with everything she could possibly want; and when her toilet was finished she found dinner was waiting in the room next to hers. But dinner does not take very long when you are all by yourself, and very soon she sat down cosily in the corner of a sofa, and began to think about the charming Prince she had seen in her dream.

"He said I could make him happy," said Beauty to herself.

"It seems, then, that this horrible Beast keeps him a prisoner. How can I set him free? I wonder why they both told me not to trust to appearances? I don't understand it. But, after all, it was only a dream, so why should I trouble myself about it? I had better go and find something to do to amuse myself."

So she got up and began to explore some of the many rooms of the palace.

The first she entered was lined with mirrors, and Beauty saw herself reflected on every side, and thought she had never seen such a charming room. Then a bracelet which was hanging from a chandelier caught her eye, and on taking it down she was greatly surprised to find that it held a portrait of her unknown admirer, just as she had seen him in her dream. With great delight she slipped the bracelet on her arm, and went on into a gallery of pictures, where she soon found a portrait of the same handsome Prince, as large as life, and so well painted that as she studied it he seemed to smile kindly at her. Tearing herself away from the portrait at last, she passed through into a room which contained every musical instrument under the sun, and here she amused herself for a long while in trying some

of them, and singing until she was tired. The next room
was a library, and she saw everything she had ever
wanted to read, as well as everything she had read, and
it seemed to her that a whole lifetime would not be
enough even to read the names of the books, there
were so many. By this time it was growing dusk, and
wax candles in diamond and ruby candlesticks were
beginning to light themselves in every room.

Beauty found her supper served just at the time she
preferred to have it, but she did not see anyone or
hear a sound, and, though her father had warned her
that she would be alone, she began to find it rather
dull.

But presently she heard the Beast coming, and wondered tremblingly if he meant to eat her up now.

However, as he did not seem at all ferocious, and
only said gruffly:

"Good-evening, Beauty," she answered cheerfully and
managed to conceal her terror. Then the Beast asked
her how she had been amusing herself, and she told
him all the rooms she had seen.

Then he asked if she thought she could be happy in
his palace; and Beauty answered that everything was so
beautiful that she would be very hard to please if she
could not be happy. And after about an hour's talk
Beauty began to think that the Beast was not nearly so
terrible as she had supposed at first. Then he got up to
leave her, and said in his gruff voice:

"Do you love me, Beauty? Will you marry me?"

"Oh! what shall I say?" cried Beauty, for she was
afraid to make the Beast angry by refusing.

"Say 'yes' or 'no' without fear," he replied.

"Oh! no, Beast," said Beauty hastily.

"Since you will not, good-night, Beauty," he said.
And she answered:

"Good-night, Beast," very glad to find that her re-
fusal had not provoked him. And after he was gone she
was very soon in bed and asleep, and dreaming of her
unknown Prince. She thought he came and said to her:

"Ah, Beauty! why are you so unkind to me? I fear I am fated to be unhappy for many a long day still."

And then her dreams changed, but the charming Prince figured in them all; and when morning came her first thought was to look at the portrait and see if it was really like him, and she found that it certainly was.

This morning she decided to amuse herself in the garden, for the sun shone, and all the fountains were playing; but she was astonished to find that every place was familiar to her, and presently she came to the brook where the myrtle trees were growing where she had first met the Prince in her dream, and that made her think more than ever that he must be kept a prisoner by the Beast. When she was tired she went back to the palace, and found a new room full of materials for every kind of work—ribbons to make into bows, and silks to work into flowers. Then there was an aviary full of rare birds, which were so tame that they flew to Beauty as soon as they saw her, and perched upon her shoulders and her head.

"Pretty little creatures," she said, "how I wish that your cage was nearer to my room, that I might often hear you sing!"

So saying she opened a door, and found to her delight that it led into her own room, though she had thought it was quite the other side of the palace.

There were more birds in a room farther on, parrots and cockatoos that could talk, and they greeted Beauty by name; indeed, she found them so entertaining that she took one or two back to her room, and they talked to her while she was at supper; after which the Beast paid her his usual visit, and asked the same questions as before, and then with a gruff "good-night" he took his departure, and Beauty went to bed to dream of her mysterious Prince. The days passed swiftly in different amusements, and after a while Beauty found out another strange thing in the palace, which often pleased her when she was tired of being alone. There was one

room which she had not noticed particularly; it was
empty, except that under each of the windows stood a
very comfortable chair; and the first time she had looked
out of the window it had seemed to her that a black
curtain prevented her from seeing anything outside.
But the second time she went into the room, happening
to be tired, she sat down in one of the chairs, when
instantly the curtain was rolled aside, and a most amusing pantomime was acted before her; there were dances,
and coloured lights, and music, and pretty dresses, and
it was all so gay that Beauty was in ecstacies. After that
she tried the other seven windows in turn, and there
was some new and surprising entertainment to be seen
from each of them, so that Beauty never could feel
lonely any more. Every evening after supper the Beast
came to see her, and always before saying good-night
asked her in his terrible voice:

"Beauty, will you marry me?"

And it seemed to Beauty, now she understood him
better, that when she said, "No, Beast," he went away
quite sad. But her happy dreams of the handsome
young Prince soon made her forget the poor Beast, and
the only thing that at all disturbed her was to be constantly told to distrust appearances, to let her heart
guide her, and not her eyes, and many other equally
perplexing things, which, consider as she would, she
could not understand.

So everything went on for a long time, until at last,
happy as she was, Beauty began to long for the sight of
her father and her brothers and sisters; and one night,
seeing her look very sad, the Beast asked her what was
the matter. Beauty had quite ceased to be afraid of him.
Now she knew that he was really gentle in spite of his
ferocious looks and his dreadful voice. So she answered
that she was longing to see her home once more. Upon
hearing this the Beast seemed sadly distressed, and
cried miserably.

"Ah! Beauty, have you the heart to desert an unhappy Beast like this? What more do you want to make you happy? Is it because you hate me that you want to escape?"

"No, dear Beast," answered Beauty softly, "I do not hate you, and I should be very sorry never to see you any more, but I long to see my father again. Only let me go for two months, and I promise to come back to you and stay for the rest of my life."

The Beast, who had been sighing dolefully while she spoke, now replied:

"I cannot refuse you anything you ask, even though it should cost me my life. Take the four boxes you will find in the room next to your own, and fill them with everything you wish to take with you. But remember your promise and come back when the two months are over, or you may have cause to repent it, for if you do not come in good time you will find your faithful Beast dead. You will not need any chariot to bring you back. Only say good-bye to all your brothers and sisters the night before you come away, and when you have gone to bed turn this ring around upon your finger and say firmly: 'I wish to go back to my palace and see my Beast again.' Good-night, Beauty. Fear nothing, sleep peacefully, and before long you shall see your father once more."

As soon as Beauty was alone she hastened to fill the boxes with all the rare and precious things she saw about her, and only when she was tired of heaping things into them did they seem to be full.

Then she went to bed, but could hardly sleep for joy. And when at last she did begin to dream of her beloved Prince she was grieved to see him stretched upon a grassy bank sad and weary, and hardly like himself.

"What is the matter?" she cried.

But he looked at her reproachfully, and said:

"How can you ask me, cruel one? Are you not leaving me to my death perhaps?"

"Ah! don't be so sorrowful," cried Beauty; "I am only

going to assure my father that I am safe and happy. I
have promised the Beast faithfully that I will come
back, and he would die of grief if I did not keep my
word!"

"What would that matter to you?" said the Prince.
"Surely you would not care?"

"Indeed I should be ungrateful if I did not care for
such a kind Beast," cried Beauty indignantly. "I would
die to save him from pain. I assure you it is not his fault
that he is so ugly."

Just then a strange sound woke her—someone was
speaking not very far away; and opening her eyes she
found herself in a room she had never seen before,
which was certainly not nearly so splendid as those she
was used to in the Beast's palace. Where could she be?
She got up and dressed hastily, and then saw that the
boxes she had packed the night before were all in
the room. While she was wondering by what magic the
Beast had transported them and herself to this strange
place she suddenly heard her father's voice, and rushed
out and greeted him joyfully. Her brothers and sisters
were all astonished at her appearance, as they had
never expected to see her again, and there was no end
to the questions they asked her. She had also much to
hear about what had happened to them while she was
away, and of her father's journey home. But when they
heard that she had only come to be with them for a
short time, and then must go back to the Beast's palace
for ever, they lamented loudly. Then Beauty asked her
father what he thought could be the meaning of her
strange dreams, and why the Prince constantly begged
her not to trust to appearances. After much consideration he answered: "You tell me yourself that the Beast,
frightful as he is, loves you dearly, and deserves your
love and gratitude for his gentleness and kindness; I
think the Prince must mean you to understand that you
ought to reward him by doing as he wishes you to, in
spite of his ugliness."

Beauty could not help seeing that this seemed very probable; still, when she thought of her dear Prince who was so handsome, she did not feel at all inclined to marry the Beast. At any rate, for two months she need not decide, but could enjoy herself with her sisters. But though they were rich now, and lived in a town again, and had plenty of acquaintances, Beauty found that nothing amused her very much; and she often thought of the palace, where she was so happy, especially as at home she never once dreamed of her dear Prince, and she felt quite sad without him.

Then her sisters seemed to have got quite used to being without her, and even found her rather in the way, so she would not have been sorry when the two months were over but for her father and brothers, who begged her to stay, and seemed so grieved at the thought of her departure that she had not the courage to say good-bye to them. Every day when she got up she meant to say it at night, and when night came she put it off again, until at last she had a dismal dream which helped her to make up her mind. She thought she was wandering in a lonely path in the palace gardens, when she heard groans which seemed to come from some bushes hiding the entrance of a cave, and running quickly to see what could be the matter, she found the Beast stretched out upon his side, apparently dying. He reproached her faintly with being the cause of his distress, and at the same moment a stately lady appeared, and said very gravely:

"Ah! Beauty, you are only just in time to save his life. See what happens when people do not keep their promises! If you had delayed one day more, you would have found him dead."

Beauty was so terrified by this dream that the next morning she announced her intention of going back at once, and that very night she said good-bye to her father and all her brothers and sisters, and as soon as she was in bed she turned her ring around upon her finger, and said firmly:

"I wish to go back to my palace and see my Beast again," as she had been told to do.

Then she fell asleep instantly, and only woke up to hear the clock saying, "Beauty, Beauty," twelve times in its musical voice, which told her at once that she was really in the palace once more. Everything was just as before, and her birds were so glad to see her! but Beauty thought she had never known such a long day, for she was so anxious to see the Beast again that she felt as if supper-time would never come.

But when it did come and no Beast appeared she was really frightened; so, after listening and waiting for a long time, she ran down into the garden to search for him. Up and down the paths and avenues ran poor Beauty, calling him in vain, for no one answered, and not a trace of him could she find; until at last, quite tired, she stopped for a minute's rest, and saw that she was standing opposite the shady path she had seen in her dream. She rushed down it, and, sure enough, there was the cave, and in it lay the Beast—asleep, as Beauty thought. Quite glad to have found him, she ran up and stroked his head, but to her horror he did not move or open his eyes.

"Oh! he is dead; and it is all my fault," said Beauty, crying bitterly.

But then, looking at him again, she fancied he still breathed, and, hastily fetching some water from the nearest fountain, she sprinkled it over his face, and to her great delight he began to revive.

"Oh! Beast, how you frightened me!" she cried. "I never knew how much I loved you until just now, when I feared I was too late to save your life."

"Can you really love such an ugly creature as I am?" said the Beast faintly. "Ah! Beauty, you only came just in time. I was dying because I thought you had forgotten your promise. But go back now and rest, I shall see you again by-and-by."

Beauty, who had half expected that he would be

angry with her, was reassured by his gentle voice, and went back to the palace, where supper was awaiting her; and afterwards the Beast came in as usual, and talked about the time she had spent with her father, asking if she had enjoyed herself, and if they had all been very glad to see her.

Beauty answered politely, and quite enjoyed telling him all that had happened to her. And when at last the time came for him to go, and he asked, as he had so often asked before:

"Beauty, will you marry me?" she answered softly: "Yes, dear Beast."

As she spoke a blaze of light sprang up before the windows of the palace; fireworks crackled and guns banged, and across the avenue of orange trees, in letters all made of fire-flies, was written: "Long live the Prince and his Bride."

Turning to ask the Beast what it could all mean, Beauty found that he had disappeared, and in his place stood her long-loved Prince! At the same moment the wheels of a chariot were heard upon the terrace, and two ladies entered the room. One of them Beauty recognized as the stately lady she had seen in her dreams; the other was also so grand and queenly that Beauty hardly knew which to greet first.

But the one she already knew said to her companion:

"Well, Queen, this is Beauty, who has had the courage to rescue your son from the terrible enchantment. They love one another, and only your consent to their marriage is wanting to make them perfectly happy."

"I consent with all my heart," cried the Queen. "How can I ever thank you enough, charming girl, for having restored my dear son to his natural form?"

And then she tenderly embraced Beauty and the Prince, who had meanwhile been greeting the Fairy and receiving her congratulations.

"Now," said the Fairy to Beauty, "I suppose you

would like me to send for all your brothers and sisters to dance at your wedding?"

And so she did, and the marriage was celebrated the very next day with the utmost splendour, and Beauty and the Prince lived happily ever after.

—*The Blue Fairy Book* (1889)

Cannetella

ITALIAN

———◆◆———

THERE was once upon a time a king who reigned over a country called "Bello Puojo." He was very rich and powerful, and had everything in the world he could desire except a child. But at last, after he had been married for many years, and was quite an old man, his wife Renzolla presented him with a fine daughter, whom they called Cannetella.

She grew up into a beautiful girl, and was as tall and straight as a young fir-tree. When she was eighteen years old her father called her to him and said: "You are of an age now, my daughter, to marry and settle down; but as I love you more than anything else in the world, and desire nothing but your happiness, I am determined to leave the choice of a husband to yourself. Choose a man after your own heart, and you are sure to satisfy me." Cannetella thanked her father very much for his kindness and consideration, but told him that she had not the slightest wish to marry, and was quite determined to remain single.

The king, who felt himself growing old and feeble, and longed to see an heir to the throne before he died, was very unhappy at her words, and begged her earnestly not to disappoint him.

When Cannetella saw that the king had set his heart

31

on her marriage, she said: "Very well, dear father, I
will marry to please you, for I do not wish to appear
ungrateful for all your love and kindness; but you must
find me a husband handsomer, cleverer, and more charming than anyone else in the world."

The king was overjoyed by her words, and from early
in the morning till late at night he sat at the window
and looked carefully at all the passers-by, in the hopes
of finding a son-in-law among them.

One day, seeing a very good-looking man crossing
the street, the king called his daughter and said: "Come
quickly, dear Cannetella, and look at this man, for I
think he might suit you as a husband."

They called the young man into the palace, and set a
sumptuous feast before him, with every sort of delicacy
you can imagine. In the middle of the meal the youth
let an almond fall out of his mouth, which, however, he
picked up again very quickly and hid under the table-
cloth.

When the feast was over the stranger went away, and
the king asked Cannetella: "Well, what did you think of
the youth?"

"I think he was a clumsy wretch," replied Cannetella.
"Fancy a man of his age letting an almond fall out of his
mouth!"

When the king heard her answer he returned to his
watch at the window, and shortly afterwards a very
handsome young man passed by. The king instantly
called his daughter to come and see what she thought of
the new comer.

"Call him in," said Cannetella, "that we may see him
close."

Another splendid feast was prepared, and when the
stranger had eaten and drunk as much as he was able,
and had taken his departure, the king asked Cannetella
how she liked him.

"Not at all," replied his daughter; "what could you do
with a man who requires at least two servants to help

him on with his cloak, because he is too awkward to put it on properly himself?"

"If that's all you have against him," said the king, "I see how the land lies. You are determined not to have a husband at all; but marry someone you shall, for I do not mean my name and house to die out."

"Well, then, my dear parent," said Cannetella, "I must tell you at once that you had better not count upon me, for I never mean to marry unless I can find a man with a gold head and gold teeth."

The king was very angry at finding his daughter so obstinate; but as he always gave the girl her own way in everything, he issued a proclamation to the effect that any man with a gold head and gold teeth might come forward and claim the princess as his bride, and the kingdom of Bello Puojo as a wedding gift.

Now the king had a deadly enemy called Scioravante, who was a very powerful magician. No sooner had this man heard of the proclamation than he summoned his attendant spirits and commanded them to gild his head and teeth. The spirits said, at first, that the task was beyond their powers, and suggested that a pair of golden horns attached to his forehead would both be easier to make and more comfortable to wear; but Scioravante would allow no compromise, and insisted on having a head and teeth made of the finest gold. When it was fixed on his shoulders he went for a stroll in front of the palace. And the king, seeing the very man he was in search of, called his daughter, and said: "Just look out of the window, and you will find exactly what you want."

Then, as Scioravante was hurrying past, the king shouted out to him: "Just stop a minute, brother, and don't be in such desperate haste. If you will step in here you shall have my daughter for a wife, and I will send attendants with her, and as many horses and servants as you wish."

"A thousand thanks," returned Scioravante; "I shall be delighted to marry your daughter, but it is quite

SCIORAVANTE LEAVES
CANNETELLA IN THE STABLE

unnecessary to send anyone to accompany her. Give me a horse and I will carry off the princess in front of my saddle, and will bring her to my own kingdom, where there is no lack of courtiers or servants, or, indeed, of anything your daughter can desire."

At first the king was very much against Cannetella's departing in this fashion; but finally Scioravante got his way, and placing the princess before him on his horse, he set out for his own country.

Towards evening he dismounted, and entering a stable he placed Cannetella in the same stall as his horse, and said to her: "Now listen to what I have to say. I am going to my home now, and that is a seven years' journey from here; you must wait for me in this stable, and never move from the spot, or let yourself be seen by a living soul. If you disobey my commands, it will be the worse for you."

The princess answered meekly: "Sir, I am your servant, and will do exactly as you bid me; but I should like to know what I am to live on till you come back?"

"You can take what the horses leave," was Scioravante's reply.

When the magician had left her Cannetella felt very miserable, and bitterly cursed the day she was born. She spent all her time weeping and bemoaning the cruel fate that had driven her from a palace into a stable, from soft down cushions to a bed of straw, and from the dainties of her father's table to the food that the horses left.

She led this wretched life for a few months, and during that time she never saw who fed and watered the horses, for it was all done by invisible hands.

One day, when she was more than usually unhappy, she perceived a little crack in the wall, through which she could see a beautiful garden, with all manner of delicious fruits and flowers growing in it. The sight and smell of such delicacies were too much for poor Cannetella, and she said to herself, "I will slip quietly out, and pick a few oranges and grapes, and I don't care what happens. Who is there to tell my husband what I do? and even if he should hear of my disobedience, he cannot make my life more miserable than it is already."

So she slipped out and refreshed her poor, starved body with the fruit she plucked in the garden.

But a short time afterwards her husband returned unexpectedly, and one of the horses instantly told him that Cannetella had gone into the garden, in his absence, and had stolen some oranges and grapes.

Scioravante was furious when he heard this, and seizing a huge knife from his pocket he threatened to kill his wife for her disobedience. But Cannetella threw herself at his feet and implored him to spare her life, saying that hunger drove even the wolf from the wood. At last she succeeded in so far softening her husband's heart that he said, "I will forgive you this time, and spare your life; but if you disobey me again, and I hear, on my return, that you have as much as moved out of the stall, I will certainly kill you. So, beware; for I am going away once more, and shall be absent for seven years."

With these words he took his departure, and Cannetella burst into a flood of tears, and, wringing her hands, she moaned: "Why was I ever born to such a hard fate? Oh! father, how miserable you have made your poor daughter! But, why should I blame my father? for I have only myself to thank for all my sufferings. I got the cursed head of gold, and it has brought all this misery on me. I am indeed punished for not doing as my father wished!"

When a year had gone by, it chanced, one day, that the king's cooper passed the stables where Cannetella was kept prisoner. She recognised the man, and called him to come in. At first he did not know the poor princess, and could not make out who it was that called him by name. But when he heard Cannetella's tale of woe, he hid her in a big empty barrel he had with him, partly because he was sorry for the poor girl, and, even more, because he wished to gain the king's favour.

Then he slung the barrel on a mule's back, and in this way the princess was carried to her own home. They arrived at the palace about four o'clock in the morning, and the cooper knocked loudly at the door. When the servants came in haste and saw only the cooper standing at the gate, they were very indignant, and scolded him soundly for coming at such an hour and waking them all out of their sleep.

The king, hearing the noise and the cause of it, sent for the cooper, for he felt certain the man must have some important business, to have come and disturbed the whole palace at such an early hour.

The cooper asked permission to unload his mule, and Cannetella crept out of the barrel. At first the king refused to believe that it was really his daughter, for she had changed so terribly in a few years, and had grown so thin and pale, that it was pitiful to see her. At last the princess showed her father a mole she had on her right arm, and then he saw that the poor girl was indeed his long-lost Cannetella. He kissed her a thousand times, and instantly had the choicest food and drink set before her.

After she had satisfied her hunger, the king said to her: "Who would have thought, my dear daughter, to have found you in such a state? What, may I ask, has brought you to this pass?"

Cannetella replied: "That wicked man with the gold head and teeth treated me worse than a dog, and many a time, since I left you, have I longed to die. But I couldn't tell you all that I have suffered, for you would never believe me. It is enough that I am once more with you, and I shall never leave you again, for I would rather be a slave in your house than queen in any other."

In the meantime Scioravante had returned to the stables, and one of the horses told him that Cannetella had been taken away by a cooper in a barrel.

When the wicked magician heard this he was beside himself with rage, and, hastening to the kingdom of

Bello Puojo, he went straight to an old woman who
lived exactly opposite the royal palace, and said to her:
"If you will let me see the king's daughter, I will give
you whatever reward you like to ask for."

The woman demanded a hundred ducats of gold, and
Scioravante counted them out of his purse and gave
them to her without a murmur. Then the old woman
led him to the roof of the house, where he could see
Cannetella combing out her long hair in a room in the
top story of the palace.

The princess happened to look out of the window,
and when she saw her husband gazing at her, she got
such a fright that she flew downstairs to the king, and
said: "My lord and father, unless you shut me up instantly in a room with seven iron doors, I am lost."

"If that's all," said the king, "it shall be done at
once." And he gave orders for the doors to be closed on
the spot.

When Scioravante saw this he returned to the old
woman, and said: "I will give you whatever you like if
you will go into the palace, hide under the princess's
bed, and slip this little piece of paper beneath her
pillow, saying, as you do so: 'May everyone in the
palace except the princess, fall into a sound sleep.' "

The old woman demanded another hundred golden
ducats, and then proceeded to carry out the magician's
wishes. No sooner had she slipped the piece of paper
under Cannetella's pillow, than all the people in the
palace fell fast asleep, and only the princess remained
awake.

Then Scioravante hurried to the seven doors and
opened them one after the other. Cannetella screamed
with terror when she saw her husband, but no one
came to help, for all in the palace lay as if they were
dead. The magician seized her in the bed on which she
lay, and was going to carry her off with him, when the
little piece of paper which the old woman had placed
under her pillow fell on the floor.

In an instant all the people in the palace woke up,

and as Cannetella was still screaming for help, they rushed to her rescue. They seized Scioravante and put him to death; so he was caught in the trap which he had laid for the princess—and, as is so often the case in this world, the biter himself was bit.

—*The Grey Fairy Book* (1900)

East of the Sun
and West of the Moon

NORSE

———◆·◆———

ONCE upon a time there was a poor husbandman who had many children and little to give them in the way either of food or clothing. They were all pretty, but the prettiest of all was the youngest daughter, who was so beautiful that there were no bounds to her beauty.

So once—it was late on a Thursday evening in autumn, and wild weather outside, terribly dark, and raining so heavily and blowing so hard that the walls of the cottage shook again—they were all sitting together by the fireside, each of them busy with something or other, when suddenly some one rapped three times against the window-pane. The man went out to see what could be the matter, and when he got out there stood a great big white bear.

"Good-evening to you," said the White Bear.

"Good-evening," said the man.

"Will you give me your youngest daughter?" said the White Bear; "if you will, you shall be as rich as you are now poor."

Truly the man would have had no objection to be rich, but he thought to himself: "I must first ask my daughter about this," so he went in and told them that there was a great white bear outside who had faithfully promised to make them all rich if he might but have the youngest daughter.

She said no, and would not hear of it; so the man went out again, and settled with the White Bear that he should come again next Thursday evening, and get her answer. Then the man persuaded her, and talked so much to her about the wealth that they would have, and what a good thing it would be for herself, that at last she made up her mind to go, and washed and mended all her rags, made herself as smart as she could, and held herself in readiness to set out. Little enough had she to take away with her.

Next Thursday evening the White Bear came to fetch her. She seated herself on his back with her bundle, and thus they departed. When they had gone a great part of the way, the White Bear said: "Are you afraid?"

"No, that I am not," said she.

"Keep tight hold of my fur, and then there is no danger," said he.

And thus she rode far, far away, until they came to a great mountain. Then the White Bear knocked on it, and a door opened, and they went into a castle where there were many brilliantly lighted rooms which shone with gold and silver, likewise a large hall in which there was a well-spread table, and it was so magnificent that it would be hard to make anyone understand how splendid it was. The White Bear gave her a silver bell, and told her that when she needed anything she had but to ring this bell, and what she wanted would appear. So after she had eaten, and night was drawing near, she grew sleepy after her journey, and thought she would like to go to bed. She rang the bell, and scarcely had she touched it before she found herself in a chamber where a bed stood ready made for her, which was as pretty as anyone could wish to sleep in. It had pillows of silk, and curtains of silk fringed with gold, and everything that was in the room was of gold or silver; but when she had lain down and put out the light a man came and lay down beside her, and behold it was the

White Bear, who cast off the form of a beast during the night. She never saw him, however, for he always came after she had put out her light, and went away before daylight appeared.

So all went well and happily for a time, but then she began to be very sad and sorrowful, for all day long she had to go about alone; and she did so wish to go home to her father and mother and brothers and sisters. Then the White Bear asked what it was that she wanted, and she told him that it was so dull there in the mountain, and that she had to go about all alone, and that in her parents' house at home there were all her brothers and sisters, and it was because she could not go to them that she was so sorrowful.

"There might be a cure for that," said the White Bear, "if you would but promise me never to talk with your mother alone, but only when the others are there too; for she will take hold of your hand," he said, "and will want to lead you into a room to talk with you alone; but that you must by no means do, or you will bring great misery on both of us."

So one Sunday the White Bear came and said that they could now set out to see her father and mother, and they journeyed thither, she sitting on his back, and they went a long, long way, and it took a long, long time; but at last they came to a large white farmhouse, and her brothers and sisters were running about outside it, playing, and it was so pretty that it was a pleasure to look at it.

"Your parents dwell here now," said the White Bear; "but do not forget what I said to you, or you will do much harm both to yourself and me."

"No, indeed," said she, "I shall never forget"; and as soon as she was at home the White Bear turned round and went back again.

There were such rejoicings when she went in to her parents that it seemed as if they would never come to an end. Everyone thought that he could never be sufficiently grateful to her for all she had done for them all.

Now they had everything that they wanted, and everything was as good as it could be. They all asked her how she was getting on where she was. All was well with her too, she said; and she had everything that she could want. What other answers she gave I cannot say, but I am pretty sure that they did not learn much from her. But in the afternoon, after they had dined at mid-day, all happened just as the White Bear had said. Her mother wanted to talk with her alone in her own chamber. But she remembered what the White Bear had said, and would on no account go. "What we have to say can be said at any time," she answered. But somehow or other her mother at last persuaded her, and she was forced to tell the whole story. So she told how every night a man came and lay down beside her when the lights were all put out, and how she never saw him, because he always went away before it grew light in the morning, and how she continually went about in sadness, thinking how happy she would be if she could but see him, and how all day long she had to go about alone, and it was so dull and solitary. "Oh!" cried the mother, in horror, "you are very likely sleeping with a troll! But I will teach you a way to see him. You shall have a bit of one of my candles, which you can take away with you hidden in your breast. Look at him with that when he is asleep, but take care not to let any tallow drop upon him."

So she took the candle, and hid it in her breast, and when evening drew near the White Bear came to fetch her away. When they had gone some distance on their way, the White Bear asked her if everything had not happened just as he had foretold, and she could not but own that it had. "Then, if you have done what your mother wished," said he, "you have brought great misery on both of us." "No," she said, "I have not done anything at all." So when she had reached home and gone to bed it was just the same as it had been before, and a man came and lay down beside her, and late at night, when she could hear that he was sleeping, she got up and kindled a light, lit her candle, let her light shine on him, and saw him, and he was the handsomest prince that eyes had ever beheld, and she loved him so much that it seemed to her that she must die if she did not kiss him that very moment. So she did kiss him; but while she was doing it she let three drops of hot tallow fall upon his shirt, and he awoke. "What have you done now?" said he; "you have brought misery on both of us. If you had but held out for the space of one year I should have been free. I have a stepmother who has bewitched me so that I am a white bear by day and a man by night; but now all is at an end between you and me, and I must leave you, and go to her. She lives in a castle which lies east of the sun and west of the moon, and there too is a princess with a nose which is three ells long, and she now is the one whom I must marry."

She wept and lamented, but all in vain, for go he must. Then she asked him if she could not go with him. But no, that could not be. "Can you tell me the way then, and I will seek you—that I may surely be allowed to do!"

"Yes, you may do that," said he; "but there is no way thither. It lies east of the sun and west of the moon, and never would you find your way there."

When she awoke in the morning both the Prince and the castle were gone, and she was lying on a small green patch in the midst of a dark, thick wood. By her side lay the self-same bundle of rags which she had brought with her from her own home. So when she had rubbed the sleep out of her eyes, and wept till she was weary, she set out on her way, and thus she walked for many and many a long day, until at last she came to a great mountain. Outside it an aged woman was sitting, playing with a golden apple. The girl asked her if she knew the way to the Prince who lived with his stepmother in the castle which lay east of the sun and west of the moon, and who was to marry a princess with a nose which was three ells long. "How do you happen to know about him?" enquired the old woman; "maybe you are she who ought to have had him." "Yes, indeed, I am," she said. "So it is you, then?" said the old woman; "I know nothing about him but that he dwells in a castle which is east of the sun and west of the moon. You will be a long time in getting to it, if ever you get to it at all; but you shall have the loan of my horse, and then you can ride on it to an old woman who is a neighbour of mine: perhaps she can tell you about him. When you have got there you must just strike the horse beneath the left ear and bid it go home again; but you may take the golden apple with you."

So the girl seated herself on the horse, and rode for a long, long way, and at last she came to the mountain, where an aged woman was sitting outside with a gold carding-comb. The girl asked her if she knew the way to the castle which lay east of the sun and west of the moon; but she said what the first old woman had said: "I know nothing about it, but that it is east of the sun and west of the moon, and that you will be a long time in getting to it, if ever you get there at all; but you shall have the loan of my horse to an old woman who lives the nearest to me: perhaps she may know where the castle is, and when you have got to her you may just strike the horse beneath the left ear and bid it go home again." Then she gave her the gold carding-comb, for it might, perhaps, be of use to her, she said.

So the girl seated herself on the horse, and rode a wearisome long way onwards again, and after a very long time she came to a great mountain, where an aged woman was sitting, spinning at a golden spinning-wheel. Of this woman, too, she enquired if she knew the way to the Prince, and where to find the castle which lay east of the sun and west of the moon. But it was only the same thing once again. "Maybe it was you who should have had the Prince," said the old woman. "Yes, indeed, I should have been the one," said the girl. But this old crone knew the way no better than the others—it was east of the sun and west of the moon, she knew that, "and you will be a long time in getting to it, if

ever you get to it at all," she said; "but you may have
the loan of my horse, and I think you had better ride to
the East Wind, and ask him: perhaps he may know
where the castle is, and will blow you thither. But
when you have got to him you must just strike the
horse beneath the left ear, and he will come home
again." And then she gave her the golden spinning-
wheel, saying: "Perhaps you may find that you have a
use for it."

The girl had to ride for a great many days, and for a
long and wearisome time, before she got there; but at
last she did arrive, and then she asked the East Wind if
he could tell her the way to the Prince who dwelt east
of the sun and west of the moon. "Well," said the East
Wind, "I have heard tell of the Prince, and of his castle,
but I do not know the way to it, for I have never blown
so far; but, if you like, I will go with you to my brother
the West Wind: he may know that, for he is much
stronger than I am. You may sit on my back, and then I
can carry you there." So she seated herself on his back,
and they did go so swiftly! When they got there, the
East Wind went in and said that the girl whom he had
brought was the one who ought to have had the Prince
up at the castle which lay east of the sun and west of
the moon, and that now she was travelling about to find
him again, so he had come there with her, and would
like to hear if the West Wind knew whereabouts the
castle was. "No," said the West Wind; "so far as that
have I never blown: but if you like I will go with you to
the South Wind, for he is much stronger than either of
us, and he has roamed far and wide, and perhaps he
can tell you what you want to know. You may seat
yourself on my back, and then I will carry you to him."

So she did this, and journeyed to the South Wind,
neither was she very long on the way. When they had
got there, the West Wind asked him if he could tell her
the way to the castle that lay east of the sun and west of
the moon, for she was the girl who ought to marry the
Prince who lived there. "Oh, indeed!" said the South

Wind, "is that she? Well," said he, "I have wandered about a great deal in my time, and in all kinds of places, but I have never blown so far as that. If you like, however, I will go with you to my brother the North Wind; he is the oldest and strongest of all of us, and if he does not know where it is no one in the whole world will be able to tell you. You may sit upon my back, and then I will carry you there." So she seated herself on his back, and off he went from his house in great haste, and they were not long on the way. When they came near the North Wind's dwelling, he was so wild and frantic that they felt cold gusts a long while before they got there. "What do you want?" he roared out from afar, and they froze as they heard. Said the South Wind: "It is I, and this is she who should have had the Prince who lives in the castle which lies east of the sun and west of the moon. And now she wishes to ask you if you have ever been there, and can tell her the way, for she would gladly find him again."

"Yes," said the North Wind, "I know where it is. I once blew an aspen leaf there, but I was so tired that for many days afterwards I was not able to blow at all. However, if you really are anxious to go there, and are not afraid to go with me, I will take you on my back, and try if I can blow you there."

"Get there I must," said she; "and if there is any way of going I will; and I have no fear, no matter how fast you go."

"Very well then," said the North Wind; "but you must sleep here to-night, for if we are ever to get there we must have the day before us."

The North Wind woke her betimes next morning, and puffed himself up, and made himself so big and so strong that it was frightful to see him, and away they went, high up through the air, as if they would not stop until they had reached the very end of the world. Down below there was such a storm! It blew down woods and houses, and when they were above the sea the ships were wrecked by hundreds. And thus they

tore on and on, and a long time went by, and then yet
more time passed, and still they were above the sea,
and the North Wind grew tired, and more tired, and at
last so utterly weary that he was scarcely able to blow
any longer, and he sank and sank, lower and lower,
until at last he went so low that the crests of the waves
dashed against the heels of the poor girl he was carrying. "Art thou afraid?" said the North Wind. "I have no
fear," said she; and it was true. But they were not very,
very far from land, and there was just enough strength
left in the North Wind to enable him to throw her on to
the shore, immediately under the windows of a castle
which lay east of the sun and west of the moon; but
then he was so weary and worn out that he was forced
to rest for several days before he could go to his own
home again.

Next morning she sat down beneath the walls of the
castle to play with the golden apple, and the first person she saw was the maiden with the long nose, who
was to have the Prince. "How much do you want for
that gold apple of yours, girl?" said she, opening the
window. "It can't be bought either for gold or money,"
answered the girl. "If it cannot be bought either for
gold or money, what will buy it? You may say what you
please," said the Princess.

"Well, if I may go to the Prince who is here, and be
with him to-night, you shall have it," said the girl who
had come with the North Wind. "You may do that,"
said the Princess, for she had made up her mind what
she would do. So the Princess got the golden apple, but
when the girl went up to the Prince's apartment that
night he was asleep, for the Princess had so contrived it.
The poor girl called to him, and shook him, and between whiles she wept; but she could not wake him. In
the morning, as soon as day dawned, in came the
Princess with the long nose, and drove her out again. In
the daytime she sat down once more beneath the windows of the castle, and began to card with her golden
carding-comb; and then all happened as it had hap-

pened before. The princess asked her what she wanted for it, and she replied that it was not for sale, either for gold or money, but that if she could get leave to go to the Prince, and be with him during the night, she should have it. But when she went up to the Prince's room he was again asleep, and, let her call him, or shake him, or weep as she would, he still slept on, and she could not put any life in him. When daylight came in the morning, the Princess with the long nose came too, and once more drove her away. When day had quite come, the girl seated herself under the castle windows, to spin with her golden spinning-wheel, and the Princess with the long nose wanted to have that also. So she opened the window, and asked what she would take for it. The girl said what she had said on each of the former occasions—that it was not for sale either for gold or for money, but if she could get leave to go to the Prince who lived there, and be with him during the night, she should have it.

"Yes," said the Princess, "I will gladly consent to that."

But in that place there were some Christian folk who had been carried off, and they had been sitting in the chamber which was next to that of the Prince, and had heard how a woman had been in there who had wept and called on him two nights running, and they told the Prince of this. So that evening, when the Princess came once more with her sleeping-drink, he pretended to drink, but threw it away behind him, for he suspected that it was a sleeping-drink. So, when the girl went into the Prince's room this time he was awake, and she had to tell him how she had come there. "You have come just in time," said the Prince, "for I should have been married to-morrow; but I will not have the long-nosed Princess, and you alone can save me. I will say that I want to see what my bride can do, and bid her wash the shirt which has the three drops of tallow on it. This she will consent to do, for she does not know that it is you who let them fall on it; but no one can wash them out but one born of Christian folk: it cannot be done by one of a pack of trolls; and then I will say that no one shall ever be my bride but the woman who can do this, and I know that you can." There was great joy and gladness between them all that night, but the next day, when the wedding was to take place, the Prince said, "I must see what my bride can do." "That you may do," said the stepmother.

"I have a fine shirt which I want to wear as my wedding shirt, but three drops of tallow have got upon it which I want to have washed off, and I have vowed to marry no one but the woman who is able to do it. If she cannot do that, she is not worth having."

Well, that was a very small matter, they thought, and agreed to do it. The Princess with the long nose began to wash as well as she could, but, the more she washed and rubbed, the larger the spots grew. "Ah! you can't wash at all," said the old troll-hag, who was her mother. "Give it to me." But she too had not had the shirt very long in her hands before it looked worse still, and, the more she washed it and rubbed it, the larger and blacker grew the spots.

So the other trolls had to come and wash, but, the more they did, the blacker and uglier grew the shirt, until at length it was as black as if it had been up the chimney. "Oh," cried the Prince, "not one of you is good for anything at all! There is a beggar-girl sitting outside the window, and I'll be bound that she can wash better than any of you! Come in, you girl there!" he cried. So she came in. "Can you wash this shirt clean?" he cried. "Oh! I don't know," she said; "but I will try." And no sooner had she taken the shirt and dipped it in the water than it was white as driven snow, and even whiter than that. "I will marry you," said the Prince.

Then the old troll-hag flew into such a rage that she burst, and the Princess with the long nose and all the little trolls must have burst too, for they have never been heard of since. The Prince and his bride set free all the Christian folk who were imprisoned there, and took away with them all the gold and silver that they could carry, and moved far away from the castle which lay east of the sun and west of the moon.

—*The Blue Fairy Book* (1889)

The Enchanted Head

ASIA MINOR

———◆◆◆———

ONCE upon a time an old woman lived in a small cottage near the sea with her two daughters. They were very poor, and the girls seldom left the house, as they worked all day long making veils for the ladies to wear over their faces, and every morning, when the veils were finished, the mother took them over the bridge and sold them in the city. Then she bought the food that they needed for the day, and returned home to do her share of veil-making.

One morning the old woman rose even earlier than usual, and set off for the city with her wares. She was just crossing the bridge when, suddenly, she knocked up against a human head, which she had never seen there before. The woman started back in horror; but what was her surprise when the head spoke, exactly as if it had a body joined on to it.

"Take me with you, good mother!" it said imploringly; "take me with you back to your house."

At the sound of these words the poor woman nearly went mad with terror. Have that horrible thing always at home? Never! never! And she turned and ran back as fast as she could, not knowing that the head was jumping, dancing, and rolling after her. But when she reached her own door it bounded in before her, and stopped in

52

front of the fire, begging and praying to be allowed to stay.

All that day there was no food in the house, for the veils had not been sold, and they had no money to buy anything with. So they all sat silent at their work, inwardly cursing the head which was the cause of their misfortunes.

When evening came, and there was no sign of supper, the head spoke, for the first time that day:

"Good mother, does no one ever eat here? During all the hours I have spent in your house not a creature has touched anything."

"No," answered the old woman, "we are not eating anything."

"And why not, good mother?"

"Because we have no money to buy any food."

"Is it your custom never to eat?"

"No, for every morning I go into the city to sell my veils, and with the few shillings I get for them I buy all we want. To-day I did not cross the bridge, so of course I had nothing for food."

"Then *I* am the cause of your having gone hungry all day?" asked the head.

"Yes, you are," answered the old woman.

"Well, then, I will give you money and plenty of it, if you will only do as I tell you. In an hour, as the clock strikes twelve, you must be on the bridge at the place where you met me. When you get there call out 'Ahmed,' three times, as loud as you can. Then a negro will appear, and you must say to him: 'The head, your master, desires you to open the trunk, and to give me the green purse which you will find in it.' "

"Very well, my lord," said the old woman, "I will set off at once for the bridge." And wrapping her veil round her she went out.

Midnight was striking as she reached the spot where she had met the head so many hours before.

"Ahmed! Ahmed! Ahmed!" cried she, and immedi-

ately a huge negro, as tall as a giant, stood on the
bridge before her.

"What do you want?" asked he.

"The head, your master, desires you to open the
trunk, and to give me the green purse which you will
find in it."

"I will be back in a moment, good mother," said he.
And three minutes later he placed a purse full of se-
quins in the old woman's hand.

No one can imagine the joy of the whole family at the
sight of all this wealth. The tiny, tumble-down cottage
was rebuilt, the girls had new dresses, and their mother
ceased selling veils. It was such a new thing to them to
have money to spend, that they were not as careful as
they might have been, and by-and-by there was not a
single coin left in the purse. When this happened their
hearts sank within them, and their faces fell.

"Have you spent your fortune?" asked the head from
its corner, when it saw how sad they looked. "Well,
then, go at midnight, good mother, to the bridge, and
call out 'Mahomet!' three times, as loud as you can. A
negro will appear in answer, and you must tell him to
open the trunk, and to give you the red purse which he
will find there."

The old woman did not need twice telling, but set off
at once for the bridge.

"Mahomet! Mahomet! Mahomet!" cried she, with all
her might; and in an instant a negro, still larger than
the last, stood before her.

"What do you want?" asked he.

"The head, your master, bids you open the trunk,
and to give me the red purse which you will find in it."

"Very well, good mother, I will do so," answered the
negro, and, the moment after he had vanished, he
reappeared with the purse in his hand.

This time the money seemed so endless that the old
woman built herself a new house, and filled it with the
most beautiful things that were to be found in the
shops. Her daughters were always wrapped in veils that

looked as if they were woven out of sunbeams, and their dresses shone with precious stones. The neighbours wondered where all this sudden wealth had sprung from, but nobody knew about the head.

"Good mother," said the head, one day, "this morning you are to go to the city and ask the sultan to give me his daughter for my bride."

"Do what?" asked the old woman in amazement. "How can I tell the sultan that a head without a body wishes to become his son-in-law? They will think that I am mad, and I shall be hooted from the palace and stoned by the children."

"Do as I bid you," replied the head; "it is my will."

The old woman was afraid to say anything more, and, putting on her richest clothes, started for the palace. The sultan granted her an audience at once, and, in a trembling voice, she made her request.

"Are you mad, old woman?" said the sultan, staring at her.

"The wooer is powerful, O Sultan, and nothing is impossible to him."

"Is that true?"

"It is, O Sultan; I swear it," answered she.

"Then let him show his power by doing three things, and I will give him my daughter."

"Command, O gracious prince," said she.

"Do you see that hill in front of the palace?" asked the sultan.

"I see it," answered she.

"Well, in forty days the man who has sent you must make that hill vanish, and plant a beautiful garden in its place. That is the first thing. Now go, and tell him what I say."

So the old woman returned and told the head the sultan's first condition.

"It is well," he replied; and said no more about it.

For thirty-nine days the head remained in its favourite corner. The old woman thought that the task set before him was beyond his powers, and that no more would be heard about the sultan's daughter. But on the thirty-ninth evening after her visit to the palace, the head suddenly spoke.

"Good mother," he said, "you must go to-night to the bridge, and when you are there cry 'Ali! Ali! Ali!' as loud as you can. A negro will appear before you, and you will tell him that he is to level the hill, and to make, in its place, the most beautiful garden that ever was seen."

"I will go at once," answered she.

It did not take her long to reach the bridge which led to the city, and she took up her position on the spot where she had first seen the head, and called loudly "Ali! Ali! Ali." In an instant a negro appeared before her, of such a huge size that the old woman was half frightened; but his voice was mild and gentle as he said: "What is it that you want?"

"Your master bids you level the hill that stands in front of the sultan's palace and in its place to make the most beautiful garden in the world."

"Tell my master he shall be obeyed," replied Ali; "it shall be done this moment." And the old woman went home and gave Ali's message to the head.

Meanwhile the sultan was in his palace waiting till the fortieth day should dawn, and wondering that not one spadeful of earth should have been dug out of the hill.

"If that old woman has been playing me a trick," thought he, "I will hang her! And I will put up a gallows to-morrow on the hill itself."

But when to-morrow came there was no hill, and when the sultan opened his eyes he could not imagine why the room was so much lighter than usual, and what was the reason of the sweet smell of flowers that filled the air.

"Can there be a fire?" he said to himself; "the sun never came in at this window before. I must get up and see." So he rose and looked out, and underneath him flowers from every part of the world were blooming, and creepers of every colour hung in chains from tree to tree.

Then he remembered. "Certainly that old woman's son is a clever magician!" cried he; "I never met anyone as clever as that. What shall I give him to do next? Let me think. Ah! I know." And he sent for the old woman, who by orders of the head, was waiting below.

"Your son has carried out my wishes very nicely," he said. "The garden is larger and better than that of any other king. But when I walk across it I shall need some place to rest on the other side. In forty days he must build me a palace, in which every room shall be filled with different furniture from a different country, and each more magnificent than any room that ever was seen." And having said this he turned round and went away.

"Oh! he will never be able to do that," thought she; "it is much more difficult than the hill." And she walked home slowly, with her head bent.

"Well, what am I to do next?" asked the head cheerfully. And the old woman told her story.

"Dear me! is that all? why it is child's play," answered the head; and troubled no more about the palace for thirty-nine days. Then he told the old woman to go to the bridge and call for Hassan.

"What do you want, old woman?" asked Hassan, when he appeared, for he was not as polite as the others had been.

"Your master commands you to build the most magnificent palace that ever was seen," replied she; "and you are to place it on the borders of the new garden."

"He shall be obeyed," answered Hassan. And when the sultan woke he saw, in the distance, a palace built of soft blue marble, resting on slender pillars of pure gold.

"That old woman's son is certainly all-powerful," cried he; "what shall I bid him do now?" And after thinking some time he sent for the old woman, who was expecting the summons.

THE PRINCESS SEES THE MAGIC HEAD

"The garden is wonderful, and the palace the finest in the world," said he, "so fine, that my servants would cut but a sorry figure in it. Let your son fill it with forty slaves whose beauty shall be unequalled, all exactly like each other, and of the same height."

This time the king thought he had invented something totally impossible, and was quite pleased with himself for his cleverness.

Thirty-nine days passed, and at midnight on the night of the last the old woman was standing on the bridge.

"Bekir! Bekir! Bekir!" cried she. And a negro appeared, and inquired what she wanted.

"The head, your master, bids you find forty slaves of unequalled beauty, and of the same height, and place them in the sultan's palace on the other side of the garden."

And when, on the morning of the fortieth day, the sultan went to the blue palace, and was received by the forty slaves, he nearly lost his wits from surprise.

"I will assuredly give my daughter to the old woman's son," thought he. "If I were to search all the world through I could never find a more powerful son-in-law."

And when the old woman entered his presence he informed her that he was ready to fulfil his promise, and she was to bid her son appear at the palace without delay.

This command did not at all please the old woman, though, of course, she made no objections to the sultan.

"All has gone well so far," she grumbled, when she told her story to the head, "but what do you suppose the sultan will say, when he sees his daughter's husband?"

"Never mind what he says! Put me on a silver dish and carry me to the palace."

So it was done, though the old woman's heart beat as she laid down the dish with the head upon it.

At the sight before him the king flew into a violent rage.

"I will never marry my daughter to such a monster,"

he cried. But the princess placed her hand gently on his arm.

"You have given your word, my father, and you cannot break it," said she.

"But, my child, it is impossible for you to marry such a being," exclaimed the sultan.

"Yes, I will marry him. He has a beautiful head, and I love him already."

So the marriage was celebrated, and great feasts were held in the palace, though the people wept tears to think of the sad fate of their beloved princess. But when the merry-making was done, and the young couple were alone, the head suddenly disappeared, or, rather, a body was added to it, and one of the handsomest young men that ever was seen stood before the princess.

"A wicked fairy enchanted me at my birth," he said, "and for the rest of the world I must always be a head only. But for you, and you only, I am a man like other men."

"And that is all I care about," said the princess.

—*The Brown Fairy Book* (1904)

The Fairy Nurse

CELTIC

———•◆•———

THERE was once a little farmer and his wife living near Coolgarrow. They had three children, and my story happened while the youngest was a baby. The wife was a good wife enough, but her mind was all on her family and her farm, and she hardly ever went to her knees without falling asleep, and she thought the time spent in the chapel was twice as long as it need be. So, friends, she let her man and her two children go before her one day to Mass, while she called to consult a fairy man about a disorder one of her cows had. She was late at the chapel, and was sorry all the day after, for her husband was in grief about it, and she was very fond of him.

Late that night he was wakened up by the cries of his children calling out "Mother! mother!" When he sat up and rubbed his eyes, there was no wife by his side; and when he asked the little ones what was become of their mother, they said they saw the room full of nice little men and women, dressed in white and red and green, and their mother in the middle of them, going out by the door as if she was walking in her sleep. Out he ran, and searched everywhere round the house, but neither tale nor tidings did he get of her for many a day.

Well, the poor man was miserable enough, for he

The Fairies go off with the Farmer's Wife

was as fond of his woman as she was of him. It used to bring the salt tears down his cheeks to see his poor children neglected and dirty, as they often were, and they'd be bad enough only for a kind neighbour that used to look in whenever she could spare time. The infant was away with a nurse.

About six weeks after—just as he was going out to his work one morning—a neighbour, that used to mind women when they were ill, came up to him, and kept step by step with him to the field, and this is what she told him.

"Just as I was falling asleep last night, I heard a horse's tramp on the grass and a knock at the door, and there, when I came out, was a fine-looking dark man, mounted on a black horse, and he told me to get ready in all haste, for a lady was in great want of me. As soon as I put on my cloak and things, he took me by the hand, and I was sitting behind him before I felt myself stirring. "Where are we going, sir?" says I. "You'll soon know," says he; and he drew his fingers across my eyes, and not a ray could I see. I kept a tight grip of him, and I little knew whether he was going backwards or forwards, or how long we were about it, till my hand was taken again, and I felt the ground under me. The fingers went the other way across my eyes, and there we were before a castle door, and in we went through a big hall and great rooms all painted in fine green colours, with red and gold bands and ornaments, and the finest carpets and chairs and tables and window curtains, and grand ladies and gentlemen walking about. At last we came to a bedroom, with a beautiful lady in bed, with a fine bouncing boy beside her. The lady clapped her hands, and in came the Dark Man and kissed her and the baby, and praised me, and gave me a bottle of green ointment to rub the child all over.

"Well, the child I rubbed, sure enough; but my right eye began to smart, and I put up my finger and gave it a rub, and then stared, for never in all my life was I so frightened. The beautiful room was a big, rough cave,

with water oozing over the edges of the stones and
through the clay; and the lady, and the lord, and the
child weazened, poverty-bitten creatures—nothing but
skin and bone—and the rich dresses were old rags. I
didn't let on that I found any difference, and after a bit
says the Dark Man, "Go before me to the hall door, and
I will be with you in a few moments, and see you safe
home." Well, just as I turned into the outside cave,
who should I see watching near the door but poor
Molly. She looked round all terrified, and says she to
me in a whisper, 'I'm brought here to nurse the child
of the king and queen of the fairies; but there is one
chance of saving me. All the court will pass the cross
near Temple-shambo next Friday night, on a visit to
the fairies of Old Ross. If John can catch me by the
hand or cloak when I ride by, and has courage not to let
go his grip, I'll be safe. Here's the king. Don't open
your mouth to answer. I saw what happened with the
ointment.'

"The Dark Man didn't once cast his eye towards
Molly, and he seemed to have no suspicion of me.
When we came out I looked about me, and where do
you think we were but in the dyke of the Rath of
Cromogue. I was on the horse again, which was nothing
but a big rag-weed, and I was in dread every minute I'd
fall off; but nothing happened till I found myself in my
own cabin. The king slipped five guineas into my hand
as soon as I was on the ground, and thanked me, and
bade me good night. I hope I'll never see his face again.
I got into bed, and couldn't sleep for a long time; and
when I examined my five guineas this morning, that I
left in the table drawer the last thing, I found five
withered leaves of oak—bad luck to the giver!"

Well, you may all think the fright, and the joy, and
the grief the poor man was in when the woman finished
her story. They talked and they talked, but we needn't
mind what they said till Friday night came, when both
were standing where the mountain road crosses the one
going to Ross.

There they stood, looking towards the bridge of Thuar, in the dead of the night, with a little moonlight shining from over Kilachdiarmid. At last she gave a start, and "By this and by that," says she, "here they come, bridles jingling and feathers tossing!" He looked, but could see nothing; and she stood trembling and her eyes wide open, looking down the way to the ford of Ballinacoola. "I see your wife," says she, "riding on the outside just so as to rub against us. We'll walk on quietly, as if we suspected nothing, and when we are passing I'll give you a shove. If you don't do *your* duty then, woe be with you!"

Well, they walked on easy, and the poor hearts beating in both their breasts; and though he could see nothing, he heard a faint jingle and trampling and rustling, and at last he got the push that she promised. He spread out his arms, and there was his wife's waist within them, and he could see her plain; but such a hullabulloo rose as if there was an earthquake, and he found himself surrounded by horrible-looking things, roaring at him and striving to pull his wife away. But he made the sign of the cross and bid them begone in God's name, and held his wife as if it was iron his arms were made of. Bedad, in one moment everything was as silent as the grave, and the poor woman lying in a faint in the arms of her husband and her good neighbour. Well, all in good time she was minding her family and her business again; and I'll go bail, after the fright she got, she spent more time on her knees, and avoided fairy men all the days of the week, and particularly on Sunday.

It is hard to have anything to do with the good people without getting a mark from them. My brave nurse didn't escape no more than another. She was one Thursday at the market of Enniscorthy, when what did she see walking among the tubs of butter but the Dark Man, very hungry-looking, and taking a scoop out of one tub and out of another. "Oh, sir," says she, very foolish, "I hope your lady is well, and the baby." "Pretty well, thank you," says he, rather frightened like. "How do I look in this new suit?" says he, getting to one side of her. "I can't see you plain at all, sir," says she. "Well, now?" says he, getting round her back to the other side. "Musha, indeed, sir, your coat looks no better than a withered dock-leaf." "Maybe, then," says he, "it will be different now," and he struck the eye next him with a switch.

Friends, she never saw a glimmer after with that one till the day of her death.

—*The Lilac Fairy Book* (1910)

The Fairy of the Dawn

ROUMANIAN

———◆◆———

ONCE upon a time what should happen *did* happen; and
if it had not happened this tale would never have been
told.

There was once an emperor, very great and mighty,
and he ruled over an empire so large that no one knew
where it began and where it ended. But if nobody
could tell the exact extent of his sovereignty everybody
was aware that the emperor's right eye laughed, while
his left eye wept. One or two men of valour had the
courage to go and ask him the reason of this strange
fact, but he only laughed and said nothing; and the
reason of the deadly enmity between his two eyes was a
secret only known to the monarch himself.

And all the while the emperor's sons were growing
up. And such sons! All three like the morning stars in
the sky!

Florea, the eldest, was so tall and broad-shouldered
that no man in the kingdom could approach him.

Costan, the second, was quite different. Small of
stature, and slightly built, he had a strong arm and
stronger wrist.

Petru, the third and youngest, was tall and thin,
more like a girl than a boy. He spoke very little, but
laughed and sang, sang and laughed, from morning till

night. He was very seldom serious, but then he had a
way when he was thinking of stroking his hair over his
forehead, which made him look old enough to sit in his
father's council!

"You are grown up, Florea," said Petru one day to his
eldest brother; "do go and ask father why one eye
laughs and the other weeps."

But Florea would not go. He had learnt by experience that this question always put the emperor in a
rage.

Petru next went to Costan, but did not succeed any
better with him.

"Well, well, as everyone else is afraid, I suppose I
must do it myself," observed Petru at length. No sooner
said than done; the boy went straight to his father and
put his question.

"May you go blind!" exclaimed the emperor in wrath;
"what business is it of yours?" and boxed Petru's ears
soundly.

Petru returned to his brothers, and told them what
had befallen him; but not long after it struck him that
his father's left eye seemed to weep less, and the right
to laugh more.

"I wonder if it has anything to do with my question,"
thought he. "I'll try again! After all, what do two boxes
on the ear matter?"

So he put his question for the second time, and had
the same answer; but the left eye only wept now and
then, while the right eye looked ten years younger.

"It really *must* be true," thought Petru. "Now I know
what I have to do. I shall have to go on putting that
question, and getting boxes on the ear, till both eyes
laugh together."

No sooner said than done. Petru never, never for-
swore himself.

"Petru, my dear boy," cried the emperor, both his
eyes laughing together. "I see you have got this on the
brain. Well, I will let you into the secret. My right eye
laughs when I look at my three sons, and see how

strong and handsome you all are, and the other eye
weeps because I fear that after I die you will not be
able to keep the empire together, and to protect it from
its enemies. But if you can bring me water from the
spring of the Fairy of the Dawn, to bathe my eyes, then
they will laugh for evermore; for I shall know that my
sons are brave enough to overcome any foe."

Thus spoke the emperor, and Petru picked up his hat
and went to find his brothers.

The three young men took counsel together, and
talked the subject well over, as brothers should do. And
the end of it was that Florea, as the eldest, went to the
stables, chose the best and handsomest horse they contained, saddled him, and took leave of the court.

"I am starting at once," said he to his brothers, "and
if after a year, a month, and a day I have not returned
with the water from the spring of the Fairy of the
Dawn, you, Costan, had better come after me." So
saying he disappeared round a corner of the palace.

For three days and three nights he never drew rein.
Like a spirit the horse flew over mountains and valleys
till he came to the borders of the empire. Here was a
deep, deep trench that girdled it the whole way round,
and there was only a single bridge by which the trench
could be crossed. Florea made instantly for the bridge,
and there pulled up to look around him once more, to
take leave of his native land. Then he turned, but
before him was standing a dragon—oh! *such* a dragon!—a
dragon with three heads and three horrible faces, all
with their mouths wide open, one jaw reaching to heaven
and the other to earth.

At this awful sight Florea did not wait to give battle.
He put spurs to his horse and dashed off, *where* he
neither knew nor cared.

The dragon heaved a sigh and vanished without leaving a trace behind him.

A week went by. Florea did not return home. Two
passed; and nothing was heard of him. After a month
Costan began to haunt the stables and to look out a

horse for himself. And the moment the year, the month, the week, and the day were over Costan mounted his horse and took leave of his youngest brother.

"If I fail, then you come," said he, and followed the path that Florea had taken.

The dragon on the bridge was more fearful and his three heads more terrible than before, and the young hero rode away still faster than his brother had done.

Nothing more was heard either of him or Florea; and Petru remained alone.

"I must go after my brothers," said Petru one day to his father.

"Go, then," said his father, "and may you have better luck than they"; and he bade farewell to Petru, who rode straight to the borders of the kingdom.

The dragon on the bridge was yet more dreadful than the one Florea and Costan had seen, for this one had seven heads instead of only three.

Petru stopped for a moment when he caught sight of this terrible creature. Then he found his voice.

"Get out of the way!" cried he. "Get out of the way!" he repeated again, as the dragon did not move. "Get out of the way!" and with this last summons he drew his sword and rushed upon him. In an instant the heavens seemed to darken round him and he was surrounded by fire—fire to right of him, fire to left of him, fire to front of him, fire to rear of him; nothing but fire whichever way he looked, for the dragon's seven heads were vomiting flame.

The horse neighed and reared at the horrible sight, and Petru could not use the sword he had in readiness.

"Be quiet! this won't do!" he said, dismounting hastily, but holding the bridle firmly in his left hand and grasping his sword in his right.

But even so he got on no better, for he could see nothing but fire and smoke.

"There is no help for it; I must go back and get a better horse," said he, and mounted again and rode homewards.

At the gate of the palace his nurse, old Birscha, was waiting for him eagerly.

"Ah, Petru, my son, I knew you would have to come back," she cried. "You did not set about the matter properly."

"How ought I to have set about it?" asked Petru, half angrily, half sadly.

"Look here, my boy," replied old Birscha. "You can never reach the spring of the Fairy of the Dawn unless you ride the horse which your father, the emperor, rode in his youth. Go and ask where it is to be found, and then mount it and be off with you."

Petru thanked her heartily for her advice, and went at once to make inquiries about the horse.

"By the light of my eyes!" exclaimed the emperor when Petru had put his question. "Who has told you anything about that? It must have been that old witch of a Birscha? Have you lost your wits? Fifty years have passed since I was young, and who knows where the bones of my horse may be rotting, or whether a scrap of his reins still lie in his stall? I have forgotten all about him long ago."

Petru turned away in anger, and went back to his old nurse.

"Do not be cast down," she said with a smile; "if that is how the affair stands all will go well. Go and fetch the scrap of the reins; I shall soon know what must be done."

The place was full of saddles, bridles, and bits of leather. Petru picked out the oldest, and blackest, and most decayed pair of reins, and brought them to the old woman, who murmured something over them and sprinkled them with incense, and held them out to the young man.

"Take the reins," said she, "and strike them violently against the pillars of the house."

Petru did what he was told, and scarcely had the reins touched the pillars when something happened—*how* I have no idea—that made Petru stare with surprise. A horse stood before him—a horse whose equal in beauty the world had never seen; with a saddle on him of gold and precious stones, and with such a dazzling bridle you hardly dared to look at it, lest you should lose your sight. A splendid horse, a splendid saddle, and a splendid bridle, all ready for the splendid young prince!

"Jump on the back of the brown horse," said the old woman, and she turned round and went into the house.

The moment Petru was seated on the horse he felt his arm three times as strong as before, and even his heart felt braver.

"Sit firmly in the saddle, my lord, for we have a long way to go and no time to waste," said the brown horse, and Petru soon saw that they were riding as no man and horse had ever ridden before.

On the bridge stood a dragon, but not the same one as he had tried to fight with, for this dragon had twelve heads, each more hideous and shooting forth more terrible flames than the other. But, horrible though he was, he had met his match. Petru showed no fear, but rolled up his sleeves, that his arms might be free.

"Get out of the way!" he said when he had done, but the dragon's heads only breathed forth more flames and smoke. Petru wasted no more words, but drew his sword and prepared to throw himself on the bridge.

"Stop a moment; be careful, my lord," put in the horse, "and be sure you do what I tell you. Dig your spurs in my body up to the rowel, draw your sword, and keep yourself ready, for we shall have to leap over both bridge and dragon. When you see that we are right above the dragon cut off his biggest head, wipe the blood off the sword, and put it back clean in the sheath before we touch earth again."

So Petru dug in his spurs, drew his sword, cut off the head, wiped the blood, and put the sword back in the sheath before the horse's hoofs touched the ground again.

And in this fashion they passed the bridge.

"But we have got to go further still," said Petru, after he had taken a farewell glance at his native land.

"Yes, forwards," answered the horse; "but you must tell me, my lord, at what speed you wish to go. Like the wind? Like thought? Like desire? or like a curse?"

Petru looked about him, up at the heavens and down again to the earth. A desert lay spread out before him, whose aspect made his hair stand on end.

"We will ride at different speeds," said he, "not so fast as to grow tired nor so slow as to waste time."

And so they rode, one day like the wind, the next like thought, the third and fourth like desire and like a curse, till they reached the borders of the desert.

"Now walk, so that I may look about, and see what I have never seen before," said Petru, rubbing his eyes like one who wakes from sleep, or like him who beholds something so strange that it seems as if . . . Before Petru lay a wood made of copper, with copper trees and copper leaves, with bushes and flowers of copper also.

Petru stood and stared as a man does when he sees something that he has never seen, and of which he has never heard.

Then he rode right into the wood. On each side of the way the rows of flowers began to praise Petru, and to try and persuade him to pick some of them and make himself a wreath.

"Take me, for I am lovely, and can give strength to whoever plucks me," said one.

"No, take me, for whoever wears me in his hat will be loved by the most beautiful woman in the world," pleaded the second; and then one after another bestirred itself, each more charming than the last, all promising, in soft sweet voices, wonderful things to Petru, if only he would pick them.

Petru was not deaf to their persuasion, and was just stooping to pick one when the horse sprang to one side.

"Why don't you stay still?" asked Petru roughly.

"Do not pick the flowers; it will bring you bad luck," answered the horse.

"Why should it do that?"

"These flowers are under a curse. Whoever plucks them must fight the Welwa of the woods."

"What kind of a goblin is the Welwa?"

"Oh, do leave me in peace! But listen. Look at the flowers as much as you like, but pick none," and the horse walked on slowly.

Petru knew by experience that he would do well to attend to the horse's advice, so he made a great effort and tore his mind away from the flowers.

But in vain! If a man is fated to be unlucky, unlucky he will be, whatever he may do!

The flowers went on beseeching him, and his heart grew ever weaker and weaker.

"What must come will come," said Petru at length; "at any rate I shall see the Welwa of the woods, what she is like, and which way I had best fight her. If she is ordained to be the cause of my death, well, then it will be so; but if not I shall conquer her though she were twelve hundred Welwas," and once more he stooped down to gather the flowers.

"You have done very wrong," said the horse sadly. "But it can't be helped now. Get yourself ready for battle, for here is the Welwa!"

Hardly had he done speaking, scarcely had Petru twisted his wreath, when a soft breeze arose on all sides at once. Out of the breeze came a storm wind, and the storm wind swelled and swelled till everything around was blotted out in darkness, and darkness covered them as with a thick cloak, while the earth swayed and shook under their feet.

"Are you afraid?" asked the horse, shaking his mane.

"Not yet," replied Petru stoutly, though cold shivers were running down his back. "What must come will come, whatever is it."

"Don't be afraid," said the horse. "I will help you. Take the bridle from my neck, and try to catch the Welwa with it."

The words were hardly spoken, and Petru had no time even to unbuckle the bridle, when the Welwa herself stood before him; and Petru could not bear to look at her, so horrible was she.

She had not exactly a head, yet neither was she without one. She did not fly through the air, but neither did she walk upon the earth. She had a mane like a horse, horns like a deer, a face like a bear, eyes like a polecat; while her body had something of each. And that was the Welwa.

Petru planted himself firmly in his stirrups, and began to lay about him with his sword, but could feel nothing.

A day and a night went by, and the fight was still undecided, but at last the Welwa began to pant for breath.

"Let us wait a little and rest," gasped she.

Petru stopped and lowered his sword.

"You must not stop an instant," said the horse, and Petru gathered up all his strength, and laid about him harder than ever.

The Welwa gave a neigh like a horse and a howl like a wolf, and threw herself afresh on Petru. For another day and night the battle raged more furiously than before. And Petru grew so exhausted he could scarcely move his arm.

"Let us wait a little and rest," cried the Welwa for the second time, "for I see you are as weary as I am."

"You must not stop an instant," said the horse.

And Petru went on fighting, though he barely had strength to move his arm. But the Welwa had ceased to throw herself upon him, and began to deliver her blows cautiously, as if she had no longer power to strike.

And on the third day they were still fighting, but as the morning sky began to redden Petru somehow managed—how I cannot tell—to throw the bridle over the head of the tired Welwa. In a moment, from the Welwa sprang a horse—the most beautiful horse in the world.

"Sweet be your life, for you have delivered me from my enchantment," said he, and began to rub his nose against his brother's. And he told Petru all his story, and how he had been bewitched for many years.

So Petru tied the Welwa to his own horse and rode on. Where did he ride? That I cannot tell you, but he rode on fast till he got out of the copper wood.

"Stay still, and let me look about, and see what I never have seen before," said Petru again to his horse. For in front of him stretched a forest that was far more wonderful, as it was made of glistening trees and shining flowers. It was the silver wood.

As before, the flowers began to beg the young man to gather them.

"Do not pluck them," warned the Welwa, trotting beside him, "for my brother is seven times stronger than I"; but though Petru knew by experience what this meant, it was no use, and after a moment's hesitation he began to gather the flowers, and to twist himself a wreath.

Then the storm wind howled louder, the earth trembled more violently, and the night grew darker, than the first time, and the Welwa of the silver wood came rushing on with seven times the speed of the other. For three days and three nights they fought, but at last Petru cast the bridle over the head of the second Welwa.

"Sweet be your life, for you have delivered me from enchantment," said the second Welwa, and they all journeyed on as before.

But soon they came to a gold wood more lovely far than the other two, and again Petru's companions pleaded with him to ride through it quickly, and to leave the flowers alone. But Petru turned a deaf ear to all they said, and before he had woven his golden crown he felt that something terrible, that he could not see, was coming near him right out of the earth. He drew his sword and made himself ready for the fight. "I will die!" cried he, "or he shall have my bridle over his head."

He had hardly said the words when a thick fog wrapped itself around him, and so thick was it that he could not see his own hand, or hear the sound of his voice. For a day and a night he fought with his sword, without ever once seeing his enemy, then suddenly the fog began to lighten. By dawn of the second day it had vanished altogether, and the sun shone brightly in the heavens. It seemed to Petru that he had been born again.

And the Welwa? She had vanished.

"You had better take breath now you can, for the fight will have to begin all over again," said the horse.

"What was it?" asked Petru.

"It was the Welwa," replied the horse, "changed into a fog! Listen! She is coming!"

And Petru had hardly drawn a long breath when he felt something approaching from the side, though *what* he could not tell. A river, yet not a river, for it seemed not to flow over the earth, but to go where it liked, and to leave no trace of its passage.

"Woe be to me!" cried Petru, frightened at last.

"Beware, and never stand still," called the brown horse, and more he could not say, for the water was choking him.

The battle began anew. For a day and a night Petru fought on, without knowing at whom or what he struck. At dawn on the second, he felt that both his feet were lame.

"Now I am done for," thought he, and his blows fell thicker and harder in his desperation. And the sun came out and the water disappeared, without his knowing how or when.

"Take breath," said the horse, "for you have no time to lose. The Welwa will return in a moment."

Petru made no reply, only wondered how, exhausted as he was, he should ever be able to carry on the fight. But he settled himself in his saddle, grasped his sword, and waited.

And then something came to him—*what* I cannot tell you. Perhaps, in his dreams, a man may see a creature which has what it has not got, and has not got what it has. At least, that was what the Welwa seemed like to Petru. She flew with her feet, and walked with her wings; her head was in her back, and her tail was on top of her body; her eyes were in her neck, and her neck in her forehead, and how to describe her further I do not know.

Petru felt for a moment as if he was wrapped in a garment of fear; then he shook himself and took heart, and fought as he had never yet fought before.

As the day wore on, his strength began to fail, and when darkness fell he could hardly keep his eyes open. By midnight he knew he was no longer on his horse, but standing on the ground, though he could not have told how he got there. When the grey light of morning came, he was past standing on his feet, but fought now upon his knees.

"Make one more struggle; it is nearly over now," said the horse, seeing that Petru's strength was waning fast.

Petru wiped the sweat from his brow with his gauntlet, and with a desperate effort rose to his feet.

"Strike the Welwa on the mouth with the bridle," said the horse, and Petru did it.

The Welwa uttered a neigh so loud that Petru thought he would be deaf for life, and then, though she too was nearly spent, flung herself upon her enemy; but Petru was on the watch and threw the bridle over her head, as she rushed on, so that when the day broke there were three horses trotting beside him.

"May your wife be the most beautiful of women," said the Welwa, "for you have delivered me from my enchantment." So the four horses galloped fast, and by nightfall they were at the borders of the golden forest.

Then Petru began to think of the crowns that he wore, and what they had cost him.

"After all, what do I want with so many? I will keep

The Fairy of the Dawn

the best," he said to himself; and taking off first the copper crown and then the silver, he threw them away.

"Stay!" cried the horse, "do not throw them away! Perhaps we shall find them of use. Get down and pick them up." So Petru got down and picked them up, and they all went on.

In the evening, when the sun is getting low, and all the midges are beginning to bite, Petru saw a wide heath stretching before him.

At the same instant the horse stood still of itself.

"What is the matter?" asked Petru.

"I am afraid that something evil will happen to us," answered the horse.

"But why should it?"

"We are going to enter the kingdom of the goddess Mittwoch,[1] and the further we ride into it the colder we shall get. But all along the road there are huge fires, and I dread lest you should stop and warm yourself at them."

"And why should I not warm myself?"

"Something fearful will happen to you if you do," replied the horse sadly.

"Well, forward!" cried Petru lightly, "and if I have to bear cold, I must bear it!"

With every step they went into the kingdom of Mittwoch, the air grew colder and more icy, till even the marrow in their bones was frozen. But Petru was no coward; the fight he had gone through had strengthened his powers of endurance, and he stood the test bravely.

Along the road on each side were great fires, with men standing by them, who spoke pleasantly to Petru as he went by, and invited him to join them. The breath froze in his mouth, but he took no notice, only bade his horse ride on the faster.

How long Petru may have waged battle silently with the cold one cannot tell, for everybody knows that the

---

[1] In German "Mittwoch," the feminine form of Mercury.

kingdom of Mittwoch is not to be crossed in a day, but he struggled on, though the frozen rocks burst around, and though his teeth chattered, and even his eyelids were frozen.

At length they reached the dwelling of Mittwoch herself, and, jumping from his horse, Petru threw the reins over his horse's neck and entered the hut.

"Good-day, little mother!" said he.

"Very well, thank you, my frozen friend!"

Petru laughed, and waited for her to speak.

"You have borne yourself bravely," went on the goddess, tapping him on the shoulder. "Now you shall have your reward," and she opened an iron chest, out of which she took a little box.

"Look!" said she; "this little box has been lying here for ages, waiting for the man who could win his way through the Ice Kingdom. Take it, and treasure it, for some day it may help you. If you open it, it will tell you anything you want, and give you news of your fatherland."

Petru thanked her gratefully for her gift, mounted his horse, and rode away.

When he was some distance from the hut, he opened the casket.

"What are your commands?" asked a voice inside.

"Give me news of my father," he replied, rather nervously.

"He is sitting in council with his nobles," answered the casket.

"Is he well?"

"Not particularly, for he is furiously angry."

"What has angered him?"

"Your brothers Costan and Florea," replied the casket. "It seems to me they are trying to rule him and the kingdom as well, and the old man says they are not fit to do it."

"Push on, good horse, for we have no time to lose!" cried Petru; then he shut up the box, and put it in his pocket.

They rushed on as fast as ghosts, as whirlwinds, as

vampires when they hunt at midnight, and how long they rode no man can tell, for the way is far.

"Stop! I have some advice to give you," said the horse at last.

"What is it?" asked Petru.

"You have known what it is to suffer cold; you will have to endure heat, such as you have never dreamed of. Be as brave now as you were then. Let no one tempt you to try to cool yourself, or evil will befall you."

"Forwards!" answered Petru. "Do not worry yourself. If I have escaped without being frozen, there is no chance of my melting."

"Why not? This is a heat that will melt the marrow in your bones—a heat that is only to be felt in the kingdom of the Goddess of Thunder."[1]

And it *was* hot. The very iron of the horse's shoes began to melt, but Petru gave no heed. The sweat ran down his face, but he dried it with his gauntlet. What heat could be he never knew before, and on the way, not a stone's throw from the road, lay the most delicious valleys, full of shady trees and bubbling streams. When Petru looked at them his heart burned within him, and his mouth grew parched. And standing among the flowers were lovely maidens who called to him in soft voices, till he had to shut his eyes against their spells.

"Come, my hero, come and rest; the heat will kill you," said they.

Petru shook his head and said nothing, for he had lost the power of speech.

Long he rode in this awful state, how long none can tell. Suddenly the heat seemed to become less, and, in the distance, he saw a little hut on a hill. This was the dwelling of the Goddess of Thunder, and when he drew rein at her door the goddess herself came out to meet him.

[1] In the German, "Donnerstag"—the day of the Thunder God, *i.e.* Jupiter.

Among the Flowers were lovely maidens calling to him with ~soft voices~

She welcomed him, and kindly invited him in, and bade him tell her all his adventures. So Petru told her all that had happened to him, and why he was there, and then took farewell of her, as he had no time to lose. "For," he said, "who knows how far the Fairy of the Dawn may yet be?"

"Stay for one moment, for I have a word of advice to give you. You are about to enter the kingdom of Venus;[1] go and tell her, as a message from me, that I hope she will not tempt you to delay. On your way back, come to me again, and I will give you something that may be of use to you."

So Petru mounted his horse, and had hardly ridden three steps when he found himself in a new country. Here it was neither hot nor cold, but the air was warm and soft like spring, though the way ran through a heath covered with sand and thistles.

"What can that be?" asked Petru, when he saw a long, long way off, at the very end of the heath, something resembling a house.

"That is the house of the goddess Venus," replied the horse, "and if we ride hard we may reach it before dark"; and he darted off like an arrow, so that as twilight fell they found themselves nearing the house. Petru's heart leaped at the sight, for all the way along he had been followed by a crowd of shadowy figures who danced about him from right to left, and from back to front, and Petru, though a brave man, felt now and then a thrill of fear.

"They won't hurt you," said the horse; "they are just the daughters of the whirlwind amusing themselves while they are waiting for the ogre of the moon."

Then he stopped in front of the house, and Petru jumped off and went to the door.

"Do not be in such a hurry," cried the horse. "There are several things I must tell you first. You cannot enter

[1]"Vineri" is Friday, and also "Venus."

the house of the goddess Venus like that. She is always watched and guarded by the whirlwind."

"What am I to do then?"

"Take the copper wreath, and go with it to that little hill over there. When you reach it, say to yourself, 'Were there ever such lovely maidens! such angels! such fairy souls!' Then hold the wreath high in the air and cry, 'Oh! if I knew whether any one would accept this wreath from me . . . if I knew! if I knew!' and throw the wreath from you!"

"And why should I do all this?" said Petru.

"Ask no questions, but go and do it," replied the horse. And Petru did.

Scarcely had he flung away the copper wreath than the whirlwind flung himself upon it, and tore it in pieces.

Then Petru turned once more to the horse.

"Stop!" cried the horse again. "I have other things to tell you. Take the silver wreath and knock at the windows of the goddess Venus. When she says, 'Who is there?' answer that you have come on foot and lost your way on the heath. She will then tell you to go your way back again; but take care not to stir from the spot. Instead, be sure you say to her, 'No, indeed I shall do nothing of the sort, as from my childhood I have heard stories of the beauty of the goddess Venus, and it was not for nothing that I had shoes made of leather with soles of steel, and have travelled for nine years and nine months, and have won in battle the silver wreath, which I hope you may allow me to give you, and have done and suffered everything to be where I now am.' This is what you must say. What happens after is your affair."

Petru asked no more, but went towards the house.

By this time it was pitch dark, and there was only the ray of light that streamed through the windows to guide him, and at the sound of his footsteps two dogs began to bark loudly.

"Which of those dogs is barking? Is he tired of life?" asked the goddess Venus.

"It is I, O goddess!" replied Petru, rather timidly. "I have lost my way on the heath, and do not know where I am to sleep this night."

"Where did you leave your horse?" asked the goddess sharply.

Petru did not answer. He was not sure if he was to lie, or whether he had better tell the truth.

"Go away, my son, there is no place for you here," replied she, drawing back from the window.

Then Petru repeated hastily what the horse had told him to say, and no sooner had he done so than the goddess opened the window, and in gentle tones she asked him:

"Let me see this wreath, my son," and Petru held it out to her.

"Come into the house," went on the goddess; "do not fear the dogs, they always know my will." And so they did, for as the young man passed they wagged their tails to him.

"Good evening," said Petru as he entered the house, and, seating himself near the fire, listened comfortably to what the goddess might choose to talk about, which was for the most part the wickedness of men, with whom she was evidently very angry. But Petru agreed with her in everything, as he had been taught was only polite.

But was anybody ever so old as she! I do not know why Petru devoured her so with his eyes, unless it was to count the wrinkles on her face; but if so he would have had to live seven lives, and each life seven times the length of an ordinary one, before he could have reckoned them up.

But Venus was joyful in her heart when she saw Petru's eyes fixed upon her.

"Nothing was that is, and the world was not a world when I was born," said she. "When I grew up and the world came into being, everyone thought I was the most beautiful girl that ever was seen, though many hated me for it. But every hundred years there came a

wrinkle on my face. And now I am old." Then she went
on to tell Petru that she was the daughter of·an emperor, and their nearest neighbour was the Fairy of the
Dawn, with whom she had a violent quarrel, and with
that she broke out into loud abuse of her.

Petru did not know what to do. He listened in silence
for the most part, but now and then he would say,
"Yes, yes, you must have been badly treated," just for
politeness' sake; what more could he do?

"I will give you a task to perform, for you are brave,
and will carry it through," continued Venus, when she
had talked a long time, and both of them were getting
sleepy. "Close to the Fairy's house is a well, and whoever drinks from it will blossom again like a rose. Bring
me a flagon of it, and I will do anything to prove my
gratitude. It is not easy! no one knows that better than I
do! The kingdom is guarded on every side by wild
beasts and horrible dragons; but I will tell you more
about that, and I also have something to give you."
Then she rose and lifted the lid of an iron-bound chest,
and took out of it a very tiny flute.

"Do you see this?" she asked. "An old man gave it to
me when I was young: whoever listens to this flute goes
to sleep, and nothing can wake him. Take it and play on
it as long as you remain in the kingdom of the Fairy of
the Dawn, and you will be safe."

At this, Petru told her that he had another task to
fulfil at the well of the Fairy of the Dawn, and Venus
was still better pleased when she heard his tale.

So Petru bade her good-night, put the flute in its
case, and laid himself down in the lowest chamber to
sleep.

Before the dawn he was awake again, and his first
care was to give to each of his horses as much corn as
he could eat, and then to lead them to the well to
water. Then he dressed himself and made ready to
start.

"Stop," cried Venus from her window, "I have still a
piece of advice for you. Leave one of your horses here,

and only take three. Ride slowly till you get to the fairy's kingdom, then dismount and go on foot. When you return, see that all your three horses remain on the road, while you walk. But above all beware never to look the Fairy of the Dawn in the face, for she has eyes that will bewitch you, and glances that will befool you. She is hideous, more hideous than anything you can imagine, with owl's eyes, foxy face, and cat's claws. Do you hear? do you hear? Be sure you never look at her."

Petru thanked her, and managed to get off at last.

Far, far away, where the heavens touch the earth, where the stars kiss the flowers, a soft red light was seen, such as the sky sometimes has in spring, only lovelier, more wonderful.

That light was behind the palace of the Fairy of the Dawn, and it took Petru two days and nights through flowery meadows to reach it. And besides, it was neither hot nor cold, bright nor dark, but something of them all, and Petru did not find the way a step too long.

After some time Petru saw something white rise up out of the red of the sky, and when he drew nearer he saw it was a castle, and so splendid that his eyes were dazzled when they looked at it. He did not know there was such a beautiful castle in the world.

But no time was to be lost, so he shook himself, jumped down from his horse, and, leaving him on the dewy grass, began to play on his flute as he walked along.

He had hardly gone many steps when he stumbled over a huge giant, who had been lulled to sleep by the music. This was one of the guards of the castle! As he lay there on his back, he seemed so big that in spite of Petru's haste he stopped to measure him.

The further went Petru, the more strange and terrible were the sights he saw—lions, tigers, dragons with seven heads, all stretched out in the sun fast asleep. It is needless to say what the dragons were like, for nowadays everyone knows, and dragons are not things to joke about. Petru ran through them like the wind. Was it haste or fear that spurred him on?

At last he came to a river, but let nobody think for a moment that this river was like other rivers? Instead of water, there flowed milk, and the bottom was of precious stones and pearls, instead of sand and pebbles. And it ran neither fast nor slow, but both fast and slow together. And the river flowed round the castle, and on its banks slept lions with iron teeth and claws; and beyond were gardens such as only the Fairy of the Dawn can have, and on the flowers slept a fairy! All this saw Petru from the other side.

But how was he to get over? To be sure there was a bridge, but, even if it had not been guarded by sleeping lions, it was plainly not meant for man to walk on. Who could tell what it was made of? It looked like soft little woolly clouds!

So he stood thinking what was to be done, for get across he must. After a while, he determined to take the risk, and strode back to the sleeping giant. "Wake up, my brave man!" he cried, giving him a shake.

The giant woke and stretched out his hand to pick up Petru, just as we should catch a fly. But Petru played on his flute, and the giant fell back again. Petru tried this three times, and when he was satisfied that the giant was really in his power he took out a handkerchief, bound the two little fingers of the giant together, drew his sword, and cried for the fourth time, "Wake up, my brave man."

When the giant saw the trick which had been played on him he said to Petru, "Do you call this a fair fight? Fight according to rules, if you really are a hero!"

"I will by-and-by, but first I want to ask you a question! Will you swear that you will carry me over the river if I fight honourably with you?" And the giant swore.

When his hands were freed, the giant flung himself upon Petru, hoping to crush him by his weight. But he had met his match. It was not yesterday, nor the day before, that Petru had fought his first battle, and he bore himself bravely.

For three days and three nights the battle raged, and sometimes one had the upper hand, and sometimes the other, till at length they both lay struggling on the ground, but Petru was on top, with the point of his sword at the giant's throat.

"Let me go! let me go!" shrieked he. "I own that I am beaten!"

"Will you take me over the river?" asked Petru.

"I will," gasped the giant.

"What shall I do to you if you break your word?"

"Kill me, any way you like! But let me live now."

"Very well," said Petru, and he bound the giant's left hand to his right foot, tied one handkerchief round his mouth to prevent him crying out, and another round his eyes, and led him to the river.

Once they had reached the bank he stretched one leg over to the other side, and, catching up Petru in the palm of his hand, set him down on the further shore.

"That is all right," said Petru. Then he played a few notes on his flute, and the giant went to sleep again. Even the fairies who had been bathing a little lower down heard the music and fell asleep among the flowers on the bank. Petru saw them as he passed, and thought, "If they are so beautiful, why should the Fairy of the Dawn be so ugly?" But he dared not linger, and pushed on.

And now he was in the wonderful gardens, which seemed more wonderful still than they had done from afar. But Petru could see no faded flowers, nor any birds, as he hastened through them to the castle. No one was there to bar his way, for all were asleep. Even the leaves had ceased to move.

He passed through the courtyard, and entered the castle itself.

What he beheld there need not be told, for all the world knows that the palace of the Fairy of the Dawn is no ordinary place. Gold and precious stones were as common as wood with us, and the stables where the horses of the sun were kept were more splendid than the palace of the greatest emperor in the world.

Petru went up the stairs and walked quickly through eight-and-forty rooms, hung with silken stuffs, and all empty. In the forty-ninth he found the Fairy of the Dawn herself.

In the middle of this room, which was as large as a church, Petru saw the celebrated well that he had come so far to seek. It was a well just like other wells, and it seemed strange that the Fairy of the Dawn should have it in her own chamber; yet anyone could tell it had been there for hundreds of years. And by the well slept the Fairy of the Dawn—the Fairy of the Dawn—herself!

And as Petru looked at her the magic flute dropped by his side, and he held his breath.

Near the well was a table, on which stood bread made with does' milk, and a flagon of wine. It was the bread of strength and the wine of youth, and Petru longed for them. He looked once at the bread and once at the wind, and then at the Fairy of the Dawn, still sleeping on her silken cushions.

As he looked a mist came over his senses. The fairy opened her eyes slowly and looked at Petru, who lost his head still further; but he just managed to remember his flute, and a few notes of it sent the Fairy to sleep again, and he kissed her thrice. Then he stooped and laid his golden wreath upon her forehead, ate a piece of the bread and drank a cupful of the wine of youth, and this he did three times over. Then he filled a flask with water from the well, and vanished swiftly.

As he passed through the garden it seemed quite different from what it was before. The flowers were lovelier, the streams ran quicker, the sunbeams shone brighter, and the fairies seemed gayer. And all this had been caused by the three kisses Petru had given the Fairy of the Dawn.

He passed everything safely by, and was soon seated in his saddle again. Faster than the wind, faster than thought, faster than longing, faster than hatred rode Petru. At length he dismounted, and, leaving his horses at the roadside, went on foot to the house of Venus.

The goddess Venus knew that he was coming, and went to meet him, bearing with her white bread and red wine.

"Welcome back, my prince," said she.

"Good day, and many thanks," replied the young man, holding out the flask containing the magic water. She received it with joy, and after a short rest Petru set forth, for he had no time to lose.

He stopped a few minutes, as he had promised, with the Goddess of Thunder, and was taking a hasty farewell of her, when she called him back.

"Stay, I have a warning to give you," said she. "Beware of your life; make friends with no man; do not ride fast, or let the water go out of your hand; believe no one; and flee flattering tongues. Go, and take care, for the way is long, the world is bad, and you hold something very precious. But I will give you this cloth to help you. It is not much to look at, but it is enchanted, and whoever carries it will never be struck by lightning, pierced by a lance, or smitten with a sword, and the arrows will glance off his body."

Petru thanked her and rode off, and, taking out his treasure box, inquired how matters were going at home. Not well, it said. The emperor was blind altogether now, and Florea and Costan had besought him to give the government of the kingdom into their hands; but he would not, saying that he did not mean to resign the government till he had washed his eyes from the well of the Fairy of the Dawn. Then the brothers had gone to consult old Brischa, who told them that Petru was already on his way home bearing the water. They had set out to meet him, and would try to take the magic water from him, and then claim as their reward the government of the emperor.

"You are lying!" cried Petru angrily, throwing the

box on the ground, where it broke into a thousand pieces.

It was not long before he began to catch glimpses of his native land, and he drew rein near a bridge, the better to look at it. He was still gazing, when he heard a sound in the distance as if some one was calling him by his name.

"You, Petru!" it said.

"On! on!" cried the horse; "it will fare ill with you if you stop."

"No, let us stop, and see who and what it is!" answered Petru, turning his horse round, and coming face to face with his two brothers. He had forgotten the warning given him by the Goddess of Thunder, and when Costan and Florea drew near with soft and flattering words he jumped straight off his horse, and rushed to embrace them. He had a thousand questions to ask, and a thousand things to tell. But his brown horse stood sadly hanging his head.

"Petru, my dear brother," at length said Florea, "would it not be better if we carried the water for you? Some one might try to take it from you on the road, while no one would suspect us."

"So it would," added Costan. "Florea speaks well." But Petru shook his head, and told them what the Goddess of Thunder had said, and about the cloth she had given him. And both brothers understood there was only one way in which they could kill him.

At a stone's throw from where they stood ran a rushing stream, with clear deep pools.

"Don't you feel thirsty, Costan?" asked Florea, winking at him.

"Yes," replied Costan, understanding directly what was wanted. "Come, Petru, let us drink now we have the chance, and then we will set out on our way home. It is a good thing you have us with you, to protect you from harm."

The horse neighed, and Petru knew what it meant, and did not go with his brothers.

No, he went home to his father, and cured his blindness; and as for his brothers, they never returned again.

—*The Violet Fairy Book* (1901)

The Flying Ship

RUSSIAN

———◆◆———

ONCE upon a time there lived an old couple who had three sons; the two elder were clever, but the third was a regular dunce. The clever sons were very fond of their mother, gave her good clothes, and always spoke pleasantly to her; but the youngest was always getting in her way, and she had no patience with him. Now, one day it was announced in the village that the King had issued a decree, offering his daughter, the Princess, in marriage to whoever should build a ship that could fly. Immediately the two elder brothers determined to try their luck, and asked their parents' blessing. So the old mother smartened up their clothes, and gave them a store of provisions for their journey, not forgetting to add a bottle of brandy. When they had gone the poor Simpleton began to tease his mother to smarten him up and let him start off.

"What would become of a dolt like you?" she answered. "Why, you would be eaten up by wolves."

But the foolish youth kept repeating, "I will go, I will go, I will go!"

Seeing that she could do nothing with him, the mother gave him a crust of bread and a bottle of water, and took no further heed of him.

So the Simpleton set off on his way. When he had

gone a short distance he met a little old manikin. They greeted one another, and the manikin asked him where he was going.

"I am off to the King's Court," he answered. "He has promised to give his daughter to whoever can make a flying ship."

"And can you make such a ship?"

"Not I."

"Then why in the world are you going?"

"Can't tell," replied the Simpleton.

"Well, if that is the case," said the manikin, "sit down beside me; we can rest for a little and have something to eat. Give me what you have got in your satchel."

Now, the poor Simpleton was ashamed to show what was in it. However, he thought it best not to make a fuss, so he opened the satchel, and could scarcely believe his own eyes, for, instead of the hard crust, he saw two beautiful fresh rolls and some cold meat. He shared them with the manikin, who licked his lips and said:

"Now, go into that wood, and stop in front of the first tree, bow three times, and then strike the tree with your axe, fall on your knees on the ground, with your face on the earth, and remain there till you are raised up. You will then find a ship at your side, step into it and fly to the King's Palace. If you meet anyone on the way, take him with you."

The Simpleton thanked the manikin very kindly, bade him farewell, and went into the road. When he got to the first tree he stopped in front of it, did everything just as he had been told, and, kneeling on the ground with his face to the earth, fell asleep. After a little time he was aroused; he awoke and, rubbing his eyes, saw a ready-made ship at his side, and at once got into it. And the ship rose and rose, and in another minute was flying through the air, when the Simpleton, who was on the look-out, cast his eyes down to the earth and saw a man beneath him on the road, who was kneeling with his ear upon the damp ground.

"Hallo!" he called out, "what are you doing down there?"

"I am listening to what is going on in the world," replied the man.

"Come with me in my ship," said the Simpleton.

So the man was only too glad, and got in beside him; and the ship flew, and flew, and flew through the air, till again from his outlook the Simpleton saw a man on the road below, who was hopping on one leg, while his other leg was tied up behind his ear. So he hailed him, calling out:

"Hallo! what are you doing, hopping on one leg?"

"I can't help it," replied the man. "I walk so fast that unless I tied up one leg I should be at the end of the earth in a bound."

"Come with us on my ship," he answered; and the man made no objections, but joined them; and the ship flew on, and on, and on, till suddenly the Simpleton, looking down on the road below, beheld a man aiming with a gun into the distance.

"Hallo!" he shouted to him, "what are you aiming at? As far as eye can see, there is no bird in sight."

"What would be the good of my taking a near shot?" replied the man; "I can hit beast or bird at a hundred miles' distance. That is the kind of shot I enjoy."

"Come into the ship with us," answered the Simpleton; and the man was only too glad to join them, and he got in; and the ship flew on, farther and farther, till again the Simpleton from his outlook saw a man on the road below, carrying on his back a basket full of bread. And he waved to him, calling out:

"Hallo! where are you going?"

"To fetch bread for my breakfast."

"Bread? Why, you have got a whole basket-load of it on your back."

"That's nothing," answered the man; "I should finish that in one mouthful."

"Come along with us in my ship, then."

And so the glutton joined the party, and the ship mounted again into the air, and flew up and onward, till the Simpleton from his outlook saw a man walking by the shore of a great lake, and evidently looking for something.

"Hallo!" he cried to him, "what are you seeking?"

"I want water to drink, I'm so thirsty," replied the man.

"Well, there's a whole lake in front of you; why don't you drink some of that?"

"Do you call that enough?" answered the other. "Why, I should drink it up in one gulp."

"Well, come with us in the ship."

And so the mighty drinker was added to the company; and the ship flew farther, and even farther, till again the Simpleton looked out, and this time he saw a man dragging a bundle of wood, walking through the forest beneath them.

"Hallo!" he shouted to him, "why are you carrying wood through a forest?"

"This is not common wood," answered the other.

"What sort of wood is it, then?" said the Simpleton.

"If you throw it upon the ground," said the man, "it will be changed into an army of soldiers."

"Come into the ship with us, then."

And so he too joined them; and away the ship flew on, and on, and on, and once more the Simpleton looked out, and this time he saw a man carrying straw upon his back.

"Hallo! Where are you carrying that straw to?"

"To the village," said the man.

"Do you mean to say there is no straw in the village?"

"Ah! but this is quite a peculiar straw. If you strew it about even in the hottest summer the air at once becomes cold, and snow falls, and the people freeze."

Then the Simpleton asked him also to join them.

At last the ship, with its strange crew, arrived at the King's Court. The King was having his dinner, but he

at once despatched one of his courtiers to find out what
the huge, strange new bird could be that had come
flying through the air. The courtier peeped into the
ship, and, seeing what it was, instantly went back to the
King and told him that it was a flying ship, and that it
was manned by a few peasants.

Then the King remembered his royal oath; but he
made up his mind that he would never consent to let
the Princess marry a poor peasant. So he thought and
thought, and then said to himself:

"I will give him some impossible tasks to perform;
that will be the best way of getting rid of him." And he
there and then decided to despatch one of his courtiers
to the Simpleton, with the command that he was to
fetch the King the healing water from the world's end
before he had finished his dinner.

But while the King was still instructing the courtier
exactly what he was to say, the first man of the ship's
company, the one with the miraculous power of hearing, had overheard the King's words, and hastily reported them to the poor Simpleton.

"Alas, alas!" he cried; "what am I to do now? It would
take me quite a year, possibly my whole life, to find the
water."

"Never fear," said his fleet-footed comrade, "I will
fetch what the King wants."

Just then the courtier arrived, bearing the King's
command.

"Tell his Majesty," said the Simpleton, "that his orders shall be obeyed"; and forthwith the swift runner
unbound the foot that was strung up behind his ear and
started off, and in less than no time had reached the
world's end and drawn the healing water from the well.

"Dear me," he thought to himself, "that's rather tir-
ing! I'll just rest for a few minutes; it will be some little
time yet before the King has got to dessert." So he
threw himself down on the grass, and, as the sun was
very dazzling, he closed his eyes, and in a few seconds
had fallen sound asleep.

In the meantime all the ship's crew were anxiously awaiting him; the King's dinner would soon be finished, and their comrade had not yet returned. So the man with the marvellous quick hearing lay down and, putting his ear to the ground, listened.

"That's a nice sort of fellow!" he suddenly exclaimed. "He's lying on the ground, snoring hard!"

At this the marksman seized his gun, took aim, and fired in the direction of the world's end, in order to awaken the sluggard. And a moment later the swift runner reappeared, and, stepping on board the ship, handed the healing water to the Simpleton. So while the King was still sitting at table finishing his dinner news was brought to him that his orders had been obeyed to the letter.

What was to be done now? The King determined to think of a still more impossible task. So he told another courtier to go to the Simpleton with the command that he and his comrades were instantly to eat up twelve oxen and twelve tons of bread. Once more the sharp-eared comrade overheard the King's words while he was still talking to the courtier, and reported them to the Simpleton.

"Alas, alas!" he sighed; "what in the world shall I do? Why, it would take us a year, possibly our whole lives, to eat up twelve oxen and twelve tons of bread."

"Never fear," said the glutton. "It will scarcely be enough for me, I'm so hungry."

So when the courtier arrived with the royal message he was told to take back word to the King that his orders should be obeyed. Then twelve roasted oxen and twelve tons of bread were brought alongside of the ship, and at one sitting the glutton had devoured it all.

"I call that a small meal," he said. "I wish they'd brought me some more."

Next, the King ordered that forty casks of wine, containing forty gallons each, were to be drunk up on the spot by the Simpleton and his party. When these words were overheard by the sharp-eared comrade and repeated to the Simpleton, he was in despair.

"Alas, alas!" he exclaimed; "what is to be done? It would take us a year, possibly our whole lives, to drink so much."

"Never fear," said his thirsty comrade. "I'll drink it all up at a gulp, see if I don't." And sure enough, when the forty casks of wine containing forty gallons each were brought alongside of the ship, they disappeared down the thirsty comrade's throat in no time; and when they were empty he remarked:

"Why, I'm still thirsty. I should have been glad of two more casks."

Then the King took counsel with himself and sent an order to the Simpleton that he was to have a bath, in a bath-room at the royal palace, and after that the betrothal should take place. Now the bath-room was built of iron, and the King gave orders that it was to be heated to such a pitch that it would suffocate the Simpleton. And so when the poor silly youth entered the room, he discovered that the iron walls were red hot. But, fortunately, his comrade with the the straw on his back had entered behind him, and when the door was shut upon them he scattered the straw about, and suddenly the red-hot walls cooled down, and it became so very cold that the Simpleton could scarcely bear to take a bath, and all the water in the room froze. So the Simpleton climbed up upon the stove, and, wrapping himself up in the bath blankets, lay there the whole night. And in the morning when they opened the door there he lay sound and safe, singing cheerfully to himself.

Now when this strange tale was told to the King he became quite sad, not knowing what he should do to get rid of so undesirable a son-in-law, when suddenly a brilliant idea occurred to him.

"Tell the rascal to raise me an army, now at this instant!" he exclaimed to one of his courtiers. "Inform him at once of this, my royal will." And to himself he added, "I think I shall do for him this time."

SIMPLETON'S ARMY APPEARS BEFORE THE KING

As on former occasions, the quick-eared comrade had overheard the King's command and repeated it to the Simpleton.

"Alas, alas!" he groaned; "now I am quite done for."

"Not at all," replied one of his comrades (the one who had dragged the bundle of wood through the forest). "Have you quite forgotten me?"

In the meantime the courtier, who had run all the way from the palace, reached the ship panting and breathless, and delivered the King's message.

"Good!" remarked the Simpleton. "I will raise an army for the King," and he drew himself up. "But if, after that, the King refuses to accept me as his son-in-law, I will wage war against him, and carry the Princess off by force."

During the night the Simpleton and his comrade went together into a big field, not forgetting to take the bundle of wood with them, which the man spread out in all directions—and in a moment a mighty army stood upon the spot, regiment on regiment of foot and horse soldiers; the bugles sounded and the drums beat, the chargers neighed, and their riders put their lances in rest, and the soldiers presented arms.

In the morning when the King awoke he was startled by these warlike sounds, the bugles and the drums, and the clatter of the horses, and the shouts of the soldiers. And, stepping to the window, he saw the lances gleam in the sunlight and the armour and weapons glitter. And the proud monarch said to himself, "I am powerless in comparison with this man." So he sent him royal robes and costly jewels, and commanded him to come to the palace to be married to the Princess. And his son-in-law put on the royal robes, and he looked so grand and stately that it was impossible to recognise the poor Simpleton, so changed was he; and the Princess fell in love with him as soon as ever she saw him.

Never before had so grand a wedding been seen, and there was so much food and wine that even the glutton and the thirsty comrade had enough to eat and drink.

—*The Yellow Fairy Book* (1894)

Fortunatus and His Purse

ENGLISH

———◆◆◆———

ONCE upon a time there lived in the city of Famagosta, in the island of Cyprus, a rich man called Theodorus. He ought to have been the happiest person in the whole world, as he had all he could wish for, and a wife and little son whom he loved dearly; but unluckily, after a short time he always grew tired of everything, and had to seek new pleasures. When people are made like this the end is generally the same, and before Fortunatus (for that was the boy's name) was ten years old, his father had spent all his money and had not a farthing left.

But though Theodorus had been so foolish he was not quite without sense, and set about getting work at once. His wife, too, instead of reproaching him sent away the servants and sold their fine horses, and did all the work of the house herself, even washing the clothes of her husband and child.

Thus time passed till Fortunatus was sixteen. One day when they were sitting at supper, the boy said to Theodorus, "Father, why do you look so sad. Tell me what is wrong, and perhaps I can help you."

"Ah, my son, I have reason enough to be sad; but for me you would now have been enjoying every kind of pleasure, instead of being buried in this tiny house."

"Oh, do not let that trouble you," replied Fortunatus, "it is time I made some money for myself. To be sure I have never been taught any trade. Still there must be something I can do. I will go and walk on the seashore and think about it."

Very soon—sooner than he expected—a chance came, and Fortunatus, like a wise boy, seized on it at once. The post offered him was that of page to the Earl of Flanders, and as the Earl's daughter was just going to be married, splendid festivities were held in her honour, and at some of the tilting matches Fortunatus was lucky enough to win the prize. These prizes, together with presents from the lords and ladies of the court, who liked him for his pleasant ways, made Fortunatus feel quite a rich man.

But though his head was not turned by the notice taken of him, it excited the envy of some of the other pages about the Court, and one of them, called Robert, invented a plot to move Fortunatus out of his way. So he told the young man that the Earl had taken a dislike to him and meant to kill him; Fortunatus believed the story, and packing up his fine clothes and money, slipped away before dawn.

He went to a great many big towns and lived well, and as he was generous and not wiser than most youths of his age, he very soon found himself penniless. Like his father, he then began to think of work, and tramped half over Brittany in search of it. Nobody seemed to want him, and he wandered about from one place to another, till he found himself in a dense wood, without any paths, and not much light. Here he spent two whole days, with nothing to eat and very little water to drink, going first in one direction and then in another, but never being able to find his way out. During the first night he slept soundly, and was too tired to fear either man or beast, but when darkness came on for the second time, and growls were heard in the distance, he grew frightened and looked about for a high tree out of reach of his enemies. Hardly had he settled himself comfortably in one of the forked branches, when a lion walked up to a spring that burst from a rock close to the tree, and crouching down drank greedily. This was bad enough, but after all, lions do not climb trees, and as long as Fortunatus stayed up on his perch, he was quite safe. But no sooner was the lion out of sight, than his place was taken by a bear, and bears, as Fortunatus knew very well, *are* tree-climbers. His heart beat fast, and not without reason, for as the bear turned away he looked up and saw Fortunatus!

Now in those days every young man carried a sword slung to his belt, and it was a fashion that came in very handily for Fortunatus. He drew his sword, and when the bear got within a yard of him he made a fierce lunge forward. The bear, wild with pain, tried to spring, but the bough he was standing on broke with his weight, and he fell heavily to the ground. Then Fortunatus descended from his tree (first taking good care to see no other wild animals were in sight) and killed him with a single blow. He was just thinking he would light a fire and make a hearty dinner off bear's flesh, which is not at all bad eating, when he beheld a beautiful lady standing by his side leaning on a wheel, and her eyes hidden by a bandage.

"I am Dame Fortune," she said, "and I have a gift for you. Shall it be wisdom, strength, long life, riches, health, or beauty? Think well, and tell me what you will have."

But Fortunatus, who had proved the truth of the proverb that "It's ill thinking on an empty stomach," answered quickly, "Good lady, let me have riches in such plenty that I may never again be as hungry as I am now."

And the lady held out a purse and told him he had only to put his hand into it, and he and his children would always find ten pieces of gold. But when they were dead it would be a magic purse no longer.

At this news Fortunatus was beside himself with joy, and could hardly find words to thank the lady. But she

THE GIFT OF FORTUNA

told him that the best thing he could do was to find his way out of the wood, and before bidding him farewell pointed out which path he should take. He walked along it as fast as his weakness would let him, until a welcome light at a little distance showed him that a house was near. It turned out to be an inn, but before entering Fortunatus thought he had better make sure of the truth of what the lady had told him, and took out the purse and looked inside. Sure enough there were the ten pieces of gold, shining brightly. Then Fortunatus walked boldly up to the inn, and ordered them to get ready a good supper at once, as he was very hungry, and to bring him the best wine in the house. And he seemed to care so little what he spent that everybody thought he was a great lord, and vied with each other who should run quickest when he called.

After a night passed in a soft bed, Fortunatus felt so much better that he asked the landlord if he could find him some men-servants, and tell him where any good horses were to be got. The next thing was to provide himself with smart clothes, and then to take a big house where he could give great feasts to the nobles and beautiful ladies who lived in palaces round about.

In this manner a whole year soon slipped away, and Fortunatus was so busy amusing himself that he never once remembered his parents whom he had left behind in Cyprus. But though he was thoughtless, he was not bad-hearted. As soon as their existence crossed his mind, he set about making preparations to visit them, and as he was not fond of being alone he looked round for someone older and wiser than himself to travel with him. It was not long before he had the good luck to come across an old man who had left his wife and children in a far country many years before, when he went out into the world to seek the fortune which he never found. He agreed to accompany Fortunatus back to Cyprus, but only on condition he should first be allowed to return for a few weeks to his own home before venturing to set sail for an island so strange and distant. Fortunatus agreed to his proposal, and as he was always fond of anything new, said that he would go with him.

The journey was long, and they had to cross many large rivers, and climb over high mountains, and find their way through thick woods, before they reached at length the old man's castle. His wife and children had almost given up hopes of seeing him again, and crowded eagerly round him. Indeed, it did not take Fortunatus five minutes to fall in love with the youngest daughter, the most beautiful creature in the whole world, whose name was Cassandra.

"Give her to me for my wife," he said to the old man, "and let us all go together to Famagosta."

So a ship was bought big enough to hold Fortunatus, the old man and his wife, and their ten children—five of them sons and five daughters. And the day before they sailed the wedding was celebrated with magnificent rejoicings, and everybody thought that Fortunatus must certainly be a prince in disguise. But when they reached Cyprus, he learned to his sorrow that both his father and mother were dead, and for some time he shut himself up in his house and would see nobody, full of shame at having forgotten them all these years. Then he begged that the old man and his wife would remain with him, and take the place of his parents.

For twelve years Fortunatus and Cassandra and their two little boys lived happily in Famagosta. They had a beautiful house and everything they could possibly want, and when Cassandra's sisters married the purse provided them each with a fortune. But at last Fortunatus grew tired of staying at home, and thought he should like to go out and see the world again. Cassandra shed many tears at first when he told her of his wishes, and he had a great deal of trouble to persuade her to give her consent. But on his promising to return at the end of two years she agreed to let him go. Before he went away he showed her three chests of gold, which stood in a room with an iron door, and walls twelve feet thick.

"If anything should happen to me," he said, "and I should never come back, keep one of the chests for yourself, and give the others to our two sons." Then he embraced them all and took ship for Alexandria.

The wind was fair and in a few days they entered the harbour, where Fortunatus was informed by a man whom he met on landing, that if he wished to be well received in the town, he must begin by making a handsome present to the Sultan. "That is easily done," said Fortunatus, and went into a goldsmith's shop, where he bought a large gold cup, which cost five thousand pounds. This gift so pleased the Sultan that he ordered a hundred casks of spices to be given to Fortunatus; Fortunatus put them on board his ship, and commanded the captain to return to Cyprus and deliver them to his wife, Cassandra. He next obtained an audience of the Sultan, and begged permission to travel through the country, which the Sultan readily gave him, adding some letters to the rulers of other lands which Fortunatus might wish to visit.

Filled with delight at feeling himself free to roam through the world once more, Fortunatus set out on his journey without losing a day. From court to court he went, astonishing everyone by the magnificence of his dress and the splendour of his presents. At length he grew as tired of wandering as he had been of staying at home, and returned to Alexandria, where he found the same ship that had brought him from Cyprus lying in the harbour. Of course the first thing he did was to pay his respects to the Sultan, who was eager to hear about his adventures.

When Fortunatus had told them all, the Sultan observed: "Well, you have seen many wonderful things, but I have something to show you more wonderful still"; and he led him into a room where precious stones lay heaped against the walls. Fortunatus' eyes were quite dazzled, but the Sultan went on without pausing and opened a door at the farther end. As far as Fortunatus could see, the cupboard was quite bare, except for a little red cap, such as soldiers wear in Turkey.

"Look at this," said the Sultan.

"But there is nothing very valuable about it," answered Fortunatus. "I've seen a dozen better caps than that, this very day."

"Ah," said the Sultan, "you do not know what you are talking about. Whoever puts this cap on his head and wishes himself in any place, will find himself there in a moment."

"But who made it?" asked Fortunatus.

"That I cannot tell you," replied the Sultan.

"Is it very heavy to wear?" asked Fortunatus.

"No, quite light," replied the Sultan, "just feel it."

Fortunatus took the cap and put it on his head, and then, without thinking, wished himself back in the ship that was starting for Famagosta. In a second he was standing at the prow, while the anchor was being weighed, and while the Sultan was repenting of his folly in allowing Fortunatus to try on the cap, the vessel was making fast for Cyprus.

When it arrived, Fortunatus found his wife and children well, but the two old people were dead and buried. His sons had grown tall and strong, but unlike their father had no wish to see the world, and found their chief pleasure in hunting and tilting. In the main, Fortunatus was content to stay quietly at home, and if a restless fit did seize upon him, he was able to go away for a few hours without being missed, thanks to the cap, which he never sent back to the Sultan.

By-and-by he grew old, and feeling that he had not many days to live, he sent for his two sons, and showing them the purse and cap, he said to them: "Never part with these precious possessions. They are worth more than all the gold and lands I leave behind me. But never tell their secret, even to your wife or dearest friend. That purse has served me well for forty years, and no one knows whence I got my riches." Then he died and was buried by his wife Cassandra, and he was mourned in Famagosta for many years.

—*The Grey Fairy Book* (1900)

The Gifts of the Magician

FINNISH

———◆◆———

ONCE upon a time there was an old man who lived in a little hut in the middle of a forest. His wife was dead, and he had only one son, whom he loved dearly. Near their hut was a group of birch trees, in which some black-game had made their nests, and the youth had often begged his father's permission to shoot the birds, but the old man always strictly forbade him to do anything of the kind.

One day, however, when the father had gone to a little distance to collect some sticks for the fire, the boy fetched his bow, and shot at a bird that was just flying towards its nest. But he had not taken proper aim, and the bird was only wounded, and fluttered along the ground. The boy ran to catch it, but though he ran very fast, and the bird seemed to flutter along very slowly, he never could quite come up with it; it was always just a little in advance. But so absorbed was he in the chase that he did not notice for some time that he was now deep in the forest, in a place where he had never been before. Then he felt it would be foolish to go any further, and he turned to find his way home.

He thought it would be easy enough to follow the path along which he had come, but somehow it was always branching off in unexpected directions. He looked about for a house where he might stop and ask his way, but there was not a sign of one anywhere, and he was afraid to stand still, for it was cold, and there were many stories of wolves being seen in that part of the forest. Night fell, and he was beginning to start at every sound, when suddenly a magician came running towards him, with a pack of wolves snapping at his heels. Then all the boy's courage returned to him. He took his bow, and aiming an arrow at the largest wolf, shot him through the heart, and a few more arrows soon put the rest to flight. The magician was full of gratitude to his deliverer, and promised him a reward for his help if the youth would go back with him to his house.

"Indeed there is nothing that would be more welcome to me than a night's lodging," answered the boy; "I have been wandering all day in the forest, and did not know how to get home again."

"Come with me, you must be hungry as well as tired," said the magician, and led the way to his house, where the guest flung himself on a bed, and went fast asleep. But his host returned to the forest to get some food, for the larder was empty.

While he was absent the housekeeper went to the boy's room and tried to wake him. She stamped on the floor, and shook him and called to him, telling him that he was in great danger, and must take flight at once. But nothing would rouse him, and if he did ever open his eyes he shut them again directly.

Soon after, the magician came back from the forest, and told the housekeeper to bring them something to eat. The meal was quickly ready, and the magician called to the boy to come down and eat it, but he could not be wakened, and they had to sit down to supper without him. By-and-by the magician went out into the wood again for some more hunting, and on his return he tried afresh to waken the youth. But finding it quite impossible, he went back for the third time to the forest.

While he was absent the boy woke up and dressed

himself. Then he came downstairs and began to talk to the housekeeper. The girl had heard how he had saved her master's life, so she said nothing more about his running away, but instead told him that if the magician offered him the choice of a reward, he was to ask for the horse which stood in the third stall of the stable.

By-and-by the old man came back and they all sat down to dinner. When they had finished the magician said: "Now, my son, tell me what you will have as the reward of your courage?"

"Give me the horse that stands in the third stall of your stable," answered the youth. "For I have a long way to go before I get home, and my feet will not carry me so far."

"Ah! my son," replied the magician, "it is the best horse in my stable that you want! Will not anything else please you as well?"

But the youth declared that it was the horse, and the horse only, that he desired, and in the end the old man gave way. And besides the horse, the magician gave him a zither, a fiddle, and a flute, saying: "If you are in danger, touch the zither; and if no one comes to your aid, then play on the fiddle; but if that brings no help, blow on the flute."

The youth thanked the magician, and fastening his treasures about him mounted the horse and rode off. He had already gone some miles when, to his great surprise, the horse spoke, and said: "It is no use your returning home just now, your father will only beat you. Let us visit a few towns first, and something lucky will be sure to happen to us."

This advice pleased the boy, for he felt himself almost a man by this time, and thought it was high time he saw the world. When they entered the capital of the country everyone stopped to admire the beauty of the horse. Even the king heard of it, and came to see the splendid creature with his own eyes. Indeed, he wanted directly to buy it, and told the youth he would give any price he liked. The young man hesitated for a moment, but before he could speak, the horse contrived to whisper to him: "Do not sell me, but ask the king to take me to his stable, and feed me there; then his other horses will become just as beautiful as I."

The king was delighted when he was told what the horse had said, and took the animal at once to the stables, and placed it in his own particular stall. Sure enough, the horse had scarcely eaten a mouthful of corn out of the manger, when the rest of the horses seemed to have undergone a transformation. Some of them were old favourites which the king had ridden in many wars, and they bore the signs of age and of service. But now they arched their heads, and pawed the ground with their slender legs as they had been wont to do in days long gone by. The king's heart beat with delight, but the old groom who had had the care of them stood crossly by, and eyed the owner of this wonderful creature with hate and envy. Not a day passed without his bringing some story against the youth to his master, but the king understood all about the matter and paid no attention. At last the groom declared that the young man had boasted that he could find the king's war horse which had strayed into the forest several years ago, and had not been heard of since. Now the king had never ceased to mourn for his horse, so this time he listened to the tale which the groom had invented, and sent for the youth. "Find me my horse in three days," said he, "or it will be the worse for you."

The youth was thunderstruck at this command, but he only bowed, and went off at once to the stable.

"Do not worry yourself," answered his own horse. "Ask the king to give you a hundred oxen, and to let them be killed and cut into small pieces. Then we will start on our journey, and ride till we reach a certain river. There a horse will come up to you, but take no notice of him. Soon another will appear, and this also you must leave alone, but when the third horse shows itself, throw my bridle over it."

Everything happened just as the horse had said, and

the third horse was safely bridled. Then the other horse spoke again: "The magician's raven will try to eat us as we ride away, but throw it some of the oxen's flesh, and then I will gallop like the wind, and carry you safe out of the dragon's clutches."

So the young man did as he was told, and brought the horse back to the king.

The old stableman was very jealous, when he heard of it, and wondered what he could do to injure the youth in the eyes of his royal master. At last he hit upon a plan, and told the king that the young man had boasted that he could bring home the king's wife, who had vanished many months before, without leaving a trace behind her. Then the king bade the young man come into his presence, and desired him to fetch the queen home again, as he had boasted he could do. And if he failed, his head would pay the penalty.

The poor youth's heart stood still as he listened. Find the queen? But how was he to do that, when nobody in the palace had been able to do so! Slowly he walked to the stable, and laying his head on his horse's shoulder, he said: "The king has ordered me to bring his wife home again, and how can I do that when she disappeared so long ago, and no one can tell me anything about her?"

"Cheer up!" answered the horse, "we will manage to find her. You have only got to ride me back to the same river that we went to yesterday, and I will plunge into it and take my proper shape again. For I am the king's wife, who was turned into a horse by the magician from whom you saved me."

Joyfully the young man sprang into the saddle and rode away to the banks of the river. Then he threw himself off, and waited while the horse plunged in. The moment it dipped its head into the water its black skin vanished, and the most beautiful woman in the world was floating on the water. She came smiling towards the youth, and held out her hand, and he took it and led her back to the palace. Great was the king's surprise

THE MAGICIAN THROWS THE TREE AND THE KING UP INTO THE AIR

and happiness when he beheld his lost wife stand before him, and in gratitude to her rescuer he loaded him with gifts.

You would have thought that after this the poor youth would have been left in peace; but no, his enemy the stableman hated him as much as ever, and laid a new plot for his undoing. This time he presented himself before the king and told him that the youth was so puffed up with what he had done that he had declared he would seize the king's throne for himself.

At this news the king waxed so furious that he ordered a gallows to be erected at once, and the young man to be hanged without a trial. He was not even allowed to speak in his own defence, but on the very steps of the gallows he sent a message to the king and begged, as a last favour, that he might play a tune on his zither. Leave was given him, and taking the instrument from under his cloak he touched the strings. Scarcely had the first notes sounded than the hangman and his helper began to dance, and the louder grew the music the higher they capered, till at last they cried for mercy. But the youth paid no heed, and the tunes rang out more merrily than before, and by the time the sun set they both sank on the ground exhausted, and declared that the hanging must be put off till to-morrow.

The story of the zither soon spread through the town, and on the following morning the king and his whole court and a large crowd of people were gathered at the foot of the gallows to see the youth hanged. Once more he asked a favour—permission to play on his fiddle, and this the king was graciously pleased to grant. But with the first notes, the leg of every man in the crowd was lifted high, and they danced to the sound of the music the whole day till darkness fell, and there was no light to hang the musician by.

The third day came, and the youth asked leave to play on his flute. "No, no," said the king, "you made me dance all day yesterday, and if I do it again it will certainly be my death. You shall play no more tunes. Quick! the rope round his neck."

At these words the young man looked so sorrowful that the courtiers said to the king: "He is very young to die. Let him play a tune if it will make him happy." So, very unwillingly, the king gave him leave; but first he had himself bound to a big fir tree, for fear that he should be made to dance.

When he was made fast, the young man began to blow softly on his flute, and bound though he was, the king's body moved to the sound, up and down the fir tree till his clothes were in tatters, and the skin nearly rubbed off his back. But the youth had no pity, and went on blowing, till suddenly the old magician appeared and asked: "What danger are you in, my son, that you have sent for me?"

"They want to hang me," answered the young man; "the gallows are all ready and the hangman is only waiting for me to stop playing."

"Oh, I will put that right," said the magician; and taking the gallows, he tore it up and flung it into the air, and no one knows where it came down. "Who has ordered you to be hanged?" asked he.

The young man pointed to the king, who was still bound to the fir; and without wasting words the magician took hold of the tree also, and with a mighty heave both fir and man went spinning through the air, and vanished in the clouds after the gallows.

Then the youth was declared to be free, and the people elected him for their king; and the stable helper drowned himself from envy, for, after all, if it had not been for him the young man would have remained poor all the days of his life.

—*The Crimson Fairy Book* (1903)

The Girl Who Pretended
To Be a Boy

ROUMANIAN

ONCE upon a time there lived an emperor who was a great conqueror, and reigned over more countries than anyone in the world. And whenever he subdued a fresh kingdom, he only granted peace on condition that the king should deliver him one of his sons for ten years' service.

Now on the borders of his kingdom lay a country whose emperor was as brave as his neighbour, and as long as he was young he was the victor in every war. But as years passed away, his head grew weary of making plans of campaign, and his people wanted to stay at home and till their fields, and at last he too felt that he must do homage to the other emperor.

One thing, however, held him back from this step which day by day he saw more clearly was the only one possible. His new overlord would demand the service of one of his sons. And the old emperor had no son; only three daughters.

Look on which side he would, nothing but ruin seemed to lie before him, and he became so gloomy, that his daughters were frightened, and did everything they could think of to cheer him up, but all to no purpose.

At length one day when they were at dinner, the

eldest of the three summoned up all her courage and said to her father:

"What secret grief is troubling you? Are your subjects discontented? or have we given you cause for displeasure? To smooth away your wrinkles, we would gladly shed our blood, for our lives are bound up in yours; and this you know."

"My daughter," answered the emperor, "what you say is true. Never have you given me one moment's pain. Yet now you cannot help me. Ah! why is not one of you a boy!"

"I don't understand," she answered in surprise. "Tell us what is wrong: and though we are not boys, we are not quite useless!"

"But what can you do, my dear children? Spin, sew, and weave—that is all your learning. Only a warrior can deliver me now, a young giant who is strong to wield the battle-axe: whose sword deals deadly blows."

"But *why* do you need a son so much at present? Tell us all about it! It will not make matters worse if we know!"

"Listen then, my daughters, and learn the reason of my sorrow. You have heard that as long as I was young no man ever brought an army against me without it costing him dear. But the years have chilled my blood and drunk my strength. And now the deer can roam the forest, my arrows will never pierce his heart; strange soldiers will set fire to my houses and water their horses at my wells, and my arm cannot hinder them. No, my day is past, and the time has come when I too must bow my head under the yoke of my foe! But who is to give him the ten years' service that is part of the price which the vanquished must pay?"

"*I* will," cried the eldest girl, springing to her feet. But her father only shook his head sadly.

"Never will I bring shame upon you," urged the girl. "Let me go. Am I not a princess, and the daughter of an emperor?"

"Go then!" he said.

*   *   *

The brave girl's heart almost stopped beating from joy, as she set about her preparations. She was not still for a single moment, but danced about the house, turning chests and wardrobes upside down. She set aside enough things for a whole year—dresses embroidered with gold and precious stones, and a great store of provisions. And she chose the most spirited horse in the stable, with eyes of flame, and a coat of shining silver.

When her father saw her mounted and curvetting about the court, he gave her much wise advice, as to how she was to behave like the young man she appeared to be, and also how to behave as the girl she really was. Then he gave her his blessing, and she touched her horse with the spur.

The silver armour of herself and her steed dazzled the eyes of the people as she darted past. She was soon out of sight, and if after a few miles she had not pulled up to allow her escort to join her, the rest of the journey would have been performed alone.

But though none of his daughters were aware of the fact, the old emperor was a magician, and had laid his plans accordingly. He managed, unseen, to overtake his daughter, and throw a bridge of copper over a stream which she would have to cross. Then, changing himself into a wolf, he lay down under one of the arches, and waited.

He had chosen his time well, and in about half an hour the sound of a horse's hoofs was heard. His feet were almost on the bridge, when a big grey wolf with grinning teeth appeared before the princess. With a deep growl that froze the blood, he drew himself up, and prepared to spring.

The appearance of the wolf was so sudden and so unexpected, that the girl was almost paralysed, and never even dreamt of flight, till the horse leaped violently to one side. Then she turned him round, and urging him to his fullest speed, never drew rein till she saw the gates of the palace rising before her.

The old emperor, who had got back long since, came to the door to meet her, and touching her shining armour, he said, "Did I not tell you, my child, that flies do not make honey?"

The days passed on, and one morning the second princess implored her father to allow her to try the adventure in which her sister had made such a failure. He listened unwillingly, feeling sure it was no use, but she begged so hard that in the end he consented, and having chosen her arms, she rode away.

But though, unlike her sister, she was quite prepared for the appearance of the wolf when she reached the copper bridge, she showed no greater courage, and galloped home as fast as her horse could carry her. On the steps of the castle her father was standing, and as still trembling with fright she knelt at his feet, he said gently, "Did I not tell you, my child, that every bird is not caught in a net?"

The three girls stayed quietly in the palace for a little while, embroidering, spinning, weaving, and tending their birds and flowers, when early one morning, the youngest princess entered the door of the emperor's private apartments. "My father, it is my turn now. Perhaps I shall get the better of that wolf!"

"What, do you think you are braver than your sisters, vain little one? You who have hardly left your long clothes behind you!" but she did not mind being laughed at, and answered,

"For your sake, father, I would cut the devil himself into small bits, or even become a devil myself. I think I shall succeed, but if I fail, I shall come home without more shame than my sisters."

Still the emperor hesitated, but the girl petted and coaxed him till at last he said,

"Well, well, if you must go, you must. It remains to

be seen what I shall get by it, except perhaps a good
laugh when I see you come back with your head bent
and your eyes on the ground."

"He laughs best who laughs last," said the princess.

Happy at having got her way, the princess decided
that the first thing to be done was to find some old
white-haired boyard, whose advice she could trust, and
then to be very careful in choosing her horse. So she
went straight to the stables where the most beautiful
horses in the empire were feeding in the stalls, but
none of them seemed quite what she wanted. Almost in
despair she reached the last box of all, which was occupied by her father's ancient war-horse, old and worn
like himself, stretched sadly out on the straw.

The girl's eyes filled with tears, and she stood gazing
at him. The horse lifted his head, gave a little neigh,
and said softly, "You look gentle and pitiful, but I know
it is your love for your father which makes you tender
to me. Ah, what a warrior he was, and what good times
we shared together! But now I too have grown old, and
my master has forgotten me, and there is no reason to
care whether my coat is dull or shining. Yet, it is not
too late, and if I were properly tended, in a week I
could vie with any horse in the stables!"

"And how should you be tended?" asked the girl.

"I must be rubbed down morning and evening with
rain water, my barley must be boiled in milk, because
of my bad teeth, and my feet must be washed in oil."

"I should like to try the treatment, as you might help
me in carrying out my scheme."

"Try it then, mistress, and I promise you will never
repent."

So in a week's time the horse woke up one morning
with a sudden shiver through all his limbs; and when it
had passed away, he found his skin shining like a mirror, his body as fat as a water melon, his movement
light as a chamois'.

Then looking at the princess who had come early to
the stable, he said joyfully,

"May success await on the steps of my master's daughter, for she has given me back my life. Tell me what I can do for you, princess, and I will do it."

"I want to go to the emperor who is our over-lord, and I have no one to advise me. Which of all the white-headed boyards shall I choose as counsellor?"

"If you have me, you need no one else: I will serve you as I served your father, if you will only listen to what I say."

"I will listen to everything. Can you start in three days?"

"This moment, if you like," said the horse.

The preparations of the emperor's youngest daughter were much fewer and simpler than those of her sisters. They only consisted of some boy's clothes, a small quantity of linen and food, and a little money in case of necessity. Then she bade farewell to her father, and rode away.

A day's journey from the palace, she reached the copper bridge, but before they came in sight of it, the horse, who was a magician, had warned her of the means her father would take to prove her courage.

Still in spite of his warning she trembled all over when a huge wolf, as thin as if he had fasted for a month, with claws like saws, and mouth as wide as an oven, bounded howling towards her. For a moment her heart failed her, but the next, touching the horse lightly with her spur, she drew her sword from its sheath, ready to separate the wolf's head from its body at a single blow.

The beast saw the sword, and shrank back, which was the best thing it could do, as now the girl's blood was up, and the light of battle in her eyes. Then without looking round, she rode across the bridge.

The emperor, proud of this victory, took a short cut, and waited for her at the end of another day's journey, close to a river, over which he threw a bridge of silver. And this time he took the shape of a lion.

But the horse guessed this new danger and told the princess how to escape it. But it is one thing to receive advice when we feel safe and comfortable, and quite another to be able to carry it out when some awful peril is threatening us. And if the wolf had made the girl quake with terror, it seemed like a lamb beside this dreadful lion.

At the sound of his roar the very trees quivered and his claws were so large that every one of them looked like a cutlass.

The breath of the princess came and went, and her feet rattled in the stirrups. Suddenly the remembrance flashed across her of the wolf whom she had put to flight, and waving her sword, she rushed so violently on the lion that he had barely time to spring on one side, so as to avoid the blow. Then, like a flash, she crossed this bridge also.

Now during her whole life, the princess had been so carefully brought up, that she had never left the gardens of the palace, so that the sight of the hills and valleys and tinkling streams, and the song of the larks and blackbirds, made her almost beside herself with wonder and delight. She longed to get down and bathe her face in the clear pools, and pick the brilliant flowers, but the horse said "No," and quickened his pace, neither turning to the right or the left.

"Warriors," he told her, "only rest when they have won the victory. You have still another battle to fight, and it is the hardest of all."

This time it was neither a wolf nor a lion that was waiting for her at the end of the third day's journey, but a dragon with twelve heads, and a golden bridge behind it.

The princess rode up without seeing anything to frighten her, when a sudden puff of smoke and flame from beneath her feet caused her to look down, and there was the horrible creature twisted and writhing, its twelve heads reared up as if to seize her between them.

THE PRINCESS CHARGES THE LION

The bridle fell from her hand: and the sword which she had just grasped slid back into its sheath, but the horse bade her fear nothing, and with a mighty effort she sat upright and spurred straight on the dragon.

The fight lasted an hour and the dragon pressed her hard. But in the end, by a well-directed side blow, she cut off one of the heads, and with a roar that seemed to rend the heavens in two, the dragon fell back on the ground, and rose as a man before her.

Although the horse had informed the princess the dragon was really her own father, the girl had hardly believed him, and stared in amazement at the transformation. But he flung his arms round her and pressed her to his heart saying, "Now I see that you are as brave as the bravest, and as wise as the wisest. You have chosen the right horse, for without his help you would have returned with a bent head and downcast eyes. You have filled me with the hope that you may carry out the task you have undertaken, but be careful to forget none of my counsels, and above all to listen to those of your horse."

When he had done speaking, the princess knelt down to receive his blessing, and they went their different ways.

The princess rode on and on, till at last she came to the mountains which hold up the roof of the world. There she met two Genii who had been fighting fiercely for two years, without one having got the least advantage over the other. Seeing what they took to be a young man seeking adventures, one of the combatants called out, "Fet-Fruners! deliver me from my enemy, and I will give you the horn that can be heard the distance of a three days' journey"; while the other cried, "Fet-Fruners! help me to conquer this pagan thief, and you shall have my horse, Sunlight."

Before answering, the princess consulted her own horse as to which offer she should accept, and he advised her to side with the genius who was master of

Sunlight, his own younger brother, and still more active than himself.

So the girl at once attacked the other genius, and soon clove his skull; then the one who was left victor begged her to come back with him to his house and he would hand her over Sunlight, as he had promised.

The mother of the genius was rejoiced to see her son return safe and sound, and prepared her best room for the princess, who, after so much fatigue, needed rest badly. But the girl declared that she must first make her horse comfortable in his stable; but this was really only an excuse, as she wanted to ask his advice on several matters.

But the old woman had suspected from the very first that the boy who had come to the rescue of her son was a girl in disguise, and told the genius that she was exactly the wife he needed. The genius scoffed, and inquired what female hand could ever wield a sabre like that; but, in spite of his sneers, his mother persisted, and as a proof of what she said, laid at night on each of their pillows a handful of magic flowers, that fade at the touch of man, but remain eternally fresh in the fingers of a woman.

It was very clever of her, but unluckily the horse had warned the princess what to expect, and when the house was silent, she stole very softly to the genius's room, and exchanged his faded flowers for those she held. Then she crept back to her own bed and fell fast asleep.

At break of day, the old woman ran to see her son, and found, as she knew she would, a bunch of dead flowers in his hand. She next passed on to the bedside of the princess, who still lay asleep grasping the withered flowers. But she did not believe any the more that her guest was a man, and so she told her son. So they put their heads together and laid another trap for her.

After breakfast the genius gave his arm to his guest, and asked her to come with him into the garden. For some time they walked about looking at the flowers, the genius all the while pressing her to pick any she fancied. But the princess, suspecting a trap, inquired roughly why they were wasting the precious hours in the garden, when, as men, they should be in the stables looking after their horses. Then the genius told his mother that she was quite wrong, and his deliverer was certainly a man. But the old woman was not convinced for all that.

She would try once more she said, and her son must lead his visitor into the armoury, where hung every kind of weapon used all over the world—some plain and bare, others ornamented with precious stones—and beg her to make choice of one of them. The princess looked at them closely, and felt the edges and points of their blades, then she hung at her belt an old sword with a curved blade, that would have done credit to an ancient warrior. After this she informed the genius that she would start early next day and take Sunlight with her.

And there was nothing for the mother to do but to submit, though she still stuck to her own opinion.

The princess mounted Sunlight, and touched him with her spur, when the old horse, who was galloping at her side, suddenly said:

"Up to this time, mistress, you have obeyed my counsels and all has gone well. Listen to me once more, and do what I tell you. I am old, and—now that there is someone to take my place, I will confess it—I am afraid that my strength is not equal to the task that lies before me. Give me leave, therefore, to return home, and do you continue your journey under the care of my brother. Put your faith in him as you put it in me, and you will never repent. Wisdom has come early to Sunlight."

"Yes, my old comrade, you have served me well; and it is only through your help that up to now I have been victorious. So grieved though I am to say farewell, I will obey you yet once more, and will listen to your brother as I would to yourself. Only, I must have a proof that he loves me as well as you do."

"How should I not love you?" answered Sunlight; "how should I not be proud to serve a warrior such as you? Trust me, mistress, and you shall never regret the absence of my brother. I know there will be difficulties in our path, but we will face them together."

Then, with tears in her eyes, the princess took leave of her old horse, who galloped back to her father.

She had ridden only a few miles further, when she saw a golden curl lying on the road before her. Checking her horse, she asked whether it would be better to take it or let it lie.

"If you take it," said Sunlight, "you will repent, and if you don't, you will repent too: so take it." On this the girl dismounted, and picking up the curl, wound it round her neck for safety.

They passed by hills, they passed by mountains, they passed through valleys, leaving behind them thick forests, and fields covered with flowers; and at length they reached the court of the over-lord.

He was sitting on his throne, surrounded by the sons of the other emperors, who served him as pages. These youths came forward to greet their new companion, and wondered why they felt so attracted towards him.

However, there was no time for talking and concealing her fright. The princess was led straight up to the throne, and explained, in a low voice, the reason of her coming. The emperor received her kindly, and declared himself fortunate at finding a vassal so brave and so charming, and begged the princess to remain in attendance on his person.

She was, however, very careful in her behaviour towards the other pages, whose way of life did not please her. One day, however, she had been amusing herself by making sweetmeats, when two of the young princes looked in to pay her a visit. She offered them some of the food which was already on the table, and they thought it so delicious that they even licked their fingers so as not to lose a morsel. Of course they did not keep the news of their discovery to themselves, but told all their companions that they had just been enjoying the best supper they had had since they were born. And from that moment the princess was left no peace, till she had promised to cook them all a dinner.

Now it happened that, on the very day fixed, all the cooks in the palace became intoxicated, and there was no one to make up the fire.

When the pages heard of this shocking state of things, they went to their companion and implored her to come to the rescue.

The princess was fond of cooking, and was, besides, very good-natured; so she put on an apron and went down to the kitchen without delay. When the dinner was placed before the emperor he found it so nice that he ate much more than was good for him. The next morning, as soon as he woke, he sent for his head cook, and told him to send up the same dishes as before. The cook, seized with fright at this command, which he knew he could not fulfil, fell on his knees, and confessed the truth.

The emperor was so astonished that he forgot to scold, and while he was thinking over the matter, some of his pages came in and said that their new companion had been heard to boast that he knew where Iliane was to be found—the celebrated Iliane of the song which begins:

Golden Hair
The fields are green,

and that to their certain knowledge he had a curl of her hair in his possession.

When he heard that, the emperor desired the page to be brought before him, and, as soon as the princess obeyed his summons, he said to her abruptly:

"Fet-Fruners, you have hidden from me the fact that you knew the golden-haired Iliane! Why did you do this? for I have treated you more kindly than all my other pages."

Then, after making the princess show him the golden curl which she wore round her neck, he added: "Listen to me; unless by some means or other you bring me the owner of this lock, I will have your head cut off in the place where you stand. Now go!"

In vain the poor girl tried to explain how the lock of hair came into her possession; the emperor would listen to nothing, and, bowing low, she left his presence and went to consult Sunlight what she was to do.

At his first words she brightened up. "Do not be afraid, mistress; only last night my brother appeared to me in a dream and told me that a genius had carried off Iliane, whose hair you picked up on the road. But Iliane declares that, before she marries her captor, he must bring her, as a present, the whole stud of mares which belong to her. The genius, half crazy with love, thinks of nothing night and day but how this can be done, and meanwhile she is quite safe in the island swamps of the sea. Go back to the emperor and ask him for twenty ships filled with precious merchandise. The rest you shall know by-and-by."

On hearing this advice, the princess went at once into the emperor's presence.

"May a long life be yours, O Sovereign all mighty!" said she. "I have come to tell you that I can do as you command if you will give me twenty ships, and load them with the most precious wares in your kingdom."

"You shall have all that I possess if you will bring me the golden-haired Iliane," said the emperor.

The ships were soon ready, and the princess entered the largest and finest, with Sunlight at her side. Then the sails were spread and the voyage began.

For seven weeks the wind blew them straight towards the west, and early one morning they caught sight of the island swamps of the sea.

They cast anchor in a little bay, and the princess

made haste to disembark with Sunlight, but, before leaving the ship, she tied to her belt a pair of tiny gold slippers, adorned with precious stones. Then mounting Sunlight, she rode about till she came to several palaces, built on hinges, so that they could always turn towards the sun.

The most splendid of these were guarded by three slaves, whose greedy eyes were caught by the glistening gold of the slippers. They hastened up to the owner of these treasures, and inquired who he was. "A merchant," replied the princess, "who had somehow missed his road, and lost himself among the island swamps of the sea."

Not knowing if it was proper to receive him or not, the slaves returned to their mistress and told her all they had seen, but not before she had caught sight of the merchant from the roof of her palace. Luckily her gaoler was away, always trying to catch the stud of mares, so for the moment she was free and alone.

The slaves told their tale so well that their mistress insisted on going down to the shore and seeing the beautiful slippers for herself. They were even lovelier than she expected, and when the merchant besought her to come on board, and inspect some that he thought were finer still, her curiosity was too great to refuse, and she went.

Once on board ship, she was so busy turning over all the precious things stored there, that she never knew that the sails were spread, and that they were flying along with the wind behind them; and when she did know, she rejoiced in her heart, though she pretended to weep at being carried captive a second time. Thus they arrived at the court of the emperor.

They were just about to land, when the mother of the genius stood before them. She had learnt that Iliane had fled from her prison in company with a merchant, and, as her son was absent, had come herself in pursuit. Striding over the blue waters, hopping from wave to wave, one foot reaching to heaven, and the other planted in the foam, she was close at their heels, breathing fire and flame, when they stepped on shore from the ship. One glance told Iliane who the horrible old woman was, and she whispered hastily to her companion. Without saying a word, the princess swung her into Sunlight's saddle, and leaping up behind her, they were off like a flash.

It was not till they drew near the town that the princess stooped and asked Sunlight what they should do. "Put your hand into my left ear," said he, "and take out a sharp stone, which you must throw behind you."

The princess did as she was told, and a huge mountain sprang up behind them. The mother of the genius began to climb up it, and though they galloped quickly, she was quicker still.

They heard her coming, faster, faster; and again the princess stooped to ask what was to be done now. "Put your hand into my right ear," said the horse, "and throw the brush you will find there behind you." The princess did so, and a great forest sprang up behind them, and, so thick were its leaves, that even a wren could not get through. But the old woman seized hold the branches and flung herself like a monkey from one to the others, and always she drew nearer—always, always—till their hair was singed by the flames of her mouth.

Then, in despair, the princess again bent down and asked if there was nothing more to be done, and Sunlight replied "Quick, quick, take off the betrothal ring on the finger of Iliane and throw it behind you."

This time there sprang up a great tower of stone, smooth as ivory, hard as steel, which reached up to heaven itself. And the mother of the genius gave a howl of rage, knowing that she could neither climb it nor get through it. But she was not beaten yet, and gathering herself together, she made a prodigious leap, which landed her on the top of the tower, right in the middle of Iliane's ring which lay there, and held her tight. Only her claws could be seen grasping the battlements.

All that could be done the old witch did; but the fire that poured from her mouth never reached the fugitives, though it laid waste the country a hundred miles round the tower, like the flames of a volcano. Then, with one last effort to free herself, her hands gave way, and, falling down to the bottom of the tower, she was broken in pieces.

When the flying princess saw what had happened she rode back to the spot, as Sunlight counselled her, and placed her finger on the top of the tower, which was gradually shrinking into the earth. In an instant the tower had vanished as if it had never been, and in its place was the finger of the princess with a ring round it.

The emperor received Iliane with all the respect that was due to her, and fell in love at first sight besides.

But this did not seem to please Iliane, whose face was sad as she walked about the palace or gardens, wondering how it was that, while other girls did as they liked, she was always in the power of someone whom she hated.

So when the emperor asked her to share his throne, Iliane answered:

"Noble Sovereign, I may not think of marriage till my stud of horses has been brought me, with their trappings all complete."

When he heard this, the emperor once more sent for Fet-Fruners, and said:

"Fet-Fruners, fetch me instantly the stud of mares, with their trappings all complete. If not, your head shall pay the forfeit."

"Mighty Emperor, I kiss your hands! I have but just returned from doing your bidding, and, behold, you send me on another mission, and stake my head on its fulfilment, when your court is full of valiant young men, pining to win their spurs. They say you are a just man; then why not entrust this quest to one of them? Where am I to seek these mares that I am to bring you?"

"How do I know? They may be anywhere in heaven or earth; but, wherever they are, you will have to find them."

The princess bowed and went to consult Sunlight. He listened while she told her tale, and then said:

"Fetch quickly nine buffalo skins; smear them well with tar, and lay them on my back. Do not fear; you will succeed in this also; but, in the end, the emperor's desires will be his undoing."

The buffalo skins were soon got, and the princess started off with Sunlight. The way was long and difficult, but at length they reached the place where the mares were grazing. Here the genius who had carried off Iliane was wandering about, trying to discover how to capture them, all the while believing that Iliane was safe in the palace where he had left her.

As soon as she caught sight of him, the princess went up and told him that Iliane had escaped, and that his mother, in her efforts to recapture her, had died of rage. At this news a blind fury took possession of the genius, and he rushed madly upon the princess, who awaited his onslaught with perfect calmness. As he came on, with his sabre lifted high in the air, Sunlight bounded right over his head, so that the sword fell harmless. And when in her turn the princess prepared to strike, the horse sank upon his knees, so that the blade pierced the genius's thigh.

The fight was so fierce that it seemed as if the earth would give way under them, and for twenty miles round the beasts in the forests fled to their caves for shelter. At last, when her strength was almost gone, the genius lowered his sword for an instant. The princess saw her chance, and, with one swoop of her arm, severed her enemy's head from his body. Still trembling from the long struggle, she turned away, and went to the meadow where the stud were feeding.

By the advice of Sunlight, she took care not to let them see her, and climbed a thick tree, where she could see and hear without being seen herself. Then he neighed, and the mares came galloping up, eager to see the new comer—all but one horse, who did not like strangers, and thought they were very well as they were. As Sunlight stood his ground, well pleased with the attention paid him, this sulky creature suddenly advanced to the charge, and bit so violently that had it not been for the nine buffalo skins Sunlight's last moment would have come. When the fight was ended, the buffalo skins were in ribbons, and the beaten animal writhing with pain on the grass.

Nothing now remained to be done but to drive the whole stud to the emperor's court. So the princess came down from the tree and mounted Sunlight, while the stud followed meekly after, the wounded horse bringing up the rear. On reaching the palace, she drove them into a yard, and went to inform the emperor of her arrival.

The news was told at once to Iliane, who ran down directly and called them to her one by one, each mare by its name. And at the first sight of her the wounded animal shook itself quickly, and in a moment its wounds were healed, and there was not even a mark on its glossy skin.

By this time the emperor, on hearing where she was, joined her in the yard, and at her request ordered the mares to be milked, so that both he and she might bathe in the milk and keep young for ever. But they would suffer no one to come near them, and the princess was commanded to perform this service also.

At this, the heart of the girl swelled within her. The hardest tasks were always given to her, and long before the two years were up, she would be worn out and useless. But while these thoughts passed through her mind, a fearful rain fell, such as no man remembered before, and rose till the mares were standing up to their knees in water. Then as suddenly it stopped, and, behold! the water was ice, which held the animals firmly in its grasp. And the princess's heart grew light again, and she sat down gaily to milk them, as if she had done it every morning of her life.

The love of the emperor for Iliane waxed greater day by day, but she paid no heed to him, and always had an excuse ready to put off their marriage. At length, when she had come to the end of everything she could think of, she said to him one day: "Grant me, Sire, just one request more, and then I will really marry you; for you have waited patiently this long time."

"My beautiful dove," replied the emperor, "both I and all I possess are yours, so ask your will, and you shall have it."

"Get me, then," she said, "a flask of the holy water that is kept in a little church beyond the river Jordan, and I will be your wife."

Then the emperor ordered Fet-Fruners to ride without delay to the river Jordan, and to bring back, at whatever cost, the holy water for Iliane.

"This, my mistress," said Sunlight, when she was saddling him, "is the last and most difficult of your tasks. But fear nothing, for the hour of the emperor has struck."

So they started; and the horse, who was not a wizard for nothing, told the princess exactly where she was to look for the holy water.

"It stands," he said, "on the altar of a little church, and is guarded by a troop of nuns. They never sleep, night or day, but every now and then a hermit comes to visit them, and from him they learn certain things it is needful for them to know. When this happens, only one of the nuns remains on guard at a time, and if we are lucky enough to hit upon this moment, we may get hold of the vase at once; if not, we shall have to wait the arrival of the hermit, however long it may be; for there is no other means of obtaining the holy water."

They came in sight of the church beyond the Jordan, and, to their great joy, beheld the hermit just arriving at the door. They could hear him calling the nuns round him, and saw them settle themselves under a tree, with the hermit in their midst—all but one, who remained on guard, as was the custom.

The hermit had a great deal to say, and the day was very hot, so the nun, tired of sitting by herself, lay down right across the threshold, and fell sound asleep.

Then Sunlight told the princess what she was to do, and the girl stepped softly over the sleeping nun, and crept like a cat along the dark aisle, feeling the wall with her fingers, lest she should fall over something and ruin it all by a noise. But she reached the altar in safety, and found the vase of holy water standing on it. This she thrust into her dress, and went back with the same care as she came. With a bound she was in the saddle, and seizing the reins bade Sunlight take her home as fast as his legs could carry him.

The sound of the flying hoofs aroused the nun, who understood instantly that the precious treasure was stolen, and her shrieks were so loud and piercing that all the rest came flying to see what was the matter. The hermit followed at their heels, but seeing it was impossible to overtake the thief, he fell on his knees and called his most deadly curse down on her head, praying that if the thief was a man, he might become a woman; and if she was a woman, that she might become a man. In either case he thought that the punishment would be severe.

But punishments are things about which people do not always agree, and when the princess suddenly felt she was really the man she had pretended to be, she was delighted, and if the hermit had only been within reach she would have thanked him from her heart.

By the time she reached the emperor's court, Fet-Fruners looked a young man all over in the eyes of everyone; and even the mother of the genius would now have had her doubts set at rest. He drew forth the vase from his tunic and held it up to the emperor, saying: "Mighty Sovereign, all hail! I have fulfilled this task also, and I hope it is the last you have for me; let another now take his turn."

"I am content, Fet-Fruners," replied the emperor, "and when I am dead it is you who will sit upon my throne: for I have yet no son to come after me. But if one is given me, and my dearest wish is accomplished, then you shall be his right hand, and guide him with your counsels."

But though the emperor was satisfied, Iliane was not, and she determined to revenge herself on the emperor for the dangers which he had caused Fet-Fruners to run. And as for the vase of holy water, she thought that, in common politeness, her suitor ought to have fetched it himself, which he could have done without any risk at all.

So she ordered the great bath to be filled with the milk of her mares, and begged the emperor to clothe himself in white robes, and enter the bath with her, an invitation he accepted with joy. Then, when both were standing with the milk reaching to their necks, she sent for the horse which had fought Sunlight, and made a secret sign to him. The horse understood what he was to do, and from one nostril he breathed fresh air over Iliane, and from the other, he snorted a burning wind which shrivelled up the emperor where he stood, leaving only a little heap of ashes.

His strange death, which no one could explain, made a great sensation throughout the country, and the funeral his people gave him was the most splendid ever known. When it was over, Iliane summoned Fet-Fruners before her, and addressed him thus:

"Fet-Fruners! it is you who brought me and have saved my life, and obeyed my wishes. It is you who gave me back my stud; you who killed the genius, and the old witch his mother; you who brought me the holy water. And you, and none other, shall be my husband."

"Yes, I will marry you," said the young man, with a voice almost as soft as when he was a princess. "But know that in *our* house, it will be the cock who sings and not the hen!"

—*The Violet Fairy Book* (1901)

The Golden Crab

GREEK

ONCE upon a time there was a fisherman who had a wife and three children. Every morning he used to go out fishing, and whatever fish he caught he sold to the King. One day, among the other fishes, he caught a golden crab. When he came home he put all the fishes together into a great dish, but he kept the Crab separate because it shone so beautifully, and placed it upon a high shelf in the cupboard. Now while the old woman, his wife, was cleaning the fish, and had tucked up her gown so that her feet were visible, she suddenly heard a voice, which said:

> "Let down, let down thy petticoat
> That lets thy feet be seen."

She turned round in surprise, and then she saw the little creature, the Golden Crab.

"What! You can speak, can you, you ridiculous crab?" she said, for she was not quite pleased at the Crab's remarks. Then she took him up and placed him on a dish.

When her husband came home and they sat down to dinner, they presently heard the Crab's little voice saying, "Give me some too." They were all very much surprised, but they gave him something to eat. When

144

the old man came to take away the plate which had contained the Crab's dinner, he found it full of gold, and as the same thing happened every day he soon became very fond of the Crab.

One day the Crab said to the fisherman's wife, "Go to the King and tell him I wish to marry his younger daughter."

The old woman went accordingly, and laid the matter before the King, who laughed a little at the notion of his daughter marrying a crab, but did not decline the proposal altogether, because he was a prudent monarch, and knew that the Crab was likely to be a prince in disguise. He said, therefore, to the fisherman's wife, "Go, old woman, and tell the Crab I will give him my daughter if by to-morrow morning he can build a wall in front of my castle much higher than my tower, upon which all the flowers of the world must grow and bloom."

The fisherman's wife went home and gave this message.

Then the Crab gave her a golden rod, and said, "Go and strike with this rod three times upon the ground on the place which the King showed you, and to-morrow morning the wall will be there."

The old woman did so and went away again.

The next morning, when the King awoke, what do you think he saw? The wall stood there before his eyes, exactly as he had bespoken it!

Then the old woman went back to the King and said to him, "Your Majesty's orders have been fulfilled."

"That is all very well," said the King, "but I cannot give away my daughter until there stands in front of my palace a garden in which there are three fountains, of which the first must play gold, the second diamonds, and the third brilliants."

So the old woman had to strike again three times upon the ground with the rod, and the next morning the garden was there. The king now gave his consent, and the wedding was fixed for the very next day.

Then the Crab said to the old fisherman, "Now take

this rod; go and knock with it on a certain mountain; then a black man will come out and ask you what you wish for. Answer him thus: 'Your master, the King, has sent me to tell you that you must send him his golden garment that is like the sun.' Make him give you, besides, the queenly robes of gold and precious stones which are like the flowery meadows, and bring them both to me. And bring me also the golden cushion."

The old man went and did his errand. When he had brought the precious robes, the Crab put on the golden garment and then crept upon the golden cushion, and in this way the fisherman carried him to the castle, where the Crab presented the other garment to his bride. Now the ceremony took place, and when the married pair were alone together the Crab made himself known to his young wife, and told her how he was the son of the greatest king in the world, and how he was enchanted, so that he became a crab by day and was a man only at night; and he could also change himself into an eagle as often as he wished. No sooner had he said this than he shook himself, and immediately became a handsome youth, but the next morning he was forced to creep back again into his crab-shell. And the same thing happened every day. But the Princess's affection for the Crab, and the polite attention with which she behaved to him, surprised the royal family very much. They suspected some secret, but though they spied and spied, they could not discover it. Thus a year passed away, and the Princess had a son, whom she called Benjamin. But her mother still thought the whole matter very strange. At last she said to the King that he ought to ask his daughter whether she would not like to have another husband instead of the Crab? But when the daughter was questioned she only answered:

"I am married to the Crab, and him only will I have."

Then the King said to her, "I will appoint a tournament in your honour, and I will invite all the princes in the world to it, and if any one of them pleases you, you shall marry him."

In the evening the Princess told this to the Crab, who said to her, "Take this rod, go to the garden gate and knock with it, then a black man will come out and say to you, 'Why have you called me, and what do you require of me?' Answer him thus: "Your master the King has sent me hither to tell you to send him his golden armour and his steed and the silver apple.' And bring them to me."

The Princess did so, and brought him what he desired.

The following evening the Prince dressed himself for the tournament. Before he went he said to his wife, "Now mind you do not say when you see me that I am the Crab. For if you do this evil will come of it. Place yourself at the window with your sisters; I will ride by and throw you the silver apple. Take it in your hand, but if they ask you who I am, say that you do not know." So saying, he kissed her, repeated his warning once more, and went away.

The Princess went with her sisters to the window and looked on at the tournament. Presently her husband rode by and threw the apple up to her. She caught it in her hand and went with it to her room, and by-and-by her husband came back to her. But her father was much surprised that she did not seem to care about any of the Princes; he therefore appointed a second tournament.

The Crab then gave his wife the same directions as before, only this time the apple which she received from the black man was of gold. But before the Prince went to the tournament he said to his wife, "Now I know you will betray me to-day."

But she swore to him that she would not tell who he was. He then repeated his warning and went away.

In the evening, while the Princess, with her mother and sisters, was standing at the window, the Prince suddenly galloped past on his steed and threw her the golden apple.

Then her mother flew into a passion, gave her a box on the ear, and cried out, "Does not even that prince please you, you fool?"

The Princess in her fright exclaimed, "That is the Crab himself!"

Her mother was still more angry because she had not been told sooner, ran into her daughter's room where the crab-shell was still lying, took it up and threw it into the fire. Then the poor Princess cried bitterly, but it was of no use; her husband did not come back.

Now we must leave the Princess and turn to the other persons in the story. One day an old man went to a stream to dip in a crust of bread which he was going to eat, when a dog came out of the water, snatched the bread from his hand, and ran away. The old man ran after him, but the dog reached a door, pushed it open, and ran in, the old man following him. He did not overtake the dog, but found himself above a staircase, which he descended. Then he saw before him a stately palace, and, entering, he found in a large hall a table set for twelve persons. He hid himself in the hall behind a great picture, that he might see what would happen. At noon he heard a great noise, so that he trembled with fear. When he took courage to look out from behind the picture, he saw twelve eagles flying in. At this sight his fear became still greater. The eagles flew to the basin of a fountain that was there and bathed themselves, when suddenly they were changed into twelve handsome youths. Now they seated themselves at the table, and one of them took up a goblet filled with wine, and said, "A health to my father!" And another said, "A health to my mother!" and so the healths went round. Then one of them said:

> "A health to my dearest lady,
>   Long may she live and well!
> But a curse on the cruel mother
>   That burnt my golden shell!"

The Prince Throws the apple To the Princess

And so saying he wept bitterly. Then the youths rose from the table, went back to the great stone fountain, turned themselves into eagles again, and flew away.

Then the old man went away too, returned to the light of day, and went home. Soon after he heard that the Princess was ill, and that the only thing that did her good was having stories told to her. He therefore went to the royal castle, obtained an audience of the Princess, and told her about the strange things he had seen in the underground palace. No sooner had he finished than the Princess asked him whether he could find the way to that palace.

"Yes," he answered, "certainly."

And now she desired him to guide her thither at once. The old man did so, and when they came to the palace he hid her behind the great picture and advised her to keep quite still, and he placed himself behind the picture also. Presently the eagles came flying in, and changed themselves into young men, and in a moment the Princess recognised her husband amongst them all, and tried to come out of her hiding-place; but the old man held her back. The youths seated themselves at the table; and now the Prince said again, while he took up the cup of wine:

> "A health to my dearest lady,
> Long may she live and well!
> But a curse on the cruel mother
> That burnt my golden shell!"

Then the Princess could restrain herself no longer, but ran forward and threw her arms round her husband. And immediately he knew her again, and said:

"Do you remember how I told you that day that you would betray me? Now you see that I spoke the truth. But all that bad time is past. Now listen to me: I must still remain enchanted for three months. Will you stay here with me till that time is over?"

So the Princess stayed with him, and said to the old

man, "Go back to the castle and tell my parents that I am staying here."

Her parents were very much vexed when the old man came back and told them this, but as soon as the three months of the Prince's enchantment were over, he ceased to be an eagle and became once more a man, and they returned home together. And then they lived happily, and we who hear the story are happier still.

—*The Yellow Fairy Book* (1894)

The Golden Lion

SICILIAN

———◆◆———

THERE was once a rich merchant who had three sons, and when they were grown up the eldest said to him, "Father, I wish to travel and see the world. I pray you let me."

So the father ordered a beautiful ship to be fitted up, and the young man sailed away in it. After some weeks the vessel cast anchor before a large town, and the merchant's son went on shore.

The first thing he saw was a large notice written on a board saying that if any man could find the king's daughter within eight days he should have her to wife, but that if he tried and failed his head must be the forfeit.

"Well," thought the youth as he read this proclamation, "that ought not to be a very difficult matter"; and he asked an audience of the king, and told him that he wished to seek for the princess.

"Certainly," replied the king. "You have the whole palace to search in; but remember, if you fail it will cost you your head."

So saying, he commanded the doors to be thrown open, and food and drink to be set before the young man, who, after he had eaten, began to look for the princess. But though he visited every corner and chest and cupboard, she was not in any of them, and after eight days he gave it up and his head was cut off.

All this time his father and brothers had had no news of him, and were very anxious. At last the second son could bear it no longer, and said, "Dear father, give me, I pray you, a large ship and some money, and let me go and seek for my brother."

So another ship was fitted out, and the young man sailed away, and was blown by the wind into the same harbour where his brother had landed.

Now when he saw the first ship lying at anchor his heart beat high, and he said to himself, "My brother cannot surely be far off," and he ordered a boat and was put on shore.

As he jumped on to the pier his eye caught the notice about the princess, and he thought, "He has undertaken to find her, and has certainly lost his head. I must try myself, and seek him as well as her. It cannot be such a very difficult matter." But he fared no better than his brother, and in eight days his head was cut off.

So now there was only the youngest at home, and when the other two never came he also begged for a ship that he might go in search of his lost brothers. And when the vessel started a high wind arose, and blew him straight to the harbour where the notice was set.

"Oho!" said he, as he read, "whoever can find the king's daughter shall have her to wife. It is quite clear now what has befallen my brothers. But in spite of that I think I must try my luck," and he took the road to the castle.

On the way he met an old woman, who stopped and begged.

"Leave me in peace, old woman," replied he.

"Oh, do not send me away empty," she said. "You are such a handsome young man you will surely not refuse an old woman a few pence."

"I tell you, old woman, leave me alone."

"You are in some trouble?" she asked. "Tell me what it is, and perhaps I can help you."

Then he told her how he had set his heart on finding the king's daughter.

"I can easily manage that for you as long as you have enough money."

"Oh, as to that, I have plenty," answered he.

"Well, you must take it to a goldsmith and get him to make it into a golden lion, with eyes of crystal; and inside it must have something that will enable it to play tunes. When it is ready bring it to me."

The young man did as he was bid, and when the lion was made the old woman hid the youth in it, and brought it to the king, who was so delighted with it that he wanted to buy it. But she replied, "It does not belong to me, and my master will not part from it at any price."

"At any rate, leave it with me for a few days," said he; "I should like to show it to my daughter."

"Yes, I can do that," answered the old woman; "but to-morrow I must have it back again." And she went away.

The king watched her till she was quite out of sight, so as to make sure that she was not spying upon him; then he took the golden lion into his room and lifted some loose boards from the floor. Below the floor there was a staircase, which he went down till he reached a door at the foot. This he unlocked, and found himself in a narrow passage closed by another door, which he also opened. The young man, hidden in the golden lion, kept count of everything, and marked that there were in all seven doors. After they had all been unlocked the king entered a lovely hall, where the princess was amusing herself with eleven friends. All twelve girls wore the same clothes, and were as like each other as two peas.

"What bad luck!" thought the youth. "Even supposing that I managed to find my way here again, I don't see how I could ever tell which was the princess."

And he stared hard at the princess as she clapped her hands with joy and ran up to them, crying, "Oh, do let

THE KING BRINGS IN THE GOLDEN LION TO HIS DAUGHTER

us keep that delicious beast for to-night; it will make such a nice plaything."

The king did not stay long, and when he left he handed over the lion to the maidens, who amused themselves with it for some time, till they got sleepy, and thought it was time to go to bed. But the princess took the lion into her own room and laid it on the floor.

She was just beginning to doze when she heard a voice quite close to her, which made her jump. "O lovely princess, if you only knew what I have gone through to find you!" The princess jumped out of bed screaming, "The lion! the lion!" but her friends thought it was a nightmare, and did not trouble themselves to get up.

"O lovely princess!" continued the voice, "fear nothing! I am the son of a rich merchant, and desire above all things to have you for my wife. And in order to get to you I have hidden myself in this golden lion."

"What use is that?" she asked. "For if you cannot pick me out from among my companions you will still lose your head."

"I look to you to help me," he said. "I have done so much for you that you might do this one thing for me."

"Then listen to me. On the eighth day I will tie a white sash round my waist, and by that you will know me."

The next morning the king came very early to fetch the lion, as the old woman was already at the palace asking for it. When they were safe from view she let the young man out, and he returned to the king and told him that he wished to find the princess.

"Very good," said the king, who by this time was almost tired of repeating the same words; "but if you fail your head will be the forfeit."

So the youth remained quietly in the castle, eating and looking at all the beautiful things around him, and every now and then pretending to be searching busily in all the closets and corners. On the eighth day he entered the room where the king was sitting. "Take up the floor in this place," he said. The king gave a cry, but stopped himself, and asked, "What do you want the floor up for? There is nothing there."

But as all his courtiers were watching him he did not like to make any more objections, and ordered the floor to be taken up, as the young man desired. The youth then went straight down the staircase till he reached the door; then he turned and demanded that the key should be brought. So the king was forced to unlock the door, and the next and the next and the next, till all seven were open, and they entered into the hall where the twelve maidens were standing all in a row, so like that none might tell them apart. But as he looked one of them silently drew a white sash from her pocket and slipped it round her waist, and the young man sprang to her and said, "This is the princess, and I claim her for my wife." And the king owned himself beaten, and commanded that the wedding feast should be held.

After eight days the bridal pair said farewell to the king, and set sail for the youth's own country, taking with them a whole shipload of treasures as the princess's dowry. But they did not forget the old woman who had brought about all their happiness, and they gave her enough money to make her comfortable to the end of her days.

—*The Pink Fairy Book* (1897)

The Golden-headed Fish

ARMENIAN

ONCE upon a time there lived in Egypt a king who lost his sight from a bad illness. Of course he was very unhappy, and became more so as months passed, and all the best doctors in the land were unable to cure him. The poor man grew so thin from misery that everyone thought he was going to die, and the prince, his only son, thought so too.

Great was therefore the rejoicing through Egypt when a traveller arrived in a boat down the river Nile, and after questioning the people as to the reason of their downcast looks, declared that he was court physician to the king of a far country, and would, if allowed, examine the eyes of the blind man. He was at once admitted into the royal presence, and after a few minutes of careful study announced that the case, though very serious, was not quite hopeless.

"Somewhere in the Great Sea," he said, "there exists a Golden-headed Fish. If you can manage to catch this creature, bring it to me, and I will prepare an ointment from its blood which will restore your sight. For a hundred days I will wait here, but if at the end of that time the fish should still be uncaught, I must return to my own master."

The next morning the young prince set forth in quest

The Prince has pity on the Gold-headed Fish

of the fish, taking with him a hundred men, each man carrying a net. Quite a little fleet of boats was awaiting them, and in these they sailed to the middle of the Great Sea. During three months they laboured diligently from sunrise to sunset, but though they caught large multitudes of fishes, not one of them had a golden head.

"It is quite useless now," said the prince on the very last night. "Even if we find it this evening, the hundred days will be over in an hour, and long before we could reach the Egyptian capital the doctor will be on his way home. Still, I will go out again, and cast the net once more myself." And so he did, and at the very moment that the hundred days were up, he drew in the net with the Golden-headed Fish entangled in its meshes.

"Success has come, but, as happens often, it is too late," murmured the young man, who had studied in the schools of philosophy; "but, all the same, put the fish in that vessel full of water, and we will take it back to show my father that we have done what we could." But when he drew near the fish it looked up at him with such piteous eyes that he could not make up his mind to condemn it to death. For he knew well that, though the doctors of his own country were ignorant of the secret of the ointment, they would do all in their power to extract something from the fish's blood. So he picked up the prize of so much labour, and threw it back into the sea, and then began his journey back to the palace. When at last he reached it he found the king in a high fever, caused by his disappointment, and he refused to believe the story told him by his son.

"Your head shall pay for it! Your head shall pay for it!" cried he; and bade the courtiers instantly summon the executioner to the palace.

But of course somebody ran at once to the queen, and told her of the king's order, and she put common clothes on the prince, and filled his pockets with gold, and hurried him on board a ship which was sailing that night for a distant island.

"Your father will repent some day, and then he will be thankful to know you are alive," said she. "But one last counsel will I give you, and that is, take no man into your service who desires to be paid every month."

The young prince thought this advice rather odd. If the servant had to be paid anyhow, he did not understand what difference it could make whether it was by the year or by the month. However, he had many times proved that his mother was wiser than he, so he promised obedience.

After a voyage of several weeks, he arrived at the island of which his mother had spoken. It was full of hills and woods and flowers, and beautiful white houses stood everywhere in gardens.

"What a charming spot to live in," thought the prince. And he lost no time in buying one of the prettiest of the dwellings.

Then servants came pressing to offer their services; but as they all declared that they must have payment at the end of every month, the young man, who remembered his mother's words, declined to have anything to say to them. At length, one morning, an Arab appeared and begged that the prince would engage him.

"And what wages do you ask?" inquired the prince, when he had questioned the new-comer and found him suitable.

"I do not want money," answered the Arab; "at the end of a year you can see what my services are worth to you, and can pay me in any way you like." And the young man was pleased, and took the Arab for his servant.

Now, although no one would have guessed it from the look of the side of the island where the prince had landed, the other part was a complete desert, owing to the ravages of a horrible monster which came up from the sea, and devoured all the corn and cattle. The governor had sent bands of soldiers to lie in wait for the creature in order to kill it; but, somehow, no one ever

happened to be awake at the moment that the ravages
were committed. It was in vain that the sleepy soldiers
were always punished severely—the same thing invari-
ably occurred next time; and at last heralds were sent
throughout the island to offer a great reward to the man
who could slay the monster.

As soon as the Arab heard the news, he went straight
to the governor's palace.

"If my master can succeed in killing the monster,
what reward will you give him?" asked he.

"My daughter and anything besides that he chooses,"
answered the governor. But the Arab shook his head.

"Give him your daughter and keep your wealth," said
he; "but, henceforeward, let her share in your gains,
whatever they are."

"It is well," replied the governor; and ordered a deed
to be prepared, which was signed by both of them.

That night the Arab stole down to the shore to watch,
but, before he set out, he rubbed himself all over with
some oil which made his skin smart so badly that there
was no chance of *his* going to sleep as the soldiers had
done. Then he hid himself behind a large rock and
waited. By-and-by a swell seemed to rise on the water,
and, a few minutes later, a hideous monster—part bird,
part beast, and part serpent—stepped noiselessly on to
the rocks. It walked stealthily up towards the fields, but
the Arab was ready for it, and, as it passed, plunged his
dagger into the soft part behind the ear. The creature
staggered and gave a loud cry, and then rolled over
dead, with its feet in the sea.

The Arab watched for a little while, in order to make
sure that there was no life left in his enemy, but as the
huge body remained quite still, he quitted his hiding-
place, and cut off the ears of his foe. These he carried to
his master, bidding him show them to the governor, and
declare that he himself, and no other, had killed
the monster.

"But it was you, and not I, who slew him," objected
the prince.

"Never mind; do as I bid you. I have a reason for it,"
answered the Arab. And though the young man did not
like taking credit for what he had never done, at length
he gave in.

The governor was so delighted at the news that he
begged the prince to take his daughter to wife that very
day; but the prince refused, saying that all he desired
was a ship which would carry him to see the world. Of
course this was granted him at once, and when he and
his faithful Arab embarked they found, heaped up in
the vessel, stores of diamonds and precious stones,
which the grateful governor had secretly placed there.

So they sailed, and they sailed, and they sailed; and
at length they reached the shores of a great kingdom.
Leaving the prince on board, the Arab went into the
town to find out what sort of a place it was. After some
hours he returned, saying that he heard that the king's
daughter was the most beautiful princess in the world,
and that the prince would do well to ask for her hand.

Nothing loth, the prince listened to this advice, and
taking some of the finest necklaces in his hand, he
mounted a splendid horse which the Arab had bought
for him, and rode up to the palace, closely followed by
his faithful attendant.

The strange king happened to be in a good humour,
and they were readily admitted to his presence. Laying
down his offerings on the steps of the throne, he prayed
the king to grant him his daughter in marriage.

The monarch listened to him in silence; but answered,
after a pause:

"Young man, I will give you my daughter to wife, if
that is your wish; but first I must tell you that she has
already gone through the marriage ceremony with a
hundred and ninety young men, and not one of them
lived for twelve hours after. So think, while there is yet
time."

The prince *did* think, and was so frightened that he
very nearly went back to his ship wihout any more

words. But just as he was about to withdraw his proposal the Arab whispered:

"Fear nothing, but take her."

"The luck must change some time," he said, at last;
"and who would not risk his head for the hand of such a
peerless princess?"

"As you will," replied the king. "Then I will give
orders that the marriage shall be celebrated to-night."

And so it was done; and after the ceremony the bride
and bridegroom retired to their own apartments to sup
by themselves, for such was the custom of the country.
The moon shone bright, and the prince walked to the
window to look out upon the river and upon the distant
hills, when his gaze suddenly fell on a silken shroud
neatly laid out on a couch, with his name embroidered
in gold thread across the front; for this also was the
pleasure of the king.

Horrified at the spectacle, he turned his head away,
and this time his glance rested on a group of men,
digging busily beneath the window. It was a strange
hour for anyone to be at work, and what was the hole
for? It was a curious shape, so long and narrow, almost
like—— Ah! yes, that was what it was! It was *his* grave
that they were digging!

The shock of the discovery rendered him speechless,
yet he stood fascinated and unable to move. At this
moment a small black snake darted from the mouth of
the princess, who was seated at the table, and wriggled
quickly towards him. But the Arab was watching for
something of the sort to happen, and seizing the serpent with some pincers that he held in one hand, he
cut off its head with a sharp dagger.

The king could hardly believe his eyes when, early
the next morning, his new son-in-law craved an audience of his Majesty.

"What, you?" he cried, as the young man entered.

"Yes, I. Why not?" asked the bridegroom, who thought
it best to pretend not to know anything that had occurred. "You remember, I told you that the luck must

turn at last, and so it has. But I came to ask whether you would be so kind as to bid the gardeners fill up a great hole right underneath my window, which spoils the view."

"Oh! certainly, yes; of course it shall be done!" stammered the king. "Is there anything else?"

"No, nothing, thank you," replied the prince, as he bowed and withdrew.

Now, from the moment that the Arab cut off the snake's head, the spell, or whatever it was, seemed to have been taken off the princess, and she lived very happily with her husband. The days passed swiftly in hunting in the forests, or sailing on the broad river that flowed past the palace, and when night fell she would sing to her harp, or the prince would tell her tales of his own country.

One evening a man in a strange garb, with a face burnt brown by the sun, arrived at court. He asked to see the bridegroom, and falling on his face announced that he was a messenger sent by the Queen of Egypt, proclaiming him king in succession to his father, who was dead.

"Her Majesty begs you will set off without delay, and your bride also, as the affairs of the kingdom are somewhat in disorder," ended the messenger.

Then the young man hastened to seek an audience of his father-in-law, who was delighted to find that his daughter's husband was not merely the governor of a province, as he had supposed, but the king of a powerful country. He at once ordered a splendid ship to be made ready, and in a week's time rode down to the harbour, to bid farewell to the young couple.

In spite of her grief of the dead king, the queen was overjoyed to welcome her son home, and commanded the palace to be hung with splendid stuffs to do honour to the bride. The people expected great things from their new sovereign, for they had suffered much from the harsh rule of the old one, and crowds presented themselves every morning with petitions in their hands, which they hoped to persuade the king to grant. Truly, he had enough to keep him busy; but he was very happy for all that, till, one night, the Arab came to him, and begged permission to return to his own land.

Filled with dismay the young man said: "Leave me! Do you really wish to leave me?" Sadly the Arab bowed his head.

"No, my master; never could I wish to leave you! But I have received a summons, and I dare not disobey it."

The king was silent, trying to choke down the grief he felt at the thought of losing his faithful servant.

"Well, I must not try to keep you," he faltered out at last. "That would be a poor return for all that you have done for me! Everything I have is yours: take what you will, for without you I should long ago have been dead!"

"And without *you*, *I* should long ago have been dead," answered the Arab. "*I* am the Golden-headed Fish."

—*The Olive Fairy Book* (1907)

Hans, The Mermaid's Son

DANISH

In a village there once lived a smith called Basmus,
who was in a very poor way. He was still a young man,
and a strong handsome fellow to boot, but he had many
little children and there was little to be earned by his
trade. He was, however, a diligent and hard-working
man, and when he had no work in the smithy he was
out at sea fishing, or gathering wreckage on the shore.

It happened one time that he had gone out to fish in
good weather, all alone in a little boat, but he did not
come home that day, nor the following one, so that all
believed that he had perished out at sea. On the third
day, however, Basmus came to shore again and had his
boat full of fish, so big and fat that no one had ever seen
their like. There was nothing the matter with him, and
he complained neither of hunger nor thirst. He had got
into a fog, he said, and could not find land again. What
he did not tell, however, was where he had been all the
time; that only came out six years later, when people
got to know that he had been caught by a mermaid out
on the deep sea, and had been her guest during the
three days that he was missing. From that time forth he
went out no more to fish; nor, indeed, did he require to
do so, for whenever he went down to the shore it never
failed that some wreckage was washed up, and in it all

Basnus & the Mermaid

kinds of valuable things. In those days everyone took
what they found and got leave to keep it, so that the
smith grew more prosperous day by day.

When seven years had passed since the smith went
out to sea, it happened one morning, as he stood in the
smithy, mending a plough, that a handsome young lad
came in to him and said, "Good-day, father; my mother
the mermaid sends her greetings, and says that *she* has
had me for six years now, and *you* can keep me for as
long."

He was a strange enough boy to be six years old, for
he looked as if he were eighteen, and was even bigger
and stronger than lads commonly are at that age.

"Will you have a bite of bread?" said the smith.

"Oh, yes," said Hans, for that was his name.

The smith then told his wife to cut a piece of bread
for him. She did so, and the boy swallowed it at one
mouthful and went out again to the smithy to his father.

"Have you got all you can eat?" said the smith.

"No," said Hans, "that was just a little bit."

The smith went into the house and took a whole loaf,
which he cut into two slices and put butter and cheese
between them, and this he gave to Hans. In a while the
boy came out to the smithy again.

"Well, have you got as much as you can eat?" said
the smith.

"No, not nearly," said Hans; "I must try to find a
better place than this, for I can see that I shall never
get my fill here."

Hans wished to set off at once, as soon as his father
would make a staff for him of such a kind as he wanted.

"It must be of iron," said he, "and one that can hold
out."

The smith brought him an iron rod as thick as an
ordinary staff, but Hans took it and twisted it round his
finger, so *that* wouldn't do. Then the smith came dragging one as thick as a waggon-pole, but Hans bent it
over his knee and broke it like a straw. The smith then
had to collect all the iron he had, and Hans held it

while his father forged for him a staff, which was heavier than the anvil. When Hans had got this he said, "Many thanks, father; now I have got my inheritance." With this he set off into the country, and the smith was very well pleased to be rid of *that* son, before he ate him out of house and home.

Hans first arrived at a large estate, and it so happened that the squire himself was standing outside the farmyard.

"Where are you going?" said the squire.

"I am looking for a place," said Hans, "where they have need of strong fellows, and can give them plenty to eat."

"Well," said the squire, "I generally have twenty-four men at this time of the year, but I have only twelve just now, so I can easily take you on."

"Very well," said Hans, "I shall easily do twelve men's work, but then I must also have as much to eat as the twelve would."

All this was agreed to, and the squire took Hans into the kitchen, and told the servant girls that the new man was to have as much food as the other twelve. It was arranged that he should have a pot to himself, and he could then use the ladle to take his food with.

It was in the evening that Hans arrived there, so he did nothing more that day than eat his supper—a big pot of buck-wheat porridge, which he cleaned to the bottom, and was then so far satisfied that he said he could sleep on that, so he went off to bed. He slept both well and long, and all the rest were up and at their work while he was still sleeping soundly. The squire was also on foot, for he was curious to see how the new man would behave who was both to eat and work for twelve.

But as yet there was no Hans to be seen, and the sun was already high in the heavens, so the squire himself went and called on him.

"Get up, Hans," he cried; "you are sleeping too long."

Hans woke up and rubbed his eyes. "Yes, that's true," he said, "I must get up and have my breakfast."

So he rose and dressed himself, and went into the kitchen, where he got his pot of porridge; he swallowed all of this, and then asked what work he was to have.

He was to thresh that day, said the squire; the other twelve men were already busy at it. There were twelve threshing-floors, and the twelve men were at work on six of them—two on each. Hans must thresh by himself all that was lying upon the other six floors. He went out to the barn and got hold of a flail. Then he looked to see how the others did it and did the same, but at the first stroke he smashed the flail in pieces. There were several flails hanging there, and Hans took the one after the the other, but they all went the same way, every one flying in splinters at the first stroke. He then looked round for something else to work with, and found a pair of strong beams lying near. Next he caught sight of a horse-hide nailed up on the barn-door. With the beams he made a flail, using the skin to tie them together. The one beam he used as a handle, and the other to strike with, and now *that* was all right. But the barn was too low, there was no room to swing the flail, and the floors were too small. Hans, however, found a remedy for this—he simply lifted the whole roof off the barn, and set it down in the field beside. He then emptied down all the corn that he could lay his hands on and threshed away. He went through one lot after another, and it was all the same to him what he got hold of, so before midday he had threshed all the squire's grain, his rye and wheat and barley and oats, all mixed through each other. When he was finished with this, he lifted the roof up on the barn again, like setting a lid on a box, and went in and told the squire that that job was done.

The squire opened his eyes at this announcement; and came out to see if it was really true. It was true, sure enough, but he was scarcely delighted with the mixed grain that he had got from all his crops. However, when he saw the flail that Hans had used, and

learned how he had made room for himself to swing it,
he was so afraid of the strong fellow, that he dared not
say anything, except that it was a good thing he had got
it threshed; but it had still to be cleaned.

"What does that mean?" asked Hans.

It was explained to him that the corn and the chaff
had to be separated; as yet both were lying in one heap,
right up to the roof. Hans began to take up a little and
sift it in his hands, but he soon saw that this would
never do. He soon thought of a plan, however; he
opened both barn-doors, and then lay down at one end
and blew, so that all the chaff flew out and lay like a
sand-bank at the other end of the barn, and the grain
was as clean as it could be. Then he reported to the
squire that that job also was done. The squire said that
that was well; there was nothing more for him to do
that day. Off went Hans to the kitchen, and got as
much as he could eat; then he went and took a midday
nap which lasted till supper-time.

Meanwhile the squire was quite miserable, and made
his moan to his wife, saying that she must help him to
find some means of getting rid of this strong fellow, for
he durst not give him his leave. She sent for the steward, and it was arranged that next day all the men
should go to the forest for fire-wood, and that they
should make a bargain among them, that the one who
came home last with his load should be hanged. They
thought they could easily manage that it would be Hans
who would lose his life, for the others would be early
on the road, while Hans would certainly oversleep himself. In the evening. therefore, the men sat and talked
together, saying that next morning they must set out
early to the forest, and as they had a hard day's work
and a long journey before them, they would, for their
amusement, make a compact, that whichever of them
came home last with his load should lose his life on the
gallows. So Hans had no objections to make.

Long before the sun was up next morning, all the
twelve men were on foot. They took all the best horses

and carts, and drove off to the forest. Hans, however, lay and slept on, and the squire said, "Just let him lie."

At last, Hans thought it was time to have his breakfast, so he got up and put on his clothes. He took plenty of time to his breakfast, and then went out to get his horse and cart ready. The others had taken everything that was any good, so that he had a difficulty in scraping together four wheels of different sizes and fixing them to an old cart, and he could find no other horses than a pair of old hacks. These he harnessed to his cart and drove off to the forest. He did not know where it lay, but he followed the track of the other carts, and in that way came to it all right. On coming to the gate leading into the forest, he was unfortunate enough to break it in pieces, so he took a huge stone that was lying on the field, seven ells long, and seven ells broad, and set this in the gap, then he went on and joined the others. These laughed at him heartily, for they had laboured as hard as they could since daybreak, and had helped each other to fell trees and put them on the carts, so that all of these were now loaded except one.

Hans got hold of a woodman's axe and proceeded to fell a tree, but he destroyed the edge and broke the shaft at the first blow. He therefore laid down the axe, put his arms round the tree, and pulled it up by the roots. This he threw upon his cart, and then another and another, and thus he went on while all the others forgot their work, and stood with open mouths, gazing at this strange woodcraft. All at once they began to hurry; the last cart was loaded, and they whipped up their horses, so as to be the first to arrive home.

When Hans had finished his work, he again put his old hacks into the cart, but they could not move it from the spot. He was annoyed at this, and took them out again, twisted a rope round the cart, and all the trees, lifted the whole affair on his back, and set off home, leading the horses behind him by the rein. When he reached the gate, he found the whole row of carts standing there, unable to get any further for the stone which lay in the gap.

"What!" said Hans, "can twelve men not move *that* stone?" With that he lifted it and threw it out of the way, and went on with his burden on his back, and the horses behind him, and arrived at the farm long before any of the others. The squire was walking about there, looking and looking, for he was very curious to know what had happened. Finally, he caught sight of Hans coming along in this fashion, and was so frightened that he did not know what to do, but he shut the gate and put on the bar. When Hans reached the gate of the courtyard, he laid down the trees and hammered at it, but no one came to open it. He then took the trees and tossed them over the barn into the yard, and the cart after them, so that every wheel flew off in a different direction.

When the squire saw this, he thought to himself, "The horses will come the same way if I don't open the door," so he did this.

"Good day, master," said Hans, and put the horses into the stable, and went into the kitchen, to get something to eat. At length the other men came home with their loads. When they came in, Hans said to them, "Do you remember the bargain we made last night? Which of you is it that's going to be hanged?" "Oh," said they, "that was only a joke; it didn't mean anything." "Oh well, it doesn't matter," said Hans, and there was no more about it.

The squire, however, and his wife and the steward, had much to say to each other about the terrible man they had got, and all were agreed that they must get rid of him in some way or other. The steward said that he would manage this all right. Next morning they were to clean the well, and they would make use of that opportunity. They would get him down into the well, and then have a big mill-stone ready to throw down on top of him—that would settle him. After that they could just fill in the well, and then escape being at any expense for his funeral. Both the squire and his wife thought this a splendid idea, and went about rejoicing at the thought that now they would get rid of Hans.

But Hans was hard to kill, as we shall see. He slept long next morning, as he always did, and finally, as he would not waken by himself, the squire had to go and call him. "Get up, Hans, you are sleeping too long," he cried. Hans woke up and rubbed his eyes. "That's so," said he, "I shall rise and have my breakfast." He got up then and dressed himself, while the breakfast stood waiting for him. When he had finished the whole of this, he asked what he was to do that day. He was told to help the other men to clean out the well. That was all right, and he went out and found the other men waiting for him. To these he said that they could choose whichever task they liked—either to go down into the well and fill the buckets while he pulled them up, and he alone would go down to the bottom of the well. They answered that they would rather stay above-ground, as there would be no room for so many of them down in the well.

Hans therefore went down alone, and began to clean out the well, but the men had arranged how they were to act, and immediately each of them seized a stone from a heap of huge blocks that lay in the farmyard, just as big as they could lift, and threw them down above him, thinking to kill him with these. Hans, however, gave no more heed to this than to shout up to them, to keep the hens away from the well, for they were scraping gravel down on the top of him.

They then saw that they could not kill him with little stones, but they had still the big one left. The whole twelve of them set to work with poles and rollers and rolled the big mill-stone to the brink of the well. It was with the greatest difficulty that they got it thrown down there, and now they had no doubt that he had got all that he wanted. But the stone happened to fall so luckily that his head went right through the hole in the middle of the mill-stone, so that it sat round his neck

like a priest's collar. At this, Hans would stay down no
longer. He came out of the well, with the mill-stone
round his neck, and went straight to the squire and
complained that the other men were trying to make a
fool of him. He would not be their priest, he said; he
had too little learning for that. Saying this, he bent
down his head and shook the stone off, so that it crushed
one of the squire's big toes.

The squire went limping in to his wife, and the
steward was sent for. He was told that he must devise
some plan for getting rid of this terrible person. The
scheme he had devised before had been of no use, and
now good counsel was scarce.

"Oh, no," said the steward, "there are good enough
ways yet. The squire can send him this evening to fish
in Devilmoss Lake: he will never escape alive from
there, for no one can go there by night for Old Eric."

That was a grand idea, both the squire and his wife
thought, and so he limped out again to Hans, and said
that he would punish his men for having tried to make a
fool of him. Meanwhile, Hans could do a little job
where he would be free from these rascals. He should
go out on the lake and fish there that night, and would
then be free from all work on the following day.

"All right," said Hans; "I am well content with that,
but I must have something with me to eat—a baking of
bread, a cask of butter, a barrel of ale, and a keg of
brandy. I can't do with less than that."

The squire said that he could easily get all that, so
Hans got all of these tied up together, hung them over
his shoulder on his good staff, and tramped away to
Devilmoss Lake.

There he got into the boat, rowed out upon the lake,
and got everything ready to fish. As he now lay out
there in the middle of the lake, and it was pretty late in
the evening, he thought he would have something to
eat first, before starting to work. Just as he was at his
busiest with this, Old Eric rose out of the lake, caught
him by the cuff of the neck, whipped him out of the

boat, and dragged him down to the bottom. It was a lucky thing that Hans had his walking-stick with him that day, and had just time to catch hold of it when he felt Old Eric's claws in his neck, so when they got down to the bottom he said, "Stop now, just wait a little; here is solid ground." With that he caught Old Eric by the back of the neck with one hand, and hammered away on his back with the staff, till he beat him out as flat as a pancake. Old Eric then began to lament and howl, begging him just to let him go, and he would never come back to the lake again.

"No, my good fellow," said Hans, "you won't get off until you promise to bring all the fish in the lake up to the squire's courtyard, before to-morrow morning,"

Old Eric eagerly promised this, if Hans would only let him go; so Hans rowed ashore, ate up the rest of his provisions, and went home to bed.

Next morning, when the squire rose and opened his front door, the fish came tumbling into the porch, and the whole yard was crammed full of them. He ran in again to his wife, for he could never devise anything himself, and said to her, "What shall we do with him now? Old Eric hasn't taken him. I am certain all the fish are out of the lake, for the yard is just filled with them."

"Yes, that's a bad business," said she; "you must see if you can't get him sent to Purgatory, to demand tribute." The squire therefore made his way to the men's quarters, to speak to Hans, and it took him all his time to push his way along the walls, under the eaves, on account of the fish that filled the yard. He thanked Hans for having fished so well, and said that now he had an errand for him, which he could only give to a trusty servant, and that was to journey to Purgatory, and demand three years' tribute, which, he said, was owing to him from that quarter.

"Willingly," said Hans; "but what road do I go, to get there?"

The squire stood, and did not know what to say, and had first to go in to his wife to ask her.

"Oh, what a fool you are!" said she, "can't you direct him straight forward, south through the wood? Whether he gets there or not, *we* shall be quit of him."

Out goes the squire again to Hans.

"The way lies straight forward, south through the wood," said he.

Hans then must have his provisions for the journey; two bakings of bread, two casks of butter, two barrels ale, and two kegs of brandy. He tied all these up together, and got them on his shoulder hanging on his good walking-stick, and off he tramped southward.

After he had got through the wood, there was more than one road, and he was in doubt which of them was the right one, so he sat down and opened up his bundle of provisions. He found he had left his knife at home, but by good chance, there was a plough lying close at hand, so he took the coulter of this to cut the bread with. As he sat there and took his bite, a man came riding past him.

"Where are you from?" said Hans.

"From Purgatory," said the man.

"Then stop and wait a little," said Hans; but the man was in a hurry, and would not stop, so Hans ran after him and caught the horse by the tail. This brought it down on its hind legs, and the man went flying over its head into a ditch. "Just wait a little," said Hans; "I am going the same way." He got his provisions tied up again, and laid them on the horse's back; then he took hold of the reins. and said to the man, "We two can go along together on foot."

As they went on their way Hans told the stranger both about the errand he had on hand and the fun he had had with Old Eric. The other said but little, but he was well acquainted with the way, and it was no long time before they arrived at the gate. There both horse and rider disappeared, and Hans was left alone outside. "They will come and let me in presently," he thought to himself; but no one came. He hammered at the gate; still no one appeared. Then he got tired of waiting, and smashed at the gate with his staff until he knocked it in pieces and got inside. A whole troop of little demons came down upon him and asked what he wanted. His master's compliments, said Hans, and he wanted three years' tribute. At this they howled at him, and were about to lay hold of him and drag him off; but when they had got some raps from his walking-stick they let go again, howled still louder than before, and ran in to Old Eric, who was still in bed, after his adventure in the lake. They told him that a messenger had come from the squire at Devilmoss to demand three years' tribute. He had knocked the gate in pieces and bruised their arms and legs with his iron staff.

"Give him three years'! give him ten!" shouted Old Eric, "only don't let him come near me."

So all the little demons came dragging so much silver and gold that it was something awful. Hans filled his bundle with gold and silver coins, put it on his neck, and tramped back to his master, who was scared beyond all measure at seeing him again.

But Hans was also tired of service now. Of all the gold and silver he brought with him he let the squire keep one half, and *he* was glad enough, both for the money and at getting rid of Hans. The other half he took home to his father the smith in Furreby. To him also he said "Farewell"; he was now tired of living on shore among mortal men, and preferred to go home again to his mother. Since that time no one has ever seen Hans, the Mermaid's son.

—*The Pink Fairy Book* (1897)

The History of
Jack the Giant-Killer

ENGLISH

———◆◆◆———

IN the reign of the famous King Arthur there lived in Cornwall a lad named Jack, who was a boy of a bold temper, and took delight in hearing or reading of conjurers, giants, and fairies; and used to listen eagerly to the deeds of the knights of King Arthur's Round Table.

In those days there lived on St. Michael's Mount, off Cornwall, a huge giant, eighteen feet high and nine feet round; his fierce and savage looks were the terror of all who beheld him.

He dwelt in a gloomy cavern on the top of the mountain, and used to wade over to the mainland in search of prey; when he would throw half-a-dozen oxen upon his back, and tie three times as many sheep and hogs round his waist, and march back to his own abode.

The giant had done this for many years when Jack resolved to destroy him.

Jack took a horn, a shovel, a pickaxe, his armour, and a dark lantern, and one winter's evening he went to the mount. There he dug a pit twenty-two feet deep and twenty broad. He covered the top over so as to make it look like solid ground. He then blew such a tantivy that the giant awoke and came out of his den, crying out: "You saucy villain! you shall pay for this. I'll broil you for my breakfast!"

He had just finished, when, taking one step further, he tumbled headlong into the pit, and Jack struck him a blow on the head with his pickaxe which killed him. Jack then returned home to cheer his friends with the news.

Another giant, call Blunderbore, vowed to be revenged on Jack if ever he should have him in his power. This giant kept an enchanted castle in the midst of a lonely wood; and some time after the death of Cormoran Jack was passing through a wood, and being weary sat down and went to sleep.

The giant, passing by and seeing Jack, carried him to his castle, where he locked him up in a large room, the floor of which was covered with the bodies, skulls, and bones of men and women.

Soon after the giant went to fetch his brother, who was likewise a giant, to take a meal off his flesh; and Jack saw with terror through the bars of the prison the two giants approaching.

Jack, perceiving in one corner of the room a strong cord, took courage, and making a slip-knot at each end, he threw them over their heads, and tied it to the window-bars; he then pulled till he had choked them. When they were black in the face he slid down the rope and stabbed them to the heart.

Jack next took a great bunch of keys from the pocket of Blunderbore, and went into the castle again. He make a strict search through all the rooms, and in one of them found three ladies tied up by the hair of their heads, and almost starved to death. They told him that their husbands had been killed by the giants, who had then condemned them to be starved to death, because they would not eat the flesh of their own dead husbands.

"Ladies," said Jack, "I have put an end to the monster and his wicked brother; and I give you this castle and all the riches it contains, to make some amends for the dreadful pains you have felt." He then very politely gave them the keys of the castle, and went further on his journey to Wales.

As Jack had but little money, he went on as fast as possible. At length he came to a handsome house. Jack knocked at the door, when there came forth a Welsh giant. Jack said he was a traveller who had lost his way, on which the giant made him welcome, and let him into a room where there there was a good bed to sleep in.

Jack took off his clothes quickly, but though he was weary he could not go to sleep. Soon after this he heard the giant walking backward and forward in the next room, and saying to himself:

"Though here you lodge with me this night,
    You shall not see the morning light;
    My club shall dash your brains out quite."

"Say you so?" thought Jack. "Are these your tricks upon travellers? But I hope to prove as cunning as you are." Then, getting out of bed, he groped about the room, and at last found a large thick billet of wood. He laid it in his own place in the bed, and then hid himself in a dark corner of the room.

The giant, about midnight, entered the apartment, and with his bludgeon struck a many blows on the bed, in the very place where Jack had laid the log; and then he went back to his own room, thinking he had broken all Jack's bones.

Early in the morning Jack put a bold face upon the matter, and walked into the giant's room to thank him for his lodging. The giant started when he saw him, and began to stammer out: "Oh! dear me; is it you? Pray how did you sleep last night? Did you hear or see anything in the dead of the night?"

"Nothing worth speaking of," said Jack carelessly: "a rat, I believe, gave me three or four slaps with its tail, and disturbed me a little; but I soon went to sleep again."

The giant wondered more and more at this: yet he did not answer a word, but went to bring two great bowls of hasty-pudding for their breakfast. Jack wanted to make the giant believe that he could eat as much as himself, so he contrived to button a leathern bag inside his coat, and slip the hasty-pudding into this bag, while he seemed to put it into his mouth.

When breakfast was over he said to the giant: "Now I will show you a fine trick. I can cure all wounds with a touch: I could cut off my head in one minute, and the next put it sound again on my shoulders. You shall see an example." He then took hold of the knife, ripped up the leathern bag, and all the hasty-pudding tumbled out upon the floor.

"Ods splutter hur nails!" cried the Welsh giant, who was ashamed to be outdone by such a little fellow as Jack, "hur can do that hurself"; so he snatched up the knife, plunged it into his own stomach, and in a moment dropped down dead.

Jack, having hitherto been successful in all his undertakings, resolved not to be idle in future; he therefore furnished himself with a horse, a cap of knowledge, a sword of sharpness, shoes of swiftness, and an invisible coat, the better to perform the wonderful enterprises that lay before him.

He travelled over high hills, and on the third day he came to a large and spacious forest through which his road lay. Scarcely had he entered the forest when he beheld a monstrous giant dragging along by the hair of their heads a handsome knight and his lady. Jack alighted from his horse, and tying him to an oak tree, put on his invisible coat, under which he carried his sword of sharpness.

When he came up to the giant he made several strokes at him, but could not reach his body, but wounded his thighs in several places; and at length putting both hands to his sword and aiming with all his might, he cut off both his legs. Then Jack, setting his foot upon his neck, plunged his sword into the giant's body, when the monster gave a groan and expired.

The knight and his lady thanked Jack for their deliverance, and invited him to their house, to receive a proper reward for his services. "No," said Jack, "I cannot be easy till I find out this monster's habitation." So taking the knight's directions, he mounted his horse, and soon after came in sight of another giant, who was sitting on a block of timber waiting for his brother's return.

Jack alighted from his horse, and, putting on his invisible coat, approached and aimed a blow at the giant's head, but missing his aim he only cut off his nose. On this the giant seized his club and laid about him most unmercifully.

"Nay," said Jack, "if this be the case I'd better dispatch you!" so jumping upon the block, he stabbed him in the back, when he dropped down dead.

Jack then proceeded on his journey, and travelled over hills and dales, till arriving at the foot of a high mountain he knocked at the door of a lonely house, when an old man let him in.

When Jack was seated the hermit thus addressed him: "My son, on the top of this mountain is an enchanted castle, kept by the giant Galligantus and a vile magician. I lament the fate of a duke's daughter, whom they seized as she was walking in her father's garden, and brought hither transformed into a deer."

Jack promised that in the morning, at the risk of his life, he would break the enchantment; and after a sound sleep he rose early, put on his invisible coat, and got ready for the attempt.

When he had climbed to the top of the mountain he saw two fiery griffins; but he passed between them without the least fear of danger, for they could not see him because of his invisible coat. On the castle gate he found a golden trumpet, under which were written these lines:—

> Whoever can this trumpet blow
> Shall cause the giant's overthrow.

As soon as Jack had read this he seized the trumpet and blew a shrill blast, which made the gates fly open and the very castle itself tremble.

The giant and the conjurer now knew that their wicked course was at an end, and they stood biting their thumbs and shaking with fear. Jack, with his sword of sharpness, soon killed the giant, and the magician was then carried away by a whirlwind; and every knight and beautiful lady who had been changed into birds and beasts returned to their proper shapes. The castle vanished away like smoke, and the head of the giant Galligantus was then sent to King Arthur.

The knights and ladies rested that night at the old man's hermitage, and next day they set out for the Court. Jack then went up to the King, and gave his Majesty an account of all his fierce battles.

Jack's fame had now spread through the whole country, and at the King's desire the duke gave him his daughter in marriage, to the joy of all his kingdom. After this the King gave him a large estate, on which he and his lady lived the rest of their days in joy and contentment.

—*The Blue Fairy Book* (1889)

Jack and the Beanstalk

ENGLISH

———◆———

JACK SELLS THE COW

ONCE upon a time there was a poor widow who lived in a little cottage with her only son Jack.

Jack was a giddy, thoughtless boy, but very kind-hearted and affectionate. There had been a hard winter, and after it the poor woman had suffered from fever and ague. Jack did no work as yet, and by degrees they grew dreadfully poor. The widow saw that there was no means of keeping Jack and herself from starvation but by selling her cow; so one morning she said to her son, "I am too weak to go myself, Jack, so you must take the cow to market for me, and sell her."

Jack liked going to market to sell the cow very much; but as he was on the way, he met a butcher who had some beautiful beans in his hand. Jack stopped to look at them, and the butcher told the boy that they were of great value, and persuaded the silly lad to sell the cow for these beans.

When he brought them home to his mother instead of the money she expected for her nice cow, she was very vexed and shed many tears, scolding Jack for his folly. He was very sorry, and mother and son went to bed very sadly that night; their last hope seemed gone.

At daybreak Jack rose and went out into the garden.

"At least," he thought, "I will sow the wonderful beans. Mother says that they are just common scarlet-runners, and nothing else; but I may as well sow them."

So he took a piece of stick, and made some holes in the ground, and put in the beans.

That day they had very little dinner, and went sadly to bed, knowing that for the next day there would be none and Jack, unable to sleep from grief and vexation, got up at day-dawn and went out into the garden.

What was his amazement to find that the beans had grown up in the night, and climbed up and up till they covered the high cliff that sheltered the cottage, and disappeared above it! The stalks had twined and twisted themselves together till they formed quite a ladder.

"It would be easy to climb it," thought Jack.

And, having thought of the experiment, he at once resolved to carry it out, for Jack was a good climber. However, after his late mistake about the cow, he thought he had better consult his mother first.

WONDERFUL GROWTH OF THE BEANSTALK

So Jack called his mother, and they both gazed in silent wonder at the Beanstalk, which was not only of great height, but was thick enough to bear Jack's weight.

"I wonder where it ends," said Jack to his mother; "I think I will climb up and see."

His mother wished him not to venture up this strange ladder, but Jack coaxed her to give her consent to the attempt, for he was certain there must be something wonderful in the Beanstalk; so at last she yielded to his wishes.

Jack instantly began to climb, and went up and up on the ladder-like bean till everything he had left behind him—the cottage, the village, and even the tall church tower—looked quite little, and still he could not see the top of the Beanstalk.

Jack felt a little tired, and thought for a moment that

he would go back again; but he was a very persevering
boy, and he knew that the way to succeed in anything is
not to give up. So after resting for a moment he went
on.

After climbing higher and higher, till he grew afraid
to look down for fear he should be giddy, Jack at last
reached the top of the Beanstalk, and found himself in a
beautiful country, finely wooded, with beautiful meadows covered with sheep. A crystal stream ran through
the pastures; not far from the place where he had got
off the Beanstalk stood a fine, strong castle.

Jack wondered very much that he had never heard of
or seen this castle before; but when he reflected on the
subject, he saw that it was as much separated from the
village by the perpendicular rock on which it stood as if
it were in another land.

While Jack was standing looking at the castle, a very
strange-looking woman came out of the wood, and advanced towards him.

She wore a pointed cap of quilted red satin turned up
with ermine, her hair streamed loose over her shoulders, and she walked with a staff. Jack took off his cap
and made her a bow.

"If you please, ma'am," said he, "is this your house?"

"No," said the old lady. "Listen, and I will tell you
the story of that castle.

"Once upon a time there was a noble knight, who
lived in this castle, which is on the borders of Fairyland. He had a fair and beloved wife and several lovely
children: and as his neighbours, the little people, were
very friendly towards him, they bestowed on him many
excellent and precious gifts.

"Rumour whispered of these treasures; and a monstrous giant, who lived at no great distance, and who
was a very wicked being, resolved to obtain possession
of them.

"So he bribed a false servant to let him inside the
castle, when the knight was in bed and asleep, and he
killed him as he lay. Then he went to the part of the

castle which was the nursery, and also killed all the poor little ones he found there.

"Happily for her, the lady was not to be found. She had gone with her infant son, who was only two or three months old, to visit her old nurse, who lived in the valley; and she had been detained all night there by a storm.

"The next morning, as soon as it was light, one of the servants at the castle, who had managed to escape, came to tell the poor lady of the sad fate of her husband and her pretty babes. She could scarcely believe him at first, and was eager at once to go back and share the fate of her dear ones; but the old nurse, with many tears, besought her to remember that she had still a child, and that it was her duty to preserve her life for the sake of the poor innocent.

"The lady yielded to this reasoning, and consented to remain at her nurse's house as the best place of conceal-ment; for the servant told her that the giant had vowed, if he could find her, he would kill both her and her baby. Years rolled on. The old nurse died, leaving her cottage and the few articles of furniture it contained to her poor lady, who dwelt in it, working as a peasant for her daily bread. Her spinning-wheel and the milk of a cow, which she had purchased with the little money she had with her, sufficed for the scanty subsistence of herself and her little son. There was a nice little garden attached to the cottage, in which they cultivated peas, beans, and cabbages, and the lady was not ashamed to go out at harvest time, and glean in the fields to supply her little son's wants.

"Jack, that poor lady is your mother. This castle was once your father's, and must again be yours."

Jack uttered a cry of surprise.

"My mother! oh, madam, what ought I to do? My poor father! My dear mother!"

"Your duty requires you to win it back for your mother. But the task is a very difficult one, and full of peril, Jack. Have you courage to undertake it?"

"I fear nothing when I am doing right," said Jack.

"Then," said the lady in the red cap, "you are one of those who slay giants. You must get into the castle, and if possible possess yourself of a hen that lays golden eggs, and a harp that talks. Remember, all the giant possesses is really yours." As she ceased speaking, the lady of the red hat suddenly disappeared, and of course Jack knew she was a fairy.

Jack determined at once to attempt the adventure; so he advanced, and blew the horn which hung at the castle portal. The door was opened in a minute or two by a frightful giantess, with one great eye in the middle of her forehead.

As soon as Jack saw her he turned to run away, but she caught him, and dragged him into the castle.

"Ho, ho!" she laughed terribly. "You didn't expect to see *me* here, that is clear! No, I shan't let you go again. I am weary of my life. I am so overworked, and I don't see why I should not have a page as well as other ladies. And you shall be my boy. You shall clean the knives, and black the boots, and make the fires, and help me generally when the giant is out. When he is at home I must hide you, for he has eaten up all my pages hitherto, and you would be a dainty morsel, my little lad."

While she spoke she dragged Jack right into the castle. The poor boy was very much frightened, as I am sure you and I would have been in his place. But he remembered that fear disgraces a man; so he struggled to be brave and make the best of things.

"I am quite ready to help you, and do all I can to serve you, madam," he said, "only I beg you will be good enough to hide me from your husband, for I should not like to be eaten at all."

"That's a good boy," said the Giantess, nodding her head; "it is lucky for you that you did not scream out when you saw me, as the other boys who have been here did, for it you had done so my husband would have awakened and have eaten you, as he did them, for breakfast. Come here, child; go into my wardrobe: he never ventures to open *that*; you will be safe there."

And she opened a huge wardrobe which stood in the great hall, and shut him into it. But the keyhole was so large that it admitted plenty of air, and he could see everything that took place through it. By-and-by he heard a heavy tramp on the stairs, like the lumbering along of a great cannon, and then a voice like thunder cried out:

> "Fe, fa, fi-fo-fum,
> I smell the breath of an Englishman.
> Let him be alive or let him be dead,
> I'll grind his bones to make my bread."

"Wife," cried the Giant, "there is a man in the castle: Let me have him for breakfast."

"You are grown old and stupid," cried the lady in her loud tones. "It is only a nice fresh steak off an elephant, that I have cooked for you, which you smell. There, sit down and make a good breakfast."

And she placed a huge dish before him of savoury steaming meat, which greatly pleased him, and made him forget his idea of an Englishman being in the castle. When he had breakfasted he went out for a walk; and then the Giantess opened the door, and made Jack come out to help her. He helped her all day. She fed him well, and when evening came put him back in the wardrobe.

THE HEN THAT LAYS GOLDEN EGGS

The Giant came in to supper. Jack watched him through the keyhole, and was amazed to see him pick a wolf's bone, and put half a fowl at a time into his capacious mouth.

When the supper was ended he bade his wife bring him his hen that laid the golden eggs.

"It lays as well as it did when it belonged to that

paltry knight," he said; "indeed I think the eggs are heavier than ever."

The Giantess went away, and soon returned with a little brown hen, which she placed on the table before her husband. "And now, my dear," she said, "I am going for a walk, if you don't want me any longer."

"Go," said the Giant; "I shall be glad to have a nap by-and-by."

Then he took up the brown hen and said to her:

"Lay!" And she instantly laid a golden egg.

"Lay!" said the Giant again. And she laid another.

"Lay!" he repeated the third time. And again a golden egg lay on the table.

Now Jack was sure this hen was that of which the fairy had spoken.

By-and-by the Giant put the hen down on the floor, and soon after went fast asleep, snoring so loud that it sounded like thunder.

Directly Jack perceived that the Giant was fast asleep, he pushed open the door of the wardrobe and crept out; very softly he stole across the room, and, picking up the hen, made haste to quit the apartment. He knew the way to the kitchen, the door of which he found was left ajar; he opened it, shut and locked it after him, and flew back to the Beanstalk, which he descended as fast as his feet would move.

When his mother saw him enter the house she wept for joy, for she had feared that the fairies had carried him away, or that the Giant had found him. But Jack put the brown hen down before her, and told her how he had been in the Giant's castle, and all his adventures. She was very glad to see the hen, which would make them rich once more.

THE MONEY BAGS

Jack made another journey up the Beanstalk to the Giant's castle one day while his mother had gone to market; but first he dyed his hair and disguised himself.

The old woman did not know him again, and dragged him in as she had done before, to help her to do the work; but she heard her husband coming, and hid him in the wardrobe, not thinking that it was the same boy who had stolen the hen. She bade him stay quite still there, or the Giant would eat him.

Then the Giant came in saying:

> "Fe, fa, fi-fo-fum,
> I smell the breath of an Englishman.
> Let him be alive or let him be dead,
> I'll grind his bones to make my bread."

"Nonsense!" said the wife, "it is only a roasted bullock that I thought would be a tit-bit for your supper; sit down and I will bring it up at once." The Giant sat down, and soon his wife brought up a roasted bullock on a large dish, and they began their supper. Jack was amazed to see them pick the bones of the bullock as if it had been a lark. As soon as they had finished their meal, the Giantess rose and said:

"Now, my dear, with your leave I am going up to my room to finish the story I am reading. If you want me call for me."

"First," answered the Giant, "bring me my money bags, that I may count my golden pieces before I sleep." The Giantess obeyed. She went and soon returned with two large bags over her shoulders, which she put down by her husband.

"There," she said; "that is all that is left of the knight's money. When you have spent it you must go and take another baron's castle."

"That he shan't, if I can help it," thought Jack.

The Giant, when his wife was gone, took out heaps and heaps of golden pieces, and counted them, and put them in piles, till he was tired of the amusement. Then he swept them all back into their bags, and leaning back in his chair fell fast asleep, snoring so loud that no other sound was audible.

Jack stole softly out of the wardrobe, and taking up

the bags of money (which were his very own, because
the Giant had stolen them from his father), he ran off,
and with great difficulty descending the Beanstalk, laid
the bags of gold on his mother's table. She had just
returned from town, and was crying at not finding Jack.

"There, mother, I have brought you the gold that my
father lost."

"Oh, Jack! you are a very good boy, but I wish you
would not risk your precious life in the Giant's castle.
Tell me how you came to go there again."

And Jack told her all about it.

Jack's mother was very glad to get the money, but
she did not like him to run any risk for her.

But after a time Jack made up his mind to go again to
the Giant's castle.

THE TALKING HARP

So he climbed the Beanstalk once more, and blew
the horn at the Giant's gate. The Giantess soon opened
the door; she was very stupid, and did not know him
again, but she stopped a minute before she took him in.
She feared another robbery; but Jack's fresh face looked
so innocent that she could not resist him, and so she
bade him come in, and again hid him away in the
wardrobe.

By-and-by the Giant came home, and as soon as he
had crossed the threshold he roared out:

> "Fe, fa, fi-fo-fum,
> I smell the breath of an Englishman.
> Let him be alive or let him be dead,
> I'll grind his bones to make my bread."

"You stupid old Giant," said his wife, "you only smell
a nice sheep, which I have grilled for your dinner."

And the Giant sat down, and his wife brought up a
whole sheep for his dinner. When he had eaten it all
up, he said:

"Now bring me my harp, and I will have a little music while you take your walk."

The Giantess obeyed, and returned with a beautiful harp. The framework was all sparkling with diamonds and rubies, and the strings were all of gold.

"This is one of the nicest things I took from the knight," said the Giant. "I am very fond of music, and my harp is a faithful servant."

So he drew the harp towards him, and said:

"Play!"

And the harp played a very soft, sad air.

"Play something merrier!" said the Giant.

And the harp played a merry tune.

"Now play me a lullaby," roared the Giant; and the harp played a sweet lullaby, to the sound of which its master fell asleep.

Then Jack stole softly out of the wardrobe, and went into the huge kitchen to see if the Giantess had gone out; he found no one there, so he went to the door and opened it softly, for he thought he could not do so with the harp in his hand.

Then he entered the Giant's room and seized the harp and ran away with it; but as he jumped over the threshold the harp called out:

"MASTER! MASTER!"

And the Giant woke up.

With a tremendous roar he sprang from his seat, and in two strides had reached the door.

But Jack was very nimble. He fled like lightning with the harp, talking to it as he went (for he saw it was a fairy), and telling it he was the son of its old master, the knight.

Still the Giant came on so fast that he was quite close to poor Jack, and had stretched out his great hand to catch him. But, luckily, just at that moment he stepped upon a loose stone, stumbled, and fell flat on the ground, where he lay at his full length.

This accident gave Jack time to get on the Beanstalk

and hasten down it; but just as he reached their own garden he beheld the Giant descending after him.

"Mother! mother!" cried Jack, "make haste and give me the axe."

His mother ran to him with a hatchet in her hand, and Jack with one tremendous blow cut through all the Beanstalks except one.

"Now, mother, stand out of the way!" said he.

THE GIANT BREAKS HIS NECK

Jack's mother shrank back, and it was well she did so, for just as the Giant took hold of the last branch of the Beanstalk, Jack cut the stem quite through and darted from the spot.

Down came the Giant with a terrible crash, and as he fell on his head, he broke his neck, and lay dead at the feet of the woman he had so much injured.

Before Jack and his mother had recovered from their alarm and agitation, a beautiful lady stood before them.

"Jack," said she, "you have acted like a brave knight's son, and deserve to have your inheritance restored to you. Dig a grave and bury the Giant, and then go and kill the Giantess."

"But," said Jack, "I could not kill anyone unless I were fighting with him; and I could not draw my sword upon a woman. Moreover, the Giantess was very kind to me."

The Fairy smiled on Jack.

"I am very much pleased with your generous feeling," she said. "Nevertheless, return to the castle, and act as you will find needful."

Jack asked the Fairy if she would show him the way to the castle, as the Beanstalk was now down. She told him that she would drive him there in her chariot which was drawn by two peacocks. Jack thanked her, and sat down in the chariot with her.

The Fairy drove him a long distance round, till they reached a village which lay at the bottom of the hill.

Here they found a number of miserable-looking men assembled. The Fairy stopped her carriage and addressed them:

"My friends," said she, "the cruel giant who oppressed you and ate up all your flocks and herds is dead, and this young gentleman was the means of your being delivered from him, and is the son of your kind old master, the knight."

The men gave a loud cheer at these words, and pressed forward to say that they would serve Jack as faithfully as they had served his father. The Fairy bade them follow her to the castle, and they marched thither in a body, and Jack blew the horn and demanded admittance.

The old Giantess saw them coming from the turret loop-hole. She was very much frightened, for she guessed that something had happened to her husband; and as she came downstairs very fast she caught her foot in her dress, and fell from the top to the bottom and broke her neck.

When the people outside found that the door was not opened to them, they took crowbars and forced the portal. Nobody was to be seen, but on leaving the hall they found the body of the Giantess at the foot of the stairs.

Thus Jack took possession of the castle. The Fairy went and brought his mother to him, with the hen and the harp. He had the Giantess buried, and endeavoured as much as lay in his power to do right to those whom the Giant had robbed.

Before her departure for fairyland, the Fairy explained to Jack that she had sent the butcher to meet him with the beans, in order to try what sort of lad he was.

"If you had looked at the gigantic Beanstalk and only stupidly wondered about it," she said, "I should have left you where misfortune had placed you, only restoring her cow to your mother. But you showed an inquiring mind, and great courage and enterprise, therefore you deserve to rise; and when you mounted the Beanstalk you climbed the Ladder of Fortune."

She then took her leave of Jack and his mother.

—*The Red Fairy Book* (1890)

King Kojata

RUSSIAN

————◆·◆————

THERE was once upon a time a king called Kojata, whose
beard was so long that it reached below his knees.
Three years had passed since his marriage; and he lived
very happily with his wife, but Heaven granted him no
heir, which grieved the King greatly. One day he set
forth from his capital, in order to make a journey through
his kingdom. He travelled for nearly a year through the
different parts of his territory, and then, having seen all
there was to be seen, he set forth on his homeward
way. As the day was very hot and sultry he commanded
his servants to pitch tents in the open field, and there
await the cool of the evening. Suddenly a frightful thirst
seized the King, and as he saw no water near, he
mounted his horse, and rode through the neighbourhood
looking for a spring. Before long he came to a well filled
to the brim with water clear as crystal, and on the
bosom of which a golden jug was floating. King Kojata
at once tried to seize the vessel, but though he endeavoured to grasp it with his right hand, and then with his
left, the wretched thing always eluded his efforts and
refused to let itself be caught. First with one hand, and
then with two, did the King try to seize it, but like a fish
the goblet always slipped through his fingers and bobbed

to the ground only to reappear at some other place, and mock the King.

"Plague on you!" said King Kojata. "I can quench my thirst without you," and bending over the well he lapped up the water so greedily that he plunged his face, beard and all, right into the crystal mirror. But when he had satisfied his thirst, and wished to raise himself up, he couldn't lift his head, because someone held his beard fast in the water. "Who's there? let me go!" cried King Kojata, but there was no answer; only an awful face looked up from the bottom of the well with two great green eyes, glowing like emeralds, and a wide mouth reaching from ear to ear showing two rows of gleaming white teeth, and the King's beard was held, not by mortal hands, but by two claws. At last a hoarse voice sounded from the depths. "Your trouble is all in vain, King Kojata; I will only let you go on condition that you give me something you know nothing about, and which you will find on your return home."

The King didn't pause to ponder long, "for what," thought he, "could be in my palace without my knowing about it—the thing is absurd"; so he answered quickly:

"Yes, I promise that you shall have it."

The voice replied, "Very well; but it will go ill with you if you fail to keep your promise." Then the claws relaxed their hold, and the face disappeared in the depths. The King drew his chin out of the water, and shook himself like a dog; then he mounted his horse and rode thoughtfully home with his retinue. When they approached the capital, all the people came out to meet them with great joy and acclamation, and when the King reached his palace the Queen met him on the threshold; beside her stood the Prime Minister, holding a little cradle in his hands, in which lay a new-born child as beautiful as the day. Then the whole thing dawned on the King, and groaning deeply he muttered to himself, "So this is what I did not know about," and the tears rolled down his cheeks. All the courtiers standing round were much amazed at the King's grief, but no one dared to ask him the cause of it. He took the child in his arms and kissed it tenderly; then laying it in its cradle, he determined to control his emotion and began to reign again as before.

The secret of the King remained a secret, though his grave, careworn expression escaped no one's notice. In the constant dread that his child would be taken from him, poor Kojata knew no rest night or day. However, time went on and nothing happened. Days and months and years passed, and the Prince grew up into a beautiful youth, and at last the King himself forgot all about the incident that had happened so long ago.

One day the Prince went out hunting, and going in pursuit of a wild boar he soon lost the other huntsmen, and found himself quite alone in the middle of a dark wood. The trees grew so thick and near together that it was almost impossible to see through them, only straight in front of him lay a little patch of meadowland, overgrown with thistles and rank weeds, in the centre of which a leafy lime tree reared itself. Suddenly a rustling sound was heard in the hollow of the tree, and an extraordinary old man with green eyes and chin crept out of it.

"A fine day, Prince Milan," he said; "you've kept me waiting a good number of years; it was high time for you to come and pay me a visit."

"Who are you, in the name of wonder?" demanded the astonished Prince.

"You'll find out soon enough, but in the meantime do as I bid you. Greet your father King Kojata from me, and don't forget to remind him of his debt; the time has long passed since it was due, but now he will have to pay it. Farewell for the present; we shall meet again."

With these words the old man disappeared into the tree, and the Prince returned home rather startled, and told his father all that he had seen and heard.

The King grew as white as a sheet when he heard the Prince's story, and said, "Woe is me, my son! The time

has come when we must part," and with a heavy heart
he told the Prince what had happened at the time of his
birth.

"Don't worry or distress yourself, dear father," answered Prince Milan. "Things are never as bad as they
look. Only give me a horse for my journey, and I wager
you'll soon see me back again."

The King gave him a beautiful charger, with golden
stirrups, and a sword. The Queen hung a little cross
round his neck, and after much weeping and lamentation the Prince bade them all farewell and set forth on
his journey.

He rode straight on for two days, and on the third he
came to a lake as smooth as glass and as clear as crystal.
Not a breath of wind moved, not a leaf stirred, all was
silent as the grave, only on the still bosom of the lake
thirty ducks, with brilliant plumage, swam about in the
water. Not far from the shore Prince Milan noticed
thirty little white garments lying on the grass, and
dismounting from his horse, he crept down under the
high bulrushes, took one of the garments and hid himself with it behind the bushes which grew round the
lake. The ducks swam about all over the place, dived
down into the depths and rose again and glided through
the waves. At last, tired of disporting themselves, they
swam to the shore, and twenty-nine of them put on
their little white garments and instantly turned into so
many beautiful maidens. Then they finished dressing
and disappeared. Only the thirtieth little duck couldn't
come to the land; it swam about close to the shore, and,
giving out a piercing cry, it stretched its neck up timidly, gazed wildly around, and then dived under again.
Prince Milan's heart was so moved with pity for the
poor little creature that he came out from behind the
bulrushes, to see if he could be of any help. As soon as
the duck perceived him, it cried in a human voice,
"Oh, dear Prince Milan, for the love of Heaven give me
back my garment, and I will be so grateful to you." The
Prince lay the little garment on the bank beside her,

and stepped back into the bushes. In a few seconds a beautiful girl in a white robe stood before him, so fair and sweet and young that no pen could describe her. She gave the Prince her hand and spoke.

"Many thanks, Prince Milan, for your courtesy. I am the daughter of a wicked magician, and my name is Hyacinthia. My father has thirty young daughters, and is a mighty ruler in the underworld, with many castles and great riches. He has been expecting you for ages, but you need have no fear if you will only follow my advice. As soon as you come into the presence of my father, throw yourself at once on the ground and approach him on your knees. Don't mind if he stamps furiously with his feet and curses and swears. I'll attend to the rest, and in the meantime we had better be off."

With these words the beautiful Hyacinthia stamped on the ground with her little foot, and the earth opened and they both sank down into the lower world.

The palace of the Magician was all hewn out of a single carbuncle, lighting up the whole surrounding region, and Prince Milan walked into it gaily.

The Magician sat on a throne, a sparkling crown on his head; his eyes blazed like a green fire, and instead of hands he had claws. As soon as Prince Milan entered he flung himself on his knees. The Magician stamped loudly with his feet, glared frightfully out of his green eyes, and cursed so loudly that the whole underworld shook. But the Prince, mindful of the counsel he had been given, wasn't the least afraid, and approached the throne still on his knees. At last the Magician laughed aloud and said, "You rogue, you have been well advised to make me laugh; I won't be your enemy any more. Welcome to the underworld! All the same, for your delay in coming here, we must demand three services from you. For to-day you may go, but to-morrow I shall have something more to say to you."

Then two servants led Prince Milan to a beautiful apartment, and he lay down fearlessly on the soft bed that had been prepared for him, and was soon fast asleep.

Early the next morning the Magician sent for him, and said, "Let's see now what you've learnt. In the first place you must build me a palace to-night, the roof of purest gold, the walls of marble, and the windows of crystal; all round you must lay out a beautiful garden, with fishponds and artistic waterfalls. If you do all this, I will reward you richly; but if you don't, you shall lose your head."

"Oh, you wicked monster!" thought Prince Milan, "you might as well have put me to death at once." Sadly he returned to his room, and with bent head sat brooding over his cruel fate till evening. When it grew dark, a little bee flew by, and knocking at the window, it said, "Open, and let me in."

Milan opened the window quickly, and as soon as the bee had entered it changed into the beautiful Hyacinthia.

"Good evening, Prince Milan. Why are you so sad?"

"How can I help being sad? Your father threatens me with death, and I see myself already without a head."

"And what have you made up your mind to do?"

"There's nothing to be done, and after all I suppose one can only die once."

"Now, don't be so foolish, my dear Prince; but keep up your spirits, for there is no need to despair. Go to bed, and when you wake up to-morrow morning the palace will be finished. Then you must go all round it, giving a tap here and there on the walls to look as if you had just finished it."

And so it all turned out just as she had said. As soon as it was daylight Prince Milan stepped out of his room, and found a palace which was quite a work of art down to the very smallest detail. The Magician himself was not a little astonished at its beauty, and could hardly believe his eyes.

"Well, you certainly are a splendid workman," he said to the Prince. "I see you are very clever with your hands, now I must see if you are equally accomplished

with your head. I have thirty daughters in my house, all beautiful princesses. To-morrow I will place the whole thirty in a row. You must walk past them three times, and the third time you must show me which is my youngest daughter Hyacinthia. If you don't guess rightly, you shall lose your head."

"This time you've made a mistake," thought Prince Milan, and going to his room he sat down at the window. "Just fancy my not recognising the beautiful Hyacinthia! Why, that's the easiest thing in the world."

"Not so easy as you think," cried the little bee, who was flying past. "If I weren't to help you, you'd never guess. We are thirty sisters so exactly alike that our own father can hardly distinguish us apart."

"Then what am I to do?" asked Prince Milan.

"Listen," answered Hyacinthia. "You will recognise me by a tiny fly I shall have on my left cheek, but be careful, for you might easily make a mistake."

The next day the Magician again commanded Prince Milan to be led before him. His daughters were all arranged in a straight row in front of him, dressed exactly alike, and with their eyes bent on the ground.

"Now, you genius," said the Magician, "look at these beauties three times, and then tell us which is the Princess Hyacinthia."

Prince Milan went past them and looked at them closely. But they were all so precisely alike that they looked like one face reflected in thirty mirrors, and the fly was nowhere to be seen; the second time he passed them he still saw nothing; but the third time he perceived a little fly stealing down one cheek, causing it to blush a faint pink. Then the Prince seized the girl's hand and cried out, "This is the Princess Hyacinthia!"

"You're right again," said the Magician in amazement; "but I've still another task for you to do. Before this candle, which I shall light, burns to the socket, you must have made me a pair of boots reaching to my knees. If they aren't finished in that time, off comes your head."

The Prince returned to his room in despair; then the Princess Hyacinthia came to him once more changed into the likeness of a bee, and asked him, "Why so sad, Prince Milan?"

"How can I help being sad? Your father has set me this time an impossible task. Before a candle which he has lit burns to the socket, I am to make a pair of boots. But what does a prince know of shoemaking? If I can't do it, I lose my head."

"And what do you mean to do?" asked Hyacinthia.

"Well, what is there to be done? What he demands I can't and won't do, so he must just make an end of me."

"Not so, dearest. I love you dearly, and you shall marry me, and I'll either save your life or die with you. We must fly now as quickly as we can, for there is no other way of escape."

With these words she breathed on the window, and her breath froze on the pane. Then she led Milan out of the room with her, shut the door, and threw the key away. Hand in hand, they hurried to the spot where they had descended into the lower world, and at last reached the banks of the lake. Prince Milan's charger was still grazing on the grass which grew near the water. The horse no sooner recognised his master, then it neighed loudly with joy, and springing towards him, it stood as if rooted to the ground, while Prince Milan and Hyacinthia jumped on its back. Then it sped onwards like an arrow from a bow.

In the meantime the Magician was waiting impatiently for the Prince. Enraged by the delay, he sent his servants to fetch him, for the appointed time was past.

The servants came to the door, and finding it locked, they knocked; but the frozen breath on the window replied in Prince Milan's voice, "I am coming directly." With this answer they returned to the Magician. But when the Prince still did not appear, after a time he sent his servants a second time to bring him. The frozen breath always gave the same answer, but the Prince never came. At last the Magician lost all patience, and commanded the door to be burst open. But when his servants did so, they found the room empty, and the frozen breath laughed aloud. Out of his mind with rage, the Magician ordered the Prince to be pursued.

Then a wild chase began. "I hear horses' hoofs behind us," said Hyacinthia to the Prince. Milan sprang from the saddle, put his ear to the ground and listened. "Yes," he answered, "they are pursuing us, and are quite close." "Then no time must be lost," said Hyacinthia, and she immediately turned herself into a river, Prince Milan into an iron bridge, and the charger into a blackbird. Behind the bridge the road branched off into three ways.

The Magician's servants hurried after the fresh tracks, but when they came to the bridge, they stood, not knowing which road to take, as the footprints stopped suddenly, and there were three paths for them to choose from. In fear and trembling they returned to tell the Magician what had happened. He flew into a dreadful rage when he saw them, and screamed out, "Oh, you fools! the river and bridge were they! Go back and bring them to me at once, or it will be the worse for you."

Then the pursuit began afresh. "I hear horses' hoofs," sighed Hyacinthia. The Prince dismounted and put his ear to the ground. "They are hurrying after us, and are already quite near." In a moment the Princess Hyacinthia had changed herself, the Prince, and his charger into a thick wood where a thousand paths and roads crossed each other. Their pursuers entered the forest, but searched in vain for Prince Milan and his bride. At last they found themselves back at the same spot they had started from, and in despair they returned once more with empty hands to the Magician.

"Then I'll go after the wretches myself," he shouted. "Bring a horse at once; they shan't escape me."

Once more the beautiful Hyacinthia murmured, "I hear horses' hoofs quite near." And the prince answered, "They are pursuing us hotly and are quite close."

"We are lost now, for that is my father himself. But at the first church we come to his power ceases; he may chase us no further. Hand me your cross."

Prince Milan loosened from his neck the little gold cross his mother had given him, and as soon as Hyacinthia grasped it, she had changed herself into a church, Milan into a monk, and the horse into a belfry. They had hardly done this when the Magician and his servants rode up.

"Did you see no one pass by on horseback, reverend father?" he asked the monk.

"Prince Milan and Princess Hyacinthia have just gone on this minute; they stopped for a few minutes in the church to say their prayers, and bade me light this wax candle for you, and give you their love."

"I'd like to wring their necks," said the Magician, and made all haste home, where he had every one of his servants beaten to within an inch of their lives.

Prince Milan rode on slowly with his bride without fearing any further pursuit. The sun was just setting, and its last rays lit up a large city they were approaching. Prince Milan was suddenly seized with an ardent desire to enter the town.

"Oh my beloved," implored Hyacinthia, "please don't go; for I am frightened and fear some evil."

"What are you afraid of?" asked the Prince. "We'll only go and look at what's to be seen in the town for about an hour, and then we'll continue our journey to my father's kingdom."

"The town is easy to get into, but more difficult to get out of," sighed Hyacinthia. "But let it be as you wish. Go, and I will await you here, but I will first change myself into a white milestone; only I pray you be very careful. The King and Queen of the town will come out to meet you, leading a little child with them. Whatever you do, don't kiss the child, or you will forget me and all that has happened to us. I will wait for you here for three days."

The Prince hurried to the town, but Hyacinthia remained behind disguised as a white milestone on the road. The first day passed, and then the second, and at last the third also, but Prince Milan did not return, for he had not taken Hyacinthia's advice. The King and Queen came out to meet him as she had said, leading with them a lovely fair-haired little girl, whose eyes shone like two clear stars. The child at once caressed the Prince, who, carried away by its beauty, bent down and kissed it on the cheek. From that moment his memory became a blank, and he forgot all about the beautiful Hyacinthia.

When the Prince did not return, poor Hyacinthia wept bitterly and changing herself from a milestone into a little blue field flower, she said, "I will grow here on the wayside till some passer-by tramples me under foot." And one of her tears remained as a dewdrop and sparkled on the little blue flower.

Now it happened shortly after this that an old man passed by, and seeing the flower, he was delighted with its beauty. He pulled it up carefully by the roots and carried it home. Here he planted it in a pot, and watered and tended the little plant carefully. And now the most extraordinary thing happened, for from this moment everything in the old man's house was changed. When he awoke in the morning he always found his room tidied and put into such beautiful order that not a speck of dust was to be found anywhere. When he came home at midday, he found a table laid out with the most dainty food, and he had only to sit down and enjoy himself to his heart's content. At first he was so surprised he didn't know what to think, but after a time he grew a little uncomfortable, and went to an old witch to ask for advice.

The witch said, "Get up before the cock crows, and watch carefully till you see something move, and then throw this cloth quickly over it, and you'll see what will happen."

All night the old man never closed an eye. When the first ray of light entered the room, he noticed that the little blue flower began to tremble, and at last it rose out of the pot and flew about the room, put everything in order, swept away the dust, and lit the fire. In great haste the old man sprang from his bed, and covered the flower with the cloth the old witch had given him, and in a moment the beautiful Princess Hyacinthia stood before him.

"What have you done?" she cried. "Why have you called me back to life? For I have no desire to live since my bridegroom, the beautiful Prince Milan, has deserted me."

"Prince Milan is just going to be married," replied the old man. "Everything is being got ready for the feast, and all the invited guests are flocking to the palace from all sides."

The beautiful Hyacinthia cried bitterly when she heard this; then she dried her tears, and went into the town dressed as a peasant woman. She went straight to the King's kitchen, where the white-aproned cooks were running about in great confusion. The Princess went up to the head cook, and said, "Dear cook, please listen to my request, and let me make a wedding-cake for Prince Milan."

The busy cook was just going to refuse her demand and order her out of the kitchen, but the words died on his lips when he turned and beheld the beautiful Hyacinthia, and he answered politely, "You have just come in the nick of time, fair maiden. Bake your cake, and I myself will lay it before Prince Milan."

The cake was soon made. The invited guests were already thronging round the table, when the head cook entered the room, bearing a beautiful wedding cake on a silver dish, and laid it before Prince Milan. The guests were all lost in admiration, for the cake was quite a work of art. Prince Milan at once proceeded to cut it open, when to his surprise two white doves sprang out of it, and one of them said to the other: "My dear mate, do not fly away and leave me, and forget me as Prince Milan forgot his beloved Hyacinthia."

Milan sighed deeply when he heard what the little dove said. Then he jumped up suddenly from the table and ran to the door, where he found the beautiful Hyacinthia waiting for him. Outside stood his faithful charger, pawing the ground. Without pausing for a moment, Milan and Hyacinthia mounted him and galloped as fast as they could into the country of King Kojata. The King and Queen received them with such joy and gladness as had never been heard of before, and they all lived happily for the rest of their lives.

—*The Green Fairy Book* (1892)

King Lindorm

SWEDISH

———◆◆———

THERE once lived a king and a queen who ruled over a
very great kingdom. They had large revenues, and lived
happily with each other; but, as the years went past,
the king's heart became heavy, because the queen had
no children. She also sorrowed greatly over it, because,
although the king said nothing to her about this trouble, yet she could see that it vexed him that they had
no heir to the kingdom; and she wished every day that
she might have one.

One day a poor old woman came to the castle and
asked to speak with the queen. The royal servants
answered that they could not let such a poor beggar-
woman go in to their royal mistress. They offered her a
penny, and told her to go away. Then the woman
desired them to tell the queen that there stood at the
palace gate one who would help her secret sorrow. This
message was taken to the queen, who gave orders to
bring the old woman to her. This was done, and the old
woman said to her:

"I know your secret sorrow, O queen, and am come
to help you in it. You wish to have a son; you shall have
two if you follow my instructions."

The queen was greatly surprised that the old woman

knew her secret wish so well, and promised to follow her advice.

"You must have a bath set in your room, O queen," said she, "and filled with running water. When you have bathed in this you will find under the bath two red onions. These you must carefully peel and eat, and in time your wish will be fulfilled."

The queen did as the poor woman told her; and after she had bathed she found the two onions under the bath. They were both alike in size and appearance. When she saw these she knew that the woman had been something more than she seemed to be, and in her delight she ate up one of the onions, skin and all. When she had done so she remembered that the woman had told her to peel them carefully before she ate them. It was now too late for the one of them, but she peeled the other and then ate it too.

In due time it happened as the woman had said; but the first that the queen gave birth to was a hideous lindorm, or serpent. No one saw this but her waiting-woman, who threw it out of the window into the forest beside the castle. The next that came into the world was the most beautiful little prince, and he was shown to the king and queen, who knew nothing about his brother the lindorm.

There was now joy in all the palace and over the whole country on account of the beautiful prince; but no one knew that the queen's first-born was a lindorm, and lay in the wild forest. Time passed with the king, the queen, and the young prince in all happiness and prosperity, until he was twenty years of his age. Then his parents said to him that he should journey to another kingdom and seek for himself a bride, for they were beginning to grow old, and would fain see their son married before they were laid in their grave. The prince obeyed, had his horses harnessed to his gilded chariot, and set out to woo his bride. But when he came to the first cross-ways there lay a huge and terrible lindorm right across the road, so that his horses had to come to a standstill.

"Where are you driving to?" asked the lindorm with a hideous voice.

"That does not concern you," said the prince. "I am the prince, and can drive where I please."

"Turn back," said the lindorm. "I know your errand, but you shall get no bride until I have got a mate and slept by her side."

The prince turned home again, and told the king and the queen what he had met at the cross-roads; but they thought that he should try again on the following day, and see whether he could not get past it, so that he might seek a bride in another kingdom.

The prince did so, but got no further than the first cross-roads; there lay the lindorm again, who stopped him in the same way as before.

The same thing happened on the third day when the prince tried to get past: the lindorm said, with a threatening voice, that before the prince could get a bride he himself must find a mate.

When the king and queen heard this for the third time they could think of no better plan than to invite the lindorm to the palace, and they would find him a mate. They thought that a lindorm would be quite well satisfied with anyone that they might give him, and so they would get some slave-woman to marry the monster. The lindorm came to the palace and received a bride of this kind, but in the morning she lay torn in pieces. So it happened every time that the king and queen compelled any woman to be his bride.

The report of this soon spread over all the country. Now it happened that there was a man who had married a second time, and his wife heard of the lindorm with great delight. Her husband had a daughter by his first wife who was more beautiful than all other maidens, and so gentle and good that she won the heart of all who knew her. His second wife, however, had also a grownup daughter, who by herself would have been

ugly and disagreeable enough, but beside her good and
beautiful stepsister seemed still more ugly and wicked,
so that all turned from her with loathing.

The stepmother had long been annoyed that her
husband's daughter was so much more beautiful than
her own, and in her heart she conceived a bitter hatred
for her stepdaughter. When she now heard that there
was in the king's palace a lindorm which tore in pieces
all the women that were married to him, and demanded
a beautiful maiden for his bride, she went to the king,
and said that her stepdaughter wished to wed the
lindorm, so that the country's only prince might travel
and seek a bride. At this the king was greatly delighted,
and gave orders that the young girl should be brought
to the palace.

When the messengers came to fetch her she was
terribly frightened, for she knew that it was her wicked
stepmother who in this way was aiming at her life. She
begged that she might be allowed to spend another
night in her father's house. This was granted her, and
she went to her mother's grave. There she lamented
her hard fate in being given over to the lindorm, and
earnestly prayed her mother for counsel. How long she
lay there by the grave and wept one cannot tell, but
sure it is that she fell asleep and slept until the sun
rose. Then she rose up from the grave, quite happy at
heart, and began to search about in the fields. There
she found three nuts, which she carefully put away in
her pocket.

"When I come into very great danger I must break
one of these," she said to herself. Then she went home,
and set out quite willingly with the king's messengers.

When these arrived at the palace with the beautiful
young maiden everyone pitied her fate; but she herself
was of good courage, and asked the queen for another
bridal chamber than the one the lindorm had had before. She got this, and then she requested them to put
a pot full of strong lye on the fire and lay down three
new scrubbing brushes. The queen gave orders that

everything should be done as she desired; and then the maiden dressed herself in seven clean snow-white shirts, and held her wedding with the lindorm.

When they were left alone in the bridal chamber the lindorm, in a threatening voice, ordered her to undress herself.

"Undress yourself first!" said she.

"None of the others bade me do that," said he in surprise.

"But I bid you," said she.

Then the lindorm began to writhe, and groan, and breathe heavily; and after a little he had cast his outer skin, which lay on the floor, hideous to behold. Then his bride took off one of her snow-white shirts, and cast it on the lindorm's skin. Again he ordered her to undress, and again she commanded him to do so first. He had to obey, and with groaning and pain cast off one skin after another, and for each skin the maiden threw off one one of her shirts, until there lay on the floor seven lindorm skins and six snow-white shirts; the seventh she still had on. The lindorm now lay before her as a formless, slimy mass, which she with all her might began to scrub with the lye and new scrubbing brushes.

When she had nearly worn out the last of these there stood before her the loveliest youth in the world. He thanked her for having saved him from his enchantment, and told her that he was the king and queen's eldest son, and heir to the kingdom. Then he asked her whether she would keep the promise she had made to the lindorm, to share everything with him. To this she was well content to answer "Yes."

Each time that the lindorm had held his wedding one of the king's retainers was sent next morning to open the door of the bridal chamber and see whether the bride was alive. This next morning also he peeped in at the door, but what he saw there surprised him so much that he shut the door in a hurry, and hastened to the king and queen, who were waiting for his report. He told them of the wonderful sight he had seen. On the floor lay seven lindorm skins and six snow-white shirts, and beside these three worn-out scrubbing brushes, while in the bed a beautiful youth was lying asleep beside the fair young maiden.

The king and queen marvelled greatly what this could mean; but just then the old woman who was spoken of in the beginning of the story was again brought in to the queen. She reminded her how she had not followed her instructions, but had eaten the first onion with all its skins, on which account her first-born had been a lindorm. The waiting-woman was then summoned, and admitted that she had thrown it out through the window into the forest. The king and queen now sent for their eldest son and his young bride. They took them both in their arms, and asked him to tell about his sorrowful lot during the twenty years he had lived in the forest as a hideous lindorm. This he did, and then his parents had it proclaimed over the whole country that he was their eldest son, and along with his spouse should inherit the country and kingdom after them.

Prince Lindorm and his beautiful wife now lived in joy and prosperity for a time in the palace; and when his father was laid in the grave, not long after this, he obtained the whole kingdom. Soon afterwards his mother also departed from this world.

Now it happened that an enemy declared war against the young king; and, as he foresaw that it would be three years at the least before he could return to his country and his queen, he ordered all his servants who remained at home to guard her most carefully. That they might be able to write to each other in confidence, he had two seal rings made, one for himself and one for his young queen, and issued an order that no one, under pain of death, was to open any letter that was sealed with one of these. Then he took farewell of his queen, and marched out to war.

The queen's wicked stepmother had heard with great grief that her beautiful stepdaughter had prospered so well that she had not only preserved her life, but had

The Bride & The Lindorm

even become queen of the country. She now plotted
continually how she might destroy her good fortune.
While King Lindorm was away at the war the wicked
woman came to the queen, and spoke fair to her, saying
that she had always foreseen that her stepdaughter was
destined to be something great in the world, and that
she had on this account secured that she should be the
enchanted prince's bride. The queen, who did not imagine that any person could be so deceitful, bade her
stepmother welcome, and kept her beside her.

Soon after this the queen had two children, the prettiest boys that anyone could see. When she had written
a letter to the king to tell him of this her stepmother
asked leave to comb her hair for her, as her own mother
used to do. The queen gave her permission, and the
stepmother combed her hair until she fell asleep. Then
she took the seal ring off her neck, and exchanged the
letter for another, in which she had written that the
queen had given birth to two whelps.

When the king received this letter he was greatly
distressed, but he remembered how he himself had
lived for twenty years as a lindorm, and had been freed
from the spell by his young queen. He therefore wrote
back to his most trusted retainer that the queen and her
two whelps should be taken care of while he was away.

The stepmother, however, took this letter as well,
and wrote a new one, in which the king ordered that
the queen and the two little princes should be burnt at
the stake. This she also sealed with the queen's seal,
which was in all respects like the king's.

The retainer was greatly shocked and grieved at the
king's orders, for which he could discover no reason;
but, as he had not the heart to destroy three innocent
beings, he had a great fire kindled, and in this he
burned a sheep and two lambs, so as to make people
believe that he had carried out the king's commands.
The stepmother had made these known to the people,
adding that the queen was a wicked sorceress.

The faithful servant, however, told the queen that it

was the king's command that during the years he was
absent in the war she should keep herself concealed in
the castle, so that no one but himself should see her
and the little princes.

The queen obeyed, and no one knew but that both
she and her children had been burned. But when the
time came near for King Lindorm to return home from
the war the old retainer grew frightened because he
had not obeyed his orders. He therefore went to the
queen, and told her everything, at the same time showing her the king's letter containing the command to
burn her and the princes. He then begged her to leave
the palace before the king returned.

The queen now took her two little sons, and wandered out into the wild forest. They walked all day
without finding a human habitation, and became very
tired. The queen then caught sight of a man who carried some venison. He seemed very poor and wretched,
but the queen was glad to see a human being, and
asked him whether he knew where she and her little
children could get a house over their heads for the
night.

The man answered that he had a little hut in the
forest, and that she could rest there; but he also said
that he was one who lived entirely apart from men, and
owned no more than the hut, a horse, and a dog, and
supported himself by hunting.

The queen followed him to the hut and rested there
overnight with her children, and when she awoke in
the morning the man had already gone out hunting.
The queen then began to put the room in order and
prepare food, so that when the man came home he
found everything neat and tidy, and this seemed to give
him some pleasure. He spoke but little, however, and
all that he said about himself was that his name was
Peter.

Later in the day he rode out into the forest, and the
queen thought that he looked very unhappy. While he
was away she looked about her in the hut a little more

closely, and found a tub full of shirts stained with blood, lying among water. She was surprised at this, but thought that the man would get the blood on his shirt when he was carrying home venison. She washed the shirts, and hung them up to dry, and said nothing to Peter about the matter.

After some time had passed she noticed that every day he came riding home from the forest he took off a blood-stained shirt and put on a clean one. She then saw that it was something else than the blood of the deer that stained his shirts, so one day she took courage and asked him about it.

At first he refused to tell her, but she then related to him her own story, and how she had succeeded in delivering the lindorm. He then told her that he had formerly lived a wild life, and had finally entered into a written compact with the Evil Spirit. Before this contract had expired he had repented and turned from his evil ways, and withdrawn himself to this solitude. The Evil One had then lost all power to take him, but so long as he had the contract he could compel him to meet him in the forest each day at a certain time, where the evil spirits then scourged him till he bled.

Next day, when the time came for the man to ride into the forest, the queen asked him to stay at home and look after the princes, and she would go to meet the evil spirits in his place. The man was amazed, and said that this would not only cost her her life, but would also bring upon him a greater misfortune than the one he was already under. She bade him be of good courage, looked to see that she had the three nuts which she had found beside her mother's grave, mounted her horse, and rode out into the forest. When she had ridden for some time the evil spirits came forth and said, "Here comes Peter's horse and Peter's hound; but Peter himself is not with them."

Then at a distance she heard a terrible voice demanding to know what she wanted.

"I have come to get Peter's contract," said she.

At this there arose a terrible uproar among the evil spirits, and the worst voice among them all said, "Ride home and tell Peter that when he comes to-morrow he shall get twice as many strokes as usual."

The queen then took one of her nuts and cracked it, and turned her horse about. At this sparks of fire flew out of all the trees, and the evil spirits howled as if they were being scourged back to their abode.

Next day at the same time the queen again rode out into the forest; but on this occasion the spirits did not dare to come so near her. They would not, however, give up the contract, but threatened both her and the man. Then she cracked her second nut, and all the forest behind her seemed to be in fire and flames, and the evil spirits howled even worse than on the previous day; but the contract they would not give up.

The queen had only one nut left now, but even that she was ready to give up in order to deliver the man. This time she cracked the nut as soon as she came near the place where the spirits appeared, and what then happened to them she could not see, but amid wild screams and howls the contract was handed to her at the end of a long branch. The queen rode happy home to the hut, and happier still was the man, who had been sitting there in great anxiety, for now he was freed from all the power of the evil spirits.

Meanwhile King Lindorm had come home from the war, and the first question he asked when he entered the palace was about the queen and the whelps. The attendants were surprised: they knew of no whelps. The queen had had two beautiful princes; but the king had sent orders that all these were to be burned.

The king grew pale with sorrow and anger, and ordered them to summon his trusted retainer, to whom he had sent the instructions that the queen and the whelps were to be carefully looked after. The retainer, however, showed him the letter in which there was written that the queen and her children were to be burned, and everyone then understood that some great treachery had been enacted.

When the king's trusted retainer saw his master's deep sorrow he confessed to him that he had spared the lives of the queen and the princes, and had only burned a sheep and two lambs, and had kept the queen and her children hidden in the palace for three years, but had sent her out into the wild forest just when the king was expected home. When the king heard this his sorrow was lessened, and he said that he would wander out into the forest and search for his wife and children. If he found them he would return to his palace; but if he did not find them he would never see it again, and in that case the faithful retainer who had saved the lives of the queen and the princes should be king in his stead.

The king then went forth alone into the wild forest, and wandered there the whole day without seeing a single human being. So it went with him the second day also, but on the third day he came by roundabout ways to the little hut. He went in there, and asked for leave to rest himself for a little on the bench. The queen and the princes were there, but she was poorly clad and so sorrowful that the king did not recognise her, neither did he think for a moment that the two children, who were dressed only in rough skins, were his own sons.

He lay down on the bench, and, tired as he was, he soon fell asleep. The bench was a narrow one, and as he slept his arm fell down and hung by the side of it.

"My son, go and lift your father's arm up on the bench," said the queen to one of the princes, for she easily knew the king again, although she was afraid to make herself known to him. The boy went and took the king's arm, but, being only a child, he did not lift it up very gently on to the bench.

The king woke at this, thinking at first that he had fallen into a den of robbers, but he decided to keep quiet and pretend that he was asleep until he should find out what kind of folk were in the house. He lay still for a little, and, as no one moved in the room, he again let his arm glide down off the bench. Then he heard a woman's voice say, "My son, go you and lift your father's arm up on the bench, but don't do it so roughly as your brother did." Then he felt a pair of little hands softly clasping his arm; he opened his eyes, and saw his queen and her children.

He sprang up and caught all three in his arms, and afterwards took them, along with the man and his horse and his hound, back to the palace with great joy. The most unbounded rejoicing reigned there then, as well as over the whole kingdom, but the wicked stepmother was burned.

King Lindorm lived long and happily with his queen, and there are some who say that if they are not dead now they are still living to this day.

—*The Pink Fairy Book* (1897)

Long, Broad, and Quickeye

BOHEMIAN

———◆◆◆———

ONCE upon a time there lived a king who had an only son whom he loved dearly. Now one day the king sent for his son and said to him:

"My dearest child, my hair is grey and I am old, and soon I shall feel no more the warmth of the sun, or look upon the trees and flowers. But before I die I should like to see you with a good wife; therefore marry, my son, as speedily as possible."

"My father," replied the prince, "now and always, I ask nothing better than to do your bidding, but I know of no daughter-in-law that I could give you."

On hearing these words the old king drew from his pocket a key of gold, and gave it to his son, saying:

"Go up the staircase, right up to the top of the tower. Look carefully round you, and then come and tell me which you like best of all that you see."

So the young man went up. He had never before been in the tower, and had no idea what it might contain.

The staircase wound round and round and round, till the prince was almost giddy, and every now and then he caught sight of a large room that opened out from the side. But he had been told to go to the top, and to the top he went. Then he found himself in a hall, which had an iron door at one end. This door he unlocked with his golden key, and he passed through into a vast chamber which had a roof of blue sprinkled with golden stars, and a carpet of green silk soft as turf. Twelve windows framed in gold let in the light of the sun, and on every window was painted the figure of a young girl, each more beautiful than the last. While the prince gazed at them in surprise, not knowing which he liked best, the girls began to lift their eyes and smile at him. He waited, expecting them to speak, but no sound came.

Suddenly he noticed that one of the windows was covered by a curtain of white silk.

He lifted it, and saw before him the image of a maiden beautiful as the day and sad as the tomb, clothed in a white robe, having a girdle of silver and a crown of pearls. The prince stood and gazed at her, as if he had been turned into stone, but as he looked the sadness which was on her face seemed to pass into his heart, and he cried out:

"This one shall be my wife. This one and no other."

As he said the words the young girl blushed and hung her head, and all the other figures vanished.

The young prince went quickly back to his father, and told him all he had seen and which wife he had chosen. The old man listened to him full of sorrow, and then he spoke:

"You have done ill, my son, to search out that which was hidden, and you are running to meet a great danger. This young girl has fallen into the power of a wicked sorcerer, who lives in an iron castle. Many young men have tried to deliver her, and none have ever come back. But what is done is done! You have given your word, and it cannot be broken. Go, dare your fate, and return to me safe and sound."

So the prince embraced his father, mounted his horse, and set forth to seek his bride. He rode on gaily for several hours, till he found himself in a wood where he had never been before, and soon lost his way among its

winding paths and deep valleys. He tried in vain to see
where he was: the thick trees shut out the sun, and he
could not tell which was north and which was south, so
that he might know what direction to make for. He felt
in despair, and had quite given up all hope of getting
out of this horrible place, when he heard a voice calling
to him.

"Hey! hey! stop a minute!"

The prince turned round and saw behind him a very
tall man, running as fast as his legs would carry him.

"Wait for me," he panted, "and take me into your
service. If you do, you will never be sorry."

"Who are you?" asked the prince, "and what can you
do?"

"Long is my name, and I can lengthen my body at
will. Do you see that nest up there on the top of that
pine-tree? Well, I can get it for you without taking the
trouble of climbing the tree," and Long stretched himself up and up and up, till he was very soon as tall as
the pine itself. He put the nest in his pocket, and
before you could wink your eyelid he made himself
small again, and stood before the prince.

"Yes; you know your business," said he, "but birds'
nests are no use to me. I am too old for them. Now if
you were only able to get me out of this wood, you
would indeed be good for something."

"Oh, there's no difficulty about that," replied Long,
and he stretched himself up and up and up till he was
three times as tall as the tallest tree in the forest. Then
he looked all round and said, "We must go in this
direction in order to get out of the wood," and shorten-
ing himself again, he took the prince's horse by the
bridle, and led him along. Very soon they got clear of
the forest, and saw before them a wide plain ending in
a pile of high rocks, covered here and there with trees,
and very much like the fortifications of a town.

As they left the wood behind, Long turned to the
prince and said, "My lord, here comes my comrade.

You should take him into your service too, as you will find him a great help."

"Well, call him then, so that I can see what sort of a man he is."

"He is a little too far off for that," replied Long. "He would hardly hear my voice, and he couldn't be here for some time yet, as he has so much to carry. I think I had better go and bring him myself," and this time he stretched himself to such a height that his head was lost in the clouds. He made two or three strides, took his friend on his back, and set him down before the prince. The new-comer was a very fat man, and as round as a barrel.

"Who are you?" asked the prince, "and what can you do?"

"Your worship, Broad is my name, and I can make myself as wide as I please."

"Let me see how you manage it."

"Run, my lord, as fast as you can, and hide yourself in the wood," cried Broad, and he began to swell himself out.

The prince did not understand why he should run to the wood, but when he saw Long flying towards it, he thought he had better follow his example. He was only just in time, for Broad had so suddenly inflated himself that he very nearly knocked over the prince and his horse too. He covered all the space for acres round. You would have thought he was a mountain!

At length Broad ceased to expand, drew a deep breath that made the whole forest tremble, and shrank into his usual size.

"You have made me run away," said the prince. "But it is not every day one meets with a man of your sort. I will take you into my service."

So the three companions continued their journey, and when they were drawing near the rocks they met a man whose eyes were covered by a bandage.

"Your excellency," said Long, "this is our third comrade. You will do well to take him into your service, and, I assure you, you will find him worth his salt."

"Who are you?" asked the prince. "And why are your eyes bandaged? You can never see your way!"

"It is just the contrary, my lord! It is because I see only too well that I am forced to bandage my eyes. Even so I see as well as people who have no bandage. When I take it off my eyes pierce through everything. Everything I look at catches fire, or, if it cannot catch fire, it falls into a thousand pieces. They call me Quickeye."

And so saying he took off his bandage and turned towards the rock. As he fixed his eyes upon it a crack was heard, and in a few moments it was nothing but a heap of sand. In the sand something might be detected glittering brightly. Quickeye picked it up and brought it to the prince. It turned out to be a lump of pure gold.

"You are a wonderful creature," said the prince, "and I should be a fool not to take you into my service. But since your eyes are so good, tell me if I am very far from the Iron Castle, and what is happening there just now."

"If you were travelling alone," replied Quickeye, "it would take you at least a year to get to it; but as we are with you, we shall arrive there to-night. Just now they are preparing supper."

"There is a princess in the castle. Do you see her?"

"A wizard keeps her in a high tower, guarded by iron bars."

"Ah, help me to deliver her!" cried the prince.

And they promised they would.

Then they all set out through the grey rocks, by the breach made by the eyes of Quickeye, and passed over great mountains and through deep woods. And every time they met with any obstacle the three friends contrived somehow to put it aside. As the sun was setting, the prince beheld the towers of the Iron Castle, and before it sank beneath the horizon he was crossing the iron bridge which led to the gates. He was only just in time, for no sooner had the sun disappeared altogether, than the bridge drew itself up and the gates shut themselves.

There was no turning back now!

The prince put up his horse in the stable, where everything looked as if a guest was expected, and then the whole party marched straight up to the castle. In the court, in the stables, and all over the great halls, they saw a number of men richly dressed, but every one turned into stone. They crossed an endless set of rooms, all opening into each other, till they reached the dining-hall. It was brilliantly lighted; the table was covered with wine and fruit, and was laid for four. They waited a few minutes expecting someone to come, but as nobody did, they sat down and began to eat and drink, for they were very hungry.

When they had done their supper they looked about for some place to sleep. But suddenly the door burst open, and the wizard entered the hall. He was old and hump-backed, with a bald head and a grey beard that fell to his knees. He wore a black robe, and instead of a belt three iron circlets clasped his waist. He led by the hand a lady of wonderful beauty, dressed in white, with a girdle of silver and a crown of pearls, but her face was pale and sad as death itself.

The prince knew her in an instant, and moved eagerly forward; but the wizard gave him no time to speak, and said:

"I know why you are here. Very good; you may have her if for three nights following you can prevent her making her escape. If you fail in this, you and your servants will all be turned into stone, like those who have come before you." And offering the princess a chair, he left the hall.

The prince could not take his eyes from the princess, she was so lovely! He began to talk to her, but she neither answered nor smiled, and sat as if she were made of marble. He seated himself by her, and determined not to close his eyes that night, for fear she should escape him. And in order that she should be doubly guarded, Long stretched himself like a strap all round the room, Broad took his stand by the door and puffed himself out, so that not even a mouse could slip by, and Quickeye leant against a pillar which stood in the middle of the floor and supported the roof. But in half a second they were all sound asleep, and they slept sound the whole night long.

In the morning, at the first peep of dawn, the prince awoke with a start. But the princess was gone. He aroused his servants and implored them to tell him what he must do.

"Calm yourself, my lord," said Quickeye. "I have found her already. A hundred miles from here there is a forest. In the middle of the forest, an old oak, and on the top of the oak, an acorn. This acorn is the princess. If Long will take me on his shoulders, we shall soon bring her back." And sure enough, in less time than it takes to walk round a cottage, they had returned from the forest, and Long presented the acorn to the prince.

"Now, your excellency, throw it on the ground."

The prince obeyed, and was enchanted to see the princess appear at his side. But when the sun peeped for the first time over the mountains, the door burst open as before, and the wizard entered with a loud laugh. Suddenly he caught sight of the princess; his face darkened, he uttered a low growl, and one of the iron circlets gave way with a crash. He seized the young girl by the hand and bore her away with him.

All that day the prince wandered about the castle, studying the curious treasures it contained, but everything looked as if life had suddenly come to a standstill. In one place he saw a prince who had been turned into stone in the act of brandishing a sword round which his two hands were clasped. In another, the same doom had fallen upon a knight in the act of running away. In a third, a serving man was standing eternally trying to convey a piece of beef to his mouth, and all around them were others, still preserving for evermore the attitudes they were in when the wizard had commanded

"From henceforth be turned into marble." In the castle, and round the castle, all was dismal and desolate. Trees there were, but without leaves; fields there were, but no grass grew on them. There was one river, but it never flowed and no fish lived in it. No flowers blossomed, and no birds sang.

Three times during the day food appeared, as if by magic, for the prince and his servants. And it was not until supper was ended that the wizard appeared, as on the previous evening, and delivered the princess into the care of the prince.

All four determined that this time they would keep awake at any cost. But it was no use. Off they went as they had done before, and when the prince awoke the next morning the room was again empty.

With a pang of shame, he rushed to find Quickeye. "Awake! Awake! Quickeye! Do you know what has become of the princess?"

Quickeye rubbed his eyes and answered: "Yes, I see her. Two hundred miles from here there is a mountain. In this mountain is a rock. In the rock, a precious stone. This stone is the princess. Long shall take me there, and we will be back before you can turn round."

So Long took him on his shoulders and they set out. At every stride they covered twenty miles, and as they drew near Quickeye fixed his burning eyes on the mountain; in an instant it split into a thousand pieces, and in one of these sparkled the precious stone. They picked it up and brought it to the prince, who flung it hastily down, and as the stone touched the floor the princess stood before him. When the wizard came, his eyes shot forth flames of fury. Cric-crac was heard, and another of his iron bands broke and fell. He seized the princess by the hand and led her off, growling louder than ever.

All that day things went on exactly as they had done the day before. After supper the wizard brought back the princess, and looking him straight in the eyes he said, "We shall see which of us two will gain the prize after all!"

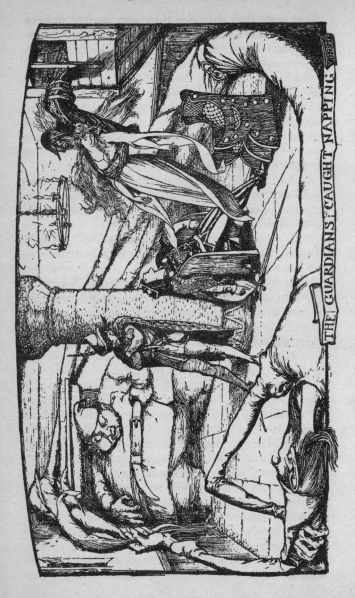

THE GUARDIANS CAUGHT NAPPING

That night they struggled their very hardest to keep awake, and even walked about instead of sitting down. But it was quite useless. One after another they had to give in, and for the third time the princess slipped through their fingers.

When morning came, it was as usual the prince who awoke the first, and as usual, the princess being gone, he rushed to Quickeye.

"Get up, get up, Quickeye, and tell me where is the princess?"

Quickeye looked about for some time without answering. "Oh, my lord, she is far, very far. Three hundred miles away there lies a black sea. In the middle of this sea there is a little shell, and in the middle of the shell is fixed a gold ring. That gold ring is the princess. But do not vex your soul; we will get her. Only to-day, Long must take Broad with him. He will be wanted badly."

So Long took Quickeye on one shoulder, and Broad on the other, and they set out. At each stride they left thirty miles behind them. When they reached the black sea, Quickeye showed them the spot where they must seek the shell. But though Long stretched down his hand as far as it would go, he could not find the shell, for it lay at the bottom of the sea.

"Wait a moment, comrades, it will be all right. I will help you," said Broad.

Then he swelled himself out so that you would have thought the world could hardly have held him, and stooping down he drank. He drank so much at every mouthful, that only a minute or so passed before the water had sunk enough for Long to put his hand to the bottom. He soon found the shell, and pulled the ring out. But time had been lost, and Long had a double burden to carry. The dawn was breaking fast before they got back to the castle, where the prince was waiting for them in an agony of fear.

Soon the first rays of the sun were seen peeping over the tops of the mountains. The door burst open, and

finding the prince standing alone the wizard broke into
peals of wicked laughter. But as he laughed a loud crash
was heard, the window fell into a thousand pieces, a
gold ring glittered in the air, and the princess stood
before the enchanter. For Quickeye, who was watching
from afar, had told Long of the terrible danger now
threatening the prince, and Long, summoning all his
strength for one gigantic effort, had thrown the ring
right through the window.

The wizard shrieked and howled with rage, till the
whole castle trembled to its foundations. Then a crash
was heard, the third band split in two, and a crow flew
out of the window.

Then the princess at length broke the enchanted
silence, and blushing like a rose, gave the prince her
thanks for her unlooked-for deliverance.

But it was not only the princess who was restored to
life by the flight of the wicked black crow. The marble
figures became men once more, and took up their
occupations just as they had left them off. The horses
neighed in the stables, the flowers blossomed in the
garden, the birds flew in the air, the fish darted in the
water. Everywhere you looked, all was life, all was joy!

And the knights who had been turned into stone
came in a body to offer their homage to the prince who
had set them free.

"Do not thank me," he said, "for I have done nothing. Without my faithful servants, Long, Broad, and
Quickeye, I should even have been as one of you."

With these words he bade them farewell, and departed with the princess and his faithful companions for
the kingdom of his father.

The old king, who had long since given up all hope,
wept for joy at the sight of his son, and insisted that the
wedding should take place as soon as possible.

All the knights who had been enchanted in the Iron
Castle were invited to the ceremony, and after it had
taken place, Long, Broad, and Quickeye took leave of

the young couple, saying that they were going to look for more work.

The prince offered them all their hearts could desire if they would only remain with him, but they replied that an idle life would not please them, and that they could never be happy unless they were busy, so they went away to seek their fortunes, and for all I know are seeking still.

—*The Grey Fairy Book* (1900)

The Mermaid and the Boy

LAPLAND

———◆◆◆———

Long, long ago, there lived a king who ruled over a country by the sea. When he had been married about a year, some of his subjects, inhabiting a distant group of islands, revolted against his laws, and it became needful for him to leave his wife and go in person to settle their disputes. The queen feared that some ill would come of it, and implored him to stay at home, but he told her that nobody could do his work for him, and the next morning the sails were spread, and the king started on his voyage.

The vessel had not gone very far when she ran upon a rock, and stuck so fast in a cleft that the strength of the whole crew could not get her off again. To make matters worse, the wind was rising too, and it was quite plain that in a few hours the ship would be dashed to pieces and everybody would be drowned, when suddenly the form of a mermaid was seen dancing on the waves which threatened every moment to overwhelm them.

"There is only one way to free yourselves," she said to the king, bobbing up and down in the water as she spoke, "and that is to give me your solemn word that you will deliver to me the first child that is born to you."

238

The king hesitated at this proposal. He hoped that some day he might have children in his home, and the thought that he must yield up the heir to his crown was very bitter to him; but just then a huge wave broke with great force on the ship's side, and his men fell on their knees and entreated him to save them.

So he promised, and this time a wave lifted the vessel clean off the rocks, and she was in the open sea once more.

The affairs of the islands took longer to settle than the king had expected, and some months passed away before he returned to his palace. In his absence a son had been born to him, and so great was his joy that he quite forgot the mermaid and the price he had paid for the safety of his ship. But as the years went on, and the baby grew into a fine big boy, the remembrance of it came back, and one day he told the queen the whole story. From that moment the happiness of both their lives was ruined. Every night they went to bed wondering if they should find his room empty in the morning, and every day they kept him by their sides, expecting him to be snatched away before their very eyes.

At last the king felt that this state of things could not continue, and he said to his wife:

"After all, the most foolish thing in the world one can do is to keep the boy here in exactly the place in which the mermaid will seek him. Let us give him food and send him on his travels, and perhaps, if the mermaid ever *does* come to seek him, she may be content with some other child." And the queen agreed that his plan seemed the wisest.

So the boy was called, and his father told him the story of the voyage, as he had told his mother before him. The prince listened eagerly, and was delighted to think that he was to go away all by himself to see the world, and was not in the least frightened; for though he was now sixteen, he had scarcely been allowed to walk alone beyond the palace gardens. He began busily to make his preparations, and took off his smart velvet

THE MERMAID ASKS FOR THE KING'S CHILD

coat, putting on instead one of green cloth, while he refused a beautiful bag which the queen offered him to hold his food, and slung a leather knapsack over his shoulders instead, just as he had seen other travellers do. Then he bade farewell to his parents and went his way.

All through the day he walked, watching with interest the strange birds and animals that darted across his path in the forest or peeped at him from behind a bush. But as evening drew on he became tired, and looked about as he walked for some place where he could sleep. At length he reached a soft mossy bank under a tree, and was just about to stretch himself out on it, when a fearful roar made him start and tremble all over. In another moment something passed swiftly through the air and a lion stood before him.

"What are you doing here?" asked the lion, his eyes glaring fiercely at the boy.

"I am flying from the mermaid," the prince answered, in a quaking voice.

"Give me some food then," said the lion, "it is past my supper time, and I am very hungry."

The boy was so thankful that the lion did not want to eat *him*, that he gladly picked up his knapsack which lay on the ground, and held out some bread and a flask of wine.

"I feel better now," said the lion when he had done, "so now I shall go to sleep on this nice soft moss, and if you like you can lie down beside me." So the boy and the lion slept soundly side by side, till the sun rose.

"I must be off now," remarked the lion, shaking the boy as he spoke; "but cut off the tip of my ear, and keep it carefully, and if you are in any danger just wish yourself a lion and you will become one on the spot. One good turn deserves another, you know."

The prince thanked him for his kindness, and did as he was bid, and the two then bade each other farewell.

"I wonder how it feels to be a lion," thought the boy, after he had gone a little way; and he took out the tip of the ear from the breast of his jacket and wished with all his might. In an instant his head had swollen to several times its usual size, and his neck seemed very hot and heavy; and, somehow, his hands became paws, and his skin grew hairy and yellow. But what pleased him most was his long tail with a tuft at the end, which he lashed and switched proudly. "I like being a lion very much," he said to himself, and trotted gaily along the road.

After a while, however, he got tired of walking in this unaccustomed way—it made his back ache and his front paws felt sore. So he wished himself a boy again, and in the twinkling of an eye his tail disappeared and his head shrank, and the long thick mane became short and curly. Then he looked out for a sleeping place, and found some dry ferns, which he gathered and heaped up.

But before he had time to close his eyes there was a great noise in the trees near by, as if a big heavy body was crashing through them. The boy rose and turned his head, and saw a huge black bear coming towards him.

"What are you doing here?" cried the bear.

"I am running away from the mermaid," answered the boy; but the bear took no interest in the mermaid, and only said: "I am hungry; give me something to eat."

The knapsack was lying on the ground among the fern, but the prince picked it up, and, unfastening the strap, took out his second flask of wine and another loaf of bread. "We will have supper together," he remarked politely; but the bear, who had never been taught manners, made no reply, and ate as fast as he could. When he had quite finished, he got up and stretched himself.

"You have got a comfortable-looking bed there," he observed. "I really think that, bad sleeper as I am, I might have a good night on it. I can manage to squeeze you in," he added; "you don't take up a great deal of room." The boy was rather indignant at the bear's cool way of talking; but as he was too tired to gather more fern, they lay down side by side, and never stirred till sunrise next morning.

"I must go now," said the bear, pulling the sleepy prince on to his feet; "but first you shall cut off the tip of my ear, and when you are in any danger just wish yourself a bear and you will become one. One good turn deserves another, you know." And the boy did as he was bid, and he and the bear bade each other farewell.

"I wonder how it feels to be a bear," thought he to himself when he had walked a little way; and he took out the tip from the breast of his coat and wished hard that he might become a bear. The next moment his body stretched out and thick black fur covered him all over. As before, his hands were changed into paws, but when he tried to switch his tail he found to his disgust that it would not go any distance. "Why it is hardly worth calling a tail!" said he. For the rest of the day he remained a bear and continued his journey, but as evening came on the bear-skin, which had been so useful when plunging through brambles in the forest, felt rather heavy, and he wished himself a boy again. He was too much exhausted to take the trouble of cutting any fern or seeking for moss, but just threw himself down under a tree, when exactly above his head he heard a great buzzing as a bumble-bee alighted on a honeysuckle branch. "What are you doing here?" asked the bee in a cross voice; "at your age you ought to be safe at home."

"I am running away from the mermaid," replied the boy; but the bee, like the lion and the bear, was one of those people who never listen to the answers to their questions, and only said: "I am hungry. Give me something to eat."

The boy took his last loaf and flask out of his knapsack and laid them on the ground, and they had supper together. "Well, now I am going to sleep," observed the bee when the last crumb was gone, "but as you are not very big I can make room for you beside me," and he curled up his wings, and tucked in his legs, and he and the prince both slept soundly till morning. Then the bee got up and carefully brushed every scrap of dust off his velvet coat and buzzed loudly in the boy's ear to waken him.

"Take a single hair from one of my wings," said he, "and if you are in danger just wish yourself a bee and you will become one. One good turn deserves another, so farewell, and thank you for your supper." And the bee departed after the boy had pulled out the hair and wrapped it carefully in a leaf.

"It must feel quite different to be a bee from what it does to be a lion or bear," thought the boy to himself when he had walked for an hour or two. "I dare say I should get on a great deal faster," so he pulled out his hair and wished himself a bee.

In a moment the strangest thing happened to him. All his limbs seemed to draw together, and his body to become very short and round; his head grew quite tiny, and instead of his white skin he was covered with the richest, softest velvet. Better than all, he had two lovely gauze wings which carried him the whole day without getting tired.

Late in the afternoon the boy fancied he saw a vast heap of stones a long way off, and he flew straight towards it. But when he reached the gates he saw that it was really a great town, so he wished himself back in his own shape and entered the city.

He found the palace doors wide open and went boldly into a sort of hall which was full of people, and where men and maids were gossiping together. He joined their talk and soon learned from them that the king had only one daughter who had such a hatred to men that she would never suffer one to enter her presence. Her father was in despair, and had had pictures painted of the handsomest princes of all the courts in the world, in the hope that she might fall in love with one of them; but it was no use; the princess would not even allow the pictures to be brought into her room.

"It is late," remarked one of the women at last; "I must go to my mistress." And, turning to one of the lackeys, she bade him find a bed for the youth.

"It is not necessary," answered the prince, "this bench is good enough for me. I am used to nothing better." And when the hall was empty he lay down for a few minutes. But as soon as everything was quiet in the palace he took out the hair and wished himself a bee, and in this shape he flew upstairs, past the guards, and through the keyhole into the princess's chamber. Then he turned himself into a man again.

At this dreadful sight the princess, who was broad awake, began to scream loudly. "A man! a man!" cried she; but when the guards rushed in there was only a bumble-bee buzzing about the room. They looked under the bed, and behind the curtains, and into the cupboards, then came to the conclusion that the princess had had a bad dream, and bowed themselves out. The door had scarcely closed on them than the bee disappeared, and a handsome youth stood in his place.

"I *knew* a man was hidden somewhere," cried the princess, and screamed more loudly than before. Her shrieks brought back the guards, but though they looked in all kinds of impossible places no man was to be seen, and so they told the princess.

"He was here a moment ago—I saw him with my own eyes," and the guards dared not contradict her, though they shook their heads and whispered to each other that the princess had gone mad on this subject, and saw a man in every table and chair. And they made up their minds that—let her scream as loudly as she might—they would take no notice.

Now the princess saw clearly what they were thinking, and that in future her guards would give her no help, and would perhaps, besides, tell some stories about her to the king, who would shut her up in a lonely tower and prevent her walking in the gardens among her birds and flowers. So when, for the third time, she beheld the prince standing before her, she did not scream but sat up in bed gazing at him in silent terror.

"Do not be afraid," he said, "I shall not hurt you"; and he began to praise her gardens, of which he had heard the servants speak, and the birds and flowers which she loved, till the princess's anger softened, and she answered him with gentle words. Indeed, they soon became so friendly that she vowed she would marry no one else, and confided to him that in three days her father would be off to the wars, leaving his sword in her room. If any man could find it and bring it to him he would receive her hand as a reward. At this point a cock crew, and the youth jumped up hastily saying: "Of course I shall ride with the king to the war, and if I do not return, take your violin every evening to the seashore and play on it, so that the very sea-kobolds who live at the bottom of the ocean may hear it and come to you."

Just as the princess had foretold, in three days the king set out for the war with a large following, and among them was the young prince, who had presented himself at court as a young noble in search of adventures. They had left the city many miles behind them, when the king suddenly discovered that he had forgotten his sword, and though all his attendants instantly offered theirs, he declared that he could fight with none but his own.

"The first man who brings it to me from my daughter's room," cried he, "shall not only have her to wife, but after my death shall reign in my stead."

At this the Red Knight, the young prince, and several more turned their horses to ride as fast as the wind back to the palace. But suddenly a better plan entered the prince's head, and, letting the others pass him, he took his precious parcel from his breast and wished himself a lion. Then on he bounded, uttering such dreadful roars that the horses were frightened and grew unmanageable, and he easily outstripped them, and soon reached the gates of the palace. Here he hastily

changed himself into a bee, and flew stright into the
princess's room, where he became a man again. She
showed him where the sword hung concealed behind a
curtain, and he took it down, saying as he did so: "Be
sure not to forget what you have promised to do."

The princess made no reply, but smiled sweetly, and
slipping a golden ring from her finger she broke it in
two and held half out silently to the prince, while the
other half she put in her own pocket. He kissed it, and
ran down the stairs bearing the sword with him. Some
way off he met the Red Knight and the rest, and the
Red Knight at first tried to take the sword from him by
force. But as the youth proved too strong for him, he
gave it up, and resolved to wait for a better opportunity.

This soon came, for the day was hot and the prince
was thirsty. Perceiving a little stream that ran into the
sea, he turned aside, and, unbuckling the sword, flung
himself on the ground for a long drink. Unluckily, the
mermaid happened at that moment to be floating on
the water not very far off, and knew he was the boy
who had been given her before he was born. So she
floated gently in to where he was lying, she seized him
by the arm, and the waves closed over them both.
Hardly had they disappeared, when the Red Knight
stole cautiously up, and could hardly believe his eyes
when he saw the king's sword on the bank. He wondered what had become of the youth, who an hour
before had guarded his treasure so fiercely; but, after
all, that was no affair of his! So, fastening the sword to
his belt, he carried it to the king.

The war was soon over, and the king returned to his
people, who welcomed him with shouts of joy. But
when the princess from her window saw that her
betrothed was not among the attendants riding behind
her father, her heart sank, for she knew that some evil
must have befallen him, and she feared the Red Knight.
She had long ago learned how clever and how wicked
he was, and something whispered to her that it was *he*
who would gain the credit of having carried back the

sword, and would claim her as his bride, though he had never even entered her chamber. And she could do nothing; for although the king loved her, he never let her stand in the way of his plans.

The poor princess was only too right, and everything came to pass exactly as she had foreseen it. The king told her that the Red Knight had won her fairly, and that the wedding would take place next day, and there would be a great feast after it.

In those days feasts were much longer and more splendid than they are now; and it was growing dark when the princess, tired out with all she had gone through, stole up to her own room for a little quiet. But the moon was shining so brightly over the sea that it seemed to draw her towards it, and taking her violin under her arm, she crept down to the shore.

"Listen! listen!" said the mermaid to the prince, who was lying stretched on a bed of seaweeds at the bottom of the sea. "Listen! that is your old love playing, for mermaids know everything that happens upon earth."

"I hear nothing," answered the youth, who did not look happy. "Take me up higher, where the sounds can reach me."

So the mermaid took him on her shoulders and bore him up midway to the surface. "Can you hear now?" she asked.

"No," answered the prince, "I hear nothing but the water rushing; I must go higher still."

Then the mermaid carried him to the very top. "You must surely be able to hear *now?*" said she.

"Nothing but the water," repeated the youth. So she took him right to the land.

"At any rate you can hear *now?*" she said again.

"The water is still rushing in my ears," answered he; "but wait a little, that will soon pass off." And as he spoke he put his hand into his breast, and seizing the hair wished himself a bee, and flew straight into the pocket of the princess. The mermaid looked in vain for him, and floated all night upon the sea; but he never came back, and never more did he gladden her eyes. But the princess felt that something strange was about her, though she knew not what, and returned quickly to the palace, where the young man at once resumed his own shape. Oh, what joy filled her heart at the sight of him! But there was no time to be lost, and she led him right into the hall, where the king and his nobles were still sitting at the feast. "Here is a man who boasts that he can do wonderful tricks," said she, "better even than the Red Knight's! That cannot be true, of course; but it might be well to give this impostor a lesson. He pretends, for instance, that he can turn himself into a lion; but that I do not believe. I know that you have studied the art of magic," she went on, turning to the Red Knight, "so suppose you just show him how it is done, and bring shame upon him."

Now the Red Knight had never opened a book of magic in his life; but he was accustomed to think that he could do everything better than other people without any teaching at all. So he turned and twisted himself about, and bellowed and made faces; but he did not become a lion for all that.

"Well, perhaps it *is* very difficult to change into a lion. Make yourself a bear," said the princess. But the Red Knight found it no easier to become a bear than a lion.

"Try a bee," suggested she. "I have always read that anyone who can do magic at all can do that." And the old knight buzzed and hummed, but he remained a man and not a bee.

"Now it is your turn," said the princess to the youth. "Let us see if you can change yourself into a lion." And in a moment such a fierce creature stood before them, that all the guests rushed out of the hall, treading each other underfoot in their fright. The lion sprang at the Red Knight, and would have torn him in pieces had not the princess held him back, and bidden him to change himself into a man again. And in a second a man took the place of the lion.

"Now become a bear," said she; and a bear advanced panting and stretching out his arms to the Red Knight, who shrank behind the princess.

By this time some of the guests had regained their courage, and returned as far as the door, thinking that if it was safe for the princess perhaps it was safe for them. The king, who was braver than they, and felt it needful to set them a good example besides, had never left his seat, and when at a new command of the princess the bear once more turned into a man, he was silent from astonishment, and a suspicion of the truth began to dawn on him. "Was it *he* who fetched the sword?" asked the king.

"Yes, it was," answered the princess; and she told him the whole story, and how she had broken her gold ring and given him half of it. And the prince took out his half of the ring, and the princess took out hers, and they fitted exactly. Next day the Red Knight was hanged, as he richly deserved, and there was a new marriage feast for the prince and princess.

—*The Brown Fairy Book* (1904)

The Nine Pea-Hens and the Golden Apples

SERBIAN

———◆◆———

ONCE upon a time there stood before the palace of an emperor a golden apple tree, which blossomed and bore fruit each night. But every morning the fruit was gone, and the boughs were bare of blossom, without anyone being able to discover who was the thief.

At last the emperor said to his eldest son, "If only I could prevent those robbers from stealing my fruit, how happy I should be!"

And his son replied, "I will sit up to-night and watch the tree, and I shall soon see who it is!"

So directly it grew dark the young man went and hid himself near the apple tree to begin his watch, but the apples had scarcely begun to ripen before he fell asleep, and when he awoke at sunrise the apples were gone. He felt very much ashamed of himself, and went with lagging feet to tell his father!

Of course, though the eldest son had failed, the second made sure that he would do better, and set out gaily at nightfall to watch the apple tree. But no sooner had he lain himself down than his eyes grew heavy, and when the sunbeams roused him from his slumbers there was not an apple left on the tree.

Next came the turn of the youngest son, who made himself a comfortable bed under the apple tree, and prepared himself to sleep. Towards midnight he awoke, and sat up to look at the tree. And behold! the apples were beginning to ripen, and lit up the whole palace with their brightness. At the same moment nine golden pea-hens flew swiftly through the air, and while eight alighted upon the boughs laden with fruit, the ninth fluttered to the ground where the prince lay, and instantly was changed into a beautiful maiden, more beautiful far than any lady in the emperor's court. The prince at once fell in love with her, and they talked together for some time, till the maiden said her sisters had finished plucking the apples, and now they must all go home again. The prince, however, begged her so hard to leave him a little of the fruit that the maiden gave him two apples, one for himself and one for his father. Then she changed herself back into a peahen, and the whole nine flew away.

As soon as the sun rose the prince entered the palace, and held out the apple to his father, who was rejoiced to see it, and praised his youngest son heartily for his cleverness. That evening the prince returned to the apple tree, and everything passed as before, and so it happened for several nights. At length the other brothers grew angry at seeing that he never came back without bringing two golden apples with him, and they went to consult an old witch, who promised to spy after him, and discover how he managed to get the apples. So, when the evening came, the old woman hid herself under the tree and waited for the prince. Before long he arrived and laid down on his bed, and was soon fast asleep. Towards midnight there was a rush of wings, and the eight pea-hens settled on the tree, while the ninth became a maiden, and ran to greet the prince. Then the witch stretched out her hand, and cut off a lock of the maiden's hair, and in an instant the girl sprang up, a pea-hen once more, spread her wings and flew away, while her sisters, who were busily stripping the boughs, flew after her.

When he had recovered from his surprise at the

UNDER THE GOLDEN APPLE TREE

unexpected disappearance of the maiden, the prince exclaimed, "What can be the matter?" and, looking about him, discovered the old witch hidden under the bed. He dragged her out, and in his fury called his guards, and ordered them to put her to death as fast as possible. But that did no good as far as the pea-hens went. They never came back any more, though the prince returned to the tree every night, and wept his heart out for his lost love. This went on for some time, till the prince could bear it no longer, and made up his mind he would search the world through for her. In vain his father tried to persuade him that his task was hopeless, and that other girls were to be found as beautiful as this one. The prince would listen to nothing, and, accompanied by only one servant, set out on his quest.

After travelling for many days, he arrived at length before a large gate, and through the bars he could see the streets of a town, and even the palace. The prince tried to pass in, but the way was barred by the keeper of the gate, who wanted to know who he was, why he was there, and how he had learnt the way, and he was not allowed to enter unless the empress herself came and gave him leave. A message was sent to her, and when she stood at the gate the prince thought he had lost his wits, for there was the maiden he had left his home to seek. And she hastened to him, and took his hand, and drew him into the palace. In a few days they were married, and the prince forgot his father and his brothers, and made up his mind that he would live and die in the castle.

One morning the empress told him that she was going to take a walk by herself, and that she would leave the keys of twelve cellars to his care. "If you wish to enter the first eleven cellars," said she, "you can; but beware of even unlocking the door of the twelfth, or it will be the worse for you."

The prince, who was left alone in the castle, soon got

tired of being by himself, and began to look about for something to amuse him.

"What *can* there be in that twelfth cellar," he thought to himself, "which I must not see?" And he went downstairs and unlocked the doors, one after the other. When he got to the twelfth he paused, but his curiosity was too much for him, and in another instant the key was turned and the cellar lay open before him. It was empty, save for a large cask, bound with iron hoops, and out of the cask a voice was saying entreatingly, "For goodness' sake, brother, fetch me some water; I am dying of thirst!"

The prince, who was very tender-hearted, brought some water at once, and pushed it through a hole in the barrel; and as he did so one of the iron hoops burst.

He was turning away, when a voice cried the second time, "Brother, for pity's sake fetch me some water; I'm dying of thirst!"

So the prince went back, and brought some more water, and again a hoop sprang.

And for the third time the voice still called for water; and when water was given it the last hoop was rent, the cask fell in pieces, and out flew a dragon, who snatched up the empress just as she was returning from her walk, and carried her off. Some servants who saw what had happened came rushing to the prince, and the poor young man went nearly mad when he heard the result of his own folly, and could only cry out that he would follow the dragon to the ends of the earth, until he got his wife again.

For months and months he wandered about, first in this direction and then in that, without finding any traces of the dragon or his captive. At last he came to a stream, and as he stopped for a moment to look at it he noticed a little fish lying on the bank, beating its tail convulsively, in a vain effort to get back into the water.

"Oh, for pity's sake, my brother," shrieked the little creature, "help me, and put me back into the river, and I will repay you some day. Take one of my scales, and when you are in danger twist it in your fingers, and I will come!"

The prince picked up the fish and threw it into the water; then he took off one of its scales, as he had been told, and put it in his pocket, carefully wrapped in a cloth. Then he went on his way till, some miles further down the road, he found a fox caught in a trap.

"Oh! be a brother to me!" called the fox, "and free me from this trap, and I will help you when you are in need. Pull out one of my hairs, and when you are in danger twist it in your fingers, and I will come."

So the prince unfastened the trap, pulled out one of the fox's hairs, and continued his journey. And as he was going over the mountain he passed a wolf entangled in a snare, who begged to be set at liberty.

"Only deliver me from death," he said, "and you will never be sorry for it. Take a lock of my fur, and when you need me twist it in your fingers." And the prince undid the snare and let the wolf go.

For a long time he walked on, without having any more adventures, till at length he met a man travelling on the same road.

"Oh, brother!" asked the prince, "tell me, if you can, where the dragon-emperor lives?"

The man told him where he would find the palace, and how long it would take him to get there, and the prince thanked him, and followed his directions, till that same evening he reached the town where the dragon-emperor lived. When he entered the palace, to his great joy he found his wife sitting alone in a vast hall, and they began hastily to invent plans for her escape. There was no time to waste, as the dragon might return directly, so they took two horses out of the stable, and rode away at lightning speed. Hardly were they out of sight of the palace than the dragon came home and found that his prisoner had flown. He sent at once for his talking horse, and said to him:

"Give me your advice; what shall I do—have my supper as usual, or set out in pursuit of them?"

"Eat your supper with a free mind first," answered the horse, "and follow them afterwards."

So the dragon ate till it was past mid-day, and when he could eat no more he mounted his horse and set out after the fugitives. In a short time he had come up with them, and as he snatched the empress out of her saddle he said to the prince:

"This time I will forgive you, because you brought me the water when I was in the cask; but beware how you return here, or you will pay for it with your life."

Half mad with grief, the prince rode sadly on a little further, hardly knowing what he was doing. Then he could bear it no longer and turned back to the palace, in spite of the dragon's threats. Again the empress was sitting alone, and once more they began to think of a scheme by which they could escape the dragon's power.

"Ask the dragon when he comes home," said the prince, "where he got that wonderful horse from, and then you can tell me, and I will try to find another like it."

Then, fearing to meet his enemy, he stole out of the castle.

Soon after the dragon came home, and the empress sat down near him, and began to coax and flatter him into a good humour, and at last she said:

"But tell me about that wonderful horse you were riding yesterday. There cannot be another like it in the whole world. Where *did* you get it from?"

And he answered:

"The way I got it is a way which no one else can take. On the top of a high mountain dwells an old woman, who has in her stables twelve horses, each one more beautiful than the other. And in one corner is a thin, wretched-looking animal whom no one would glance at a second time, but he is in reality the best of the lot. He is twin brother to my own horse, and can fly as high as the clouds themselves. But no one can ever get this horse without first serving the old woman for three whole days. And besides the horses she has a foal and its mother, and the man who serves her must look after them for three whole days, and if he does not let them run away he will in the end get the choice of any horse as a present from the old woman. But if he fails to keep the foal and its mother safe on any one of the three nights his head will pay."

The next day the prince watched till the dragon left the house, and then he crept in to the empress, who told him all she had learnt from her gaoler. The prince at once determined to seek the old woman on the top of the mountain, and lost no time in setting out. It was a long and steep climb, but at last he found her, and with a low bow he began:

"Good greeting to you, little mother!"

"Good greeting to you, my son! What are you doing here?"

"I wish to become your servant," answered he.

"So you shall," said the old woman. "If you can take care of my mare for three days I will give you a horse for wages, but if you let her stray you will lose your head"; and as she spoke she led him into a courtyard surrounded with palings, and on every post a man's head was stuck. One post only was empty, and as they passed it cried out:

"Woman, give me the head I am waiting for!"

The old woman made no answer, but turned to the prince and said:

"Look! all those men took service with me, on the same conditions as you, but not one was able to guard the mare!"

But the prince did not waver, and declared he would abide by his words.

When evening came he led the mare out of the stable and mounted her, and the colt ran behind. He managed to keep his seat for a long time, in spite of all her efforts to throw him, but at length he grew so weary that he fell fast asleep, and when he woke he found himself sitting on a log, with the halter in his hands. He jumped up in terror, but the mare was nowhere to be seen, and he started with a beating heart in search of her. He had gone some way without a single trace to guide him, when he came to a little river. The sight of the water brought back to his mind the fish whom he had saved from death, and he hastily drew the scale from his pocket. It had hardly touched his fingers when the fish appeared in the stream beside him.

"What is it, my brother?" asked the fish anxiously.

"The old woman's mare strayed last night, and I don't know where to look for her."

"Oh, I can tell you that: she has changed herself into a big fish, and her foal into a little one. But strike the water with the halter and say, 'Come here, O mare of the mountain witch!' and she will come."

The prince did as he was bid, and the mare and her foal stood before him. Then he put the halter round her neck, and rode her home, the foal always trotting behind them. The old woman was at the door to receive them, and gave the prince some food while she led the mare back to the stable.

"You should have gone among the fishes," cried the old woman, striking the animal with a stick.

"I did go among the fishes," replied the mare; "but they are no friends of mine, for they betrayed me at once."

"Well, go among the foxes this time," said she, and returned to the house, not knowing that the prince had overheard her.

So when it began to grow dark the prince mounted the mare for the second time and rode into the meadows, and the foal trotted behind its mother. Again he managed to stick on till midnight: then a sleep overtook him that he could not battle against, and when he woke up he found himself, as before, sitting on the log, with the halter in his hands. He gave a shriek of dismay, and sprang up in search of the wanderers. As he went he suddenly remembered the words that the old woman had said to the mare, and he drew out the fox hair and twisted it in his fingers.

"What is it, my brother?" asked the fox, who instantly appeared before him.

"The old witch's mare has run away from me, and I do not know where to look for her."

"She is with us," replied the fox, "and has changed herself into a big fox, and her foal into a little one, but strike the ground with a halter and say, 'Come here, O mare of the mountain witch!' "

The prince did so, and in a moment the fox became a mare and stood before him, with the little foal at her heels. He mounted and rode back, and the old woman placed food on the table, and led the mare back to the stable.

"You should have gone to the foxes, as I told you," said she, striking the mare with a stick.

"I did go to the foxes," replied the mare, "but they are no friends of mine and betrayed me."

"Well, this time you had better go to the wolves," said she, not knowing that the prince had heard all she had been saying.

The third night the prince mounted the mare and rode her out to the meadows, with the foal trotting after. He tried hard to keep awake, but it was of no use, and in the morning there he was again on the log, grasping the halter. He started to his feet, and then stopped, for he remembered what the old woman had said, and pulled out the wolf's grey lock.

"What is it, my brother?" asked the wolf as it stood before him.

"The old witch's mare has run away from me," replied the prince, "and I don't know where to find her."

"Oh, she is with us," answered the wolf, "and she has changed herself into a she-wolf, and the foal into a cub; but strike the earth here with the halter, and cry, 'Come to me, O mare of the mountain witch.' "

The prince did as he was bid, and as the hair touched his fingers the wolf changed back into a mare, with the foal beside her. And when he had mounted and ridden her home the old woman was on the steps to receive them, and she set some food before the prince, but led the mare back to her stable.

"You should have gone among the wolves," said she, striking her with a stick.

"So I did," replied the mare, "but they are no friends of mine and betrayed me."

The old woman made no answer, and left the stable, but the prince was at the door waiting for her.

"I have served you well," said he, "and now for my reward."

"What I promised that will I perform," answered she. "Choose one of these twelve horses; you can have which you like."

"Give me, instead, that half-starved creature in the corner," asked the prince. "I prefer him to all those beautiful animals."

"You can't really mean what you say?" replied the woman.

"Yes, I do," said the prince, and the old woman was forced to let him have his way. So he took leave of her, and put the halter round his horse's neck and led him into the forest, where he rubbed him down till his skin was shining like gold. Then he mounted, and they flew straight through the air to the dragon's palace. The empress had been looking for him night and day, and stole out to meet him, and he swung her on to his saddle, and the horse flew off again.

Not long after the dragon came home, and when he found the empress was missing he said to his horse, "What shall we do? Shall we eat and drink, or shall we follow the runaways?" and the horse replied, "Whether you eat or don't eat, drink or don't drink, follow them or stay at home, matters nothing now, for you can never, never catch them."

But the dragon made no reply to the horse's words, but sprang on his back and set off in chase of the fugitives. And when they saw him coming they were frightened, and urged the prince's horse faster and faster, till he said, "Fear nothing; no harm can happen to us," and their hearts grew calm, for they trusted his wisdom.

Soon the dragon's horse was heard panting behind, and he cried out, "Oh, my brother, do not go so fast! I shall sink to the earth if I try to keep up with you."

And the prince's horse answered, "Why do you serve a monster like that? Kick him off, and let him break in pieces on the ground, and come and join us."

And the dragon's horse plunged and reared, and the dragon fell on a rock, whick broke him in pieces. Then the empress mounted his horse, and rode back with her husband to her kingdom, over which they ruled for many years.

—*The Violet Fairy Book* (1901)

The Ogre

ITALIAN

————◆◆————

THERE lived, once upon a time, in the land of Mari-
gliano, a poor woman called Masella, who had six pretty
daughters, all as upright as young fir-trees, and an only
son called Antonio, who was so simple as to be almost
an idiot. Hardly a day passed without his mother saying
to him, "What are you doing, you useless creature? If
you weren't too stupid to look after yourself, I would
order you to leave the house and never to let me see
your face again."

Every day the youth committed some fresh piece of
folly, till at last Masella, losing all patience, gave him a
good beating, which so startled Antonio that he took to
his heels and never stopped running till it was dark and
the stars were shining in the heavens. He wandered on
for some time, not knowing where to go, and at last he
came to a cave, at the mouth of which sat an ogre,
uglier than anything you can conceive.

He had a huge head and wrinkled brow—eyebrows
that met, squinting eyes, a flat broad nose, and a great
gash of a mouth from which two huge tusks stuck out.
His skin was hairy, his arms enormous, his legs like
sword blades, and his feet as flat as ducks'. In short,
he was the most hideous and laughable object in the
world.

ANTONIO · IS · NOT · AFRAID ·
OF · THE OGRE

But Antonio, who, with all his faults, was no coward, and was moreover a very civil-spoken lad, took off his hat, and said: "Good-day, sir; I hope you are pretty well. Could you kindly tell me how far it is from here to the place where I wish to go?"

When the ogre heard this extraordinary question he burst out laughing, and as he liked the youth's polite manners he said to him: "Will you enter my service?"

"What wages do you give?" replied Antonio.

"If you serve me faithfully," returned the ogre, "I'll be bound you'll get enough wages to satisfy you."

So the bargain was struck, and Antonio agreed to become the ogre's servant. He was very well treated, in every way, and he had little or no work to do, with the result that in a few days he became as fat as a quail, as round as a barrel, as red as a lobster, and as impudent as a bantam-cock.

But, after two years, the lad got weary of this idle life, and longed desperately to visit his home again. The ogre, who could see into his heart and knew how unhappy he was, said to him one day: "My dear Antonio, I know how much you long to see your mother and sisters again, and because I love you as the apple of my eye, I am willing to allow you to go home for a visit. Therefore, take this donkey, so that you may not have to go on foot; but see that you never say 'Bricklebrit' to him, for if you do you'll be sure to regret it."

Antonio took the beast without as much as saying thank you, and jumping on its back he rode away in great haste; but he hadn't gone two hundred yards when he dismounted and called out "Bricklebrit."

No sooner had he pronounced the word than the donkey opened its mouth and poured forth rubies, emeralds, diamonds and pearls, as big as walnuts.

Antonio gazed in amazement at the sight of such wealth, and joyfully filling a huge sack with the precious stones, he mounted the donkey again and rode on till he came to an inn. Here he got down, and going straight to the landlord, he said to him: "My good man, I must ask you to stable this donkey for me. Be sure you give the poor beast plenty of oats and hay, but beware of saying the word 'Bricklebrit' to him, for if you do I can promise you will regret it. Take this heavy sack, too, and put it carefully away for me."

The landlord, who was no fool, on receiving this strange warning, and seeing the precious stones sparkling through the canvas of the sack, was most anxious to see what would happen if he used the forbidden word. So he gave Antonio an excellent dinner, with a bottle of fine old wine, and prepared a comfortable bed for him. As soon as he saw the poor simpleton close his eyes and had heard his lusty snores, he hurried to the stables and said to the donkey "Bricklebrit," and the animal as usual poured out any number of precious stones.

When the landlord saw all these treasures he longed to get possession of so valuable an animal, and determined to steal the donkey from his foolish guest. As soon as it was light next morning Antonio awoke, and having rubbed his eyes and stretched himself about a hundred times he called the landlord and said to him: "Come here, my friend, and produce your bill, for short reckonings make long friends."

When Antonio had paid his account he went to the stables and took out his donkey, as he thought, and fastening a sack of gravel, which the landlord had substituted for his precious stones, on the creature's back, he set out for his home.

No sooner had he arrived there than he called out: "Mother, come quickly, and bring table-cloths and sheets with you, and spread them out on the ground. Antonio placed the donkey on them, and called out "Bricklebrit." But this time he met with no success, for the donkey took no more notice of the magic word than he would have done if a lyre had been twanged in his ear. Two, three, and four times did Antonio pronounce "Bricklebrit," but all in vain, and he might as well have spoken to the wind.

Disgusted and furious with the poor creature, he seized a thick stick and began to beat it so hard that he nearly broke every bone in its body. The miserable donkey was so distracted at such treatment that, for from pouring out precious stones, it only tore and dirtied all the fine linen.

When poor Masella saw her table-cloths and sheets being destroyed, and that instead of becoming rich she had only been made a fool of, she seized another stick and belaboured Antonio so unmercifully with it, that he fled before her, and never stopped till he reached the ogre's cave.

When his master saw the lad returning in such a sorry plight, he understood at once what had happened to him, and making no bones about the matter, he told Antonio what a fool he had been to allow himself to be so imposed upon by the landlord, and to let a worthless animal be palmed off on him instead of his magic donkey.

Antonio listened humbly to the ogre's words, and vowed solemnly that he would never act so foolishly again. And so a year passed, and once more Antonio was overcome by a fit of home-sickness, and felt a great longing to see his own people again.

Now the ogre, although he was so hideous to look upon, had a very kind heart, and when he saw how restless and unhappy Antonio was, he at once gave him leave to go home on a visit. At parting he gave him a beautiful table-cloth, and said: "Give this to your mother; but see that you don't lose it as you lost the donkey, and till you are safely in your own house beware of saying 'Table-cloth, open,' and 'Table-cloth, shut.' If you do, the misfortune be on your own head, for I have given you fair warning."

Antonio set out on his journey, but hardly had he got

out of sight of the cave than he laid the table-cloth on the ground and said, "Table-cloth, open." In an instant the table-cloth unfolded itself and disclosed a whole mass of precious stones and other treasures.

When Antonio perceived this he said, "Table-cloth, shut," and continued his journey. He came to the same inn again, and calling the landlord to him, he told him to put the table-cloth carefully away, and whatever he did not to say "Table-cloth, open," or "Table-cloth, shut," to it.

The landlord, who was a regular rogue, answered, "Just leave it to me, I will look after it as if it were my own."

After he had given Antonio plenty to eat and drink, and had provided him with a comfortable bed, he went straight to the table-cloth and said, "Table-cloth, open." It opened at once, and displayed such costly treasures that the landlord made up his mind on the spot to steal it.

When Antonio awoke next morning, the host handed him over a table-cloth exactly like his own, and carrying it carefully over his arm, the foolish youth went straight to his mother's house, and said: "Now we shall be rich beyond the dreams of avarice, and need never go about in rags again, or lack the best of food."

With these words he spread the table-cloth on the ground and said, "Table-cloth, open."

But he might repeat the injunction as often as he pleased, it was only waste of breath, for nothing happened. When Antonio saw this he turned to his mother and said: "That old scoundrel of a landlord has done me once more; but he will live to repent it, for if I ever enter his inn again, I will make him suffer for the loss of my donkey and the other treasures he has robbed me of."

Masella was in such a rage over her fresh disappointment that she could not restrain her impatience, and, turning on Antonio, she abused him soundly, and told him to get out of her sight at once, for she would never acknowledge him as a son of hers again. The poor boy was very depressed by her words, and slunk back to his master like a dog with his tail between his legs. When the ogre saw him, he guessed at once what had happened. He gave Antonio a good scolding, and said, "I don't know what prevents me smashing your head in, you useless ne'er-do-well! You blurt everything out, and your long tongue never ceases wagging for a moment. If you had remained silent in the inn this misfortune would never have overtaken you, so you have only yourself to blame for your present suffering."

Antonio listened to his master's words in silence, looking for all the world like a whipped dog. When he had been three more years in the ogre's service he had another bad fit of home-sickness, and longed very much to see his mother and sisters again.

So he asked for permission to go home on a visit, and it was at once granted to him. Before he set out on his journey the ogre presented him with a beautifully carved stick and said, "Take this stick as a remembrance of me; but beware of saying, 'Rise up, Stick,'' and 'Lie down, Stick,' for if you do, I can only say I wouldn't be in your shoes for something."

Antonio took the stick and said, "Don't be in the least alarmed, I'm not such a fool as you think, and know better than most people what two and two make."

"I'm glad to hear it," replied the ogre, "but words are women, deeds are men. You have heard what I said, and forewarned is forearmed."

This time Antonio thanked his master warmly for all his kindness, and started on his homeward journey in great spirits; but he had not gone half a mile when he said "Rise up, Stick."

The words were hardly out of his mouth when the stick rose and began to rain down blows on poor Antonio's back with such lightning-like rapidity that he had hardly strength to call out, "Lie down, Stick"; but as soon as he uttered the words the stick lay down, and ceased beating his back black and blue.

Although he had learnt a lesson at some cost to himself, Antonio was full of joy, for he saw a way now of revenging himself on the wicked landlord. Once more he arrived at the inn, and was received in the most friendly and hospitable manner by his host. Antonio greeted him cordially, and said: "My friend, will you kindly take care of this stick for me? But, whatever you do, don't say 'Rise up, Stick.' If you do, you will be sorry for it, and you needn't expect any sympathy from me."

The landlord, thinking he was coming in for a third piece of good fortune, gave Antonio an excellent supper; and after he had seen him comfortably to bed, he ran to the stick, and calling to his wife to come and see the fun, he lost no time in pronouncing the words "Rise up, Stick."

The moment he spoke the stick jumped up and beat the landlord so unmercifully that he and his wife ran screaming to Antonio, and, waking him up, pleaded for mercy.

When Antonio saw how successful his trick had been, he said: "I refuse to help you, unless you give me all that you have stolen from me, otherwise you will be beaten to death."

The landlord, who felt himself at death's door already, cried out: "Take back your property, only release me from this terrible stick"; and with these words he ordered the donkey, the table-cloth, and other treasures to be restored to their rightful owner.

As soon as Antonio had recovered his belongings he said "Stick, lie down," and it stopped beating the landlord at once.

Then he took his donkey and table-cloth and arrived safely at his home with them. This time the magic words had the desired effect, and the donkey and table-cloth provided the family with treasures untold. Antonio very soon married off his sister, made his mother rich for life, and they all lived happily for ever after.

—*The Grey Fairy Book* (1900)

Paperarello

SICILIAN

———— ◆◆◆ ————

ONCE upon a time there lived a king and a queen who had one son. The king loved the boy very much, but the queen, who was a wicked woman, hated the sight of him; and this was the more unlucky for, when he was twelve years old, his father died, and he was left alone in the world.

Now the queen was very angry because the people, who knew how bad she was, seated her son on the throne instead of herself, and she never rested till she had formed a plan to get him out of the way. Fortunately, however, the young king was wise and prudent, and knew her too well to trust her.

One day, when his mourning was over, he gave orders that everything should be made ready for a grand hunt. The queen pretended to be greatly delighted that he was going to amuse himself once more, and declared that she would accompany him. "No, mother, I cannot let you come," he answered; "the ground is rough, and you are not strong." But he might as well have spoken to the winds: when the horn was sounded at daybreak the queen was there with the rest.

All that day they rode, for game was plentiful, but towards evening the mother and son found themselves alone in a part of the country that was strange to them.

The Horse brings the boy to the Fairies' House

They wandered on for some time, without knowing where they were going, till they met with a man whom they begged to give them shelter. "Come with me," said the man gladly, for he was an ogre, and fed on human flesh; and the king and his mother went with him, and he led them to his house. When they got there they found to what a dreadful place they had come, and, falling on their knees, they offered him great sums of money, if he would only spare their lives. The ogre's heart was moved at the sight of the queen's beauty, and he promised that he would do her no harm; but he stabbed the boy at once, and binding his body on a horse, turned him loose in the forest.

The ogre had happened to choose a horse which he had bought only the day before, and he did not know it was a magician, or he would not have been so foolish as to fix upon it on this occasion. The horse no sooner had been driven off with the prince's body on its back than it galloped straight to the home of the fairies, and knocked at the door with its hoof. The fairies heard the knock, but were afraid to open till they had peeped from an upper window to see that it was no giant or ogre who could do them harm. "Oh, look, sister!" cried the first to reach the window, "it is a horse that has knocked, and on its back there is bound a dead boy, the most beautiful boy in all the world!" Then the fairies ran to open the door, and let in the horse and unbound the ropes which fastened the young king on its back. And they gathered round to admire his beauty, and whispered one to the other: "We will make him alive again, and will keep him for our brother." And so they did, and for many years they all lived together as brothers and sisters.

By-and-by the boy grew into a man, as boys will, and then the oldest of the fairies said to her sisters: "Now I will marry him, and he shall be really your brother." So the young king married the fairy, and they lived happily together in the castle; but though he loved his wife he still longed to see the world.

At length this longing grew so strong on him that he could bear it no more; and, calling the fairies together, he said to them: "Dear wife and sisters, I must leave you for a time, and go out and see the world. But I shall think of you often, and one day I shall come back to you."

The fairies wept and begged him to stay, but he would not listen, and at last the eldest, who was his wife, said to him: "If you really will abandon us, take this lock of my hair with you; you will find it useful in time of need." So she cut off a long curl, and handed it to him.

The prince mounted his horse, and rode on all day without stopping once. Towards evening he found himself in a desert, and, look where he would, there was no such thing as a house or a man to be seen. "What am I to do now?" he thought. "If I go to sleep here wild beasts will come and eat me! Yet both I and my horse are worn out, and can go no further." Then suddenly he remembered the fairy's gift, and taking out the curl he said to it: "I want a castle here, and servants, and dinner, and everything to make me comfortable to-night; and besides that, I must have a stable and fodder for my horse." And in a moment the castle was before him just as he had wished.

In this way he travelled through many countries, till at last he came to a land that was ruled over by a great king. Leaving his horse outside the walls, he clad himself in the dress of a poor man, and went up to the palace. The queen, who was looking out of the window, saw him approaching, and filled with pity sent a servant to ask who he was and what he wanted. "I am a stranger here," answered the young king, "and very poor. I have come to beg for some work." "We have everybody we want," said the queen, when the servant told her the young man's reply. "We have a gate-keeper, and a hall porter, and servants of all sorts in the palace; the only person we have not got is a goose-boy. Tell him that he can be our goose-boy if he likes." The youth answered

that he was quite content to be goose-boy; and that was
how he got his nickname of Paperarello. And in order
that no one should guess that he was any better than a
goose-boy should be, he rubbed his face and his rags
over with mud, and made himself altogether such a
disgusting object that every one crossed over to the
other side of the road when he was seen coming.

"Do go and wash yourself, Paperarello!" said the
queen sometimes, for he did his work so well that she
took an interest in him. "Oh, I should not feel comfortable if I was clean, your Majesty," answered he, and
went whistling after his geese.

It happened one day that, owing to some accident to
the great flour mills which supplied the city, there was
no bread to be had, and the king's army had to do
without. When the king heard of it, he sent for the
cook, and told him that by the next morning he must
have all the bread that the oven, heated seven times
over, could bake. "But, your Majesty, it is not possible," cried the poor man in despair. "The mills have
only just begun working, and the flour will not be
ground till evening, and how can I heat the oven seven
times in one night?" "That is your affair," answered the
King, who, when he took anything into his head, would
listen to nothing. "If you succeed in baking the bread
you shall have my daughter to wife, but if you fail your
head will pay for it."

Now Paperarello, who was passing through the hall
where the king was giving his orders, heard these words,
and said: "Your Majesty, have no fears; I will bake your
bread." "Very well," answered the king; "but if you fail,
you will pay for it with your head!" and signed that both
should leave his presence.

The cook was still trembling with the thought of what
he had escaped, but to his surprise Paperarello did not
seem disturbed at all, and when night came he went to
sleep as usual. "Paperarello," cried the other servants,
when they saw him quietly taking off his clothes, "you
cannot go to bed; you will need every moment of the

night for your work. Remember, the king is not to be played with!"

"I really must have some sleep first," replied Paperarello, stretching himself and yawning; and he flung himself on his bed, and was fast asleep in a moment. In an hour's time, the servants came and shook him by the shoulder. "Paperarello, are you mad?" said they. "Get up, or you will lose your head." "Oh, do let me sleep a little more," answered he. And this was all he would say, though the servants returned to wake him many times in the night.

At last the dawn broke, and the servants rushed to his room, crying: "Paperarello! Paperarello! get up, the king is coming. You have baked no bread, and of a surety he will have your head."

"Oh, don't scream so," replied Paperarello, jumping out of bed as he spoke; and taking the lock of hair in his hand, he went into the kitchen. And, behold! there stood the bread piled high—four, five, six ovens full, and the seventh still waiting to be taken out of the oven. The servants stood and stared in surprise, and the king said: "Well done, Paperarello, you have won my daughter." And he thought to himself: "This fellow must really be a magician."

But when the princess heard what was in store for her she wept bitterly, and declared that never, never would she marry that dirty Paperarello! However, the king paid no heed to her tears and prayers, and before many days were over the wedding was celebrated with great splendour, though the bridegroom had not taken the trouble to wash himself, and was as dirty as before.

When night came he went as usual to sleep among his geese, and the princess went to the king and said: "Father, I entreat you to have that horrible Paperarello put to death." "No, no!" replied her father, "he is a great magician, and before I put him to death, I must first find out the secret of his power, and then—we shall see."

Soon after this a war broke out, and everybody about

the palace was very busy polishing up armour and sharpening swords, for the king and his sons were to ride at the head of the army. Then Paperarello left his geese, and came and told the king that he wished to go to fight also. The king gave him leave, and told him that he might go to the stable and take any horse he liked from the stables. So Paperarello examined the horses carefully, but instead of picking out one of the splendid well-groomed creatures, whose skin shone like satin, he chose a poor lame thing, put a saddle on it, and rode after the other men-at-arms who were attending the king. In a short time he stopped, and said to them: "My horse can go no further; you must go on to the war without me, and I will stay here, and make some little clay soldiers, and will play at a battle." The men laughed at him for being so childish, and rode on after their master.

Scarcely were they out of sight than Paperarello took out his curl, and wished himself the best armour, the sharpest sword, and the swiftest horse in the world, and the next minute was riding as fast as he could to the field of battle. The fight had already begun, and the enemy was getting the best of it, when Paperarello rode up, and in a moment the fortunes of the day had changed. Right and left this strange knight laid about him, and his sword pierced the stoutest breast-plate, and the strongest shield. He was indeed "a host in himself," and his foes fled before him thinking he was only the first of a troop of such warriors, whom no one could withstand. When the battle was over, the king sent for him to thank him for his timely help, and to ask what reward he should give him. "Nothing but your little finger, your Majesty," was his answer; and the king cut off his little finger and gave it to Paperarello, who bowed and hid it in his surcoat. Then he left the field, and when the soldiers rode back they found him still sitting in the road making whole rows of little clay dolls.

The next day the king went out to fight another battle, and again Paperarello appeared, mounted on his lame horse. As on the day before, he halted on the road, and sat down to make his clay soldiers; then a second time he wished himself armour, sword, and a horse, all sharper and better than those he had previously had, and galloped after the rest. He was only just in time: the enemy had almost beaten the king's army back, and men whispered to each other that if the strange knight did not soon come to their aid, they would be all dead men. Suddenly someone cried: "Hold on a little longer, I see him in the distance; and his armour shines brighter, and his horse runs swifter, than yesterday." Then they took fresh heart and fought desperately on till the knight came up, and threw himself into the thick of the battle. As before, the enemy gave way before him, and in a few minutes the victory remained with the king.

The first thing that the victor did was to send for the knight to thank him for his timely help, and to ask what gift he could bestow on him in token of gratitude. "Your Majesty's ear," answered the knight; and as the king could not go back from his word, he cut it off and gave it to him. Paperarello bowed, fastened the ear inside his surcoat and rode away. In the evening, when they all returned from the battle, there he was, sitting in the road, making clay dolls.

On the third day the same thing happened, and this time he asked for the king's nose as the reward of his aid. Now, to lose one's nose, is worse even than losing one's ear or one's finger, and the king hesitated as to whether he should comply. However, he had always prided himself on being an honourable man, so he cut off his nose, and handed it to Paperarello. Paperarello bowed, put the nose in his surcoat, and rode away. In the evening, when the king returned from the battle, he found Paperarello sitting in the road making clay dolls. And Paperarello got up and said to him: "Do you know who I am? I am your dirty goose-boy, yet you have given me your finger, and your ear, and your nose."

That night, when the king sat at dinner, Paperarello came in, and laying down the ear, and the nose, and the finger on the table, turned and said to the nobles and courtiers who were waiting on the king: "I am the invincible knight, who rode three times to your help, and I also am a king's son, and no goose-boy as you all think." And he went away and washed himself, and dressed himself in fine clothes and entered the hall again, looking so handsome that the proud princess fell in love with him on the spot. But Paperarello took no notice of her, and said to the king: "It was kind of you to offer me your daughter in marriage, and for that I thank you; but I have a wife at home whom I love better, and it is to her that I am going. But as a token of farewell, I wish that your ear, and nose, and finger may be restored to their proper places." So saying, he bade them all goodbye, and went back to his home and his fairy bride, with whom he lived happily till the end of his life.

—*The Crimson Fairy Book* (1903)

The Prince and the Dragon

SERBIAN

———◆◆———

ONCE upon a time there lived an emperor who had three sons. They were all fine young men, and fond of hunting, and scarcely a day passed without one or other of them going out to look for game.

One morning the eldest of the three princes mounted his horse and set out for a neighbouring forest, where wild animals of all sorts were to be found. He had not long left the castle, when a hare sprang out of a thicket and dashed across the road in front. The young man gave chase at once, and pursued it over hill and dale, till at last the hare took refuge in a mill which was standing by the side of a river. The prince followed and entered the mill, but stopped in terror by the door, for, instead of a hare, before him stood a dragon, breathing fire and flame. At this fearful sight the prince turned to fly, but a fiery tongue coiled round his waist, and drew him into the dragon's mouth, and he was seen no more.

A week passed away, and when the prince never came back everyone in the town began to grow uneasy. At last his next brother told the emperor that he likewise would go out to hunt, and that perhaps he would find some clue as to his brother's disappearance. But hardly had the castle gates closed on the prince than the hare sprang out of the bushes as before, and led the

HOW THE DRAGON CAUGHT THE PRINCE

huntsman up hill and down dale, till they reached the mill. Into this the hare flew with the prince at his heels, when, lo! instead of the hare, there stood a dragon breathing fire and flame; and out shot a fiery tongue which coiled round the prince's waist, and lifted him straight into the dragon's mouth, and he was seen no more.

Days went by, and the emperor waited and waited for the sons who never came, and could not sleep at night for wondering where they were and what had become of them. His youngest son wished to go in search of his brothers, but for long the emperor refused to listen to him, lest he should lose him also. But the prince prayed so hard for leave to make the search, and promised so often that he would be very cautious and careful, that at length the emperor gave him permission, and ordered the best horse in the stables to be saddled for him.

Full of hope the young prince started on his way, but no sooner was he outside the city walls than a hare sprang out of the bushes and ran before him, till they reached the mill. As before, the animal dashed in through the open door, but this time he was not followed by the prince. Wiser than his brothers, the young man turned away, saying to himself: "There are as good hares in the forest as any that have come out of it, and when I have caught them, I can come back and look for you."

For many hours he rode up and down the mountain, but saw nothing, and at last, tired of waiting, he went back to the mill. Here he found an old woman sitting, whom he greeted pleasantly.

"Good morning to you, little mother," he said; and the old woman answered: "Good morning, my son."

"Tell me, little mother," went on the prince, "where shall I find my hare?"

"My son," replied the old woman, "that was no hare, but a dragon who has led many men hither, and then has eaten them all." At these words the prince's heart grew heavy, and he cried, "Then my brothers must have come here, and have been eaten by the dragon!"

"You have guessed right," answered the old woman; "and I can give you no better counsel than to go home at once, before the same fate overtakes you."

"Will you not come with me out of this dreadful place?" said the young man.

"He took me prisoner, too," answered she, "and I cannot shake off his chains."

"Then listen to me," cried the prince. "When the dragon comes back, ask him where he always goes when he leaves here, and what makes him so strong; and when you have coaxed the secret from him, tell me the next time I come."

So the prince went home, and the old woman remained in the mill, and as soon as the dragon returned she said to him:

"Where have you been all this time—you must have traveled far?"

"Yes, little mother, I have indeed travelled far," answered he. Then the old woman began to flatter him, and to praise his cleverness; and when she thought she had got him into a good temper, she said: "I have wondered so often where you get your strength from; I do wish you would tell me. I would stoop and kiss the place out of pure love!" The dragon laughed at this, and answered:

"In the hearthstone yonder lies the secret of my strength."

Then the old woman jumped up and kissed the hearth; whereat the dragon laughed the more, and said:

"You foolish creature! I was only jesting. It is not in the hearthstone, but in that tall tree that lies the secret of my strength." Then the old woman jumped up again and put her arms round the tree, and kissed it heartily. Loudly laughed the dragon when he saw what she was doing.

"Old fool," he cried, as soon as he could speak, "did

you really believe that my strength came from that tree?"

"Where is it then?" asked the old woman, rather crossly, for she did not like being made fun of.

"My strength," replied the dragon, "lies far away; so far that you could never reach it. Far, far from here is a kingdom, and by its capital city is a lake, and in the lake is a dragon, and inside the dragon is a wild boar, and inside the wild boar is a pigeon, and inside the pigeon a sparrow, and inside the sparrow is my strength." And when the old woman heard this, she thought it was no use flattering him any longer, for never, never, could she take his strength from him.

The following morning, when the dragon had left the mill, the prince came back, and the old woman told him all that the creature had said. He listened in silence, and then returned to the castle, where he put on a suit of shepherd's clothes, and taking a staff in his hand, he went forth to seek a place as tender of sheep.

For some time he wandered from village to village and from town to town, till he came at length to a large city in a distant kingdom, surrounded on three sides by a great lake, which happened to be the very lake in which the dragon lived. As was his custom, he stopped everybody whom he met in the streets that looked likely to want a shepherd and begged them to engage him, but they all seemed to have shepherds of their own, or else not to need any. The prince was beginning to lose heart, when a man who had overhead his question turned round and said that he had better go and ask the emperor, as he was in search of some one to see after his flocks.

"Will you take care of my sheep?" said the emperor, when the young man knelt before him.

"Most willingly, your Majesty," answered the young man, and he listened obediently while the emperor told him what he was to do.

"Outside the city walls," went on the emperor, "you will find a large lake, and by its banks lie the richest meadows in my kingdom. When you are leading out your flocks to pasture, they will all run straight to these meadows, and none that have gone there have ever been known to come back. Take heed, therefore, my son, not to suffer your sheep to go where they will, but drive them to any spot that you think best."

. With a low bow the prince thanked the emperor for his warning, and promised to do his best to keep the sheep safe. Then he left the palace and went to the market-place, where he bought two greyhounds, a hawk, and a set of pipes; after that he took the sheep out to pasture. The instant the animals caught sight of the lake lying before them, they trotted off as fast as their legs would go to the green meadows lying round it. The prince did not try to stop them; he only placed his hawk on the branch of a tree, laid his pipes on the grass, and bade the greyhounds sit still; then, rolling up his sleeves and trousers, he waded into the water crying as he did so: "Dragon! dragon! If you are not a coward, come out and fight with me!" And a voice answered from the depths of the lake:

"I am waiting for you, O prince"; and the next minute the dragon reared himself out of the water, huge and horrible to see. The prince sprang upon him and they grappled with each other and fought together till the sun was high, and it was noonday. Then the dragon gasped:

"O prince, let me dip my burning head once into the lake, and I will hurl you up to the top of the sky." But the prince answered, "Oh, ho! my good dragon, do not crow too soon! If the emperor's daughter were only here, and would kiss me on the forehead, I would throw you up higher still!" And suddenly the dragon's hold loosened, and he fell back into the lake.

As soon as it was evening, the prince washed away all signs of the fight, took his hawk upon his shoulder, and his pipes under his arm, and with his greyhounds in front and his flock following after him he set out for the city. As they all passed through the streets the people stared in wonder, for never before had any flock returned from the lake.

The next morning he rose early, and led his sheep down the road to the lake. This time, however, the emperor sent two men on horseback to ride behind him, with orders to watch the prince all day long. The horsemen kept the prince and his sheep in sight, without being seen themselves. As soon as they beheld the sheep running towards the meadows, they turned aside up a steep hill, which overhung the lake. When the shepherd reached the place he laid, as before, his pipes on the grass and bade the greyhounds sit beside them, while the hawk he perched on the branch of the tree. Then he rolled up his trousers and his sleeves, and waded into the water crying:

"Dragon! dragon! if you are not a coward, come out and fight with me!" And the dragon answered:

"I am waiting for you, O prince," and the next minute he reared himself out of the water, huge and horrible to see. Again they clasped each other tight round the body and fought till it was noon, and when the sun was at its hottest, the dragon gasped:

"O prince, let me dip my burning head once in the lake, and I will hurl you up to the top of the sky." But the prince answered:

"Oh, ho! my good dragon, do not crow too soon! If the emperor's daughter were only here, and would kiss me on the forehead, I would throw you up higher still!" And suddenly the dragon's hold loosened, and he fell back into the lake.

As soon as it was evening the prince again collected his sheep, and playing on his pipes he marched before them into the city. When he passed through the gates all the people came out of their houses to stare in wonder, for never before had any flock returned from the lake.

Meanwhile the two horsemen had ridden quickly back, and told the emperor all that they had seen and heard. The emperor listened eagerly to their tale, then called his daughter to him and repeated it to her.

"To-morrow," he said, when he had finished, "you shall go with the shepherd to the lake, and then you shall kiss him on the forehead as he wishes."

But when the princess heard these words, she burst into tears, and sobbed out:

"Will you really send me, your only child, to that dreadful place, from which most likely I shall never come back?"

"Fear nothing, my little daughter, all will be well. Many shepherds have gone to that lake and none have ever returned; but this one has in these two days fought twice with the dragon and has escaped without a wound. So I hope to-morrow he will kill the dragon altogether, and deliver this land from the monster who has slain so many of our bravest men."

Scarcely had the sun begun to peep over the hills next morning, when the princess stood by the shepherd's side, ready to go to the lake. The shepherd was brimming over with joy, but the princess only wept bitterly. "Dry your tears, I implore you," said he. "If you will just do what I ask you, and when the time comes, run and kiss my forehead, you have nothing to fear."

Merrily the shepherd blew on his pipes as he marched at the head of his flock, only stopping every now and then to say to the weeping girl at his side:

"Do not cry so, Heart of Gold; trust me and fear nothing." And so they reached the lake.

In an instant the sheep were scattered all over the meadows, and the prince placed his hawk on the tree, and his pipes on the grass, while he bade his greyhounds lie beside them. Then he rolled up his trousers and his sleeves, and waded into the water, calling:

"Dragon! dragon! if you are not a coward, come forth, and let us have one more fight together." And the dragon answered: "I am waiting for you, O prince'; and the next minute he reared himself out of the water, huge and horrible to see. Swiftly he drew near to the bank, and the prince sprang to meet him, and they grasped each other round the body and fought till it was noon. And when the sun was at its hottest, the dragon cried:

"O prince, let me dip my burning head in the lake, and I will hurl you to the top of the sky." But the prince answered:

"Oh, ho! my good dragon, do not crow too soon! If the emperor's daughter were only here, and she would kiss my forehead, I would throw you higher still."

Hardly had he spoken, when the princess, who had been listening, ran up and kissed him on the forehead. Then the prince swung the dragon straight up into the clouds, and when he touched the earth again, he broke into a thousand pieces. Out of the pieces there sprang a wild boar and galloped away, but the prince called his hounds to give chase, and they caught the boar and tore it to bits. Out of the pieces there sprang a hare, and in a moment the greyhounds were after it, and they caught it and killed it; and out of the hare there came a pigeon. Quickly the prince let loose his hawk, which soared straight into the air, then swooped upon the bird and brought it to his master. The prince cut open its body and found the sparrow inside, as the old woman had said.

"Now," cried the prince, holding the sparrow in his hand, "now you shall tell me where I can find my brothers."

"Do not hurt me," answered the sparrow, "and I will tell you with all my heart. Behind your father's castle stands a mill, and in the mill are three slender twigs. Cut off these twigs and strike their roots with them, and the iron door of a cellar will open. In the cellar you will find as many people, young and old, women and children, as would fill a kingdom, and among them are your brothers."

By this time twilight had fallen, so the prince washed himself in the lake, took the hawk on his shoulder and

the pipes under his arm, and with his greyhounds before him and his flock behind him, marched gaily into
the town, the princess following them all, still trembling
with fright. And so they passed through the streets,
thronged with a wondering crowd, till they reached the
castle.

Unknown to anyone, the emperor had stolen out on
horseback, and had hidden himself on the hill, where
he could see all that happened. When all was over, and
the power of the dragon was broken for ever, he rode
quickly back to the castle, and was ready to receive the
prince with open arms, and to promise him his daughter to wife. The wedding took place with great splendour,
and for a whole week the town was hung with coloured
lamps, and tables were spread in the hall of the castle
for all who chose to come and eat. And when the feast
was over, the prince told the emperor and the people
who he really was, and at this everyone rejoiced still
more, and preparations were made for the prince and
princess to return to their own kingdom, for the prince
was impatient to set free his brothers.

The first thing he did when he reached his native
country was to hasten to the mill, where he found the
three twigs as the sparrow had told him. The moment
that he struck the root the iron door flew open, and
from the cellar a countless multitude of men and women
streamed forth. He bade them go one by one whereso-
ever they would, while he himself waited by the door
till his brothers passed through. How delighted they
were to meet again, and to hear all that the prince had
done to deliver them from their enchantment. And
they went home with him and served him all the days
of their lives, for they said that he only who had proved
himself brave and faithful was fit to be king.

—*The Crimson Fairy Book* (1903)

The Prince Who Would
Seek Immortality

HUNGARIAN

———————◆•◆———————

ONCE upon a time, in the very middle of the middle of a large kingdom, there was a town, and in the town a palace, and in the palace a king. This king had one son whom his father thought was wiser and cleverer than any son ever was before, and indeed his father had spared no pains to make him so. He had been very careful in choosing his tutors and governors when he was a boy, and when he became a youth he sent him to travel, so that he might see the ways of other people, and find that they were often as good as his own.

It was now a year since the prince had returned home, for his father felt that it was time that his son should learn how to rule the kingdom which would one day be his. But during his long absence the prince seemed to have changed his character altogether. From being a merry and light-hearted boy, he had grown into a gloomy and thoughtful man. The king knew of nothing that could have produced such an alteration. He vexed himself about it from morning till night, till at length an explanation occurred to him—the young man was in love!

Now the prince never talked about his feelings—for the matter of that he scarcely talked at all; and the father knew that if he was to come to the bottom of the prince's dismal face, he would have to begin. So one day, after dinner, he took his son by the arm and led him into another room, hung entirely with the pictures of beautiful maidens, each one more lovely than the other.

"My dear boy," he said, "you are very sad; perhaps after all your wanderings it is dull for you here all alone with me. It would be much better if you would marry, and I have collected here the portraits of the most beautiful women in the world of a rank equal to your own. Choose which among them you would like for a wife, and I will send an embassy to her father to ask for her hand."

"Alas! your Majesty," answered the prince, "it is not love or marriage that makes me so gloomy; but the thought, which haunts me day and night, that all men, even kings, must die. Never shall I be happy again till I have found a kingdom where death is unknown. And I have determined to give myself no rest till I have discovered the Land of Immortality."

The old king heard him with dismay; things were worse than he thought. He tried to reason with his son, and told him that during all these years he had been looking forward to his return, in order to resign his throne and its cares, which pressed so heavily upon him. But it was in vain that he talked; the prince would listen to nothing, and the following morning buckled on his sword and set forth on his journey.

He had been travelling for many days, and had left his fatherland behind him, when close to the road he came upon a huge tree, and on its topmost bough an eagle was sitting shaking the branches with all his might. This seemed so strange and so unlike an eagle, that the prince stood still with surprise, and the bird saw him and flew to the ground. The moment its feet touched the ground he changed into a king.

"Why do you look so astonished?" he asked.

"I was wondering why you shook the boughs so fiercely," answered the prince.

"I am condemned to do this, for neither I nor any of my kindred can die till I have rooted up this great tree," replied the king of the eagles. "But it is now evening, and I need work no more to-day. Come to my house with me, and be my guest for the night."

The prince accepted gratefully the eagle's invitation, for he was tired and hungry. They were received at the palace by the king's beautiful daughter, who gave orders that dinner should be laid for them at once. While they were eating, the eagle questioned his guest about his travels, and if he was wandering for pleasure's sake, or with any special aim. Then the prince told him everything, and how he could never turn back till he had discovered the Land of Immortality.

"Dear brother," said the eagle, "you have discovered it already, and it rejoices my heart to think that you will stay with us. Have you not just heard me say that death has no power either over myself or any of my kindred till that great tree is rooted up? It will take me six hundred years' hard work to do that; so marry my daughter and let us all live happily together here. After all, six hundred years is an eternity!"

"Ah, dear king," replied the young man, "your offer is very tempting! But at the end of six hundred years we should have to die, so we should be no better off! No, I must go on till I find the country where there is no death at all."

Then the princess spoke, and tried to persuade the guest to change his mind, but he sorrowfully shook his head. At length, seeing that his resolution was firmly fixed, she took from a cabinet a little box which contained her picture, and gave it to him saying:

"As you will not stay with us, prince, accept this box, which will sometimes recall us to your memory. If you are tired of travelling before you come to the Land of Immortality, open this box and look at my picture, and you will be borne along either on earth or in the air, quick as thought, or swift as the whirlwind."

The prince thanked her for her gift, which he placed

The Baldheaded Man on The Mountain

in his tunic, and sorrowfully bade the eagle and his daughter farewell.

Never was any present in the world as useful as that little box, and many times did he bless the kind thought of the princess. One evening it had carried him to the top of a high mountain, where he saw a man with a bald head, busily engaged in digging up spadefuls of earth and throwing them in a basket. When the basket was full he took it away and returned with an empty one, which he likewise filled. The prince stood and watched him for a little, till the bald-headed man looked up and said to him: "Dear brother, what surprises you so much?"

"I was wondering why you were filling the basket," replied the prince.

"Oh!" replied the man, "I am condemned to do this, for neither I nor any of my family can die till I have dug away the whole of this mountain and made it level with the plain. But, come, it is almost dark, and I shall work no longer." And he plucked a leaf from a tree close by, and from a rough digger he was changed into a stately bald-headed king. "Come home with me," he added; "you must be tired and hungry, and my daughter will have supper ready for us." The prince accepted gladly, and they went back to the palace, where the bald-headed king's daughter, who was still more beautiful than the other princess, welcomed them at the door and led the way into a large hall and to a table covered with silver dishes. While they were eating, the bald-headed king asked the prince how he had happened to wander so far, and the young man told him all about it, and how he was seeking the Land of Immortality. "You have found it already," answered the king, "for, as I said, neither I nor my family can die till I have levelled this great mountain; and that will take full eight hundred years longer. Stay here with us and marry my daughter. Eight hundred years is surely long enough to live."

"Oh, certainly," answered the prince; "but, all the

same, I would rather go and seek the land where there is no death at all."

So next morning he bade them farewell, though the princess begged him to stay with all her might; and when she found that she could not persuade him she gave him as a remembrance a gold ring. This ring was still more useful than the box, because when one wished oneself at any place one was there directly, without even the trouble of flying to it through the air. The prince put it on his finger, and thanking her heartily, went his way.

He walked on for some distance, and then he recollected the ring and thought he would try if the princess had spoken truly as to its powers. "I wish I was at the end of the world," he said, shutting his eyes, and when he opened them he was standing in a street full of marble palaces. The men who passed him were tall and strong, and their clothes were magnificent. He stopped some of them and asked in all the twenty-seven languages he knew what was the name of the city, but no one answered him. Then his heart sank within him; what should he do in this strange place if nobody could understand anything? he said. Suddenly his eyes fell upon a man dressed after the fashion of his native country, and he ran up to him and spoke to him in his own tongue. "What city is this, my friend?" he inquired.

"It is the capital city of the Blue Kingdom," replied the man, "but the king himself is dead, and his daughter is now the ruler."

With this news the prince was satisfied, and begged his countryman to show him the way to the young queen's palace. The man led him through several streets into a large square, one side of which was occupied by a splendid building that seemed borne up on slender pillars of soft green marble. In front was a flight of steps, and on these the queen was sitting wrapped in a veil of shining silver mist, listening to the complaints of her people and dealing out justice. When the prince came up she saw directly that he was no ordinary man, and telling her chamberlain to dismiss the rest of her petitioners for that day, she signed to the prince to follow her into the palace. Luckily she had been taught his language as a child, so they had no difficulty in talking together.

The prince told all his story and how he was journeying in search of the Land of Immortality. When he had finished, the princess, who had listened attentively, rose, and taking his arm, led him to the door of another room, the floor of which was made entirely of needles, stuck so close together that there was not room for a single needle more.

"Prince," she said, turning to him, "you see these needles? Well, know that neither I nor any of my family can die till I have worn out these needles in sewing. It will take at least a thousand years for that. Stay here, and share my throne; a thousand years is long enough to live!"

"Certainly," answered he; "still, at the end of the thousand years I should have to die! No, I must find the land where there is no death."

The queen did all she could to persuade him to stay, but as her words proved useless, at length she gave it up. Then she said to him: "As you will not stay, take this little golden rod as a remembrance of me. It has the power to become anything you wish it to be, when you are in need."

So the prince thanked her, and putting the rod in his pocket, went his way.

Scarcely had he left the town behind him when he came to a broad river which no man might pass, for he was standing at the end of the world, and this was the river which flowed round it. Not knowing what to do next, he walked a little distance up the bank, and there, over his head, a beautiful city was floating in the air. He longed to get to it, but how? neither road nor bridge was anywhere to be seen, yet the city drew him upwards, and he felt that here at last was the country which he sought. Suddenly he remembered the golden rod which the mist-veiled queen had given him. With a beating heart he flung it to the ground, wishing with all his might that it should turn into a bridge, and fearing that, after all, this might prove beyond its power. But no, instead of the rod, there stood a golden ladder, leading straight up to the city of the air. He was about to enter the golden gates, when there sprang at him a wondrous beast, whose like he had never seen. "Out sword from the sheath," cried the prince, springing back with a cry. And the sword leapt from the scabbard and cut off some of the monster's heads, but others grew again directly, so that the prince, pale with terror, stood where he was, calling for help, and put his sword back in the sheath again.

The queen of the city heard the noise and looked from her window to see what was happening. Summoning one of her servants, she bade him go and rescue the stranger, and bring him to her. The prince thankfully obeyed her orders, and entered her presence.

The moment she looked at him, the queen also felt that he was no ordinary man, and she welcomed him graciously, and asked him what had brought him to the city. In answer the prince told all his story, and how he had travelled long and far in search of the Land of Immortality.

"You have found it," said she, "for I am queen over life and over death. Here you can dwell among the immortals."

A thousand years had passed since the prince first entered the city, but they had flown so fast that the time seemed no more than six months. There had not been one instant of the thousand years that the prince was not happy till one night when he dreamed of his father and mother. Then the longing for his home came upon him with a rush, and in the morning he told the Queen of the Immortals that he must go and see his father and mother once more. The queen stared at him with amazement, and cried: "Why, prince, are you out of your senses? It is more than eight hundred years since your father and mother died! There will not even be their dust remaining."

"I must go all the same," said he.

"Well, do not be in a hurry," continued the queen, understanding that he would not be prevented. "Wait till I make some preparations for your journey." So she unlocked her great treasure chest, and took out two beautiful flasks, one of gold and one of silver, which she hung round his neck. Then she showed him a little trap-door in one corner of the room, and said: "Fill the silver flask with this water, which is below the trap-door. It is enchanted, and whoever you sprinkle with the water will become a dead man at once, even if he had lived a thousand years. The golden flask you must fill with the water here," she added, pointing to a well in another corner. "It springs from the rock of eternity; you have only to sprinkle a few drops on a body and it will come to life again, if it had been a thousand years dead."

The prince thanked the queen for her gifts, and, bidding her farewell, went on his journey.

He soon arrived in the town where the mist-veiled queen reigned in her palace, but the whole city had changed, and he could scarcely find his way through the streets. In the palace itself all was still, and he wandered through the rooms without meeting anyone to stop him. At last he entered the queen's own chamber, and there she lay, with her embroidery still in her hands, fast asleep. He pulled at her dress, but she did not waken. Then a dreadful idea came over him, and he ran to the chamber where the needles had been kept, but it was quite empty. The queen had broken the last over the work she held in her hand, and with it the spell was broken too, and she lay dead.

Quick as thought the prince pulled out the golden flask, and sprinkled some drops of the water over the queen. In a moment she moved gently, and raising her head, opened her eyes.

"Oh, my dear friend, I am so glad you wakened me; I must have slept a long while!"

"You would have slept till eternity," answered the prince, "if I had not been here to waken you."

At these words the queen remembered about the needles. She knew now that she had been dead, and that the prince had restored her to life. She gave him thanks from her heart for what he had done, and vowed she would repay him if she ever got a chance.

The prince took his leave, and set out for the country of the bald-headed king. As he drew near the place he saw that the whole mountain had been dug away, and that the king was lying dead on the ground, his spade and bucket beside him. But as soon as the water from the golden flask touched him he yawned and stretched himself, and slowly rose to his feet. "Oh, my dear friend, I am so glad to see you," cried he, "I must have slept a long while!"

"You would have slept till eternity if I had not been here to waken you," answered the prince. And the king remembered the mountain, and the spell, and vowed to repay the service if he ever had a chance.

Further along the road which led to his old home the prince found the great tree torn up by its roots, and the king of the eagles sitting dead on the ground, with his wings outspread as if for flight. A flutter ran through the feathers as the drops of water fell on them, and the eagle lifted his beak from the ground and said: "Oh, how long I must have slept! How can I thank you for having awakened me, my dear, good friend!"

"You would have slept till eternity if I had not been here to waken you"; answered the prince. Then the king remembered about the tree, and knew that he had been dead, and promised, if ever he had the chance, to repay what the prince had done for him.

At last he reached the capital of his father's kingdom, but on reaching the place where the royal palace had stood, instead of the marble galleries where he used to play, there lay a great sulphur lake, its blue flames darting into the air. How was he to find his father and mother, and bring them back to life, if they were lying at the bottom of that horrible water? He turned away sadly and wandered back into the streets, hardly knowing where he was going; when a voice behind him cried: "Stop, prince, I have caught you at last! It is a thousand years since I first began to seek you." And there beside him stood the old, white-bearded, figure of Death. Swiftly he drew the ring from his finger, and the king of the eagles, the bald-headed king, and the mist-veiled queen, hastened to his rescue. In an instant they had seized upon Death and held him tight, till the prince should have time to reach the Land of Immortality. But they did not know how quickly Death could fly, and the prince had only one foot across the border, when he felt the other grasped from behind, and the voice of Death calling: "Halt! now you are mine."

The Queen of the Immortals was watching from her window, and cried to Death that he had no power in her kingdom, and that he must seek his prey elsewhere.

"Quite true," answered Death; "but his foot is in *my* kingdom, and that belongs to me!"

"At any rate half of him is mine," replied the Queen, "and what good can the other half do you? Half a man is no use, either to you or to me! But this once I will allow you to cross into my kingdom, and we will decide by a wager whose he is."

And so it was settled. Death stepped across the narrow line that surrounds the Land of Immortality, and the queen proposed the wager which was to decide the prince's fate. "I will throw him up into the sky," she said, "right to the back of the morning star, and if he falls down into this city, then he is mine. But if he should fall outside the walls, he shall belong to you."

In the middle of the city was a great open square, and here the queen wished the wager to take place. When all was ready, she put her foot under the foot of the prince and swung him into the air. Up, up, he went, high amongst the stars, and no man's eyes could follow him. Had she thrown him up straight? the queen wondered anxiously, for, if not, he would fall outside the walls, and she would lose him for ever. The moments seemed long while she and Death stood gazing up into the air, waiting to know whose prize the prince would be. Suddenly they both caught sight of a tiny speck no bigger than a wasp, right up in the blue. Was he coming straight? No! Yes! But as he was nearing the city, a light wind sprang up, and swayed him in the direction of the wall. Another second and he would have fallen half over it, when the queen sprang forward, seized him in her arms, and flung him into the castle. Then she commanded her servants to cast Death out of the city, which they did, with such hard blows that he never dared to show his face again in the Land of Immortality.

—*The Crimson Fairy Book* (1903)

The Princess
on the Glass Hill

NORSE

———◆◆◆———

ONCE upon a time there was a man who had a meadow
which lay on the side of a mountain, and in the meadow
there was a barn in which he stored hay. But there had
not been much hay in the barn for the last two years,
for every St. John's eve, when the grass was in the
height of its vigour, it was all eaten clean up, just as if a
whole flock of sheep had gnawed it down to the ground
during the night. This happened once, and it happened
twice, but then the man got tired of losing his crop, and
said to his sons—he had three of them, and the third
was called Cinderlad—that one of them must go and
sleep in the barn on St. John's night, for it was absurd
to let the grass be eaten up again, blade and stalk, as it
had been the last two years, and the one who went to
watch must keep a sharp look-out, the man said.

The eldest was quite willing to go to the meadow; he
would watch the grass, he said, and he would do it so
well that neither man, nor beast, nor even the devil
himself should have any of it. So when evening came he
went to the barn, and lay down to sleep, but when
night was drawing near there was such a rumbling and
such an earthquake that the walls and roof shook again,
and the lad jumped up and took to his heels as fast as
he could, and never even looked back, and the barn

remained empty that year just as it had been for the last two.

Next St. John's eve the man again said that he could not go on in this way, losing all the grass in the outlying field year after year, and that one of his sons must just go there and watch it, and watch well too. So the next oldest son was willing to show what he could do. He went to the barn and lay down to sleep, as his brother had done; but when night was drawing near there was a great rumbling, and then an earthquake, which was even worse than that on the former St. John's night, and when the youth heard it he was terrified, and went off, running as if for a wager.

The year after, it was Cinderlad's turn, but when he made ready to go the others laughed at him, and mocked him. "Well, you are just the right one to watch the hay, you who have never learnt anything but how to sit among the ashes and bake yourself!" said they. Cinderlad, however, did not trouble himself about what they said, but when evening drew near rambled away to the outlying field. When he got there he went into the barn and lay down, but in about an hour's time the rumbling and creaking began, and it was frightful to hear it. "Well, if it gets no worse than that, I can manage to stand it," thought Cinderlad. In a little time the creaking began again, and the earth quaked so that all the hay flew about the boy. "Oh, if it gets no worse than that I can manage to stand it," thought Cinderlad. But then came a third rumbling, and a third earthquake; so violent that the boy thought the walls and roof had fallen down, but when that was over everything suddenly grew as still as death around him. "I am pretty sure that it will come again," thought Cinderlad; but no, it did not. Everything was quiet, and everything stayed quiet, and when he had lain still a short time he heard something that sounded as if a horse were standing chewing just outside the barn door. He stole away to the door, which was ajar, to see what was there, and a horse was standing eating. It was so big, and fat, and

fine a horse that Cinderlad had never seen one like it
before, and a saddle and bridle lay upon it, and a
complete suit of armour for a knight, and everything
was of copper, and so bright that it shone again. "Ha,
ha! it is thou who eatest up our hay then," thought the
boy; "but I will stop that." So he made haste, and took
out his steel for striking fire, and threw it over the
horse, and then it had no power to stir from the spot,
and became so tame that the boy could do what he
liked with it. So he mounted it and rode away to a place
which no one knew of but himself, and there he tied it
up. When he went home again his brothers laughed
and asked how he had got on.

"You didn't lie long in the barn, if even you have
been so far as the field!" said they.

"I lay in the barn till the sun rose, but I saw nothing
and heard nothing, not I," said the boy. "God knows
what there was to make you two so frightened."

"Well, we shall soon see whether you have watched
the meadow or not," answered the brothers, but when
they got there the grass was all standing just as long and
as thick as it had been the night before.

The next St. John's eve it was the same thing once
again: neither of the two brothers dared to go to the
outlying field to watch the crop, but Cinderlad went,
and everything happened exactly the same as on the
previous St. John's eve: first there was a rumbling and
an earthquake, and then there was another, and then a
third; but all three earthquakes were much, very much
more violent than they had been the year before. Then
everything became still as death again, and the boy
heard something chewing outside the barn door, so he
stole as softly as he could to the door, which was
slightly ajar, and again there was a horse standing close
by the wall of the house, eating and chewing, and it was
far larger and fatter than the first horse, and it had a
saddle on its back, and a bridle was on it too, and a full
suit of armour for a knight, all of bright silver, and as
beautiful as anyone could wish to see. "Ho, ho!" thought

the boy, "is it thou who eatest up our hay in the night? but I will put a stop to that." So he took out his steel for striking fire, and threw it over the horse's mane, and the beast stood there as quiet as a lamb. Then the boy rode this horse, too, away to the place where he kept the other, and then went home again.

"I suppose you will tell us that you have watched well again this time," said the brothers.

"Well, so I have," said Cinderlad. So they went there again, and there the grass was, standing as high and as thick as it had been before, but that did not make them any kinder to Cinderlad.

When the third St. John's night came neither of the two elder brothers dared to lie in the outlying barn to watch the grass, for they had been so heartily frightened the night that they had slept there that they could not get over it, but Cinderlad dared to go, and everything happened just the same as on the two former nights. There were three earthquakes, each worse than the other, and the last flung the boy from one wall of the barn to the other, but then everything suddenly became still as death. When he had lain quietly a short time, he heard something chewing outside the barn door; then he once more stole to the door, which was slightly ajar, and behold, a horse was standing just outside it, which was much larger and fatter than the two others he had caught. "Ho, ho! it is thou, then, who art eating up our hay this time," thought the boy; "but I will put a stop to that." So he pulled out his steel for striking fire, and threw it over the horse, and it stood as still as if it had been nailed to the field, and the boy could do just what he liked with it. Then he mounted it and rode away to the place where he had the two others, and then he went home again. Then the two brothers mocked him just as they had done before, and told him that they could see that he must have watched the grass very carefully that night, for he looked just as if he were walking in his sleep; but Cinderlad did not trouble himself about that, but just bade them go to the field and see. They did go, and this time too the grass was standing, looking as fine and as thick as ever.

The King of the country in which Cinderlad's father dwelt had a daughter whom he would give to no one who could not ride up to the top of the glass hill, for there was a high, high hill of glass, slippery as ice, and it was close to the King's palace. Upon the very top of this the King's daughter was to sit with three gold apples in her lap, and the man who could ride up and take the three golden apples should marry her, and have half the kingdom. The King had this proclaimed in every church in the whole kingdom, and in many other kingdoms too. The Princess was very beautiful, and all who saw her fell violently in love with her, even in spite of themselves. So it is needless to say that all the princes and knights were eager to win her, and half the kingdom besides, and that for this cause they came riding thither from the very end of the world, dressed so splendidly that their raiments gleamed in the sunshine, and riding on horses which seemed to dance as they went, and there was not one of these princes who did not think that he was sure to win the Princess.

When the day appointed by the King had come, there was such a host of knights and princes under the glass hill that they seemed to swarm, and everyone who could walk or even creep was there too, to see who won the King's daughter. Cinderlad's two brothers were there too, but they would not hear of letting him go with them, for he was so dirty and black with sleeping and grubbing among the ashes that they said everyone would laugh at them if they were seen in the company of such an oaf.

"Well, then, I will go all alone by myself," said Cinderlad.

When the two brothers got to the glass hill, all the princes and knights were trying to ride up it, and their horses were in a foam; but it was all in vain, for no sooner did the horses set foot upon the hill than down they slipped, and there was not one which could get even so much as a couple of yards up. Nor was that strange, for the hill was as smooth as glass window-pane, and as steep as the side of a house. But they were all eager to win the King's daughter and half the kingdom, so they rode and they slipped, and thus it went on. At length all the horses were so tired that they could do no more, and so hot that the foam dropped from them and the riders were forced to give up the attempt. The King was just thinking that he would cause it to be proclaimed that the riding should begin afresh on the following day, when perhaps it might go better, when suddenly a knight came riding up on so fine a horse that no one had ever seen the like of it before, and the knight had armour of copper, and his bridle was of copper too, and all his accoutrements were so bright that they shone again. The other knights all called out to him that he might just as well spare himself the trouble of trying to ride up the glass hill, for it was of no use to try; but he did not heed them, and rode straight off to it, and went up as if it were nothing at all. Thus he rode for a long way—it may have been a third part of the way up—but when he had got so far he turned his horse round and rode down again. But the Princess thought that she had never yet seen so handsome a knight, and while he was riding up she was sitting thinking: "Oh! how I hope he may be able to come up to the top!" And when she saw that he was turning his horse back she threw one of the golden apples down after him, and it rolled into his shoe. But when he had come down from off the hill he rode away, and that so fast that no one knew what had become of him.

So all the princes and knights were bidden to present themselves before the King that night, so that he who had ridden so far up the glass hill might show the golden apple which the King's daughter had thrown down. But no one had anything to show. One knight presented himself after the other, and none could show the apple.

At night, too, Cinderlad's brothers came home again and had a long story to tell about the riding up the glass hill. At first, they said, there was not one who was able to get even so much as one step up, but then came a knight who had armour of copper, and a bridle of copper, and his armour and trappings were so bright that they shone to a great distance, and it was something like a sight to see him riding. He rode one-third of the way up the glass hill, and he could easily have ridden the whole of it if he had liked; but he had turned back, for he had made up his mind that that was enough for once. "Oh! I should have liked to see him too, that I should," said Cinderlad, who was as usual sitting by the chimney among the cinders. "You indeed!" said the brothers, "you look as if you were fit to be among such great lords, nasty beast that you are to sit there!"

Next day the brothers were for setting out again, and this time too Cinderlad begged them to let him go with them and see who rode; but no, they said he was not fit to do that, for he was much too ugly and dirty. "Well, well, then I will go all alone by myself," said Cinderlad. So the brothers went to the glass hill, and all the princes and knights began to ride again, and this time they had taken care to rough the shoes of their horses; but that did not help them: they rode and they slipped as they had done the day before, and not one of them could even get so far as a yard up the hill. When they had tired out their horses, so that they could do no more, they again had to stop altogether. But just as the King was thinking that it would be well to proclaim that the riding should take place next day for the last time, so that they might have one more chance, he suddenly bethought himself that it would be well to wait a little longer to see if the knight in copper armour would come on this day too. But nothing was to be seen of him. Just as they were still looking for him, however, came a knight riding on a steed that was much, much finer than that which the knight in copper armour had ridden, and this knight had silver armour and a silver

saddle and bridle, and all were so bright that they
shone and glistened when he was a long way off. Again
the other knights called to him, and said that he might
just as well give up the attempt to ride up the glass hill,
for it was useless to try; but the knight paid no heed to
that, but rode straight away to the glass hill, and went
still farther up than the knight in copper armour had
gone; but when he had ridden two-thirds of the way up
he turned his horse round, and rode down again. The
Princess liked this knight still better than she had liked
the other, and sat longing that he might be able to get up
above, and when she saw him turning back she threw
the second apple after him, and it rolled into his shoe,
and as soon as he had got down the glass hill he rode
away so fast that no one could see what had become of
him.

In the evening, when everyone was to appear before
the King and Princess, in order that he who had the
golden apple might show it, one knight went in after
the other, but none of them had a golden apple to
show.

At night the two brothers went home as they had
done the night before, and told how things had gone,
and how everyone had ridden, but no one had been
able to get up the hill. "But last of all," they said,
"came one in silver armour, and he had a silver bridle
on his horse, and a silver saddle, and oh, but he could
ride! He took his horse two-thirds of the way up the
hill, but then he turned back. He was a fine fellow,"
said the brothers, "and the Princess threw the second
golden apple to him!"

"Oh, how I should have liked to see him too!" said
Cinderlad.

"Oh, indeed! He was a little brighter than the ashes
that you sit grubbing among, you dirty black creature!"
said the brothers.

On the third day everything went just as on the
former days. Cinderlad wanted to go with them to look
at the riding, but the two brothers would not have him

in their company, and when they got to the glass hill there was no one who could ride even so far as a yard up it, and everyone waited for the knight in silver armour, but he was neither to be seen nor heard of. At last, after a long time, came a knight riding upon a horse that was such a fine one, its equal had never yet been seen. The knight had golden armour, and the horse a golden saddle and bridle, and these were all so bright that they shone and dazzled everyone, even while the knight was still at a great distance. The other princes and knights were not able even to call to tell him how useless it was to try to ascend the hill, so amazed were they at the sight of his magnificence. He rode straight away to the glass hill, and galloped up it as if it were no hill at all, so that the Princess had not even time to wish that he might get up the whole way. As soon as he had ridden to the top, he took the third golden apple from the lap of the Princess, and then turned his horse about and rode down again, and vanished from their sight before anyone was able to say a word to him.

When the two brothers came home again at night, they had much to tell of how the riding had gone off that day, and at last they told about the knight in the golden armour too. "He was a fine fellow, that was! Such another splendid knight is not to be found on earth!" said the brothers.

"Oh, how I should have liked to see him too!" said Cinderlad.

"Well, he shone nearly as brightly as the coal-heaps that thou art always lying raking amongst, dirty black creature that thou art!" said the brothers.

Next day all the knights and princes were to appear before the King and the Princess—it had been too late for them to do it the night before—in order that he who had the golden apple might produce it. They all went in turn, first princes, and then knights, but none of them had a golden apple.

"But somebody must have it," said the King, "for

with our own eyes we all saw a man ride up and take it."
So he commanded that everyone in the kingdom should
come to the palace, and see if he could show the apple.
And one after the other they all came, but no one had
the golden apple, and after a long, long time Cinderlad's
two brothers came likewise. They were the last of all,
so the King inquired of them if there was no one else in
the kingdom left to come.

"Oh, yes, we have a brother," said the two, "but he
never got the golden apple! He never left the cinder-
heap on any of the three days."

"Never mind that," said the King; "as everyone else
has come to the palace, let him come too."

So Cinderlad was forced to go to the King's palace.

"Hast thou the golden apple?" asked the King.

"Yes, here is the first, and here is the second, and
here is the third, too," said Cinderlad, and he took all
the three apples out of his pocket, and with that threw
off his sooty rags, and appeared there before them in
his bright golden armour, which gleamed as he stood.

"Thou shalt have my daughter, and the half of my
kingdom, and thou hast well earned both!" said the
King. So there was a wedding, and Cinderlad got the
King's daughter, and everyone made merry at the wedding, for all of them could make merry, though they
could not ride up the glass hill, and if they have not left
off their merry-making they must be at it still.

—*The Blue Fairy Book* (1889)

Puddocky

GERMAN

———— ◆◆◆ ————

THERE was once upon a time a poor woman who had
one little daughter called "Parsley." She was so called
because she liked eating parsley better than any other
food, indeed she would hardly eat anything else. Her
poor mother hadn't enough money always to be buying
parsley for her, but the child was so beautiful that she
could refuse her nothing, and so she went every night
to the garden of an old witch who lived near and stole
great branches of the coveted vegetable, in order to
satisfy her daughter.

This remarkable taste of the fair Parsley soon became
known, and the theft was discovered. The witch called
the girl's mother to her, and proposed that she should
let her daughter come and live with her, and then she
could eat as much parsley as she liked. The mother was
quite pleased with this suggestion, and so the beautiful
Parsley took up her abode with the old witch.

One day three Princes, whom their father had sent
abroad to travel, came to the town where Parsley lived
and perceived the beautiful girl combing and plaiting
her long black hair at the window. In one moment they
all fell hopelessly in love with her, and longed ardently
to have the girl for their wife; but hardly had they with
one breath expressed their desire than, mad with jeal-

313

ousy, they drew their swords and all three set upon each other. The struggle was so violent and the noise so loud that the old witch heard it, and said at once "Of course Parsley is at the bottom of all this."

And when she had convinced herself that this was so, she stepped forward, and, full of wrath over the quarrels and feuds Parsley's beauty gave rise to, she cursed the girl and said, "I wish you were an ugly toad, sitting under a bridge at the other end of the world."

Hardly were the words out of her mouth than Parsley was changed into a toad and vanished from their sight. The Princes, now that the cause of their dispute was removed, put up their swords, kissed each other affectionately, and returned to their father.

The King was growing old and feeble, and wished to yield his sceptre and crown in favour of one of his sons, but he couldn't make up his mind which of the three he should appoint as his successor. He determined that fate should decide for him. So he called his three children to him and said, "My dear sons, I am growing old, and am weary of reigning, but I can't make up my mind to which of you three I should yield my crown, for I love you all equally. At the same time I would like the best and cleverest of you to rule over my people. I have, therefore, determined to set you three tasks to do, and the one that performs them best shall be my heir. The first thing I shall ask you to do is to bring me a piece of linen a hundred yards long, so fine that it will go through a gold ring." The sons bowed low, and, promising to do their best, they started on their journey without further delay.

The two elder brothers took many servants and carriages with them, but the youngest set out quite alone. In a short time they came to three cross roads; two of them were gay and crowded, but the third was dark and lonely.

The two elder brothers chose the more frequented ways, but the youngest, bidding them farewell, set out on the dreary road.

Wherever fine linen was to be bought, there the two elder brothers hastened. They loaded their carriages with bales of the finest linen they could find and then returned home.

The youngest brother, on the other hand, went on his weary way for many days; and nowhere did he come across any linen that would have done. So he journeyed on, and his spirits sank with every step. At last he came to a bridge which stretched over a deep river flowing through a flat and marshy land. Before crossing the bridge he sat down on the banks of the stream and sighed dismally over his sad fate. Suddenly a misshapen toad crawled out of the swamp, and, sitting down opposite him, asked: "What's the matter with you, my dear Prince?"

The Prince answered impatiently. "There's not much good my telling you, Puddocky, for you couldn't help me if I did."

"Don't be too sure of that," replied the toad; "tell me your trouble and we'll see."

Then the Prince became most confidential and told the little creature why he had been sent out of his father's kingdom.

"Prince, I will certainly help you," said the toad, and, crawling back into her swamp, she returned dragging after her a piece of linen not bigger than a finger, which she lay before the Prince, saying, "Take this home, and you'll see it will help you."

The Prince had no wish to take such an insignificant bundle with him; but he didn't like to hurt Puddocky's feelings by refusing it, so he took up the little packet, put it in his pocket, and bade the little toad farewell. Puddocky watched the Prince till he was out of sight and then crept back into the water.

The further the Prince went the more he noticed that the pocket in which the little roll of linen lay became heavier, and in proportion his heart grew lighter. And so, greatly comforted, he returned to the Court of his father, and arrived home just at the same time as his brothers with their caravans. The King was delighted to see them all again, and at once drew the ring from his finger and the trial began. In all the waggon-loads there was not one piece of linen the tenth part of which would go through the ring, and the two elder brothers, who had at first sneered at their youngest brother for returning with no baggage, began to feel rather small. But what were their feelings when he drew a bale of linen out of his pocket which in fineness, softness, and purity of colour was unsurpassable! The threads were hardly visible, and it went through the ring without the smallest difficulty, at the same time measuring a hundred yards quite correctly.

The father embraced his fortunate son, and commanded the rest of the linen to be thrown into the water; then, turning to his children he said, "Now, dear Princes, prepare yourselves for the second task. You must bring me back a little dog that will go comfortably into a walnut-shell."

The sons were all in despair over this demand, but as they each wished to win the crown, they determined to do their best, and after a very few days set out on their travels again.

At the cross roads they separated once more. The youngest went by himself along his lonely way, but this time he felt much more cheerful. Hardly had he sat down under the bridge and heaved a sigh, than Puddocky came out; and, sitting down opposite him, asked, "What's wrong with you now, dear Prince?"

The Prince, who this time never doubted the little toad's power to help him, told her his difficulty at once. "Prince, I will help you," said the toad again, and crawled back into her swamp as fast as her short little legs would carry her. She returned, dragging a hazel-nut behind her, which she laid at the Prince's feet and said, "Take this nut home with you and tell your father to crack it very carefully, and you'll see then what will happen." The Prince thanked her heartily and went on his way in the best of spirits, while the little puddock crept slowly back into the water.

When the Prince got home he found his brothers had just arrived with great waggon-loads of little dogs of all sorts. The King had a walnut shell ready, and the trial began; but not one of the dogs the two eldest sons had brought with them would in the least fit into the shell. When they had tried all their little dogs, the youngest son handed his father the hazel-nut, with a modest bow, and begged him to crack it carefully. Hardly had the old King done so than a lovely tiny dog sprang out of the nutshell, and ran about on the King's hand, wagging its tail and barking lustily at all the other little dogs. The joy of the Court was great. The father again embraced his fortunate son, commanded the rest of the small dogs to be thrown into the water and drowned, and once more addressed his sons. "The two most difficult tasks have been performed. Now listen to the third and last: whoever brings the fairest wife home with him shall be my heir."

This demand seemed so easy and agreeable and the reward was so great, that the Princes lost no time in setting forth on their travels. At the cross roads the two elder brothers debated if they should go the same way as the youngest, but when they saw how dreary and deserted it looked they made up their minds that it would be impossible to find what they sought in these wilds, and so they stuck to their former paths.

The youngest was very depressed this time and said to himself, "Anything else Puddocky could have helped me in, but this task is quite beyond her power. How could she ever find a beautiful wife for me? Her swamps are wide and empty, and no human beings dwell there; only frogs and toads and other creatures of that sort." However, he sat down as usual under the bridge, and this time he sighed from the bottom of his heart.

In a few minutes the toad stood in front of him and asked, "What's the matter with you now, my dear Prince?"

"Oh, Puddocky, this time you can't help me, for the task is beyond even your power," replied the Prince.

"Still," answered the toad, "you may as well tell me your difficulty, for who knows but I mayn't be able to help you this time also."

The Prince then told her the task they had been set to do. "I'll help you right enough, my dear Prince," said the little toad; "just you go home, and I'll soon follow you." With these words, Puddocky, with a spring quite unlike her usual slow movements, jumped into the water and disappeared.

The Prince rose up and went sadly on his way, for he didn't believe it possible that the little toad could really help him in his present difficulty. He had hardly gone a few steps when he heard a sound behind him, and, looking round, he saw a carriage made of cardboard, drawn by six big rats, coming towards him. Two hedgehogs rode in front as outriders, and on the box sat a fat mouse as coachman, and behind stood two little frogs as footmen. In the carriage itself sat Puddocky, who kissed her hand to the Prince out of the window as she passed by.

Sunk deep in thought over the fickleness of fortune that had granted him two of his wishes and now seemed about to deny him the last and best, the Prince hardly noticed the absurd equipage, and still less did he feel inclined to laugh at its comic appearance.

The carriage drove on in front of him for some time and then turned a corner. But what was his joy and surprise when suddenly, round the same corner, but coming towards him, there appeared a beautiful coach drawn by six splendid horses, with outriders, coachmen, footmen and other servants all in the most gorgeous liveries, and seated in the carriage was the most beautiful woman the Prince had ever seen, and in whom he at once recognised the beautiful Parsley, for whom his heart had formerly burned. The carriage stopped when it reached him, and the footmen sprang down and opened the door for him. He got in and sat down beside the beautiful Parsley, and thanked her heartily for her help, and told her how much he loved her.

And so he arrived at his father's capital, at the same moment as his brothers who had returned with many carriage-loads of beautiful women. But when they were all led before the King, the whole Court with one consent awarded the prize of beauty to the fair Parsley.

The old King was delighted, and embraced his thrice fortunate son and his new daughter-in-law tenderly, and appointed them as his successors to the throne. But he commanded the other women to be thrown into the water and drowned, like the bales of linen and the little dogs. The Prince married Puddocky and reigned long and happily with her, and if they aren't dead I suppose they are living still.

—*The Green Fairy Book* (1892)

The Ratcatcher

FRENCH

———◆◆◆———

A VERY long time ago the town of Hamel in Germany was invaded by bands of rats, the like of which had never been seen before nor will ever be again.

They were great black creatures that ran boldly in broad daylight through the streets, and swarmed so, all over the houses, that people at last could not put their hand or foot down anywhere without touching one. When dressing in the morning they found them in their breeches and petticoats, in their pockets and in their boots; and when they wanted a morsel to eat, the voracious horde had swept away everything from cellar to garret. The night was even worse. As soon as the lights were out, these untiring nibblers set to work. And everywhere, in the ceilings, in the floors, in the cupboards, at the doors, there was a chase and a rummage, and so furious a noise of gimlets, pincers, and saws, that a deaf man could not have rested for one hour together.

Neither cats nor dogs, nor poison nor traps, nor prayers nor candles burnt to all the saints—nothing would do anything. The more they killed the more came. And the inhabitants of Hamel began to go to the dogs (not that *they* were of much use), when one Friday there arrived in the town a man with a queer face, who played the bagpipes and sang this refrain:

"Qui vivra verra:
Le voilà,
Le preneur des rats."

He was a great gawky fellow, dry and bronzed, with a crooked nose, a long rat-tail moustache, two great yellow piercing and mocking eyes, under a large felt hat set off by a scarlet cock's feather. He was dressed in a green jacket with a leather belt and red breeches, and on his feet were sandals fastened by thongs passed round his legs in the gipsy fashion.

That is how he may be seen to this day, painted on a window of the cathedral of Hamel.

He stopped on the great market-place before the town hall, turned his back on the church and went on with his music, singing:

"Who lives shall see:
This is he,
The ratcatcher."

The town council had just assembled to consider once more this plague of Egypt, from which no one could save the town.

The stranger sent word to the counsellors that, if they would make it worth his while, he would rid them of all their rats before night, down to the very last.

"Then he is a sorcerer!" cried the citizens with one voice; "we must beware of him."

The Town Counsellor, who was considered clever, reassured them.

He said: "Sorcerer or no, if this bagpiper speaks the truth, it was he who sent us this horrible vermin that he wants to rid us of to-day for money. Well, we must learn to catch the devil in his own snares. You leave it to me."

"Leave it to the Town Counsellor," said the citizens one to another.

And the stranger was brought before them.

"Before night," said he, "I shall have despatched all the rats in Hamel if you will but pay me a *gros* a head."

"A *gros* a head!" cried the citizens, "but that will come to millions of florins!"

The Town Counsellor simply shrugged his shoulders and said to the stranger:

"A bargain! To work; the rats will be paid one *gros* a head as you ask."

The bagpiper announced that he would operate that very evening when the moon rose. He added that the inhabitants should at that hour leave the streets free, and content themselves with looking out of their windows at what was passing, and that it would be a pleasant spectacle. When the people of Hamel heard of the bargain, they too exclaimed: "A *gros* a head! but this will cost us a deal of money!"

"Leave it to the Town Counsellor," said the town council with a malicious air. And the good people of Hamel repeated with their counsellors, "Leave it to the Town Counsellor."

Towards nine at night the bagpiper re-appeared on the market-place. He turned, as at first, his back to the church, and the moment the moon rose on the horizon, "Trarira, trari!" the bagpipes resounded.

It was first a slow, caressing sound, then more and more lively and urgent, and so sonorous and piercing that it penetrated as far as the farthest alleys and retreats of the town.

Soon from the bottom of the cellars, the top of the garrets, from under all the furniture, from all the nooks and corners of the houses, out come the rats, search for the door, fling themselves into the street, and trip, trip, trip, begin to run in file towards the front of the town hall, so squeezed together that they covered the pavement like the waves of flooded torrent.

When the square was quite full the bagpiper faced about, and, still playing briskly, turned towards the river that runs at the foot of the walls of Hamel.

Arrived there he turned round; the rats were following.

"Hop! hop!" he cried, pointing with his finger to the middle of the stream, where the water whirled and was drawn down as if through a funnel. And hop! hop! without hesitating, the rats took the leap, swam straight to the funnel, plunged in head foremost and disappeared.

The plunging continued thus without ceasing till midnight.

At last, dragging himself with difficulty, came a big rat, white with age, and stopped on the bank.

It was the king of the band.

"Are they all there, friend Blanchet?" asked the bagpiper.

"They are all there," replied friend Blanchet.

"And how many were they?"

"Nine hundred and ninety thousand, nine hundred and ninety-nine."

"Well reckoned?"

"Well reckoned."

"Then go and join them, old sire, and *au revoir*."

Then the old white rat sprang in his turn into the river, swam to the whirlpool and disappeared.

When the bagpiper had thus concluded his business he went to bed at his inn. And for the first time during three months the people of Hamel slept quietly through the night.

The next morning, at nine o'clock, the bagpiper repaired to the town hall, where the town council awaited him.

"All your rats took a jump into the river yesterday," said he to the counsellors, "and I guarantee that not one of them comes back. They were nine hundred and ninety thousand, nine hundred and ninety-nine, at one *gros* a head. Reckon!"

"Let us reckon the heads first. One *gros* a head is one head the *gros*. Where are the heads?"

The ratcatcher did not expect this treacherous stroke. He paled with anger and his eyes flashed fire.

"The heads!" cried he, "if you care about them, go and find them in the river."

"So," replied the Town Counsellor, "you refuse to hold to the terms of your agreement? We ourselves could refuse you all payment. But you have been of use to us, and we will not let you go without a recompense," and he offered him fifty crowns.

"Keep your recompense for yourself," replied the ratcatcher proudly. "If you do not pay me I will be paid by your heirs."

Thereupon he pulled his hat down over his eyes, went hastily out of the hall, and left the town without speaking to a soul.

When the Hamel people heard how the affair had ended they rubbed their hands, and with no more scruple than their Town Counsellor, they laughed over the ratcatcher, who, they said, was caught in his own trap. But what made them laugh above all was his threat of getting himself paid by their heirs. Ha! they wished that they only had such creditors for the rest of their lives.

Next day, which was a Sunday, they all went gaily to church, thinking that after Mass they would at last be able to eat some good thing that the rats had not tasted before them.

They never suspected the terrible surprise that awaited them on their return home. No children anywhere, they had all disappeared!

"Our children! where are our poor children?" was the cry that was soon heard in all the streets.

Then through the east door of the town came three little boys, who cried and wept, and this is what they told:

While the parents were at church a wonderful music had resounded. Soon all the little boys and all the little girls that had been left at home had gone out, attracted by the magic sounds, and had rushed to the great market-place. There they found the ratcatcher playing his bagpipes at the same spot as the evening before.

Then the stranger had begun to walk quickly, and they had followed, running, singing and dancing to the sound of the music, as far as the foot of the mountain which one sees on entering Hamel. At their approach the mountain had opened a little, and the bagpiper had gone in with them, after which it had closed again. Only the three little ones who told the adventure had remained outside, as if by a miracle. One was bandy-legged and could not run fast enough; the other, who had left the house in haste, one foot shod the other bare, had hurt himself against a big stone and could not walk without difficulty; the third had arrived in time, but in hurrying to go in with the others had struck so violently against the wall of the mountain that he fell backwards at the moment it closed upon his comrades.

At this story the parents redoubled their lamentations. They ran with pikes and mattocks to the mountain, and searched till evening to find the opening by which their children had disappeared, without being able to find it. At last, the night falling, they returned desolate to Hamel.

But the most unhappy of all was the Town Counsellor, for he lost three little boys and two pretty little girls, and to crown all, the people of Hamel overwhelmed him with reproaches, forgetting that the evening before they had all agreed with him.

What had become of all these unfortunate children?

The parents always hoped they were not dead, and that the ratcatcher, who certainly must have come out of the mountain, would have taken them with him to his country. That is why for several years they sent in search of them to different countries, but no one ever came on the trace of the poor little ones.

It was not till much later that anything was to be heard of them.

About one hundred and fifty years after the event, when there was no longer one left of the fathers, mothers, brothers or sisters of that day, there arrived one evening in Hamel some merchants of Bremen returning from the East, who asked to speak with the citizens. They told that they, in crossing Hungary, had sojourned in a mountainous country called Transylvania, where the inhabitants only spoke German, while all around them nothing was spoken but Hungarian. These people also declared that they came from Germany, but they did not know how they chanced to be in this strange country. "Now," said the merchants of Bremen, "these Germans cannot be other than the descendants of the lost children of Hamel."

The people of Hamel did not doubt it; and since that day they regard it as certain that the Transylvanians of Hungary are their country folk, whose ancestors, as children, were brought there by the ratcatcher. There are more difficult things to believe than that.

—*The Red Fairy Book* (1890)

Rübezahl

GERMAN

————◆◆————

OVER all the vast under-world the mountain Gnome
Rübezahl was lord; and busy enough the care of his
dominions kept him. There were the endless treasure
chambers to be gone through, and the hosts of gnomes
to be kept to their tasks. Some built strong barriers to
hold back the fiery rivers in the earth's heart, and some
had scalding vapours to change dull stones to precious
metal, or were hard at work filling every cranny of the
rocks with diamonds and rubies; for Rübezahl loved all
pretty things. Sometimes the fancy would take him to
leave those gloomy regions, and come out upon the
green earth for a while, and bask in the sunshine and
hear the birds sing. And as gnomes live many hundreds
of years he saw strange things. For, the first time he
came up, the great hills were covered with thick forests, in which wild animals roamed, and Rübezahl
watched the fierce fights between bear and bison, or
chased the grey wolves, or amused himself by rolling
great rocks down into the desolate valleys, to hear the
thunder of their fall echoing among the hills. But the
next time he ventured above ground, what was his
surprise to find everything changed! The dark woods
were hewn down, and in their place appeared blossoming
orchards surrounding cosy-looking thatched cottages;

from every chimney the blue smoke curled peacefully
into the air, sheep and oxen fed in the flowery meadows, while from the shade of the hedges came the
music of the shepherd's pipe. The strangeness and pleas-
antness of the sight so delighted the gnome that he
never thought of resenting the intrusion of these unexpected guests, who, without saying "by your leave" or
"with your leave," had made themselves so very much
at home upon his hills; nor did he wish to interfere with
their doings, but left them in quiet possession of their
homes, as a good householder leaves in peace the swal-
lows who have built their nests under his eaves. He was
indeed greatly minded to make friends with this being
called "man," so, taking the form of an old field labourer,
he entered the service of a farmer. Under his care all
the crops flourished exceedingly, but the master proved
to be wasteful and ungrateful, and Rübezahl soon left
him, and went to be shepherd to his next neighbour.
He tended the flock so diligently, and knew so well
where to lead the sheep to the sweetest pastures, and
where among the hills to look for any who strayed
away, that they too prospered under his care, and not
one was lost or torn by wolves; but this new master was
a hard man, and begrudged him his well-earned wages.
So he ran away and went to serve the judge. Here he
upheld the law with might and main, and was a terror
to thieves and evildoers; but the judge was a bad man,
who took bribes, and despised the law. Rübezahl would
not be the tool of an unjust man, and so he told his
master, who thereupon ordered him to be thrown into
prison. Of course that did not trouble the gnome at all,
he simply got out through the keyhole, and went away
down to his underground palace, very much disappointed by his first experience of mankind. But, as time
went on, he forgot the disagreeable things that had
happened to him, and thought he would take another
look at the upper world.

So he stole into the valley, keeping himself carefully
hidden in copse or hedgerow, and very soon met with

The Gnome falls in love with the Princess

an adventure; for, peeping through a screen of leaves, he saw before him a green lawn where stood a charming maiden, fresh as the spring, and beautiful to look upon. Around her upon the grass lay her young companions, as if they had thrown themselves down to rest after some merry game. Beyond them flowed a little brook, into which a waterfall leapt from a high rock, filling the air with its pleasant sound, and making a coolness even in the sultry noontide. The sight of the maiden so pleased the gnome that, for the first time, he wished himself a mortal; and, longing for a better view of the gay company, he changed himself into a raven and perched upon an oaktree which overhung the brook. But he soon found that this was not at all a good plan. He could only see with a raven's eyes, and feel as a raven feels; and a nest of field-mice at the foot of the tree interested him far more than the sport of the maidens. When he understood this he flew down again in a great hurry into the thicket, and took the form of a handsome young man—that was the best way—and he fell in love with the girl then and there. The fair maiden was the daughter of the king of the country, and she often wandered in the forest with her play fellows gathering the wild flowers and fruits, till the midday heat drove the merry band to the shady lawn by the brook to rest, or to bathe in the cool waters. On this particular morning the fancy took them to wander off again into the wood. This was Master Rübezahl's opportunity. Stepping out of his hiding-place he stood in the midst of the little lawn, weaving his magic spells, till slowly all about him changed, and when the maidens returned at noon to their favourite resting-place they stood lost in amazement, and almost fancied that they must be dreaming. The red rocks had become white marble and alabaster; the stream that murmured and struggled before in its rocky bed, flowed in silence now in its smooth channel, from which a clear fountain leapt, to fall again in showers of diamond drops, now on this side now on that, as the wandering breeze scattered it.

Daisies and forget-me-nots fringed its brink, while tall hedges of roses and jasmine ringed it round, making the sweetest and daintiest bower imaginable. To the right and left of the waterfall opened out a wonderful grotto, its walls and arches glittering with many-coloured rock-crystals, while in every niche were spread out strange fruits and sweetmeats, the very sight of which made the princess long to taste them. She hesitated a while, however, scarcely able to believe her eyes, and not knowing if she should enter the enchanted spot or fly from it. But at length curiosity prevailed, and she and her companions explored to their heart's content, and tasted and examined everything, running hither and thither in high glee, and calling merrily to each other.

At last, when they were quite weary, the princess cried out suddenly that nothing would content her but to bathe in the marble pool, which certainly did look very inviting; and they all went gaily to this new amusement. The princess was ready first, but scarcely had she slipped over the rim of the pool when down—down—down she sank, and vanished in its depths before her frightened playmates could seize her by so much as a lock of her floating golden hair!

Loudly did they weep and wail, running about the brink of the pool, which looked so shallow and so clear, but which had swallowed up their princess before their eyes. They even sprang into the water and tried to dive after her, but in vain; they only floated like corks in the enchanted pool, and could not keep under water for a second.

They saw at last that there was nothing for it but to carry to the king the sad tidings of his beloved daughter's disappearance. And what great weeping and lamentation there was in the palace when the dreadful news was told! The king tore his robes, dashed his golden crown from his head, and hid his face in his purple mantle for grief and anguish at the loss of the princess. After the first outburst of wailing, however, he took heart and hurried off to see for himself the scene of this strange adventure, thinking, as people will in sorrow, that there might be some mistake after all. But when he reached the spot, behold, all was changed again! The glittering grotto described to him by the maidens had completely vanished, and so had the marble bath, the bower of jasmine; instead, all was a tangle of flowers, as it had been of old. The king was so much perplexed that he threatened the princess's playfellows with all sorts of punishments if they would not confess something about her disappearance; but as they only repeated the same story he presently put down the whole affair to the work of some sprite or goblin, and tried to console himself for his loss by ordering a grand hunt; for kings cannot bear to be troubled about anything long.

Meanwhile the princess was not at all unhappy in the palace of her elfish lover.

When the water-nymphs, who were hiding in readiness, had caught her and dragged her out of the sight of her terrified maidens, she herself had not had time to be frightened. They swam with her quickly by strange underground ways to a palace so splendid that her father's seemed but a poor cottage in comparison with it, and when she recovered from her astonishment she found herself seated upon a couch, wrapped in a wonderful robe of satin fastened with a silken girdle, while beside her knelt a young man who whispered the sweetest speeches imaginable in her ear. The gnome, for he it was, told her all about himself and his great underground kingdom, and presently led her through the many rooms and halls of the palace, and showed her the rare and wonderful things displayed in them till she was fairly dazzled at the sight of so much splendour. On three sides of the castle lay a lovely garden with masses of gay, sweet flowers, and velvet lawns all cool and shady, which pleased the eye of the princess. The fruit trees were hung with golden and rosy apples, and nightingales sang in every bush, as the gnome and the princess wandered in the leafy alleys, sometimes gazing at the moon, sometimes pausing to gather the rarest flowers for her adornment. And all the time he was thinking to himself that never, during the hundreds of years he had lived, had he seen so charming a maiden. But the princess felt no such happiness; in spite of all the magic delights around her she was sad, though she tried to seem content for fear of displeasing the gnome. However, he soon perceived her melancholy, and in a thousand ways strove to dispel the cloud, but in vain. At last he said to himself: "Men are sociable creatures, like bees or ants. Doubtless this lovely mortal is pining for company. Who is there I can find for her to talk to?"

Thereupon he hastened into the nearest field and dug up a dozen or so of different roots—carrots, turnips, and radishes—and laying them carefully in an elegant basket brought them to the princess, who sat pensive in the shade of the rose-bower.

"Loveliest daughter of earth," said the gnome, "banish all sorrow; no more shall you be lonely in my dwelling. In this basket is all you need to make this spot delightful to you. Take this little many-coloured wand, and with a touch give to each root the form you desire to see."

With this he left her, and the princess, without an instant's delay, opened the basket, and touching a turnip, cried eagerly: "Brunhilda, my dear Brunhilda! come to me quickly!" And sure enough there was Brunhilda, joyfully hugging and kissing her beloved princess, and chattering as gaily as in the old days.

This sudden appearance was so delightful that the princess could hardly believe her own eyes, and was quite beside herself with the joy of having her dear playfellow with her once more. Hand in hand they wandered about the enchanted garden, and gathered the golden apples from the trees, and when they were tired of this amusement the princess led her friend through all the wonderful rooms of the palace, until at last they came to the one in which were kept all the marvellous dresses and ornaments the gnome had given to his hoped-for bride. There they found so much to amuse them that the hours passed like minutes. Veils, girdles, and necklaces were tried on and admired, the imitation Brunhilda knew so well how to behave herself, and showed so much taste that nobody would ever have suspected that she was nothing but a turnip after all. The gnome, who had secretly been keeping an eye upon them, was very pleased with himself for having so well understood the heart of a woman; and the princess seemed to him even more charming than before. She did not forget to touch the rest of the roots with her magic wand, and soon had all her maidens about her, and even, as she had two tiny radishes to spare, her favourite cat, and her little dog whose name was Beni.

And now all went cheerfully in the castle. The princess gave to each of the maidens her task, and never was mistress better served. For a whole week she enjoyed the delight of her pleasant company undisturbed. They all sang, they danced, they played from morning to night; only the princess noticed that day by day the fresh young faces of her maidens grew pale and wan, and the mirror in the great marble hall showed her that she alone still kept her rosy bloom, while Brunhilda and the rest faded visibly. They assured her that all was well with them; but, nevertheless, they continued to waste away, and day by day it became harder to them to take part in the games of the princess, till at last, one fine morning, when the princess started from bed and hastened out to join her gay playfellows, she shuddered and started back at the sight of a group of shrivelled crones, with bent backs and trembling limbs, who supported their tottering steps with staves and crutches, and coughed dismally. A little nearer to the hearth lay the once frolicsome Beni, with all four feet stretched stiffly out, while the sleek cat seemed too weak to raise his head from his velvet cushion.

The horrified princess fled to the door to escape from the sight of this mournful company, and called loudly for the gnome, who appeared at once, humbly anxious to do her bidding.

"Malicious Sprite," she cried, "why do you begrudge me my playmates—the greatest delight of my lonely hours? Isn't this solitary life in such a desert bad enough without your turning the castle into a hospital for the aged? Give my maidens back their youth and health this very minute, or I will never love you!"

"Sweetest and fairest of damsels," cried the gnome, "do not be angry; everything that is in my power I will do—but do not ask the impossible. So long as the sap was fresh in the roots the magic staff could keep them in the forms you desired, but as the sap dried up they withered away. But never trouble yourself about that, dearest one, a basket of fresh turnips will soon set matters right, and you can speedily call up again every form you wish to see. The great green patch in the garden will provide you with a more lively company."

So saying the gnome took himself off. And the princess with her magic wand touched the wrinkled old women, and left them the withered roots they really were, to be thrown upon the rubbish heap; and with light feet skipped off across to the meadow to take possession of the freshly filled basket. But to her surprise she could not find it anywhere. Up and down the garden she searched, spying into every corner, but not a sign of it was to be found. By the trellis of grape vines she met the gnome, who was so much embarrassed at the sight of her that she became aware of his confusion while he was still quite a long way off.

"You are trying to tease me," she cried, as soon as she saw him. "Where have you hidden the basket? I have been looking for it at least an hour."

"Dear queen of my heart," answered he, "I pray you to forgive my carelessness. I promised more than I could perform. I have sought all over the land for the roots you desire; but they are gathered in, and lie drying in musty cellars, and the fields are bare and desolate, for below in the valley winter reigns, only here in your presence spring is held fast, and wherever your foot is set the gay flowers bloom. Have patience for a little, and then without fail you shall have your puppets to play with."

Almost before the gnome had finished, the disappointed princess turned away, and marched off to her own apartments, without deigning to answer him.

The gnome, however, set off above ground as speedily as possible, and disguising himself as a farmer, bought an ass in the nearest market-town, and brought it back loaded with sacks of turnip, carrot, and radish seed. With this he sowed a great field, and sent a vast army of his goblins to watch and tend it, and to bring up the fiery rivers from the heart of the earth near enough to warm and encourage the sprouting seeds. Thus fostered they grew and flourished marvellously, and promised a goodly crop.

The princess wandered about the field day by day, no other plants or fruits in all her wonderful garden pleased her as much as these roots; but still her eyes were full of discontent. And, best of all, she loved to while away the hours in a shady fir-wood, seated upon the bank of a little stream, into which she would cast the flowers she had gathered and watch them float away.

The gnome tried hard by every means in his power to please the princess and win her love, but little did he guess the real reason of his lack of success. He imagined that she was too young and inexperienced to care for him; but that was a mistake, for the truth was that another image already filled her heart. The young Prince Ratibor, whose lands joined her father's, had won the heart of the princess; and the lovers had been looking forward to the coming of their wedding-day when the bride's mysterious disappearance took place. The sad news drove Ratibor distracted, and as the days went on, and nothing could be heard of the princess, he forsook his castle and the society of men, and spent his days in the wild forests, roaming about and crying her name aloud to the trees and rocks. Meanwhile, the maiden, in her gorgeous prison, sighed in secret over her grief, not wishing to arouse the gnome's suspicions. In her own mind she was wondering if by any means she might escape from her captivity, and at last she hit upon a plan.

By this time spring once more reigned in the valley, and the gnome sent the fires back to their places in the deeps of the earth, for the roots which they had kept warm through all the cruel winter had now come to their full size. Day by day the princess pulled up some of them, and made experiments with them, conjuring up now this longed-for person, and now that, just for the pleasure of seeing them as they appeared; but she really had another purpose in view.

One day she changed a tiny turnip into a bee, and sent him off to bring her some news of her lover.

"Fly, dear little bee, towards the east," said she, "to my beloved Ratibor, and softly hum into his ear that I love him only, but that I am a captive in the gnome's palace under the mountains. Do not forget a single word of my greeting, and bring me back a message from my beloved."

So the bee spread his shining wings and flew away to do as he was bidden; but before he was out of sight a greedy swallow made a snatch at him, and to the great grief of the princess her messenger was eaten up then and there.

After that, by the power of the wonderful wand she summoned a cricket, and taught him this greeting:

"Hop, little cricket, to Ratibor, and chirp in his ear that I love him only, but that I am held captive by the gnome in his palace under the mountains."

So the cricket hopped off gaily, determined to do his best to deliver his message; but, alas! a long-legged stork who was prancing along the same road caught him in her cruel beak, and before he could say a word he had disappeared down her throat.

These two unlucky ventures did not prevent the princess from trying once more.

This time she changed the turnip into a magpie.

"Flutter from tree to tree, chattering bird," said she, "till you come to Ratibor, my love. Tell him that I am a captive, and bid him come with horses and men, the third day from this, to the hill that rises from the Thorny Valley."

The magpie listened, hopped awhile from branch to branch, and then darted away, the princess watching him anxiously as far as she could see.

Now Prince Ratibor was still spending his life in wandering about the woods, and not even the beauty of the spring could soothe his grief.

One day, as he sat in the shade of an oak tree, dreaming of his lost princess, and sometimes crying her name aloud, he seemed to hear another voice reply to his, and, starting up, he gazed around him, but he could see no one, and he had just made up his mind that he must be mistaken, when the same voice called again, and, looking up sharply, he saw a magpie which hopped to and fro among the twigs. Then Ratibor heard with surprise that the bird was indeed calling him by name.

"Poor chatterpie," said he; "who taught you to say that name, which belongs to an unlucky mortal who wishes the earth would open and swallow up him and his memory for ever?"

Thereupon he caught up a great stone, and would have hurled it at the magpie, if it had not at that moment uttered the name of the princess.

This was so unexpected that the prince's arm fell helplessly to his side at the sound, and he stood motionless.

But the magpie in the tree, who, like all the rest of his family, was not happy unless he could be for ever chattering, began to repeat the message the princess had taught him; and as soon as he understood it, Prince Ratibor's heart filled with joy. All his gloom and misery vanished in a moment, and he anxiously questioned the welcome messenger as to the fate of the princess.

But the magpie knew no more than the lesson he had learnt, so he soon fluttered away; while the prince hurried back to his castle to gather together a troop of horsemen, full of courage for whatever might befall.

The princess meanwhile was craftily pursuing her plan of escape. She left off treating the gnome with coldness and indifference; indeed, there was a look in her eyes which encouraged him to hope that she might some day return his love, and the idea pleased him mightily. The next day, as soon as the sun rose, she made her appearance decked as a bride, in the wonderful robes and jewels which the fond gnome had prepared for her. Her golden hair was braided and crowned with myrtle blossoms, and her flowing veil sparkled with gems. In these magnificent garments she went to meet the gnome upon the great terrace.

"Loveliest of maidens," he stammered, bowing low before her, "let me gaze into your dear eyes, and read in them that you will no longer refuse my love, but will make me the happiest being the sun shines upon."

So saying he would have drawn aside her veil; but the princess only held it more closely about her.

"Your constancy has overcome me," she said; "I can no longer oppose your wishes. But believe my words, and suffer this veil still to hide my blushes and tears."

"Why tears, beloved one?" cried the gnome anxiously; "every tear of yours falls upon my heart like a drop of molten gold. Greatly as I desire your love, I do not ask a sacrifice."

"Ah!" cried the false princess, "why do you misunderstand my tears? My heart answers to your tenderness, and yet I am fearful. A wife cannot always charm, and though *you* will never alter, the beauty of mortals is as a flower that fades. How can I be sure that you will always be as loving and charming as you are now?"

"Ask some proof, sweetheart," said he. "Put my obedience and my patience to some test by which you can judge of my unalterable love."

"Be it so," answered the crafty maiden. "Then give

me just one proof of your goodness. Go! count the
turnips in yonder meadow. My wedding feast must not
lack guests. They shall provide me with bride-maidens
too. But beware lest you deceive me, and do not miss a
single one. That shall be the test of your truth towards
me."

Unwilling as the gnome was to lose sight of his beautiful bride for a moment, he obeyed her commands
without delay, and hurried off to begin his task. He
skipped along among the turnips as nimbly as a grass-
hopper, and had soon counted them all; but, to be
quite certain that he had made no mistake, he thought
he would just run over them again. This time, to his
great annoyance, the number was different; so he reckoned them for the third time, but now the number was
not the same as either of the previous ones! And this
was hardly to be wondered at, as his mind was full of
the princess's pretty looks and words.

As for the maiden, no sooner was her deluded lover
fairly out of sight than she began to prepare for flight.
She had a fine fresh turnip hidden close at hand, which
she changed into a spirited horse, all saddled and bridled, and, springing upon its back, she galloped away
over hill and dale till she reached the Thorny Valley,
and flung herself into the arms of her beloved Prince
Ratibor.

Meanwhile the toiling gnome went through his task
over and over again till his back ached and his head
swam, and he could no longer put two and two together; but as he felt tolerably certain of the exact
number of turnips in the field, big and little together,
he hurried back eager to prove to his beloved one what
a delightful and submissive husband he would be. He
felt very well satisfied with himself as he crossed the
mossy lawn to the place where he had left her; but,
alas! she was no longer there.

He searched every thicket and path, he looked behind every tree, and gazed into every pond, but with-

out success; then he hastened into the palace and rushed from room to room, peering into every hole and corner and calling her by name; but only echo answered in the marble halls—there was neither voice nor footstep.

Then he began to perceive that something was amiss, and, throwing off the mortal form that encumbered him, he flew out of the palace, and soared high into the air, and saw the fugitive princess in the far distance just as the swift horse carried her across the boundary of his dominions.

Furiously did the enraged gnome fling two great clouds together, and hurl a thunderbolt after the flying maiden, splintering the rocky barriers which had stood a thousand years. But his fury was vain, the thunder-clouds melted away into a soft mist, and the gnome, after flying about for a while in despair, bewailing to the four winds his unhappy fate, went sorrowfully back to the palace, and stole once more through every room, with many sighs and lamentations. He passed through the gardens which for him had lost their charm, and the sight of the princess's footprints on the golden sand of the pathway renewed his grief. All was lonely, empty, sorrowful; and the forsaken gnome resolved that he would have no more deal-ings with such false creatures as he had found men to be.

Thereupon he stamped three times upon the earth, and the magic palace, with all its treasures, vanished away into the nothingness out of which he had called it; and the gnome fled once more to the depths of his underground kingdom.

While all this was happening, Prince Ratibor was hurrying away with his prize to a place of safety. With great pomp and triumph he restored the lovely princess to her father, and was then and there mar-ried to her, and took her back with him to his own castle.

But long after she was dead, and her children too, the villagers would tell the tale of her imprisonment underground, as they sat carving wood in the winter nights.

—*The Brown Fairy Book* (1904)

The Sister of the Sun

LAPLAND

A LONG time ago there lived a young prince whose favourite playfellow was the son of the gardener who lived in the grounds of the palace. The king would have preferred his choosing a friend from the pages who were brought up at court; but the prince would have nothing to say to them, and as he was a spoilt child, and allowed his way in all things, and the gardener's boy was quiet and well-behaved, he was suffered to be in the palace, morning, noon, and night.

The game the children loved the best was a match at archery, for the king had given them two bows exactly alike, and they would spend whole days in trying to see which could shoot the highest. This is always very dangerous, and it was a great wonder they did not put their eyes out; but somehow or other they managed to escape.

One morning, when the prince had done his lessons, he ran out to call his friend, and they both hurried off to the lawn which was their usual playground. They took their bows out of the little hut where their toys were kept, and began to see which could shoot the highest. At last they happened to let fly their arrows both together, and when they fell to earth again the tail feather of a golden hen was found sticking in one. Now the question began to arise whose was the lucky arrow, for they were both alike, and look as closely as you would you could see no difference between them. The prince declared that the arrow was his, and the gardener's boy was quite sure it was *his*—and on this occasion he was perfectly right; but, as they could not decide the matter, they went straight to the king.

When the king had heard the story, he decided that the feather belonged to his son; but the other boy would not listen to this and claimed the feather for himself. At length the king's patience gave way, and he said angrily:

"Very well; if you are so sure that the feather is yours, yours it shall be; only you will have to seek till you find a golden hen with a feather missing from her tail. And if you fail to find her your head will be the forfeit."

The boy had need of all his courage to listen silently to the king's words. He had no idea where the golden hen might be, or even, if he discovered that, how he was to get to her. But there was nothing for it but to do the king's bidding, and he felt that the sooner he left the palace the better. So he went home and put some food into a bag, and then set forth, hoping that some accident might show him which path to take.

After walking for several hours he met a fox, who seemed inclined to be friendly, and the boy was so glad to have anyone to talk to that he sat down and entered into conversation.

"Where are you going?" asked the fox.

"I have got to find a golden hen who has lost a feather out of her tail," answered the boy; "but I don't know where she lives or how I shall catch her!"

"Oh, I can show you the way!" said the fox, who was really very good-natured. "Far towards the east, in that direction, lives a beautiful maiden who is called 'The Sister of the Sun.' She has three golden hens in her house. Perhaps the feather belongs to one of them."

The boy was delighted at this news, and they walked on all day together, the fox in front, and the boy behind. When evening came they lay down to sleep, and put the knapsack under their heads for a pillow.

Suddenly, about midnight, the fox gave a low whine, and drew nearer to his bedfellow. "Cousin," he whispered very low, "there is someone coming who will take the knapsack away from me. Look over there!" And the boy, peeping through the bushes, saw a man.

"Oh, I don't think he will rob us!" said the boy; and when the man drew near, he told them his story, which so much interested the stranger that he asked leave to travel with them, as he might be of some use. So when the sun rose they set out again, the fox in front as before, the man and boy following.

After some hours they reached the castle of the Sister of the Sun, who kept the golden hens among her treasures. They halted before the gate and took counsel as to which of them should go in and see the lady herself.

"I think it would be best for me to enter and steal the hens," said the fox; but this did not please the boy at all.

"No, it is my business, so it is right that I should go," answered he.

"You will find it a very difficult matter to get hold of the hens," replied the fox.

"Oh, nothing is likely to happen to me," returned the boy.

"Well, go then," said the fox, "but be careful not to make any mistake. Steal only the hen which has the feather missing from her tail, and leave the others alone."

The man listened, but did not interfere, and the boy entered the court of the palace.

He soon spied the three hens strutting proudly about, though they were really anxiously wondering if there were not some grains lying on the ground that they might be glad to eat. And as the last one passed by him, he saw she had one feather missing from her tail.

At this sight the youth darted forward and seized the hen by the neck so that she could not struggle. Then, tucking her comfortably under his arm, he made straight for the gate. Unluckily, just as he was about to go through it he looked back and caught a glimpse of wonderful splendours from an open door of the palace. "After all, there is no hurry," he said to himself; "I may as well see something now I *am* here," and turned back, forgetting all about the hen, which escaped from under his arm, and ran to join her sisters.

He was so much fascinated by the sight of all the beautiful things which peeped through the door that he scarcely noticed that he had lost the prize he had won; and he did not remember there was such a thing as a hen in the world when he beheld the Sister of the Sun sleeping on a bed before him.

For some time he stood staring; then he came to himself with a start, and feeling that he had no business there, softly stole away, and was fortunate enough to recapture the hen, which he took with him to the gate. On the threshold he stopped again. "Why should I not look at the Sister of the Sun?" he thought to himself; "she is asleep, and will never know." And he turned back for the second time and entered the chamber, while the hen wriggled herself free as before. When he had gazed his fill he went out into the courtyard and picked up his hen who was seeking for corn.

As he drew near the gate he paused. "Why did I not give her a kiss?" he said to himself; "I shall never kiss any woman so beautiful." And he wrung his hands with regret, so that the hen fell to the ground and ran away.

"But I can do it still!" he cried with delight, and he rushed back to the chamber and kissed the sleeping maiden on the forehead. But, alas! when he came out again he found that the hen had grown so shy that she would not let him come near her. And, worse than that, her sisters began to cluck so loud that the Sister of the Sun was awakened by the noise. She jumped up in haste from her bed, and going to the door she said to the boy:

"You shall never, never, have my hen till you bring

THE GOLDEN HEN WILL BE CAUGHT AT LAST

me back my sister who was carried off by a giant to his castle, which is a long way off."

Slowly and sadly the youth left the palace and told his story to his friends, who were waiting outside the gate, how he had actually held the hen three times in his arms and had lost her.

"I knew that we should not get off so easily," said the fox, shaking his head; "but there is no more time to waste. Let us set off at once in search of the sister. Luckily, I know the way."

They walked on for many days, till at length the fox, who, as usual, was going first, stopped suddenly.

"The giant's castle is not far now," he said, "but when we reach it you two must remain outside while I go and fetch the princess. Directly I bring her out you must both catch hold of her tight, and get away as fast as you can; while I return to the castle and talk to the giants— for there are many of them—so that they may not notice the escape of the princess."

A few minutes later they arrived at the castle, and the fox, who had often been there before, slipped in without difficulty. There were several giants, both young and old, in the hall, and they were all dancing round the princess. As soon as they saw the fox they cried out: "Come and dance too, old fox; it is a long time since we have seen you."

So the fox stood up, and did his steps with the best of them; but after a while he stopped and said:

"I know a charming new dance that I should like to show you; but it can only be done by two people. If the princess will honour me for a few minutes, you will soon see how it is done."

"Ah, that is delightful; we want something new," answered they, and placed the princess between the outstretched arms of the fox. In one instant he had knocked over the great stand of lights that lighted the hall, and in the darkness had borne the princess to the gate. His comrades seized hold of her, as they had been bidden, and the fox was back again in the hall before anyone had missed him. He found the giants busy trying to kindle a fire and get some light; but after a bit someone cried out:

"Where is the princess?"

"Here, in my arms," replied the fox. "Don't be afraid; she is quite safe." And he waited until he thought that his comrades had gained a good start, and put at least five or six mountains between themselves and the giants. Then he sprang through the door, calling, as he went: "The maiden is here; take her if you can!"

At these words the giants understood that their prize had escaped, and they ran after the fox as fast as their great legs could carry them, thinking that they should soon come up with the fox, who they supposed had the princess on his back. The fox, on his side, was far too clever to choose the same path that his friends had taken, but wound in and out of the forest, till at last even *he* was tired out, and fell fast asleep under a tree. Indeed, he was so exhausted with his day's work that he never heard the approach of the giants, and their hands were already stretched out to seize his tail when his eyes opened, and with a tremendous bound he was once more beyond their reach. All the rest of the night the fox ran and ran; but when bright red spread over the east, he stopped and waited till the giants were close upon him. Then he turned, and said quietly: "Look, there is the Sister of the Sun!"

The giants raised their eyes all at once, and were instantly turned into pillars of stone. The fox then made each pillar a low bow, and set off to join his friends.

He knew a great many short cuts across the hills, so it was not long before he came up with them, and all four travelled night and day till they reached the castle of the Sister of the Sun. What joy and feasting there was throughout the palace at the sight of the princess whom they had mourned as dead! and they could not make enough of the boy who had gone through such dangers in order to rescue her. The golden hen was given to him at once, and, more than that, the Sister of

the Sun told him that, in a little time, when he was a
few years older, she would herself pay a visit to his
home and become his wife. The boy could hardly believe his ears when he heard what was in store for him,
for this was the most beautiful princess in all the world;
and however thick the darkness might be, it fled away
at once from the light of a star on her forehead.

So the boy set forth on his journey home, with his
friends for company; his heart full of gladness when he
thought of the promise of the princess. But, one by
one, his comrades dropped off at the places where they
had first met him, and he was quite alone when he
reached his native town and the gates of the palace.
With the golden hen under his arm he presented himself before the king, and told his adventures, and how
he was going to have for a wife a princess so wonderful
and unlike all other princesses, that the star on her
forehead could turn night into day. The king listened
silently, and when the boy had done, he said quietly:
"If I find that your story is not true I will have you
thrown into a cask of pitch."

"It is true—every word of it," answered the boy; and
went on to tell that the day and even the hour were
fixed when his bride was to come and seek him.

But as the time drew near, and nothing was heard of
the princess, the youth became anxious and uneasy,
especially when it came to his ears that the great cask
was being filled with pitch, and that sticks were laid
underneath to make a fire to boil it with. All day long
the boy stood at the window, looking over the sea by
which the princess must travel; but there were no signs
of her, not even the tiniest white sail. And, as he stood,
soldiers came and laid hands on him, and led him up to
the cask, where a big fire was blazing, and the horrid
black pitch boiling and bubbling over the sides. He
looked and shuddered, but there was no escape; so he
shut his eyes to avoid seeing.

The word was given for him to mount the steps
which led to the top of the cask, when, suddenly, some

men were seen running with all their might, crying as they went that a large ship with its sails spread was making straight for the city. No one knew what the ship was, or whence it came; but the king declared that he would not have the boy burned before its arrival, there would always be time enough for that.

At length the vessel was safe in port, and a whisper went through the watching crowd that on board was the Sister of the Sun, who had come to marry the young peasant, as she had promised. In a few moments more she had landed, and desired to be shown the way to the cottage which her bridegroom had so often described to her; and whither he had been led back by the king's order at the first sign of the ship.

"Don't you know me?" asked the Sister of the Sun, bending over him where he lay, almost driven out of his senses with terror.

"No, no; I don't know you," answered the youth, without raising his eyes.

"Kiss me," said the Sister of the Sun; and the youth obeyed her, but still without looking up.

"Don't you know me *now*?" asked she.

"No, I don't know you—I don't know you," he replied, with the manner of a man whom fear had driven mad.

At this the Sister of the Sun grew rather frightened, and beginning at the beginning, she told him the story of his meeting with her, and how she had come a long way in order to marry him. And just as she had finished in walked the king, to see if what the boy had said was really true. But hardly had he opened the door of the cottage when he was almost blinded by the light that filled it; and he remembered what he had been told about the star on the forehead of the princess. He staggered back as if he had been struck, then a curious feeling took hold of him, which he had never felt before, and falling on his knees before the Sister of the Sun he implored her to give up all thought of the peasant boy, and to share his throne. But she only laughed, and said she had a finer throne of her own, if she wanted to sit on it, and that she was free to please herself, and would have no husband but the boy whom she would never have seen except for the king himself.

"I shall marry him to-morrow," ended she; and ordered the preparations to be set on foot at once.

When the next day came, however, the bridegroom's father informed the princess that, by the law of the land, the marriage must take place in the presence of the king; but he hoped his majesty would not long delay his arrival. An hour or two passed, and everyone was waiting and watching, when at last the sound of trumpets was heard and a grand procession was seen marching up the street. A chair covered with velvet had been made ready for the king, and he took his seat upon it, and, looking round upon the assembled company, he said:

"I have no wish to forbid this marriage; but, before I can allow it to be celebrated, the bridegroom must prove himself worthy of such a bride by fulfilling three tasks. And the first is that in a single day he must cut down every tree in an entire forest."

The youth stood aghast at the king's words. He had never cut down a tree in his life, and had not the least idea how to begin. And as for a whole forest——! But the princess saw what was passing in his mind, and whispered to him:

"Don't be afraid. In my ship you will find an axe, which you must carry off to the forest. When you have cut down one tree with it just say: 'So let the forest fall,' and in an instant all the trees will be on the ground. But pick up three chips of the tree you have felled, and put them in your pocket."

And the young man did exactly as he was bid, and soon returned with the three chips safe in his coat.

The following morning the princess declared that she had been thinking about the matter, and that, as she was not a subject of the king, she saw no reason why she should be bound by his laws; and she meant to be married that very day. But the bridegroom's father told her that it was all very well for her to talk like that, but it was quite different for his son, who would pay with his head for any disobedience to the king's commands. However, in consideration of what the youth had done the day before, he hoped his majesty's heart might be softened, especially as he had sent a message that they might expect him at once. With this the bridal pair had to be content, and be as patient as they could till the king's arrival.

He did not keep them long, but they saw by his face that nothing good awaited them.

"The marriage cannot take place," he said shortly, "till the youth has joined to their roots all the trees he cut down yesterday."

This sounded much more difficult than what he had done before, and he turned in despair to the Sister of the Sun.

"It is all right," she whispered encouragingly. "Take this water and sprinkle it on one of the fallen trees, and say to it: 'So let all the trees of the forest stand upright,' and in a moment they will be erect again."

And the young man did what he was told, and left the forest looking exactly as it had done before.

Now, surely, thought the princess, there was no longer any need to put off the wedding; and she gave orders that all should be ready for the following day. But again the old man interfered, and declared that without the king's permission no marriage could take place. For the third time his majesty was sent for, and for the third time he proclaimed that he could not give his consent until the bridegroom should have slain a serpent which dwelt in a broad river that flowed at the back of the castle. Everyone knew stories of this terrible serpent, though no one had actually seen it; but from time to time a child strayed from home and never came back, and then mothers would forbid the other children to go near the river, which had juicy fruits and lovely flowers growing along its banks.

So no wonder the youth trembled and turned pale when he heard what lay before him.

"You will succeed in this also," whispered the Sister of the Sun, pressing his hand, "for in my ship is a magic sword which will cut through everything. Go down to the river and unfasten a boat which lies moored there, and throw the chips into the water. When the serpent rears up its body you will cut off its three heads with one blow of your sword. Then take the tip of each tongue and go with it to-morrow morning into the king's kitchen. If the king himself should enter, just say to him: 'Here are three gifts I offer you in return for the services you demanded of me!' and throw the tips of the serpent's tongues at him, and hasten to the ship as fast as your legs will carry you. But be sure you take great care never to look behind you."

The young man did exactly what the princess had told him. The three chips which he flung into the river became a boat, and, as he steered across the stream, the serpent put up its head and hissed loudly. The youth had his sword ready, and in another second the three heads were bobbing on the water. Guiding his boat till he was beside them, he stooped down and snipped off the ends of the tongues, and then rowed back to the other bank. Next morning he carried them into the royal kitchen, and when the king entered, as was his custom, to see what he was going to have for dinner, the bridegroom flung them in his face, saying: "Here is a gift for you in return for the services you asked of me." And, opening the kitchen door, he fled to the ship. Unluckily he missed the way, and in his excitement ran backwards and forwards, without knowing whither he was going. At last, in despair, he looked round, and saw to his amazement that both the city and palace had vanished completely. Then he turned his eyes in the other direction and, far, far away, he caught sight of the ship with her sails spread, and a fair wind behind her.

This dreadful spectacle seemed to take away his senses, and all day long he wandered about, without knowing where he was going, till, in the evening, he noticed some smoke from a little hut of turf near by. He went straight up to it and cried: "O mother, let me come in for pity's sake!" The old woman who lived in the hut beckoned to him to enter, and hardly was he inside when he cried again: "O mother, can you tell me anything of the Sister of the Sun?"

But the old woman only shook her head. "No, I know nothing of her," said she.

The young man turned to leave the hut, but the old woman stopped him, and, giving him a letter, begged him to carry it to her next eldest sister, saying: "If you should get tired on the way, take out the letter and rustle the paper."

This advice surprised the young man a good deal, as he did not see how it could help him; but he did not answer, and went down the road without knowing where he was going. At length he grew so tired he could walk no more; then he remembered what the old woman had said. After he had rustled the leaves only once all fatigue disappeared, and he strode gaily over the grass till he came to another little turf hut.

"Let me in, I pray you, dear mother," cried he. And the door opened in front of him. "Your sister has sent you this letter," he said, and added quickly: "O mother! can you tell me anything of the Sister of the Sun?"

"No, I know nothing of her," answered she. But as he turned hopelessly away, she stopped him.

"If you happen to pass my eldest sister's house, will you give her this letter?" said she. "And if you should get tired on the road, just take it out of your pocket and rustle the paper."

So the young man put the letter in his pocket, and walked all day over the hills till he reached a little turf hut, exactly like the other two.

"Let me in, I pray you, dear mother," cried he. And as he entered he added: "Here is a letter from your sister, and—can you tell me anything of the Sister of the Sun?"

"Yes, I can," answered the old woman. "She lives in the castle on the Banka. Her father lost a battle only a few days ago because you had stolen his sword from him, and the Sister of the Sun herself is almost dead of grief. But, when you see her, stick a pin into the palm of her hand, and suck the drops of blood that flow. Then she will grow calmer, and will know you again. Only, beware; for before you reach the castle on the Banka fearful things will happen."

He thanked the old woman with tears of gladness for the good news she had given him, and continued his journey. But he had not gone very far when, at a turn of the road, he met with two brothers, who were quarrelling over a piece of cloth.

"My good men, what are you fighting about?" said he. "That cloth does not look worth much!"

"Oh, it is ragged enough," answered they, "but it was left us by our father, and if any man wraps it round him no one can see him; and we each want it for our own."

"Let me put it round me for a moment," said the youth, "and then I will tell you whose it ought to be!"

The brothers were pleased with this idea, and gave him the stuff; but the moment he had thrown it over his shoulder he disappeared as completely as if he had never been there at all.

Meanwhile the young man walked briskly along, till he came up with two other men, who were disputing over a table-cloth.

"What is the matter?" asked he, stopping in front of them.

"If this cloth is spread on a table," answered they, "the table is instantly covered with the most delicious food; and we each want to have it."

"Let me try the table-cloth," said the youth, "and I will tell you whose it ought to be."

The two men were quite pleased with this idea, and

handed him the cloth. He then hastily threw the first piece of stuff round his shoulders and vanished from sight, leaving the two men grieving over their own folly.

The young man had not walked far before he saw two more men standing by the road-side, both grasping the same stout staff, and sometimes one seemed on the point of getting it, and sometimes the other.

"What are you quarrelling about? You could cut a dozen sticks from the wood each just as good as that!" said the young man. And as he spoke the fighters both stopped and looked at him.

"Ah! you may think so," said one, "but a blow from one end of this stick will kill a man, while a touch from the other end will bring him back to life. You won't easily find another stick like that!"

"No; that is true," answered the young man. "Let me just look at it, and I will tell you whose it ought to be."

The men were pleased with the idea, and handed him the staff.

"It is very curious, certainly," said he; "but which end is it that restores people to life? After all, anyone can be killed by a blow from a stick if it is only hard enough!" But when he was shown the end he threw the stuff over his shoulders and vanished.

At last he saw another set of men, who were struggling for the possession of a pair of shoes.

"Why can't you leave that pair of old shoes alone?" said he. "Why, you could not walk a yard in them!"

"Yes, they are old enough," answered they; "but whoever puts them on and wishes himself at a particular place, gets there without going."

"That sounds very clever," said the youth. "Let me try them, and then I shall be able to tell you whose they ought to be."

The idea pleased the men, and they handed him the shoes; but the moment they were on his feet he cried:

"I wish to be in the castle on the Banka!" And before he knew it, he was there, and found the Sister of the

Sun dying of grief. He knelt down by her side, and pulling out a pin he stuck it into the palm of her hand, so that a drop of blood gushed out. This he sucked, as he had been told to do by the old woman, and immediately the princess came to herself, and flung her arms round his neck. Then she told him all her story, and what had happened since the ship had sailed away without him. "But the worst misfortune of all," she added, "was a battle which my father lost because you had vanished with his magic sword; and out of his whole army hardly one man was left."

"Show me the battle-field," said he. And she took him to a wild heath, where the dead were lying as they fell, waiting for burial. One by one he touched them with the end of his staff, till at length they all stood before him. Throughout the kingdom there was nothing but joy; and *this* time the wedding was *really* celebrated. And the bridal pair lived happily in the castle on the Banka till they died.

—*The Brown Fairy Book* (1904)

The Story of a Gazelle

SWAHILI

———————◆◆◆———————

ONCE upon a time there lived a man who wasted all his money, and grew so poor that his only food was a few grains of corn, which he scratched like a fowl from out of a dust-heap.

One day he was scratching as usual among a dust-heap in the street, hoping to find something for breakfast, when his eye fell upon a small silver coin, called an eighth, which he greedily snatched up. "Now I can have a proper meal," he thought, and after drinking some water at a well he lay down and slept so long that it was sunrise before he woke again. Then he jumped up and returned to the dust-heap. "For who knows," he said to himself, "whether I may not have some good luck again."

As he was walking down the road, he saw a man coming towards him, carrying a cage made of twigs. "Hi! you fellow!" called he, "what have you got inside there?"

"Gazelles," replied the man.

"Bring them here, for I should like to see them."

As he spoke, some men who were standing by began to laugh, saying to the man with the cage: "You had better take care how you bargain with him, for he has nothing at all except what he picks up from a dust-heap, and if he can't feed himself, will he be able to feed a gazelle?"

But the man with the cage made answer: "Since I started from my home in the country, fifty people at the least have called me to show them my gazelles, and was there one among them who cared to buy? It is the custom for a trader in merchandise to be summoned hither and thither, and who knows where one may find a buyer?" And he took up his cage and went towards the scratcher of dust-heaps, and the men went with him.

"What do you ask for your gazelles?" said the beggar. "Will you let me have one for an eighth?"

And the man with the cage took out a gazelle, and held it out, saying, "Take this one, master!"

And the beggar took it and carried it to the dust-heap, where he scratched carefully till he found a few grains of corn, which he divided with his gazelle. This he did night and morning, till five days went by.

Then, as he slept, the gazelle woke him, saying, "Master."

And the man answered, "How is it that I see a wonder?"

"What wonder?" asked the gazelle.

"Why, that you, a gazelle, should be able to speak, for, from the beginning, my father and mother and all the people that are in the world have never told me of a talking gazelle."

"Never mind that," said the gazelle, "but listen to what I say! First, I took you for my master. Second, you gave for me all you had in the world. I cannot run away from you, but give me, I pray you, leave to go every morning and seek food for myself, and every evening I will come back to you. What you find in the dust-heaps is not enough for both of us."

"Go, then," answered the master; and the gazelle went.

When the sun had set, the gazelle came back, and

the poor man was very glad, and they lay down and slept side by side.

In the morning it said to him, "I am going away to feed."

And the man replied, "Go, my son," but he felt very lonely without his gazelle, and set out sooner than usual for the dust-heap where he generally found most corn. And glad he was when the evening came, and he could return home. He lay on the grass chewing tobacco, when the gazelle trotted up.

"Good evening, my master; how have you fared all day? I have been resting in the shade in a place where there is sweet grass when I am hungry, and fresh water when I am thirsty, and a soft breeze to fan me in the heat. It is far away in the forest, and no one knows of it but me, and to-morrow I shall go again."

So for five days the gazelle set off at daybreak for this cool spot, but on the fifth day it came to a place where the grass was bitter, and it did not like it, and scratched, hoping to tear away the bad blades. But, instead, it saw something lying in the earth, which turned out to be a diamond, very large and bright. "Oh, ho!" said the gazelle to itself, "perhaps now I can do something for my master who bought me with all the money he had; but I must be careful or they will say he has stolen it. I had better take it myself to some great rich man, and see what it will do for me."

Directly the gazelle had come to this conclusion, it picked up the diamond in its mouth, and went on and on and on through the forest, but found no place where a rich man was likely to dwell. For two more days it ran, from dawn to dark, till at last early one morning it caught sight of a large town, which gave it fresh courage.

The people were standing about the streets doing their marketing, when the gazelle bounded past, the diamond flashing as it ran. They called after it, but it took no notice till it reached the palace, where the sultan was sitting, enjoying the cool air. And the gazelle galloped up to him, and laid the diamond at his feet.

The sultan looked first at the diamond and next at the gazelle; then he ordered his attendants to bring cushions and a carpet, that the gazelle might rest itself after its long journey. And he likewise ordered milk to be brought, and rice, that it might eat and drink and be refreshed.

And when the gazelle was rested, the sultan said to it: "Give me the news you have come with."

And the gazelle answered: "I am come with this diamond, which is a pledge from my master the Sultan Darai. He has heard you have a daughter, and sends you this small token, and begs you will give her to him to wife."

And the sultan said: "I am content. The wife is his wife, the family is his family, the slave is his slave. Let him come to me empty-handed, I am content."

When the sultan had ended, the gazelle rose, and said: "Master, farewell; I go back to our town, and in eight days, or it may be in eleven days, we shall arrive as your guests."

And the sultan answered: "So let it be."

All this time the poor man far away had been mourning and weeping for his gazelle, which he thought had run away from him for ever. And when it came in at the door he rushed to embrace it with such joy that he would not allow it a chance to speak.

"Be still, master, and don't cry," said the gazelle at last; "let us sleep now, and in the morning, when I go, follow me."

With the first ray of dawn they got up and went into the forest, and on the fifth day, as they were resting near a stream, the gazelle gave its master a sound beating, and then bade him stay where he was till it returned. And the gazelle ran off, and about ten o'clock it came near the sultan's palace, where the road was all lined with soldiers who were there to do honour to Sultan Darai. And directly they caught sight of the gazelle in the distance one of the soldiers ran on and said, "Sultan Darai is coming: I have seen the gazelle."

THE GAZELLE BRINGS THE DIAMOND TO THE SULTAN

Then the sultan rose up, and called his whole court to follow him, and went out to meet the gazelle, who, bounding up to him, gave him greeting. The sultan answered politely, and inquired where it had left its master, whom it had promised to bring back.

"Alas!" replied the gazelle, "he is lying in the forest, for on our way here we were met by robbers, who, after beating and robbing him, took away all his clothes. And he is now hiding under a bush, lest a passing stranger might see him."

The sultan, on hearing what had happened to his future son-in-law, turned his horse and rode to the palace, and bade a groom to harness the best horse in the stable and order a woman slave to bring a bag of clothes, such as a man might want, out of the chest; and he chose out a tunic and a turban and a sash for the waist, and fetched himself a gold-hilted sword, and a dagger and a pair of sandals, and a stick of sweet-smelling wood.

"Now," said he to the gazelle, "take these things with the soldiers to the sultan, that he may be able to come."

And the gazelle answered: "Can I take those soldiers to go and put my master to shame as he lies there naked? I am enough by myself, my lord."

"How will you be enough," asked the sultan, "to manage this horse and all these clothes?"

"Oh, that is easily done," replied the gazelle. "Fasten the horse to my neck and tie the clothes to the back of the horse, and be sure they are fixed firmly, as I shall go faster than he does."

Everything was carried out as the gazelle had ordered, and when all was ready it said to the sultan: "Farewell, my lord, I am going."

"Farewell, gazelle," answered the sultan; "when shall we see you again?"

"To-morrow about five," replied the gazelle, and, giving a tug to the horse's rein, they set off at a gallop.

The sultan watched them till they were out of sight:

then he said to his attendants, "That gazelle comes from gentle hands, from the house of a sultan, and that is what makes it so different from other gazelles." And in the eyes of the sultan the gazelle became a person of consequence.

Meanwhile the gazelle ran on till it came to the place where its master was seated, and his heart laughed when he saw the gazelle.

And the gazelle said to him, "Get up, my master, and bathe in the stream!" and when the man had bathed it said again, "Now rub yourself well with earth, and rub your teeth well with sand to make them bright and shining." And when this was done it said, "The sun has gone down behind the hills; it is time for us to go": so it went and brought the clothes from the back of the horse, and the man put them on and was well pleased.

"Master!" said the gazelle when the man was ready, "be sure that where we are going you keep silence, except for giving greetings and asking for news. Leave all the talking to me. I have provided you with a wife, and have made her presents of clothes and turbans and rare and precious things, so it is needless for you to speak."

"Very good, I will be silent," replied the man as he mounted the horse. "You have given all this; it is you who are the master, and I who am the slave, and I will obey you in all things."

So they went their way, and they went and went till the gazelle saw in the distance the palace of the sultan. Then it said, "Master, that is the house we are going to, and you are not a poor man any longer: even your name is new."

"What *is* my name, eh, my father?" asked the man.

"Sultan Darai," said the gazelle.

Very soon some soldiers came to meet them, while others ran off to tell the sultan of their approach. And the sultan set off at once, and the viziers and the emirs, and the judges, and the rich men of the city, all followed him.

Directly the gazelle saw them coming, it said to its master: "Your father-in-law is coming to meet you; that is he in the middle, wearing a mantle of sky-blue. Get off your horse and go to greet him."

And Sultan Darai leapt from his horse, and so did the other sultan, and they gave their hands to one another and kissed each other, and went together into the palace.

The next morning the gazelle went to the rooms of the sultan, and said to him: "My lord, we want you to marry us our wife, for the soul of Sultan Darai is eager."

"The wife is ready, so call the priest," answered he, and when the ceremony was over a cannon was fired and music was played, and within the palace there was feasting.

"Master," said the gazelle the following morning, "I am setting out on a journey, and I shall not be back for seven days, and perhaps not then. But be careful not to leave the house till I come."

And the master answered, "I will not leave the house."

And it went to the sultan of the country and said to him: "My lord, Sultan Darai has sent me to his town to get the house in order. It will take me seven days, and if I am not back in seven days he will not leave the palace till I return."

"Very good," said the sultan.

And it went and it went through the forest and wilderness, till it arrived at a town full of fine houses. At the end of the chief road was a great house, beautiful exceedingly, built of sapphire and turquoise and marbles. "That," thought the gazelle, "is the house for my master, and I will call up my courage and go and look at the people who are in it, if any people there are. For in this town have I as yet seen no people. If I die, I die, and if I live, I live. Here can I think of no plan, so if anything is to kill me, it will kill me."

Then it knocked twice at the door, and cried "Open," but no one answered. And it cried again, and a voice replied:

"Who are you that are crying 'Open'?"

And the gazelle said, "It is I, great mistress, your grandchild."

"If you are my grandchild," returned the voice, "go back whence you came. Don't come and die here, and bring me to my death as well."

"Open, mistress, I entreat, I have something to say to you."

"Grandchild," replied she, "I fear to put your life in danger, and my own too."

"Oh, mistress, my life will not be lost, nor yours either; open, I pray you." So she opened the door.

"What is the news where you come from, my grandson," asked she.

"Great lady, where I come from it is well, and with you it is well."

"Ah, my son, here it is not well at all. If you seek a way to die, or if you have not yet seen death, then is to-day the day for you to know what dying is."

"If I am to know it, I shall know it," replied the gazelle; "but tell me, who is the lord of this house?"

And she said: "Ah, father! in this house is much wealth, and much people, and much food, and many horses. And the lord of it all is an exceeding great and wonderful snake."

"Oh!" cried the gazelle when he heard this; "tell me how I can get at the snake to kill him?"

"My son," returned the old woman, "do not say words like those; you risk both our lives. He has put me here all by myself, and I have to cook his food. When the great snake is coming there springs up a wind, and blows the dust about, and this goes on till the great snake glides into the courtyard and calls for his dinner, which must always be ready for him in those big pots. He eats till he has had enough, and then drinks a whole tankful of water. After that he goes away. Every second day he comes, when the sun is over the house. And he has seven heads. How then can you be a match for him, my son?"

"Mind your own business, mother," answered the gazelle, "and don't mind other people's! Has this snake a sword?"

"He has a sword, and a sharp one too. It cuts like a flash of lightning."

"Give it to me, mother!" said the gazelle, and she unhooked the sword from the wall, as she was bidden. "You must be quick," she said, "for he may be here at any moment. Hark! is not that the wind rising? He has come!"

They were silent, but the old woman peeped from behind a curtain, and saw the snake busy at the pots which she had placed ready for him in the courtyard. And after he had done eating and drinking he came to the door:

"You old body!" he cried; "what smell is that I smell inside that is not the smell of every day?"

"Oh, master!" answered she, "I am alone, as I always am! But to-day, after many days, I have sprinkled fresh scent all over me, and it is that which you smell. What else could it be, master?"

All this time the gazelle had been standing close to the door, holding the sword in one of its front paws. And as the snake put one of his heads through the hole that he had made so as to get in and out comfortably, it cut it off so clean that the snake really did not feel it. The second blow was not quite so straight, for the snake said to himself, "Who is that who is trying to scratch me?" and stretched out his third head to see; but no sooner was the neck through the hole than the head went rolling to join the rest.

When six of his heads were gone the snake lashed his tail with such fury that the gazelle and the old woman could not see each other for the dust he made. And the gazelle said to him, "You have climbed all sorts of trees, but this you can't climb," and as the seventh head came darting through it went rolling to join the rest.

Then the sword fell rattling on the ground, for the gazelle had fainted.

The old woman shrieked with delight when she saw her enemy was dead, and ran to bring water to the gazelle, and fanned it, and put it where the wind could blow on it, till it grew better and gave a sneeze. And the heart of the old woman was glad, and she gave it more water, till by-and-by the gazelle got up.

"Show me this house," it said, "from beginning to end, from top to bottom, from inside to out."

So she arose and showed the gazelle rooms full of gold and precious things, and other rooms full of slaves. "They are all yours, goods and slaves," said she.

But the gazelle answered, "You must keep them safe till I call my master."

For two days it lay and rested in the house, and fed on milk and rice, and on the third day it bade the old woman farewell and started back to its master.

And when he heard that the gazelle was at the door he felt like a man who has found the time when all prayers are granted, and he rose and kissed it, saying: "My father, you have been a long time; you have left sorrow with me. I cannot eat, I cannot drink, I cannot laugh; my heart felt no smile at anything, because of thinking of you."

And the gazelle answered: "I am well, and where I come from it is well, and I wish that after four days you would take your wife and go home."

And he said: "It is for you to speak. Where you go, I will follow."

"Then I shall go to your father-in-law and tell him this news."

"Go, my son."

So the gazelle went to the father-in-law and said: "I am sent by my master to come and tell you that after four days he will go away with his wife to his own home."

"Must he really go so quickly? We have not yet sat much together, I and Sultan Darai, nor have we yet talked much together, nor have we yet ridden out together, nor have we eaten together; yet it is fourteen days since he came."

But the gazelle replied: "My lord, you cannot help it, for he wishes to go home, and nothing will stop him."

"Very good," said the sultan, and he called all the people who were in the town, and commanded that the day his daughter left the palace ladies and guards were to attend her on her way.

And at the end of four days a great company of ladies and slaves and horses went forth to escort the wife of Sultan Darai to her new home. They rode all day, and when the sun sank behind the hills they rested, and ate of the food the gazelle gave them, and lay down to sleep. And they journeyed on for many days, and they all, nobles and slaves, loved the gazelle with a great love—more than they loved the Sultan Darai.

At last one day signs of houses appeared, far, far off. And those who saw cried out, "Gazelle!"

And it answered, "Ah, my mistresses, that is the house of Sultan Darai."

At this news the women rejoiced much, and the slaves rejoiced much, and in the space of two hours they came to the gates, and the gazelle bade them all stay behind, and it went on to the house with Sultan Darai.

When the old woman saw them coming through the courtyard she jumped and shouted for joy, and as the gazelle drew near she seized it in her arms, and kissed it. The gazelle did not like this, and said to her: "Old woman, leave me alone; the one to be carried is my master, and the one to be kissed is my master."

And she answered, "Forgive me, my son. I did not know this was our master," and she threw open all the doors so that the master might see everything that the rooms and storehouses contained. Sultan Darai looked about him, and at length he said:

"Unfasten those horses that are tied up, and let loose those people that are bound. And let some sweep, and some spread the beds, and some cook, and some draw water, and some come out and receive the mistress."

And when the sultana and her ladies and her slaves entered the house, and saw the rich stuffs it was hung with, and the beautiful rice that was prepared for them to eat, they cried: "Ah, you gazelle, we have seen great houses, we have seen people, we have heard of things. But this house, and you, such as you are, we have never seen or heard of."

After a few days, the ladies said they wished to go home again. The gazelle begged them hard to stay, but finding they would not, it brought many gifts, and gave some to the ladies and some to their slaves. And they all thought the gazelle greater a thousand times than its master, Sultan Darai.

The gazelle and its master remained in the house many weeks, and one day it said to the old woman, "I came with my master to this place, and I have done many things for my master, good things, and till to-day he has never asked me: 'Well, my gazelle, how did you get this house? Who is the owner of it? And this town, were there no people in it?' All good things I have done for the master, and he has not one day done me any good thing. But people say, 'If you want to do any one good, don't do him good only, do him evil also, and there will be peace between you.' So, mother, I have done: I want to see the favours I have done to my master, that he may do me the like."

"Good," replied the old woman, and they went to bed.

In the morning, when light came, the gazelle was sick in its stomach and feverish, and its legs ached. And it said "Mother!"

And she answered, "Here, my son?"

And it said, "Go and tell my master upstairs the gazelle is very ill."

"Very good, my son; and if he should ask me what is the matter, what am I to say?"

"Tell him all my body aches badly; I have no single part without pain."

The old woman went upstairs, and she found the mistress and master sitting on a couch of marble spread with soft cushions, and they asked her, "Well, old woman, what do you want?"

"To tell the master the gazelle is ill," said she.

"What is the matter?" asked the wife.

"All its body pains; there is no part without pain."

"Well, what can I do? Make some gruel of red millet, and give to it."

But his wife stared and said: "Oh, master, do you tell her to make the gazelle gruel out of red millet, which a horse would not eat? Eh, master, that is not well."

But he answered, "Oh, you are mad! Rice is only kept for people."

"Eh, master, this is not like a gazelle. It is the apple of your eye. If sand got into that, it would trouble you."

"My wife, your tongue is long," and he left the room.

The old woman saw she had spoken vainly, and went back weeping to the gazelle. And when the gazelle saw her it said, "Mother, what is it, and why do you cry? If it be good, give me the answer; and if it be bad, give me the answer."

But still the old woman would not speak, and the gazelle prayed her to let it know the words of the master. At last she said: "I went upstairs and found the mistress and the master sitting on a couch, and he asked me what I wanted, and I told him that you, his slave, were ill. And his wife asked what was the matter, and I told her that there was not a part of your body without pain. And the master told me to take some red millet and make you gruel, but the mistress said, 'Eh, master, the gazelle is the apple of your eye; you have no child, this gazelle is like your child; so this gazelle is not one to be done evil to. This is a gazelle in form, but not a gazelle in heart; he is in all things better than a gentleman, be he who he may.'

"And he answered her, 'Silly chatterer, your words

are many. I know its price; I bought it for an eighth. What loss will it be to me?' "

The gazelle kept silence for a few moments. Then it said, "The elders said, 'One that does good like a mother,' and I have done him good, and I have got this that the elders said. But go up again to the master, and tell him the gazelle is very ill, and it has not drunk the gruel of red millet."

So the old woman returned, and found the master and the mistress drinking coffee. And when he heard what the gazelle had said, he cried: "Hold your peace, old woman, and stay your feet and close your eyes, and stop your ears with wax; and if the gazelle bids you come to me, say your legs are bent, and you cannot walk; and if it begs you to listen, say your ears are stopped with wax; and if it wishes to talk, reply that your tongue has got a hook in it."

The heart of the old woman wept as she heard such words, because she saw that when the gazelle first came to that town it was ready to sell its life to buy wealth for its master. Then it happened to get both life and wealth, but now it had no honour with its master.

And tears sprung likewise to the eyes of the sultan's wife, and she said, "I am sorry for you, my husband, that you should deal so wickedly with that gazelle"; but he only answered, "Old woman, pay no heed to the talk of the mistress: tell it to perish out of the way. I cannot sleep, I cannot eat, I cannot drink, for the worry of that gazelle. Shall a creature that I bought for an eighth trouble me from morning till night? Not so, old woman!"

The old woman went downstairs, and there lay the gazelle, blood flowing from its nostrils. And she took it in her arms and said, "My son, the good you did is lost; there remains only patience."

And it said, "Mother, I shall die, for my soul is full of anger and bitterness. My face is ashamed, that I should have done good to my master, and that he should repay me with evil." It paused for a moment, and then went on, "Mother, of the goods that are in this house, what do I eat? I might have every day half a basinful, and would my master be any the poorer? But did not the elders say, 'He that does good like a mother!' "

And it said, "Go and tell my master that the gazelle is nearer death than life."

So she went, and spoke as the gazelle had bidden her; but he answered, "I have told you to trouble me no more."

But his wife's heart was sore, and she said to him: "Ah, master, what has the gazelle done to you? How has he failed you? The things you do to him are not good, and you will draw on yourself the hatred of the people. For this gazelle is loved by all, by small and great, by women and men. Ah, my husband! I thought you had great wisdom, and you have not even a little!"

But he answered, "You are mad, my wife."

The old woman stayed no longer, and went back to the gazelle, followed secretly by the mistress, who called a maidservant and bade her take some milk and rice and cook it for the gazelle.

"Take also this cloth," she said, "to cover it with, and this pillow for its head. And if the gazelle wants more, let it ask me, and not its master. And if it will, I will send it in a litter to my father, and he will nurse it till it is well."

And the maidservant did as her mistress bade her, and said what her mistress had told her to say, but the gazelle made no answer, but turned over on its side and died quietly.

When the news spread abroad, there was much weeping among the people, and Sultan Darai arose in wrath, and cried, "You weep for that gazelle as if you wept for me! And, after all, what is it but a gazelle, that I bought for an eighth?"

But his wife answered, "Master, we looked upon that gazelle as we looked upon you. It was the gazelle who came to ask me of my father, it was the gazelle who brought me from my father, and I was given in charge to the gazelle by my father."

And when the people heard her they lifted up their voices and spoke:

"We never saw you, we saw the gazelle. It was the gazelle who met with trouble here, it was the gazelle who met with rest here. So, then, when such an one departs from this world we weep for ourselves, we do not weep for the gazelle."

And they said furthermore:

"The gazelle did you much good, and if anyone says he could have done more for you he is a liar! Therefore, to us who have done you no good, what treatment will you give? The gazelle has died from bitterness of soul, and you ordered your slaves to throw it into the well. Ah! leave us alone that we may weep."

But Sultan Darai would not heed their words, and the dead gazelle was thrown into the well.

When the mistress heard of it, she sent three slaves, mounted on donkeys, with a letter to her father the sultan, and when the sultan had read the letter he bowed his head and wept, like a man who had lost his mother. And he commanded horses to be saddled, and called the governor and the judges and all the rich men, and said:

"Come now with me; let us go and bury it."

Night and day they travelled, till the sultan came to the well where the gazelle had been thrown. And it was a large well, built round a rock, with room for many people; and the sultan entered, and the judges and the rich men followed him. And when he saw the gazelle lying there he wept afresh, and took it in his arms and carried it away.

When the three slaves went and told their mistress what the sultan had done, and how all the people were weeping, she answered:

"I too have eaten no food, neither have I drunk water, since the day the gazelle died. I have not spoken, and I have not laughed."

The sultan took the gazelle and buried it, and ordered the people to wear mourning for it, so there was great mourning throughout the city.

Now after the days of mourning were at an end, the wife was sleeping at her husband's side, and in her sleep she dreamed that she was once more in her father's house, and when she woke up it was no dream.

And the man dreamed that he was on the dust-heap, scratching. And when he woke, behold! that also was no dream, but the truth.

—*The Violet Fairy Book* (1901)

The Story of
Dschemil and Dschemila

TRIPOLI

———◆◆◆———

THERE was once a man whose name was Dschemil, and he had a cousin who was called Dschemila. They had been betrothed by their parents when they were children, and now Dschemil thought that the time had come for them to be married, and he went two or three days' journey, to the nearest big town, to buy furniture for the new house.

While he was away, Dschemila and her friends set off to the neighbouring woods to pick up sticks, and as she gathered them she found an iron mortar lying on the ground. She placed it on her bundle of sticks, but the mortar would not stay still, and whenever she raised the bundle to put it on her shoulders it slipped off sideways. At length she saw the only way to carry the mortar was to tie it in the very middle of her bundle, and had just unfastened her sticks, when she heard her companions' voices.

"Dschemila, what are you doing? it is almost dark, and if you mean to come with us you must be quick!"

But Dschemila only replied, "You had better go back without me, for I am not going to leave my mortar behind, if I stay here till midnight."

"Do as you like," said the girls, and started on their walk home.

377

The night soon fell, and at the last ray of light the mortar suddenly became an ogre, who threw Dschemila on his back, and carried her off into a desert place, distant a whole month's journey from her native town. Here he shut her into a castle, and told her not to fear, as her life was safe. Then he went back to his wife, leaving Dschemila weeping over the fate that she had brought upon herself.

Meanwhile the other girls had reached home, and Dschemila's mother came out to look for her daughter.

"What have you done with her?" she asked anxiously.

"We had to leave her in the wood," they replied, "for she had picked up an iron mortar, and could not manage to carry it."

So the old woman set off at once for the forest, calling to her daughter as she hurried along.

"Do go home," cried the townspeople, as they heard her; "we will go and look for your daughter; you are only a woman, and it is a task that needs strong men."

But she answered, "Yes, go; but I will go with you! Perhaps it will be only her corpse that we shall find after all. She has most likely been stung by asps, or eaten by wild beasts."

The men, seeing her heart was bent on it, said no more, but told one of the girls she must come with them, and show them the place where they had left Dschemila. They found the bundle of wood lying where she had dropped it, but the maiden was nowhere to be seen.

"Dschemila! Dschemila!" cried they; but nobody answered.

"If we make a fire, perhaps she will see it," said one of the men. And they lit a fire, and then went, one this way, and one that, through the forest, to look for her, whispering to each other that if she had been killed by a lion they would be sure to find some trace of it; or if she had fallen asleep, the sound of their voices would wake her; or if a snake had bitten her, they would at least come on her corpse.

All night they searched, and when morning broke and they knew no more than before what had become of the maiden, they grew weary, and said to the mother:

"It is no use. Let us go home, nothing has happened to your daughter, except that she has run away with a man."

"Yes, I will come," answered she, "but I must first look in the river. Perhaps some one has thrown her in there." But the maiden was not in the river.

For four days the father and mother waited and watched for their child to come back; then they gave up hope, and said to each other: "What is to be done? What are we to say to the man to whom Dschemila is betrothed? Let us kill a goat, and bury its head in the grave, and when the man returns we must tell him Dschemila is dead."

Very soon the bridegroom came back, bringing with him carpets and soft cushions for the house of his bride. And as he entered the town Dschemila's father met him, saying, "Greeting to you. She is dead."

At these words the young man broke into loud cries, and it was some time before he could speak. Then he turned to one of the crowd who had gathered round him, and asked: "Where have they buried her?"

"Come to the churchyard with me," answered he; and the young man went with him, carrying with him some of the beautiful things he had brought. These he laid on the grass and then began to weep afresh. All day he stayed, and at nightfall he gathered up his stuffs and carried them to his own house. But when the day dawned he took them in his arms and returned to the grave, where he remained as long as it was light, playing softly on his flute. And this he did daily for six months.

One morning, a man who was wandering through the desert, having lost his way, came upon a lonely castle. The sun was very hot, and the man was very tired, so he said to himself, "I will rest a little in the shadow of this castle." He stretched himself out comfortably, and was almost asleep, when he heard a voice calling to him softly:

"Are you a ghost," it said, "or a man?"

He looked up, and saw a girl leaning out of a window, and he answered:

"I am a man, and a better one, too, than your father or your grandfather."

"May all good luck be with you," said she; "but what has brought you into this land of ogres and horrors?"

"Does an ogre really live in this castle?" asked he.

"Certainly he does," replied the girl, "and as night is not far off he will be here soon. So, dear friend, depart quickly, lest he return and snap you up for supper."

"But I am so thirsty!" said the man. "Be kind, and give me some drink, or else I shall die! Surely, even in this desert there must be some spring?"

"Well, I have noticed that whenever the ogre brings back water he always comes from that side; so if you follow the same direction perhaps you may find some."

The man jumped up at once and was about to start, when the maiden spoke again:

"Tell me, where are you going?"

"Why do you want to know?"

"I have an errand for you; but tell me first whether you go east or west."

"I travel to Damascus."

"Then do this for me. As you pass through our village, ask for a man called Dschemil, and say to him: 'Dschemila greets you, from the castle, which lies far away, and is rocked by the wind. In my grave lies only a goat. So take heart.' "

And the man promised, and went his way, till he came to a spring of water. And he drank a great draught and then lay on the bank and slept quietly. When he woke he said to himself, "The maiden did a good deed when she told me where to find water. A few hours more, and I should have been dead. So I will do her bidding, and seek out her native town and the man for whom the message was given."

For a whole month he travelled, till at last he reached the town where Dschemil dwelt, and as luck would have it, there was the young man sitting before his door with his beard unshaven and his shaggy hair hanging over his eyes.

"Welcome, stranger," said Dschemil, as the man stopped. "Where have you come from?"

"I come from the west, and go towards the east," he answered.

"Well, stop with us awhile, and rest and eat!" said Dschemil. And the man entered; and food was set before him, and he sat down with the father of the maiden and her brothers, and Dschemil. Only Dschemil himself was absent, squatting on the threshold.

"Why do you not eat too?" asked the stranger. But one of the young men whispered hastily:

"Leave him alone. Take no notice! It is only at night that he ever eats."

So the stranger went on silently with his food. Suddenly one of Dschemil's brothers called out and said: "Dschemil, bring us some water!" And the stranger remembered his message and said:

"Is there a man here named 'Dschemil?' I lost my way in the desert, and came to a castle, and a maiden looked out of the window and——"

"Be quiet," they cried, fearing that Dschemil might hear. But Dschemil had heard, and came forward and said:

"What did you see? Tell me truly, or I will cut off your head this instant!"

"My lord," replied the stranger, "as I was wandering, hot and tired, through the desert, I saw near me a great castle, and I said aloud, 'I will rest a little in its shadow.' And a maiden looked out of a window and said, 'Are you a ghost or a man?' And I answered, 'I am a man, and a better one, too, than your father or your grandfather.' And I was thirsty and asked for water, but she had none to give me, and I felt like to die. Then she told me that the ogre, in whose castle she dwelt, brought

in water always from the same side, and that if I too
went that way most likely I should come to it. But
before I started she begged me to go to her native
town, and if I met a man called Dschemil I was to say
to him, 'Dschemila greets you, from the castle which
lies far away, and is rocked by the wind. In my grave
lies only a goat. So take heart.' "

Then Dschemil turned to his family and said:

"Is this true? and is Dschemila not dead at all, but
simply stolen from her home?"

"No, no," replied they, "his story is a pack of lies.
Dschemila is really dead. Everybody knows it."

"That I shall see for myself," said Dschemil, and,
snatching up a spade, hastened off to the grave where
the goat's head lay buried.

And they answered, "Then hear what really happened. When you were away, she went with the other
maidens to the forest to gather wood. And there she
found an iron mortar, which she wished to bring home;
but she could not carry it, neither would she leave it.
So the maidens returned without her, and as night was
come, we all set out to look for her, but found nothing.
And we said, 'The bridegroom will be here to-morrow,
and when he learns that she is lost, he will set out to
seek her, and we shall lose him too. Let us kill a goat,
and bury it in her grave, and tell him she is dead.' Now
you know, so do as you will. Only, if you go to seek
her, take with you this man with whom she has spoken
that he may show you the way."

"Yes; that is the best plan," replied Dschemil; "so
give me food, and hand me my sword, and we will set
out directly."

But the stranger answered: "I am not going to waste
a whole month in leading you to the castle! If it were
only a day or two's journey I would not mind; but a
month—no!"

"Come with me then for three days," said Dschemil,
"and put me in the right road, and I will reward you
richly."

"Very well," replied the stranger, "so let it be."

For three days they travelled from sunrise to sunset, then the stranger said: "Dschemil?"

'Yes," replied he.

"Go straight on till you reach a spring, then go on a little farther, and soon you will see the castle standing before you."

"So I will," said Dschemil.

"Farewell, then," said the stranger, and turned back the way he had come.

It was six and twenty days before Dschemil caught sight of a green spot rising out of the sandy desert, and knew that the spring was near at last. He hastened his steps, and soon was kneeling by its side, drinking thirstily of the bubbling water. Then he lay down on the cool grass, and began to think. "If the man was right, the castle must be somewhere about. I had better sleep here to-night, and to-morrow I shall be able to see where it is." So he slept long and peacefully. When he awoke the sun was high, and he jumped up and washed his face and hands in the spring, before going on his journey. He had not walked far, when the castle suddenly appeared before him, though a moment before not a trace of it could be seen. "How am I to get in?" he thought. "I dare not knock, lest the ogre should hear me. Perhaps it would be best for me to climb up the wall, and wait to see what will happen." So he did, and after sitting on the top for about an hour, a window above him opened, and a voice said: "Dschemil!" He looked up, and at the sight of Dschemila, whom he had so long believed to be dead, he began to weep.

"Dear cousin," she whispered, "what has brought you here?"

"My grief at losing you."

"Oh! go away at once. If the ogre comes back he will kill you."

"I swear by your head, queen of my heart, that I have not found you only to lose you again! If I must die, well, I must!"

"Oh, what can I do for you?"

"Anything you like!"

"If I let you down a cord, can you make it fast under your arms, and climb up?"

"Of course I can," said he.

So Dschemila lowered the cord, and Dschemil tied it round him, and climbed up to her window. Then they embraced each other tenderly, and burst into tears of joy.

"But what shall I do when the ogre returns?" asked she.

"Trust to me," he said.

Now there was a chest in the room, where Dschemila kept her clothes. And she made Dschemil get into it, and lie at the bottom, and told him to keep very still.

He was only hidden just in time, for the lid was hardly closed when the ogre's heavy tread was heard on the stairs. He flung open the door, bringing men's flesh for himself and lamb's flesh for the maiden. "I smell the smell of a man!" he thundered. "What is he doing here?"

"How could any one have come to this desert place?" asked the girl, and burst into tears.

"Do not cry," said the ogre; "perhaps a raven has dropped some scraps from his claws."

"Ah, yes, I was forgetting," answered she. "One did drop some bones about."

"Well, burn them to powder," replied the ogre, "so that I may swallow it."

So the maiden took some bones and burned them, and gave them to the ogre, saying, "Here is the powder, swallow it."

And when he had swallowed the powder the ogre stretched himself out and went to sleep.

In a little while the man's flesh, which the maiden was cooking for the ogre's supper, called out and said:

> "Hist! Hist!
> A man lies in the kist!"

And the lamb's flesh answered:

"He is your brother,
And cousin of the other."

The ogre moved sleepily, and asked, "What did the meat say, Dschemila?"

"Only that I must be sure to add salt."

"Well, add salt."

"Yes, I have done so," said she.

The ogre was soon sound asleep again, when the man's flesh called out a second time:

"Hist! Hist!
A man lies in the kist!"

And the lamb's flesh answered:

"He is your brother,
And cousin of the other."

"What did it say, Dschemila?" asked the ogre.

"Only that I must add pepper."

"Well, add pepper."

"Yes, I have done so," said she.

The ogre had had a long day's hunting, and could not keep himself awake. In a moment his eyes were tight shut, and then the man's flesh called out for the third time:

"Hist! Hist!
A man lies in the kist."

And the lamb's flesh answered:

"He is your brother,
And cousin of the other."

"What did it say, Dschemila?" asked the ogre.

"Only that it was ready, and that I had better take it off the fire."

"Then if it is ready, bring it to me, and I will eat it."

So she brought it to him, and while he was eating she

H.J.FORD

supped off the lamb's flesh herself, and managed to put some aside for her cousin.

When the ogre had finished, and had washed his hands, he said to Dschemila: "Make my bed, for I am tired."

So she made his bed, and put a nice soft pillow for his head, and tucked him up.

"Father," she said suddenly.

"Well, what is it?"

"Dear father, if you are really asleep, why are your eyes always open?"

"Why do you ask that, Dschemila? Do you want to deal treacherously with me?"

"No, of course not, father. How could I, and what would be the use of it?"

"Well, why do you want to know?"

"Because last night I woke up and saw the whole place shining in a red light, which frightened me."

"That happens when I am fast asleep."

"And what is the good of the pin you always keep here so carefully?"

"If I throw that pin in front of me, it turns into an iron mountain."

"And this darning needle?"

"That becomes a sea."

"And this hatchet?"

"That becomes a thorn hedge, which no one can pass through. But why do you ask all these questions? I am sure you have something in your head."

"Oh, I just wanted to know; and how could anyone find me out here?" and she began to cry.

"Oh, don't cry, I was only in fun," said the ogre.

He was soon asleep again, and a yellow light shone through the castle.

"Come quick!" called Dschemil from the chest; "we must fly now while the ogre is asleep."

"Not yet," she said, "there is a yellow light shining. I don't think he is asleep."

So they waited for an hour. Then Dschemil whispered again: "Wake up! There is no time to lose!"

"Let me see if he is asleep," said she, and she peeped in, and saw a red light shining. Then she stole back to her cousin, and asked, "But how are we to get out?"

"Get the rope, and I will let you down."

So she fetched the rope, the hatchet, and the pin and the needles, and said, "Take them, and put them in the pocket of your cloak, and be sure not to lose them."

Dschemil put them carefully in his pocket, and tied the rope round her, and let her down over the wall.

"Are you safe?" he asked.

"Yes, quite."

"Then untie the rope, so that I may draw it up."

And Dschemila did as she was told, and in a few minutes he stood beside her.

Now all this time the ogre was asleep, and had heard nothing. Then his dog came to him and said, "O, sleeper, are you having pleasant dreams? Dschemila has forsaken you and run away."

The ogre got out of bed, gave the dog a kick, then went back again, and slept till morning.

When it grew light, he rose, and called, "Dschemila! Dschemila!" but he only heard the echo of his own voice! Then he dressed himself quickly; buckled on his sword and whistled to his dog, and followed the road which he knew the fugitives must have taken.

"Cousin," said Dschemila suddenly, and turning round as she spoke.

"What is it?" answered he.

"The ogre is coming after us. I saw him."

"But where is he? I don't see him."

"Over there. He only looks about as tall as a needle."

Then they both began to run as fast as they could, while the ogre and his dog kept drawing always nearer. A few more steps, and he would have been by their side, when Dschemila threw the darning needle behind her. In a moment it became an iron mountain between them and their enemy.

"We will break it down, my dog and I," cried the ogre in a rage, and they dashed at the mountain till they had forced a path through, and came ever nearer and nearer.

"Cousin!" said Dschemila suddenly.

"What is it?"

"The ogre is coming after us with his dog."

"You go on in front then," answered he; and they both ran on as fast as they could, while the ogre and the dog drew always nearer and nearer.

"They are close upon us!" cried the maiden, glancing behind, "you must throw the pin."

So Dschemil took the pin from his cloak and threw it behind him, and a dense thicket of thorns sprang up round them, which the ogre and his dog could not pass through.

"I will get through it somehow, if I burrow underground," cried he, and very soon he and the dog were on the other side.

"Cousin," said Dschemila, "they are close to us now."

"Go in front, and fear nothing," replied Dschemil.

So she ran on a little way, and then stopped.

"He is only a few yards away now," she said, and Dschemil flung the hatchet on the ground, and it turned into a lake.

"I will drink, and my dog shall drink, till it is dry," shrieked the ogre and the dog drank so much that it burst and died. But the ogre did not stop for that, and soon the whole lake was nearly dry. Then he exclaimed, "Dschemila, let your head become a donkey's head, and your hair fur!"

But when it was done, Dschemil looked at her in horror, and said, "She is really a donkey, and not a woman at all!"

And he left her, and went home.

For two days poor Dschemila wandered about alone, weeping bitterly. When her cousin drew near his native town, he began to think over his conduct, and to feel ashamed of himself.

"Perhaps by this time she has changed back to her proper shape," he said to himself, "I will go and see!"

So he made all the haste he could, and at last he saw her seated on a rock, trying to keep off the wolves, who longed to have her for dinner. He drove them off and said, "Get up, dear cousin, you have had a narrow escape."

Dschemila stood up and answered, "Bravo, my friend. You persuaded me to fly with you, and then left me helplessly to my fate."

"Shall I tell you the truth?" asked he.

"Tell it."

"I thought you were a witch, and I was afraid of you."

"Did you not see me before my transformation? and did you not watch it happen under your very eyes, when the ogre bewitched me?"

"What shall I do?" said Dschemila. "If I take you into the town, everyone will laugh, and say, 'Is that a new kind of toy you have got? It has hands like a woman, feet like a woman, the body of a woman; but its head is the head of an ass, and its hair is fur.' "

"Well, what do you mean to do with me?" asked Dschemila. "Better take me home to my mother by night, and tell no one anything about it."

"So I will," said he.

They waited where they were till it was nearly dark, then Dschemil brought his cousin home.

"Is that Dschemil?" asked the mother when he knocked softly.

"Yes, it is."

"And have you found her?"

"Yes, and I have brought her to you."

"Oh, where is she? let me see her!" cried the mother.

"Here, behind me," answered Dschemil.

But when the poor woman caught sight of her daughter, she shrieked, and exclaimed, "Are you making fun of me? When did I ever give birth to an ass?"

"Hush!" said Dschemil, "it is not necessary to let the

whole world know! And if you look at her body, you will see two scars on it."

"Mother," sobbed Dschemila, "do you really not know your own daughter?"

"Yes, of course I know her."

"What are her two scars then?"

"On her thigh is a scar from the bite of a dog, and on her breast is the mark of a burn, where she pulled a lamp over her when she was little."

"Then look at me, and see if I am not your daughter," said Dschemila, throwing off her clothes and showing her two scars.

And at the sight her mother embraced her, weeping.

"Dear daughter," she cried, "what evil fate has befallen you?"

"It was the ogre who carried me off first, and then bewitched me," answered Dschemila.

"But what is to be done with you?" asked her mother.

"Hide me away, and tell no one anything about me. And you, dear cousin, say nothing to the neighbours, and if they should put questions, you can make answer that I have not yet been found."

"So I will," replied he.

Then he and her mother took her upstairs and hid her in a cupboard, where she stayed for a whole month, only going out to walk when all the world was asleep.

Meanwhile Dschemil had returned to his own home, where his father and mother, his brothers and neighbours, greeted him joyfully.

"When did you come back?" said they, "and have you found Dschemila?"

"No, I searched the whole world after her, and could hear nothing of her."

"Did you part company with the man who started with you?"

"Yes; after three days he got so weak and useless he could not go on. It must be a month by now since he reached home again. I went on and visited every castle, and looked in every house. But there were no signs of her; and so I gave it up."

And they answered him: "We told you before that it was no good. An ogre or an ogress must have snapped her up, and how can you expect to find her?"

"I loved her too much to be still," he said.

But his friends did not understand, and soon they spoke to him again about it.

"We will seek for a wife for you. There are plenty of girls prettier than Dschemila."

"I dare say; but I don't want them."

"But what will you do with all the cushions and carpets, and beautiful things you bought for your house?"

"They can stay in the chests."

"But the moths will eat them! For a few weeks, it is of no consequence, but after a year or two they will be quite useless."

"And if they have to lie there ten years I will have Dschemila, and her only, for my wife. For a month, or even two months, I will rest here quietly. Then I will go and seek her afresh."

"Oh, you are quite mad! Is she the only maiden in the world? There are plenty of others better worth having than she is."

"If there are I have not seen them! And why do you make all this fuss? Every man knows his own business best."

"Why, it is you who are making all the fuss your-self——"

But Dschemil turned and went into the house, for he did not want to quarrel.

Three months later a Jew, who was travelling across the desert, came to the castle, and laid himself down under the wall to rest.

In the evening the ogre saw him there and said to him, "Jew, what are you doing here? Have you anything to sell?"

"I have only some clothes," answered the Jew, who was in mortal terror of the ogre.

"Oh, don't be afraid of me," said the ogre, laughing. "I shall not eat you. Indeed, I mean to go a bit of the way with you myself."

"I am ready, gracious sir," replied the Jew, rising to his feet.

"Well, go straight on till you reach a town, and in that town you will find a maiden called Dschemila and a young man called Dschemil. Take this mirror and this comb with you, and say to Dschemila, 'Your father, the ogre, greets you, and begs you to look at your face in this mirror, and it will appear as it was before, and to comb your hair with this comb, and it will be as formerly.' If you do not carry out my orders, I will eat you the next time we meet."

"Oh, I will obey you punctually," cried the Jew.

After thirty days the Jew entered the gate of the town, and sat down in the first street he came to, hungry, thirsty, and very tired.

Quite by chance, Dschemil happened to pass by, and seeing a man sitting there, full in the glare of the sun, he stopped, and said, "Get up at once, Jew; you will have a sunstroke if you sit in such a place."

"Ah, good sir," replied the Jew, "for a whole month I have been travelling, and I am too tired to move."

"Which way did you come?" asked Dschemil.

"From out there," answered the Jew pointing behind him.

"And you have been travelling for a month, you say? Well, did you see anything remarkable?"

"Yes, good sir; I saw a castle, and lay down to rest under its shadow. And an ogre woke me, and told me to come to this town, where I should find a young man called Dschemil, and a girl called Dschemila."

"My name is Dschemil. What does the ogre want with me?"

"He gave me some presents for Dschemila. How can I see her?"

"Come with me, and you shall give them into her own hands."

So the two went together to the house of Dschemil's uncle, and Dschemil led the Jew into his aunt's room.

"Aunt!" he cried, "this Jew who is with me has come from the ogre, and has brought with him, as presents, a mirror and a comb which the ogre has sent her."

"But it may be only some wicked trick on the part of the ogre," said she.

"Oh, I don't think so," answered the young man, "give her the things."

Then the maiden was called, and she came out of her hiding place, and went up to the Jew, saying, "Where have you come from, Jew?"

"From your father the ogre."

"And what errand did he send you on?"

"He told me I was to give you this mirror and this comb, and to say 'Look in this mirror, and comb your hair with this comb, and both will become as they were formerly.'"

And Dschemila took the mirror and looked into it, and combed her hair with the comb, and she had no longer an ass's head, but the face of a beautiful maiden.

Great was the joy of both mother and cousin at this wonderful sight, and the news that Dschemila had returned soon spread, and the neighbours came flocking in with greetings.

"When did you come back?"

"My cousin brought me."

"Why, he told us he could not find you!"

"Oh, I did that on purpose," answered Dschemil. "I did not want everyone to know."

Then he turned to his father and his mother, his brothers and his sisters-in-law, and said, "We must set to work at once, for the wedding will be to-day."

A beautiful litter was prepared to carry the bride to her new home, but she shrank back, saying, "I am afraid, lest the ogre should carry me off again."

"How can the ogre get at you when we are all here?" they said. "There are two thousand of us all told, and every man has his sword."

"He will manage it somehow," answered Dschemila, "he is a powerful king!"

"She is right," said an old man. "Take away the litter, and let her go on foot if she is afraid."

"But it is absurd!" exclaimed the rest; "how can the ogre get hold of her?"

"I will not go," said Dschemila again. "You do not know that monster; I do."

And while they were disputing the bridegroom arrived.

"Let her alone. She shall stay in her father's house. After all, I can live here, and the wedding feast shall be made ready."

And so they were married at last, and died without having had a single quarrel.

—*The Grey Fairy Book* (1900)

The Story of
the Hero Makóma

ZIMBABWEAN

———— ◆◆◆ ————

ONCE upon a time, at the town of Senna on the banks
of the Zambesi, was born a child. He was not like other
children, for he was very tall and strong; over his shoulder he carried a big sack, and in his hand an iron
hammer. He could also speak like a grown man, but
usually he was very silent.

One day his mother said to him: "My child, by what
name shall we know you?"

And he answered: "Call all the head men of Senna
here to the river's bank." And his mother called the
head men of the town, and when they had come he led
them down to a deep black pool in the river where all
the fierce crocodiles lived.

"O great men!" he said, while they all listened, "which
of you will leap into the pool and overcome the crocodiles?" But no one would come forward. So he turned
and sprang into the water and disappeared.

The people held their breath, for they thought: "Surely
the boy is bewitched and throws away his life, for the
crocodiles will eat him!" Then suddenly the ground
trembled, and the pool, heaving and swirling, became
red with blood, and presently the boy rising to the
surface swam on shore.

But he was no longer just a boy! He was stronger

than any man and very tall and handsome, so that the
people shouted with gladness when they saw him.

"Now, O my people!" he cried waving his hand, "you
know my name—I am Makóma, 'the Greater'; for have
I not slain the crocodiles in the pool where none would
venture?"

Then he said to his mother: "Rest gently, my mother,
for I go to make a home for myself and become a hero."
Then, entering his hut he took Nu-éndo, his iron hammer, and throwing the sack over his shoulder, he went
away.

Makóma crossed the Zambesi, and for many moons
he wandered towards the north and west until he came
to a very hilly country where, one day, he met a huge
giant making mountains.

"Greeting," shouted Makóma, "who are you?"

"I am Chi-éswa-mapíri, who makes the mountains,"
answered the giant; "and who are you?"

"I am Makóma, which signifies 'greater,' " answered
he.

"Greater than who?" asked the giant.

"Greater than you!" answered Makóma.

The giant gave a roar and rushed upon him. Makóma
said nothing, but swinging his great hammer, Nu-éndo,
he struck the giant upon the head.

He struck him so hard a blow that the giant shrank
into quite a little man, who fell upon his knees saying:
"You are indeed greater than I, O Makóma; take me
with you to be your slave!" So Makóma picked him up
and dropped him into the sack that he carried upon his
back.

He was greater than ever now, for all the giant's
strength had gone into him; and he resumed his journey, carrying his burden with as little difficulty as an
eagle might carry a hare.

Before long he came to a country broken up with
huge stones and immense clods of earth. Looking over
one of the heaps he saw a giant wrapped in dust drag-

ging out the very earth and hurling it in handfuls on either side of him.

"Who are you," cried Makóma, "that pulls up the earth in this way?"

"I am Chi-dúbula-táka," said he, "and I am making the river-beds."

"Do you know who I am?" said Makóma. "I am he that is called 'greater!' "

"Greater than who?" thundered the giant.

"Greater than you!" answered Makóma.

With a shout, Chi-dúbula-táka seized a great clod of earth and launched it at Makóma. But the hero had his sack held over his left arm and the stones and earth fell harmlessly upon it, and, tightly gripping his iron hammer, he rushed in and struck the giant to the ground. Chi-dúbula-táka grovelled before him, all the while growing smaller and smaller; and when he had become a convenient size Makóma picked him up and put him into the sack beside Chi-éswa-mapíri.

He went on his way even greater than before, as all the river-maker's power had become his; and at last he came to a forest of bao-babs and thorn trees. He was astonished at their size, for every one was full grown and larger than any trees he had ever seen, and close by he saw Chi-gwísa-míti, the giant who was planting the forest.

Chi-gwísa-míti was taller than either of his brothers, but Makóma was not afraid, and called out to him: "Who are you, O Big One?"

"I," said the giant, "am Chi-gwísa-míti, and I am planting these bao-babs and thorns as food for my children the elephants."

"Leave off!" shouted the hero, "for I am Makóma, and would like to exchange a blow with thee!"

The giant, plucking up a monster bao-bab by the roots, struck heavily at Makóma; but the hero sprang aside, and as the weapon sank deep into the soft earth, whirled Nu-éndo the hammer round his head and felled the giant with one blow.

So terrible was the stroke that Chi-gwísa-míti shrivelled up as the other giants had done; and when he had got back his breath he begged Makóma to take him as his servant. "For," said he, "it is honourable to serve a man so great as thou."

Makóma, after placing him in his sack, proceeded upon his journey, and travelling for many days he at last reached a country so barren and rocky that not a single living thing grew upon it—everywhere reigned grim desolation. And in the midst of this dead region he found a man eating fire.

"What are you doing?" demanded Makóma.

"I am eating fire," answered the man, laughing; "and my name is Chi-ídea-móto, for I am the flame-spirit, and can waste and destroy what I like."

"You are wrong," said Makóma; "for I am Makóma, who is 'greater' than you—and you cannot destroy me!"

The fire-eater laughed again, and blew a flame at Makóma. But the hero sprang behind a rock—just in time, for the ground upon which he had been standing was turned to molten glass, like an overbaked pot, by the heat of the flame-spirit's breath.

Then the hero flung his iron hammer at Chi-ídea-móto, and, striking him, it knocked him helpless; so Makóma placed him in the sack, Woro-nówu, with the other great men that he had overcome.

And now, truly, Makóma was a very great hero; for he had the strength to make hills, the industry to lead rivers over dry wastes, foresight and wisdom in planting trees, and the power of producing fire when he wished.

Wandering on he arrived one day at a great plain, well watered and full of game; and in the very middle of it, close to a large river, was a grassy spot, very pleasant to make a home upon.

Makóma was so delighted with the little meadow that he sat down under a large tree, and removing the sack from his shoulder, took out all the giants and set them before him. "My friends," said he, "I have travelled far and am weary. Is not this such a place as would suit a

hero for his home? Let us then go, to-morrow, to bring
in timber to make a kraal."

So the next day Makóma and the giants set out to get
poles to build the kraal, leaving only Chi-éswa-mapíri
to look after the place and cook some venison which
they had killed. In the evening, when they returned,
they found the giant helpless and tied to a tree by one
enormous hair!

"How is it," said Makóma, astonished, "that we find
you thus bound and helpless?"

"O Chief," answered Chi-éswa-mapíri, "at mid-day a
man came out of the river; he was of immense stature,
and his grey moustaches were of such length that I
could not see where they ended! He demanded of me
'Who is thy master?' And I answered: 'Makóma, the
greatest of heroes.' Then the man seized me, and pulling a hair from his moustache, tied me to this tree—
even as you see me."

Makóma was very wroth, but he said nothing, and
drawing his finger-nail across the hair (which was as
thick and strong as palm rope) cut it, and set free the
mountain-maker.

The three following days exactly the same thing happened, only each time with a different one of the party;
and on the fourth day Makóma stayed in camp when
the others went to cut poles, saying that he would see
for himself what sort of man this was that lived in the
river and whose moustaches were so long that they
extended beyond men's sight.

So when the giants had gone he swept and tidied the
camp and put some venison on the fire to roast. At
midday, when the sun was right overhead, he heard a
rumbling noise from the river, and looking up he saw
the head and shoulders of an enormous man emerging
from it. And behold! right down the river-bed and up
the river-bed, till they faded into the blue distance,
stretched the giant's grey moustaches!

"Who are you?" bellowed the giant, as soon as he was
out of the water.

MAKOMA Gets entangled by a hair of CHINDEBOU MAUC·IR

"I am he that is called Makóma," answered the hero; "and, before I slay thee, tell me also what is thy name and what thou doest in the river?"

"My name is Chin-débou Máu-giri," said the giant. "My home is in the river, for my moustache is the grey fever-mist that hangs above the water, and with which I bind all those that come unto me so that they die."

"You cannot bind me!" shouted Makóma, rushing upon him and striking with his hammer. But the river giant was so slimy that the blow slid harmlessly off his green chest, and as Makóma stumbled and tried to regain his balance, the giant swung one of his long hairs around him and tripped him up.

For a moment Makóma was helpless, but remembering the power of the flame-spirit which had entered into him, he breathed a fiery breath upon the giant's hair and cut himself free.

As Chin-débou Máu-giri leaned forward to seize him the hero flung his sack Woronówu over the giant's slippery head, and gripping his iron hammer, struck him again; this time the blow alighted upon the dry sack and Chin-débou Máu-giri fell dead.

When the four giants returned at sunset with the poles they rejoiced to find that Makóma had overcome the fever-spirit, and they feasted on the roast venison till far into the night; but in the morning, when they awoke, Makóma was already warming his hands at the fire, and his face was gloomy.

"In the darkness of the night, O my friends," he said presently, "the white spirits of my fathers came unto me and spoke, saying: 'Get thee hence, Makóma, for thou shalt have no rest until thou hast found and fought with Sákatirína, who has five heads, and is very great and strong; so take leave of thy friends, for thou must go alone.'"

Then the giants were very sad, and bewailed the loss of their hero; but Makóma comforted them, and gave back to each the gifts he had taken from them. Then bidding them "Farewell," he went on his way.

Makóma travelled far towards the west; over rough mountains and water-logged morasses, fording deep rivers, and tramping for days across dry deserts where most men would have died, until at length he arrived at a hut standing near some large peaks, and inside the hut were two beautiful women.

"Greeting!" said the hero. "Is this the country of Sákatiŕina of five heads, whom I am seeking?"

"We greet you, O Great One!" answered the women. "We are the wives of Sákatiŕina; your search is at an end, for there stands he whom you seek!" And they pointed to what Makóma had thought were two tall mountain peaks. "Those are his legs," they said; "his body you cannot see, for it is hidden in the clouds."

Makóma was astonished when he beheld how tall was the giant; but, nothing daunted, he went forward until he reached one of Sákatiŕina's legs, which he struck heavily with Nu-éndo. Nothing happened, so he hit again and then again until, presently, he heard a tired, far-away voice saying: "Who is it that scratches my feet?"

And Makóma shouted as loud as he could, answering: "It is I, Makóma, who is called 'Greater!' " And he listened, but there was no answer.

Then Makóma collected all the dead brushwood and trees that he could find, and making an enormous pile round the giant's legs, set a light to it.

This time the giant spoke; his voice was very terrible, for it was the rumble of thunder in the clouds. "Who is it," he said, "making that fire smoulder around my feet?"

"It is I, Makóma!" shouted the hero. "And I have come from far away to see thee, O Sákatiŕina, for the spirits of my fathers bade me go seek and fight with thee, lest I should grow fat, and weary of myself!"

There was silence for a while, and then the giant spoke softly: "It is good, O Makóma!" he said. "For I too have grown weary. There is no man as great as I, therefore I am all alone. Guard thyself!" And bending suddenly he seized the hero in his hands and dashed him upon the ground. And lo! instead of death, Makóma had found life, for he sprang to his feet mightier in strength and stature than before, and rushing in he gripped the giant by the waist and wrestled with him.

Hour by hour they fought, and mountains rolled beneath their feet like pebbles in a flood; now Makóma would break away, and summoning up his strength, strike the giant with Nu-éndo his iron hammer, and Sákatiría would pluck up the mountains and hurl them upon the hero, but neither one could slay the other. At last, upon the second day, they grappled so strongly that they could not break away; but their strength was failing, and, just as the sun was sinking, they fell together to the ground, insensible.

In the morning when they awoke, Mulímo the Great Spirit was standing by them; and he said: "O Makóma and Sákatiría! Ye are heroes so great that no man may come against you. Therefore ye will leave the world and take up your home with me in the clouds." And as he spake the heroes became invisible to the people of the Earth, and were no more seen among them.

—*The Orange Fairy Book* (1906)

The Story of Zoulvisia

ARMENIAN

———◆◆◆———

In the midst of a sandy desert, somewhere in Asia, the eyes of travellers are refreshed by the sight of a high mountain covered with beautiful trees, among which the glitter of foaming waterfalls may be seen in the sunlight. In that clear, still air it is even possible to hear the song of the birds, and smell of the flowers; but though the mountain is plainly inhabited—for here and there a white tent is visible—none of the kings or princes who pass it on the road to Babylon or Baalbec ever plunge into its forests—or, if they do, they never come back. Indeed, so great is the terror caused by the evil reputation of the mountain that fathers on their death-beds pray their sons never to try to fathom its mysteries. But in spite of its ill-fame, a certain number of young men every year announce their intention of visiting it and, as we have said, are never seen again.

Now there was once a powerful king who ruled over a country on the other side of the desert, and, when dying, gave the usual counsel to his seven sons. Hardly, however, was he dead than the eldest, who succeeded to the throne, announced his intention of hunting in the enchanted mountain. In vain the old men shook their heads and tried to persuade him to give up his mad scheme. All was useless; he went, but did not return; and in due time the throne was filled by his next brother.

And so it happened to the other five; but when the youngest became king, and he also proclaimed a hunt in the mountain, a loud lament was raised in the city. "Who will reign over us when you are dead? For dead you surely will be," cried they. "Stay with us, and we will make you happy." And for a while he listened to their prayers, and the land grew rich and prosperous under his rule. But in a few years the restless fit again took possession of him, and this time he would hear nothing. Hunt in that forest he would, and calling his friends and attendants round him, he set out one morning across the desert.

They were riding through a rocky valley, when a deer sprang up in front of them and bounded away. The king instantly gave chase, followed by his attendants; but the animal ran so swiftly that they never could get up to it, and at length it vanished in the depths of the forest.

Then the young man drew rein for the first time, and looked about him. He had left his companions far behind, and, glancing back, he beheld them entering some tents, dotted here and there amongst the trees. For himself, the fresh coolness of the woods was more attractive to him than any food, however delicious, and for hours he strolled about as his fancy led him.

By-and-by, however, it began to grow dark, and he thought that the moment had arrived for them to start for the palace. So, leaving the forest with a sigh, he made his way down to the tents, but what was his horror to find his men lying about, some dead, some dying. These were past speech, but speech was needless. It was as clear as day that the wine they had drunk contained deadly poison.

"I am too late to help you, my poor friends," he said, gazing at them sadly; "but at least I can avenge you! Those that have set the snare will certainly return to see to its working. I will hide myself somewhere, and discover who they are!"

Near the spot where he stood he noticed a large walnut tree, and into this he climbed. Night soon fell, and nothing broke the stillness of the place; but with the earliest glimpse of dawn a noise of galloping hoofs was heard.

Pushing the branches aside the young man beheld a youth approaching, mounted on a white horse. On reaching the tents the cavalier dismounted, and closely inspected the dead bodies that lay about them. Then, one by one, he dragged them to a ravine close by and threw them into a lake at the bottom. While he was doing this, the servants who had followed him led away the horses of the ill-fated men, and the courtiers were ordered to let loose the deer, which was used as a decoy, and to see that the tables in the tents were covered as before with food and wine.

Having made these arrangements he strolled slowly through the forest, but great was his surprise to come upon a beautiful horse hidden in the depths of a thicket.

"There was a horse for every dead man," he said to himself. "Then whose is this?"

"Mine!" answered a voice from a walnut tree close by. "Who are you that lure men into your power and then poison them? But you shall do so no longer. Return to your house, wherever it may be, and we will fight before it!"

The cavalier remained speechless with anger at these words; then with a great effort he replied:

"I accept your challenge. Mount, and follow me. I am Zoulvisia." And, springing on his horse, he was out of sight so quickly that the king had only time to notice that light seemed to flow from himself and his steed, and that the hair under his helmet was like liquid gold.

Clearly, the cavalier was a woman. But who could she be? Was she queen of all the queens? Or was she chief of a band of robbers? She was neither: only a beautiful maiden.

I ACCEPT YOUR CHALLENGE MOUNT AND FOLLOW ME I AM ZOULVISIA

Wrapped in these reflections, he remained standing beneath the walnut tree, long after horse and rider had vanished from sight. Then he awoke with a start, to remember that he must find the way to the house of his enemy, though where it was he had no notion. However, he took the path down which the rider had come, and walked along it for many hours till he came to three huts side by side, in each of which lived an old fairy and her sons.

The poor king was by this time so tired and hungry that he could hardly speak, but when he had drunk some milk, and rested a little, he was able to reply to the questions they eagerly put to him.

"I am going to seek Zoulvisia," said he; "she has slain my brothers and many of my subjects, and I mean to avenge them."

He had only spoken to the inhabitants of one house, but from all three came an answering murmur.

"What a pity we did not know! Twice this day has she passed our door, and we might have kept her prisoner."

But though their words were brave their hearts were not, for the mere thought of Zoulvisia made them tremble.

"Forget Zoulvisia, and stay with us," they all said, holding out their hands; "you shall be our big brother, and we will be your little brothers." But the king would not.

Drawing from his pocket a pair of scissors, a razor and a mirror, he gave one to each of the old fairies, saying:

"Though I may not give up my vengeance I accept your friendship, and therefore leave you these three tokens. If blood should appear on the face of either know that my life is in danger, and, in memory of our sworn brotherhood, come to my aid."

"We will come," they answered. And the king mounted his horse and set out along the road they showed him.

By the light of the moon he presently perceived a splendid palace, but, though he rode twice round it, he could find no door. He was considering what he should do next, when he heard the sound of loud snoring, which seemed to come from his feet. Looking down, he beheld an old man lying at the bottom of a deep pit, just outside the walls, with a lantern by his side.

"Perhaps *he* may be able to give me some counsel," thought the king; and, with some difficulty, he scrambled into the pit and laid his hand on the shoulder of the sleeper.

"Are you a bird or a snake that you can enter here?" asked the old man, awaking with a start. But the king answered that he was a mere mortal, and that he sought Zoulvisia.

"Zoulvisia? The world's curse?" replied he, gnashing his teeth. "Out of all the thousands she has slain I am the only one who has escaped, though why she spared me only to condemn me to this living death I cannot guess."

"Help me if you can," said the king. And he told the old man his story, to which he listened intently.

"Take heed then to my counsel," answered the old man. "Know that every day at sunrise Zoulvisia dresses herself in her jacket of pearls, and mounts the steps of her crystal watch-tower. From there she can see all over her lands, and behold the entrance of either man or demon. If so much as one is detected she utters such fearful cries that those who hear her die of fright. But hide yourself in a cave that lies near the foot of the tower, and plant a forked stick in front of it; then, when she has uttered her third cry, go forth boldly, and look up at the tower. And go without fear, you will have broken her power."

Word for word the king did as the old man had bidden him, and when he stepped forth from the cave, their eyes met.

"You have conquered me," said Zoulvisia, "and are worthy to be my husband, for you are the first man who has not died at the sound of my voice!" And letting down her golden hair, she drew up the king to the summit of the tower as with a rope. Then she led him into the hall of audience, and presented him to her household.

"Ask of me what you will, and I will grant it to you," whispered Zoulvisia with a smile, as they sat together on a mossy bank by the stream. And the king prayed her to set free the old man to whom he owed his life, and to send him back to his own country.

"I have finished with hunting, and with riding about my lands," said Zoulvisia, the day that they were married. "The care of providing for us all belongs henceforth to you." And turning to her attendants, she bade them bring the horse of fire before her.

"This is your master, O my steed of flame," cried she; "and you will serve him as you have served me." And kissing him between his eyes, she placed the bridle in the hand of her husband.

The horse looked for a moment at the young man, and then bent his head, while the king patted his neck and smoothed his tail, till they felt themselves old friends. After this he mounted to do Zoulvisia's bidding, but before he started she gave him a case of pearls containing one of her hairs, which he tucked into the breast of his coat.

He rode along for some time, without seeing any game to bring home for dinner. Suddenly a fine stag started up almost under his feet, and he at once gave chase. On they sped, but the stag twisted and turned so that the king had no chance of a shot till they reached a broad river, when the animal jumped in and swam across. The king fitted his cross-bow with a bolt, and took aim, but though he succeeded in wounding the stag, it contrived to gain the opposite bank, and in his excitement he never observed that the case of pearls had fallen into the water.

The stream, though deep, was likewise rapid, and the box was swirled along miles, and miles, and miles, till it was washed up in quite another country. Here it was picked up by one of the water-carriers belonging to the palace, who showed it to the king. The workmanship of the case was so curious, and the pearls so rare, that the king could not make up his mind to part with it, but he gave the man a good price and sent him away. Then, summoning his chamberlain, he bade him find out its history in three days, or lose his head.

But the answer to the riddle, which puzzled all the magicians and wise men, was given by an old woman, who came up to the palace and told the chamberlain that, for two handfuls of gold, she would reveal the mystery.

Of course the chamberlain gladly gave her what she asked, and in return she informed him that the case and the hair belonged to Zoulvisia.

"Bring her hither, old crone, and you shall have gold enough to stand up in," said the chamberlain. And the old woman answered that she would try what she could do.

She went back to her hut in the middle of the forest, and standing in the door-way, whistled softly. Soon the dead leaves on the ground began to move and to rustle, and from underneath them there came a long train of serpents. They wriggled to the feet of the witch, who stooped down and patted their heads, and gave each one some milk in a red earthen basin. When they had all finished, she whistled again, and bade two or three coil themselves round her arms and neck, while she turned one into a cane and another into a whip. Then she took a stick, and on the river bank changed it into a raft, and seating herself comfortably, she pushed off into the centre of the stream.

All that day she floated, and all the next night, and towards sunset the following evening she found herself close to Zoulvisia's garden, just at the moment that the king, on the horse of flame, was returning from hunting.

"Who are you?" he asked in surprise; for old women

travelling on rafts were not common in that country. "Who are you, and why have you come here?"

"I am a poor pilgrim, my son," answered she, "and having missed the caravan, I have wandered foodless for many days through the desert, till at length I reached the river. There I found this tiny raft, and to it I committed myself, not knowing if I should live or die. But since you have found me, give me, I pray you, bread to eat, and let me lie this night by the dog who guards your door!"

This piteous tale touched the heart of the young man, and he promised that he would bring her food, and that she should pass the night in his palace.

"But mount behind me, good woman," cried he, "for you have walked far, and it is still a long way to the palace." And as he spoke he bent down to help her, but the horse swerved on one side.

And so it happened twice and thrice, and the old witch guessed the reason, though the king did not.

"I fear to fall off," said she; "but as your kind heart pities my sorrows, ride slowly, and lame as I am, I think I can manage to keep up."

At the door he bade the witch to rest herself, and he would fetch her all she needed. But Zoulvisia his wife grew pale when she heard whom he had brought, and besought him to feed the old woman and send her away, as she would cause mischief to befall them.

The king laughed at her fears, and answered lightly:

"Why, one would think she was a witch to hear you talk! And even if she were, what harm could she do to us?" And calling to the maidens he bade them carry her food, and to let her sleep in their chamber.

Now the old woman was very cunning, and kept the maidens awake half the night with all kinds of strange stories. Indeed, the next morning, while they were dressing their mistress, one of them suddenly broke into a laugh, in which the others joined her.

"What is the matter with you?" asked Zoulvisia. And the maid answered that she was thinking of a droll adventure told them the evening before by the new-comer.

"And, oh, madam!" cried the girl, "it may be that she is a witch, as they say; but I am sure she never would work a spell to harm a fly! And as for her tales, they would pass many a dull hour for you, when my lord was absent!"

So, in an evil hour, Zoulvisia consented that the crone should be brought to her, and from that moment the two were hardly ever apart.

One day the witch began to talk about the young king, and to declare that in all the lands she had visited she had seen none like him.

"It was so clever of him to guess your secret so as to win your heart," said she. "And of course he told you his, in return?"

"No, I don't think he has got any," returned Zoulvisia.

"Not got any secrets?" cried the old woman scornfully. "That is nonsense! Every man has a secret, which he always tells to the woman he loves. And if he has not told it to *you*, it is that he does not love you!"

These words troubled Zoulvisia mightily, though she would not confess it to the witch. But the next time she found herself alone with her husband, she began to coax him to tell her in what lay the secret of his strength. For a long while he put her off with caresses, but when she would be no longer denied, he answered:

"It is my sabre that gives me strength, and day and night it lies by my side. But now that I have told you, swear upon this ring, that I will give you in exchange for yours, that you will reveal it to nobody." And Zoulvisia swore; and instantly hastened to betray the great news to the old woman.

Four nights later, when all the world was asleep, the witch softly crept into the king's chamber and took the sabre from his side as he lay sleeping. Then, opening her lattice, she flew on to the terrace and dropped the sword into the river.

The next morning everyone was surprised because the king did not, as usual, rise early and go off to hunt. The attendants listened at the keyhole and heard the sound of heavy breathing, but none dared enter, till Zoulvisia pushed past. And what a sight met their gaze! There lay the king almost dead, with foam on his mouth, and eyes that were already closed. They wept, and they cried to him, but no answer came.

Suddenly a shriek broke from those who stood hindmost, and in strode the witch, with serpents round her neck and arms and hair. At a sign from her they flung themselves with a hiss upon the maidens, whose flesh was pierced with their poisonous fangs. Then turning to Zoulvisia, she said:

"I give you your choice—will you come with me, or shall the serpents slay you also?" And as the terrified girl stared at her, unable to utter one word, she seized her by the arm and led her to the place where the raft was hidden among the rushes. When they were both on board she took the oars, and they floated down the stream till they had reached the neighbouring country, where Zoulvisia was sold for a sack of gold to the king.

Now, since the young man had entered the three huts on his way through the forest, not a morning had passed without the sons of the three fairies examining the scissors, the razor and the mirror, which the young king had left them. Hitherto the surfaces of all three things had been bright and undimmed, but on this particular morning, when they took them out as usual, drops of blood stood on the razor and the scissors, while the little mirror was clouded over.

"Something terrible must have happened to our little brother," they whispered to each other, with awestruck faces; "we must hasten to his rescue ere it be too late." And putting on their magic slippers they started for the palace.

The servants greeted them eagerly, ready to pour forth all they knew, but that was not much; only that the sabre had vanished, none knew where. The newcomers passed the whole of the day in searching for it, but it could not be found, and when night closed in, they were very tired and hungry. But how were they to get food? The king had not hunted that day, and there was nothing for them to eat. The little men were in despair, when a ray of the moon suddenly lit up the river beneath the walls.

"How stupid! Of course there are fish to catch," cried they; and running down to the bank they soon succeeded in landing some fine fish, which they cooked on the spot. Then they felt better, and began to look about them.

Further out, in the middle of the stream, there was a strange splashing, and by-and-by the body of a huge fish appeared, turning and twisting as if in pain. The eyes of all the brothers were fixed on the spot, when the fish leapt in the air, and a bright gleam flashed through the night. "The sabre!" they shouted, and plunged into the stream, and with a sharp tug, pulled out the sword, while the fish lay on the water, exhausted by its struggles. Swimming back with the sabre to land, they carefully dried it in their coats, and then carried it to the palace and placed it on the king's pillow. In an instant colour came back to the waxen face, and the hollow cheeks filled out. The king sat up, and opening his eyes he said:

"Where is Zoulvisia?"

"That is what we do not know," answered the little men; "but now that you are saved you will soon find out." And they told him what had happened since Zoulvisia had betrayed his secret to the witch.

"Let me go to my horse," was all he said. But when he entered the stable he could have wept at the sight of his favourite steed, which was nearly in as sad a plight as his master had been. Languidly he turned his head as the door swung back on its hinges, but when he beheld the king he rose up, and rubbed his head against him.

"Oh, my poor horse! How much cleverer were you

than I! If I had acted like you I should never have lost
Zoulvisia; but we will seek her together, you and I."

For a long while the king and his horse followed the
course of the stream, but nowhere could he learn anything of Zoulvisia. At length, one evening, they both
stopped to rest by a cottage not far from a great city,
and as the king was lying outstretched on the grass,
lazily watching his horse cropping the short turf, an old
woman came out with a wooden bowl of fresh milk,
which she offered him.

He drank it eagerly, for he was very thirsty, and then
laying down the bowl, began to talk to the woman, who
was delighted to have someone to listen to her conversation.

"You are in luck to have passed this way just now,"
said she, "for in five days the king holds his wedding
banquet. Ah! but the bride is unwilling, for all her blue
eyes and her golden hair! And she keeps by her side a
cup of poison, and declares that she will swallow it
rather than become his wife. Yet he is a handsome man
too, and a proper husband for her—more than she
could have looked for, having come no one knows
whither, and bought from a witch——"

The king started. Had he found her after all? His
heart beat violently, as if it would choke him; but he
gasped out:

"Is her name Zoulvisia?"

"Ay, so she says, though the old witch—— But what
ails you?" she broke off, as the young man sprang to his
feet and seized her wrists.

"Listen to me," he said. "Can you keep a secret?"

"Aye," answered the old woman again, "if I am paid
for it."

"Oh, you shall be paid, never fear—as much as your
heart can desire! Here is a handful of gold: you shall
have as much again if you will do my bidding." The old
crone nodded her head.

"Then go and buy a dress such as ladies wear at

court, and manage to get admitted into the palace, and
into the presence of Zoulvisia. When there, show her
this ring, and after that she will tell you what to do."

So the old woman set off, and clothed herself in a
garment of yellow silk, and wrapped a veil closely round
her head. In this dress she walked boldly up the palace
steps behind some merchants whom the king had sent
for to bring presents for Zoulvisia.

At first the bride would have nothing to say to any of
them; but on perceiving the ring, she suddenly grew as
meek as a lamb. And thanking the merchants for their
trouble, she sent them away, and remained alone with
her visitor.

"Grandmother," asked Zoulvisia, as soon as the door
was safely shut, "where is the owner of this ring?"

"In my cottage," answered the old woman, "waiting
for orders from you."

"Tell him to remain there for three days; and now go
to the king of this country, and say that you have
succeeded in bringing me to reason. Then he will let
me alone and will cease to watch me. On the third day
from this I shall be wandering about the garden near
the river, and there your guest will find me. The rest
concerns myself only."

The morning of the third day dawned, and with the
first rays of the sun a bustle began in the palace; for that
evening the king was to marry Zoulvisia. Tents were
being erected of fine scarlet cloth, decked with wreaths
of sweet-smelling white flowers, and in them the banquet was spread. When all was ready a procession was
formed to fetch the bride, who had been wandering in
the palace gardens since daylight, and crowds lined the
way to see her pass. A glimpse of her dress of golden
gauze might be caught, as she passed from one flowery
thicket to another; then suddenly the multitude swayed,
and shrank back, as a thunderbolt seemed to flash out
of the sky to the place where Zoulvisia was standing.
Ah! but it was no thunderbolt, only the horse of fire!

And when the people looked again, it was bounding away with two persons on its back.

Zoulvisia and her husband both learnt how to keep happiness when they had got it; and *that* is a lesson that many men and women never learn at all. And besides, it is a lesson which nobody can teach, and that every boy and girl must learn for themselves.

—*The Olive Fairy Book* (1907)

The Three Treasures
of the Giants

SLAVIC

———◆◆———

LONG, long ago, there lived an old man and his wife
who had three sons; the eldest was called Martin, the
second Michael, while the third was named Jack.

One evening they were all seated round the table,
eating their supper of bread and milk.

"Martin," said the old man suddenly, "I feel that I
cannot live much longer. You, as the eldest, will inherit
this hut; but, if you value my blessing, be good to your
mother and brothers."

"Certainly, father; how can you suppose I should do
them wrong?" replied Martin indignantly, helping himself to all the best bits in the dish as he spoke. The old
man saw nothing, but Michael looked on in surprise,
and Jack was so astonished that he quite forgot to eat
his own supper.

A little while after, the father fell ill, and sent for his
sons, who were out hunting, to bid him farewell. After
giving good advice to the two eldest, he turned to Jack.

"My boy," he said, "you have not got quite as much
sense as other people, but if Heaven has deprived you
of some of your wits, it has given you a kind heart.
Always listen to what it says, and take heed to the
words of your mother and brothers, as well as you are

able!" So saying the old man sank back on his pillows and died.

The cries of grief uttered by Martin and Michael sounded through the house, but Jack remained by the bedside of his father, still and silent, as if he were dead also. At length he got up, and going into the garden, hid himself in some trees, and wept like a child, while his two brothers made ready for the funeral.

No sooner was the old man buried than Martin and Michael agreed that they would go into the world together to seek their fortunes, while Jack stayed at home with their mother. Jack would have liked nothing better than to sit and dream by the fire, but the mother, who was very old herself, declared that there was no work for him to do, and that he must seek it with his brothers.

So, one fine morning, all three set out; Martin and Michael carried two great bags full of food, but Jack carried nothing. This made his brothers very angry, for the day was hot and the bags were heavy, and about noon they sat down under a tree and began to eat. Jack was as hungry as they were, but he knew that it was no use asking for anything; and he threw himself under another tree, and wept bitterly.

"Another time perhaps you won't be so lazy, and will bring food for yourself," said Martin, but to his surprise Jack answered:

"You are a nice pair! You talk of seeking your fortunes so as not to be a burden on our mother, and you begin by carrying off all the food she has in the house!"

This reply was so unexpected that for some moments neither of the brothers made any answer. Then they offered their brother some of their food, and when he had finished eating they went their way once more.

Towards evening they reached a small hut, and knocking at the door, asked if they might spend the night there. The man, who was a wood-cutter, invited them in, and begged them to sit down to supper. Martin thanked him, but being very proud, explained that it was only shelter they wanted, as they had plenty of food with them; and he and Michael at once opened their bags and began to eat, while Jack hid himself in a corner. The wife, on seeing this, took pity on him, and called him to come and share their supper, which he gladly did, and very good he found it. At this, Martin regretted deeply that he had been so foolish as to refuse, for his bits of bread and cheese seemed very hard when he smelt the savoury soup his brother was enjoying.

"He shan't have such a chance again," thought he; and the next morning he insisted on plunging into a thick forest where they were likely to meet nobody.

For a long time they wandered hither and thither, for they had no path to guide them; but at last they came upon a wide clearing, in the midst of which stood a castle. Jack shouted with delight, but Martin, who was in a bad temper, said sharply:

"We must have taken a wrong turning! Let us go back."

"Idiot!" replied Michael, who was hungry too, and, like many people when they are hungry, very cross also. "We set out to travel through the world, and what does it matter if we go to the right or to the left?" And, without another word, took the path to the castle, closely followed by Jack, and after a moment by Martin likewise.

The door of the castle stood open, and they entered a great hall, and looked about them. Not a creature was to be seen, and suddenly Martin—he did not know why—felt a little frightened. He would have left the castle at once, but stopped when Jack boldly walked up to a door in the wall and opened it. He could not for very shame be outdone by his younger brother, and passed behind him into another splendid hall, which was filled from floor to ceiling with great pieces of copper money.

The sight quite dazzled Martin and Michael, who emptied all the provisions that remained out of their bags, and heaped them up instead with handfuls of copper.

Scarcely had they done this when Jack threw open another door, and this time it led to a hall filled with silver. In an instant his brothers had turned their bags upside down, so that the copper money tumbled out on to the floor, and were shovelling in handfuls of the silver instead. They had hardly finished, when Jack opened yet a third door, and all three fell back in amazement, for this room was a mass of gold, so bright that their eyes grew sore as they looked at it. However, they soon recovered from their surprise, and quickly emptied their bags of the silver, and filled them with gold instead. When they would hold no more, Martin said:

"We had better hurry off now lest somebody else should come, and we might not know what to do"; and, followed by Michael, he hastily left the castle. Jack lingered behind for a few minutes to put pieces of gold, silver, and copper into his pocket, and to eat the food that his brothers had thrown down in the first room. Then he went after them, and found them lying down to rest in the midst of a forest. It was near sunset, and Martin began to feel hungry, so, when Jack arrived, he bade him return to the castle and bring the bread and cheese that they had left there.

"It is hardly worth doing that," answered Jack; "for I picked up the pieces and ate them myself."

At this reply both brothers were beside themselves with anger, and fell upon the boy, beating him, and calling him names, till they were quite tired.

"Go where you like," cried Martin with a final kick; "but never come near us again." And poor Jack ran weeping into the woods.

The next morning his brothers went home, and bought a beautiful house, where they lived with their mother like great lords.

Jack remained for some hours in hiding, thankful to be safe from his tormentors; but when no one came to trouble him, and his back did not ache so much, he began to think what he had better do. At length he made up his mind to go to the castle and take away as much money with him as would enable him to live in comfort for the rest of his life. This being decided, he sprang up, and set out along the path which led to the castle. As before, the door stood open, and he went on till he had reached the hall of gold, and there he took off his jacket and tied the sleeves together so that it might make a kind of bag. He then began to pour in the gold by handfuls, when, all at once, a noise like thunder shook the castle. This was followed by a voice, hoarse as that of a bull, which cried:

"I smell the smell of a man." And two giants entered.

"So, little worm! it is *you* who steal our treasures!" exclaimed the biggest. "Well, we have got you now, and we will cook you for supper!" But here the other giant drew him aside, and for a moment or two they whispered together. At length the first giant spoke:

"To please my friend I will spare your life on condition that, for the future, you shall guard our treasures. If you are hungry take this little table and rap on it, saying, as you do so: 'The dinner of an emperor!' and you will get as much food as you want."

With a light heart Jack promised all that was asked of him, and for some days enjoyed himself mightily. He had everything he could wish for, and did nothing from morning till night; but by-and-by he began to get very tired of it all.

"Let the giants guard their treasures themselves," he said to himself at last; "I am going away. But I will leave all the gold and silver behind me, and will take nought but you, my good little table."

So, tucking the table under his arm, he started off for the forest, but he did not linger there long, and soon found himself in the fields on the other side. There he saw an old man, who begged Jack to give him something to eat.

"You could not have asked a better person," answered Jack cheerfully. And signing to him to sit down

THE GIANTS FIND JACK IN THE TREASURE ROOM.

with him under a tree, he set the table in front of them, and struck it three times, crying:

"The dinner of an emperor!" He had hardly uttered the words when fish and meat of all kinds appeared on it!

"That is a clever trick of yours," said the old man, when he had eaten as much as he wanted. "Give it to me in exchange for a treasure I have which is still better. Do you see this cornet? Well, you have only to tell it that you wish for an army, and you will have as many soldiers as you require."

Now, since he had been left to himself, Jack had grown ambitious, so, after a moment's hesitation, he took the cornet and gave the table in exchange. The old man bade him farewell, and set off down one path, while Jack chose another, and for a long time he was quite pleased with his new possession. Then, as he felt hungry, he wished for his table back again, as no house was in sight, and he wanted some supper badly. All at once he remembered his cornet, and a wicked thought entered his mind.

"Two hundred hussars, forward!" cried he. And the neighing of horses and the clanking of swords were heard close at hand. The officer who rode at their head approached Jack, and politely inquired what he wished them to do.

"A mile or two along that road," answered Jack, "you will find an old man carrying a table. Take the table from him and bring it to me."

The officer saluted and went back to his men, who started at a gallop to do Jack's bidding.

In ten minutes they had returned, bearing the table with them.

"That is all, thank you," said Jack; and the soldiers disappeared inside the cornet.

Oh, what a good supper Jack had that night, quite forgetting that he owed it to a mean trick. The next day he breakfasted early, and then walked on towards the nearest town. On the way thither he met another old man, who begged for something to eat.

"Certainly, you shall have something to eat," replied Jack. And, placing the table on the ground, he cried:

"The dinner of an emperor!" when all sorts of good dishes appeared. At first the old man ate greedily, and said nothing; but, after his hunger was satisfied, he turned to Jack and said:

"That is a very clever trick of yours. Give the table to me, and you shall have something still better."

"I don't believe that there *is* anything better," answered Jack.

"Yes, there is. Here is my bag; it will give you as many castles as you can possibly want."

Jack thought for a moment; then he replied: "Very well, I will exchange with you." And passing the table to the old man, he hung the bag over his arm.

Five minutes later he summoned five hundred lancers out of the cornet and bade them go after the old man and fetch back the table.

Now that by his cunning he had obtained possession of the three magic objects, he resolved to return to his native place. Smearing his face with dirt, and tearing his clothes so as to look like a beggar, he stopped the passers by and, on pretence of seeking money or food, he questioned them about the village gossip. In this manner he learned that his brothers had become great men, much respected in all the country round. When he heard that, he lost no time in going to the door of their fine house and imploring them to give him food and shelter; but the only thing he got was hard words, and a command to beg elsewhere. At length, however, at their mother's entreaty, he was told that he might pass the night in the stable. Here he waited until everybody in the house was sound asleep, when he drew his bag from under his cloak, and desired that a castle might appear in that place; and the cornet gave him soldiers to guard the castle, while the table furnished him with a good supper. In the morning, he caused it all to vanish, and when his brothers entered the stable they found him lying on the straw.

Jack remained here for many days, doing nothing, and—as far as anybody knew—eating nothing. This conduct puzzled his brothers greatly, and they put such constant questions to him, that at length he told them the secret of the table, and even gave a dinner to them, which far outdid any they had ever seen or heard of. But though they had solemnly promised to reveal nothing, somehow or other the tale leaked out, and before long reached the ears of the king himself. That very evening his chamberlain arrived at Jack's dwelling, with a request from the king that he might borrow the table for three days.

"Very well," answered Jack, "you can take it back with you. But tell his majesty that if he does not return it at the end of the three days I will make war upon him."

So the chamberlain carried away the table and took it straight to the king, telling him at the same time of Jack's threat, at which they both laughed till their sides ached.

Now the king was so delighted with the table, and the dinners it gave him, that when the three days were over he could not make up his mind to part with it. Instead, he sent for his carpenter, and bade him copy it exactly, and when it was done he told his chamberlain to return it to Jack with his best thanks. It happened to be dinner time, and Jack invited the chamberlain, who knew nothing of the trick, to stay and dine with him. The good man, who had eaten several excellent meals provided by the table in the last three days, accepted the invitation with pleasure, even though he was to dine in a stable, and sat down on the straw beside Jack.

"The dinner of an emperor!" cried Jack. But not even a morsel of cheese made its appearance.

"The dinner of an emperor!" shouted Jack in a voice of thunder. Then the truth dawned on him; and, crushing the table between his hands, he turned to the chamberlain, who, bewildered and half-frightened, was wondering how to get away.

"Tell your false king that to-morrow I will destroy his castle as easily as I have broken this table."

The chamberlain hastened back to the palace, and gave the king Jack's message, at which he laughed more than before, and called all his courtiers to hear the story. But they were not quite so merry when they woke next morning and beheld ten thousand horsemen, and as many archers, surrounding the palace. The king saw it was useless to hold out, and he took the white flag of truce in one hand, and the real table in the other, and set out to look for Jack.

"I committed a crime," said he; "but I will do my best to make up for it. Here is your table, which I own with shame that I tried to steal, and you shall have besides, my daughter as your wife!"

There was no need to delay the marriage when the table was able to furnish the most splendid banquet that ever was seen, and after everyone had eaten and drunk as much as they wanted, Jack took his bag and commanded a castle filled with all sorts of treasures to arise in the park for himself and his bride.

At this proof of his power the king's heart died within him.

"Your magic is greater than mine," he said; "and you are young and strong, while I am old and tired. Take, therefore, the sceptre from my hand, and my crown from my head, and rule my people better than I have done."

So at last Jack's ambition was satisfied. He could not hope to be more than a king, and as long as he had his cornet to provide him with soldiers he was secure against his enemies. He never forgave his brothers for the way they had treated him, though he presented his mother with a beautiful castle, and everything she could possibly wish for. In the centre of his own palace was a treasure chamber, and in this chamber the table, the cornet, and the bag were kept as the most prized of all his possessions, and not a week passed without a visit from king John to make sure they were safe. He reigned long and well, and died a very old man, beloved by his people. But his good example was not followed by his sons and his grandsons. They grew so proud that they were ashamed to think that the founder of their race had once been a poor boy; and as they and all the world could not fail to remember it, as long as the table, the cornet, and the bag were shown in the treasure chamber, one king, more foolish than the rest, thrust them into a dark and damp cellar.

For some time the kingdom remained, though it became weaker and weaker every year that passed. Then, one day, a rumour reached the king that a large army was marching against him. Vaguely he recollected some tales he had heard about a magic cornet which could provide as many soldiers as would serve to conquer the earth, and which had been removed by his grandfather to a cellar. Thither he hastened that he might renew his power once more, and in that black and slimy spot he found the treasures indeed. But the table fell to pieces as he touched it, in the cornet there remained only a few fragments of leathern belts which the rats had gnawed, and in the bag nothing but broken bits of stone.

And the king bowed his head to the doom that awaited him, and in his heart cursed the ruin wrought by the pride and foolishness of himself and his forefathers.

—*The Orange Fairy Book* (1906)

The Troll's Daughter

DANISH

———————•◆•———————

THERE was once a lad who went to look for a place. As he went along he met a man, who asked him where he was going. He told him his errand, and the stranger said, "Then you can serve me; I am just in want of a lad like you, and I will give you good wages—a bushel of money the first year, two the second year, and three the third year, for you must serve me three years, and obey me in everything, however strange it seems to you. You need not be afraid of taking service with me, for there is no danger in it if you only know how to obey."

The bargain was made, and the lad went home with the man to whom he had engaged himself. It was a strange place indeed, for he lived in a bank in the middle of the wild forest, and the lad saw there no other person than his master. The latter was a great troll, and had marvellous power over both men and beasts.

Next day the lad had to begin his service. The first thing that the troll set him to was to feed all the wild animals from the forest. These the troll had tied up, and there were both wolves and bears, deer and hares, which the troll had gathered in the stalls and folds in his stable down beneath the ground, and that stable was a mile long. The boy, however, accomplished all this work on that day, and the troll praised him and said that it was very well done.

Next morning the troll said to him, "To-day the animals are not to be fed; they don't get the like of that every day. You shall have leave to play about for a little, until they are to be fed again."

Then the troll said some words to him which he did not understand, and with that the lad turned into a hare, and ran out into the wood. He got plenty to run for, too, for all the hunters aimed at him, and tried to shoot him, and the dogs barked and ran after him wherever they got wind of him. He was the only animal that was left in the wood now, for the troll had tied up all the others, and every hunter in the whole country was eager to knock him over. But in this they met with no success; there was no dog that could overtake him, and no marksman that could hit him. They shot and shot at him, and he ran and ran. It was an unquiet life, but in the long run he got used to it, when he saw that there was no danger in it, and it even amused him to befool all the hunters and dogs that were so eager after him.

Thus a whole year passed, and when it was over the troll called him home, for he was now in his power like all the other animals. The troll then said some words to him which he did not understand, and the hare immediately became a human being again. "Well, how do you like to serve me?" said the troll, "and how do you like being a hare?"

The lad replied that he liked it very well; he had never been able to go over the ground so quickly before. The troll then showed him the bushel of money that he had already earned, and the lad was well pleased to serve him for another year.

The first day of the second year the boy had the same work to do as on the previous one—namely, to feed all the wild animals in the troll's stable. When he had done this the troll again said some words to him, and with

The Troll's Daughter.

that he became a raven, and flew high up into the air. This was delightful, the lad thought; he could go even faster now than when he was a hare, and the dogs could not come after him here. This was a great delight to him, but he soon found out that he was not to be left quite at peace, for all the marksmen and hunters who saw him aimed at him and fired away, for they had no other birds to shoot at than himself, as the troll had tied up all the others.

This, however, he also got used to, when he saw that they could never hit him, and in this way he flew about all that year, until the troll called him home again, said some strange words to him, and gave him his human shape again. "Well, how did you like being a raven?" said the troll.

"I liked it very well," said the lad, "for never in all my days have I been able to rise so high." The troll then showed him the two bushels of money which he had earned that year, and the lad was well content to remain in his service for another year.

Next day he got his old task of feeding all the wild beasts. When this was done the troll again said some words to him, and at these he turned into a fish, and sprang into the river. He swam up and he swam down, and thought it was pleasant to let himself drive with the stream. In this way he came right out into the sea, and swam further and further out. At last he came to a glass palace, which stood at the bottom of the sea. He could see into all the rooms and halls, where everything was very grand; all the furniture was of white ivory, inlaid with gold and pearl. There were soft rugs and cushions of all the colours of the rainbow, and beautiful carpets that looked like the finest moss, and flowers and trees with curiously crooked branches, both green and yellow, white and red, and there were also little fountains which sprang up from the most beautiful snail-shells, and fell into bright mussel-shells, and at the same time made a most delightful music, which filled the whole palace.

The most beautiful thing of all, however, was a young girl who went about there, all alone. She went about from one room to another, but did not seem to be happy with all the grandeur she had about her. She walked in solitude and melancholy, and never even thought of looking at her own image in the polished glass walls that were on every side of her, although she was the prettiest creature anyone could wish to see. The lad thought so too while he swam round the palace and peeped in from every side.

"Here, indeed, it would be better to be a man than such a poor dumb fish as I am now," said he to himself; "if I could only remember the words that the troll says when he changes my shape, then perhaps I could help myself to become a man again." He swam and he pondered and he thought over this until he remembered the sound of what the troll said, and then he tried to say it himself. In a moment he stood in human form at the bottom of the sea.

He made haste then to enter the glass palace, and went up to the young girl and spoke to her.

At first he nearly frightened the life out of her, but he talked to her so kindly and explained how he had come down there that she soon recovered from her alarm, and was very pleased to have some company to relieve the terrible solitude that she lived in. Time passed so quickly for both of them that the youth (for now he was quite a young man, and no more a lad) forgot altogether how long he had been there.

One day the girl said to him that now it was close on the time when he must become a fish again—the troll would soon call him home, and he would have to go, but before that he must put on the shape of the fish, otherwise he could not pass through the sea alive. Before this, while he was staying down there, she had told him that she was a daughter of the same troll whom the youth served, and he had shut her up there to keep her away from everyone. She had now devised a plan by which they could perhaps succeed in getting

to see each other again, and spending the rest of their
lives together. But there was much to attend to, and he
must give careful heed to all that she told him.

She told him then that all the kings in the country
round about were in debt to her father the troll, and
the king of a certain kingdom, the name of which she
told him, was the first who had to pay, and if he could
not do so at the time appointed he would lose his head.
"And he cannot pay," said she; "I know that for certain.
Now you must, first of all, give up your service with my
father; the three years are past, and you are at liberty to
go. You will go off, with your six bushels of money, to
the kingdom that I have told you of, and there enter
the service of the king. When the time comes near for
his debt becoming due you will be able to notice by his
manner that he is ill at ease. You shall then say to him
that you know well enough what it is that is weighing
upon him—that it is the debt which he owes to the
troll, and cannot pay, but that you can lend him the
money. The amount is six bushels—just what you have.
You shall, however, only lend them to him on condition
that you may accompany him when he goes to make the
payment, and that you then have permission to run
before him as a fool. When you arrive at the troll's
abode, you must perform all kinds of foolish tricks, and
see that you break a whole lot of his windows, and do
all other damage that you can. My father will then get
very angry, and as the king must answer for what his
fool does he will sentence him, even although he has
paid his debt, either to answer three questions or to
lose his life. The first question my father will ask will
be, 'Where is my daughter?' Then you shall step forward and answer, 'She is at the bottom of the sea.' He
will then ask you whether you can recognise her, and to
this you will answer 'Yes.' Then he will bring forward a
whole troop of women, and cause them to pass before
you, in order that you may pick out the one that you
take for his daughter. You will not be able to recognise
me at all, and therefore I will catch hold of you as I go

past, so that you can notice it, and you must then make haste to catch me and hold me fast. You have then answered his first question. His next question will be, 'Where is my heart?' You shall then step forward again and answer, 'It is in a fish.' 'Do you know that fish?' he will say, and you will again answer 'Yes.' He will then cause all kinds of fish to come before you, and you shall choose between them. I shall take good care to keep by your side, and when the right fish comes I will give you a little push, and with that you will seize the fish and cut it up. Then all will be over with the troll; he will ask no more questions, and we shall be free to wed."

When the youth had got all these directions as to what he had to do when he got ashore again the next thing was to remember the words which the troll said when he changed him from a human being to an animal; but these he had forgotten, and the girl did not know them either. He went about all day in despair, and thought and thought, but he could not remember what they sounded like. During the night he could not sleep, until towards morning he fell into a slumber, and all at once it flashed upon him what the troll used to say. He made haste to repeat the words, and at the same moment he became a fish again and slipped out into the sea. Immediately after this he was called upon, and swam through the sea up the river to where the troll stood on the bank and restored him to human shape with the same words as before.

"Well, how do you like to be a fish?" asked the troll.

It was what he had liked best of all, said the youth, and that was no lie, as everybody can guess.

The troll then showed him the three bushels of money which he had earned during the past year; they stood beside the other three, and all the six now belonged to him.

"Perhaps you will serve me for another year yet," said the troll, "and you will get six bushels of money for it; that makes twelve in all, and that is a pretty penny."

"No," said the youth; he thought he had done enough, and was anxious to go some other place to serve, and learn other people's ways; but he would, perhaps, come back to the troll some other time.

The troll said that he would always be welcome; he had served him faithfully for the three years they had agreed upon, and he could make no objections to his leaving now.

The youth then got his six bushels of money, and with these he betook himself straight to the kingdom which his sweetheart had told him of. He got his money buried in a lonely spot close to the king's palace, and then went in there and asked to be taken into service. He obtained his request, and was taken on as stable-man, to tend the king's horses.

Some time passed, and he noticed how the king always went about sorrowing and grieving, and was never glad or happy. One day the king came into the stable, where there was no one present except the youth, who said straight out to him that, with his majesty's permission, he wished to ask him why he was so sorrowful.

"It's of no use speaking about that," said the king; "you cannot help me, at any rate."

"You don't know about that," said the youth; "I know well enough what it is that lies so heavy on your mind, and I know also of a plan to get the money paid."

This was quite another case, and the king had more talk with the stableman, who said that he could easily lend the king the six bushels of money, but would only do it on condition that he should be allowed to accompany the king when he went to pay the debt, and that he should then be dressed like the king's court fool, and run before him. He would cause some trouble, for which the king would be severely spoken to, but he would answer for it that no harm would befall him.

The king gladly agreed to all that the youth proposed, and it was now high time for them to set out.

When they came to the troll's dwelling it was no longer in the bank, but on the top of this there stood a large castle which the youth had never seen before. The troll could, in fact, make it visible or invisible, just as he pleased, and, knowing as much as he did of the troll's magic arts, the youth was not at all surprised at this.

When they came near to this castle, which looked as if it was of pure glass, the youth ran on in front as the king's fool. He ran sometimes facing forwards, sometimes backwards, stood sometimes on his head, and sometimes on his feet, and he dashed in pieces so many of the troll's big glass windows and doors that it was something awful to see, and overturned everything he could, and made a fearful disturbance.

The troll came rushing out, and was so angry and furious, and abused the king with all his might for bringing such a wretched fool with him, as he was sure that he could not pay the least bit of all the damage that had been done when he could not even pay off his old debt.

The fool, however, spoke up, and said that he could do so quite easily, and the king then came forward with the six bushels of money which the youth had lent him. They were measured and found to be correct. This the troll had not reckoned on, but he could make no objection against it. The old debt was honestly paid, and the king got his bond back again.

But there still remained all the damage that had been done that day, and the king had nothing with which to pay for this. The troll, therefore, sentenced the king, either to answer three questions that he would put to him, or have his head taken off, as was agreed on in the old bond.

There was nothing else to be done than to try to answer the troll's riddles. The fool then stationed himself just by the king's side while the troll came forward with his questions. He first asked, "Where is my daughter?"

The fool spoke up and said, "She is at the bottom of the sea."

"How do you know that?" said the troll.

"The little fish saw it," said the fool.

"Would you know her?" said the troll.

"Yes, bring her forward," said the fool.

The troll made a whole crowd of women go past them, one after the other, but all these were nothing but shadows and deceptions. Amongst the very last was the troll's real daughter, who pinched the fool as she went past him to make him aware of her presence. He thereupon caught her round the waist and held her fast, and the troll had to admit that his first riddle was solved.

Then the troll asked again: "Where is my heart?"

"It is in a fish," said the fool.

"Would you know that fish?" said the troll.

"Yes, bring it forward," said the fool.

Then all the fishes came swimming past them, and meanwhile the troll's daughter stood just by the youth's side. When at last the right fish came swimming along she gave him a nudge, and he seized it at once, drove his knife into it, and split it up, took the heart out of it, and cut it through the middle.

At the same moment the troll fell dead and turned into pieces of flint. With that all the bonds that the troll had bound were broken; all the wild beasts and birds which he had caught and hid under the ground were free now, and dispersed themselves in the woods and in the air.

The youth and his sweetheart entered the castle, which was now theirs, and held their wedding; and all the kings roundabout, who had been in the troll's debt,

and were now out of it, came to the wedding, and
saluted the youth as their emperor, and he ruled over
them all, and kept peace between them, and lived in
his castle with his beautiful empress in great joy and
magnificence. And if they have not died since they are
living there to this day.

—*The Pink Fairy Book* (1897)

Uraschimataro
and the Turtle

JAPANESE

———◆◆◆———

THERE was once a worthy old couple who lived on the
coast, and supported themselves by fishing. They had
only one child, a son, who was their pride and joy, and
for his sake they were ready to work hard all day long,
and never felt tired or discontented with their lot. This
son's name was Uraschimataro, which means in Japanese, "Son of the island," and he was a fine well-grown
youth and a good fisherman, minding neither wind nor
weather. Not the bravest sailor in the whole village
dared venture so far out to sea as Uraschimataro, and
many a time the neighbours used to shake their heads
and say to his parents, "If your son goes on being so
rash, one day he will try his luck once too often, and
the waves will end by swallowing him up." But Uraschimataro paid no heed to these remarks, and as he was
really very clever in managing a boat, the old people
were very seldom anxious about him.

One beautiful bright morning, as he was hauling his
well-filled nets into the boat, he saw lying among the
fishes a tiny little turtle. He was delighted with his
prize, and threw it into a wooden vessel to keep till he
got home, when suddenly the turtle found its voice,
and tremblingly begged for its life. "After all," it said,
"what good can I do you? I am so young and small, and

I would so gladly live a little longer. Be merciful and set me free, and I shall know how to prove my gratitude."

Now Uraschimataro was very good-natured, and besides, he could never bear to say no, so he picked up the turtle, and put it back into the sea.

Years flew by, and every morning Uraschimataro sailed his boat into the deep sea. But one day as he was making for a little bay between some rocks, there arose a fierce whirlwind, which shattered his boat to pieces, and she was sucked under by the waves. Uraschimataro himself very nearly shared the same fate. But he was a powerful swimmer, and struggled hard to reach the shore. Then he saw a large turtle coming towards him, and above the howling of the storm he heard what it said: "I am the turtle whose life you once saved. I will now pay my debt and show my gratitude. The land is still far distant, and without my help you would never get there. Climb on my back, and I will take you where you will." Uraschimataro did not wait to be asked twice, and thankfully accepted his friend's help. But scarcely was he seated firmly on the shell, when the turtle proposed that they should not return to the shore at once, but go under the sea, and look at some of the wonders that lay hidden there.

Uraschimataro agreed willingly, and in another moment they were deep, deep down, with fathoms of blue water above their heads. Oh, how quickly they darted through the still, warm sea! The young man held tight, and marvelled where they were going and how long they were to travel, but for three days they rushed on, till at last the turtle stopped before a splendid palace, shining with gold and silver, crystal and precious stones, and decked here and there with branches of pale pink coral and glittering pearls. But if Uraschimataro was astonished at the beauty of the outside, he was struck dumb at the sight of the hall within, which was lighted by the blaze of fish scales.

"Where have you brought me?" he asked his guide in a low voice.

"To the palace of Ringu, the house of the sea god, whose subjects we all are," answered the turtle. "I am the first waiting maid of his daughter, the lovely princess Otohimé, whom you will shortly see."

Uraschimataro was still so puzzled with the adventures that had befallen him, that he waited in a dazed condition for what would happen next. But the turtle, who had talked so much of him to the princess that she had expressed a wish to see him, went at once to make known his arrival. And directly the princess beheld him her heart was set on him, and she begged him to stay with her, and in return promised that he should never grow old, neither should his beauty fade. "Is not that reward enough?" she asked, smiling, looking all the while as fair as the sun itself. And Uraschimataro said "Yes," and so he stayed there. For how long? That he only knew later.

His life passed by, and each hour seemed happier than the last, when one day there rushed over him a terrible longing to see his parents. He fought against it hard, knowing how it would grieve the princess, but it grew on him stronger and stronger, till at length he became so sad that the princess inquired what was wrong. Then he told her of the longing he had to visit his old home, and that he must see his parents once more. The princess was almost frozen with horror, and implored him to stay with her, or something dreadful would be sure to happen. "You will never come back, and we shall meet again no more," she moaned bitterly. But Uraschimataro stood firm and repeated, "Only this once will I leave you, and then will I return to your side for ever." Sadly the princess shook her head, but she answered slowly, "One way there is to bring you safely back, but I fear you will never agree to the conditions of the bargain."

"I will do anything that will bring me back to you," exclaimed Uraschimataro, looking at her tenderly, but the princess was silent: she knew too well that when he left her she would see his face no more. Then she took

HOW URASCHIMATARO MET PRINCESS OTOHIME

from a shelf a tiny golden box, and gave it to Uraschimataro, praying him to keep it carefully, and above all things never to open it. "If you can do this," she said as she bade him farewell, "your friend the turtle will meet you at the shore, and will carry you back to me."

Uraschimataro thanked her from his heart, and swore solemnly to do her bidding. He hid the box safely in his garments, seated himself on the back of the turtle, and vanished in the ocean path, waving his hand to the princess. Three days and three nights they swam through the sea, and at length Uraschimataro arrived at the beach which lay before his old home. The turtle bade him farewell, and was gone in a moment.

Uraschimataro drew near to the village with quick and joyful steps. He saw the smoke curling through the roof, and the thatch where green plants had thickly sprouted. He heard the children shouting and calling, and from a window that he passed came the twang of the koto, and everything seemed to cry a welcome for his return. Yet suddenly he felt a pang at his heart as he wandered down the street. After all, everything was changed. Neither men nor houses were those he once knew. Quickly he saw his old home; yes, it was still there, but it had a strange look. Anxiously he knocked at the door, and asked the woman who opened it after his parents. But she did not know their names, and could give him no news of them.

Still more disturbed, he rushed to the burying ground, the only place that could tell him what he wished to know. Here at any rate he would find out what it all meant. And he was right. In a moment he stood before the grave of his parents, and the date written on the stone was almost exactly the date when they had lost their son, and he had forsaken them for the Daughter of the Sea. And so he found that since he had left his home, three hundred years had passed by.

Shuddering with horror at his discovery he turned back into the village street, hoping to meet some one who could tell him of the days of old. But when the man spoke, he knew he was not dreaming, though he felt as if he had lost his senses.

In despair he bethought him of the box which was the gift of the princess. Perhaps after all this dreadful thing was not true. He might be the victim of some enchanter's spell, and in his hand lay the counter-charm. Almost unconsciously he opened it, and a purple vapour came pouring out. He held the empty box in his hand, and as he looked he saw that the fresh hand of youth had grown suddenly shrivelled, like the hand of an old, old man. He ran to the brook, which flowed in a clear stream down from the mountain, and saw himself reflected as in a mirror. It was the face of a mummy which looked back at him. Wounded to death, he crept back through the village, and no man knew the old, old man to be the strong handsome youth who had run down the street an hour before. So he toiled wearily back, till he reached the shore, and here he sat sadly on a rock, and called loudly on the turtle. But she never came back any more, but instead, death came soon, and set him free. But before that happened, the people who saw him sitting lonely on the shore had heard his story, and when their children were restless they used to tell them of the good son who from love to his parents had given up for their sakes the splendour and wonders of the palace in the sea, and the most beautiful woman in the world besides.

—*The Pink Fairy Book* (1897)

What Came of Picking Flowers

PORTUGUESE

———◆◆———

THERE was once a woman who had three daughters whom she loved very much. One day the eldest was walking in a water-meadow, when she saw a pink growing in the stream. She stooped to pick the flower, but her hand had scarcely touched it, when she vanished altogether. The next morning the second sister went out into the meadow, to see if she could find any traces of the lost girl, and as a branch of lovely roses lay trailing across her path, she bent down to move it away, and in so doing, could not resist plucking one of the roses. In a moment she too had disappeared. Wondering what could have become of her two sisters, the youngest followed in their footsteps, and fell a victim to a branch of delicious white jessamine. So the old woman was left without any daughters at all.

She wept and wept, and wept, all day and all night, and went on weeping so long, that her son, who had been a little boy when his sisters disappeared, grew up to be a tall youth. Then one night he asked his mother to tell him what was the matter.

When he had heard the whole story, he said, "Give me your blessing, mother, and I will go and search the world till I find them."

So he set forth, and after he had travelled several

448

miles without any adventures, he came upon three big boys fighting in the road. He stopped and inquired what they were fighting about, and one of them answered:

"My lord! our father left to us, when he died, a pair of boots, a key, and a cap. Whoever puts on the boots and wishes himself in any place, will find himself there. The key will open every door in the world, and with the cap on your head no one can see you. Now our eldest brother wants to have all three things for himself, and we wish to draw lots for them."

"Oh, that is easily settled," said the youth. "I will throw this stone as far as I can, and the one who picks it up first, shall have the three things." So he took the stone and flung it, and while the three brothers were running after it, he drew hastily on the boots, and said, "Boots, take me to the place where I shall find my eldest sister."

The next moment the young man was standing on a steep mountain before the gates of a strong castle guarded by bolts and bars and iron chains. The key, which he had not forgotten to put in his pocket, opened the doors one by one, and he walked through a number of halls and corridors, till he met a beautiful and richly-dressed young lady who started back in surprise at the sight of him, and exclaimed, "Oh, sir, how did you contrive to get in here?" The young man replied that he was her brother, and told her by what means he had been able to pass through the doors. In return, she told him how happy she was, except for one thing, and that was, her husband lay under a spell, and could never break it till there should be put to death a man who could not die.

They talked together for a long time, and then the lady said he had better leave her as she expected her husband back at any moment, and he might not like him to be there; but the young man assured her she need not be afraid, as he had with him a cap which would make him invisible. They were still deep in conversation when the door suddenly opened, and a

bird flew in, but he saw nothing unusual, for, at the first noise, the youth had put on his cap. The lady jumped up and brought a large golden basin, into which the bird flew, reappearing directly after as a handsome man. Turning to his wife, he cried, "I am sure someone is in the room!" She got frightened, and declared that she was quite alone, but her husband persisted, and in the end she had to confess the truth.

"But if he is really your brother, why did you hide him?" asked he. "I believe you are telling me a lie, and if he comes back I shall kill him!"

At this the youth took off his cap, and came forward. Then the husband saw that he was indeed so like his wife that he doubted her word no longer, and embraced his brother-in-law with delight. Drawing a feather from his bird's skin, he said, "If you are in danger and cry, 'Come and help me, King of the Birds,' everything will go well with you."

The young man thanked him and went away, and after he had left the castle he told the boots that they must take him to the place where his second sister was living. As before, he found himself at the gates of a huge castle, and within was his second sister, very happy with her husband, who loved her dearly, but longing for the moment when he should be set free from the spell that kept him half his life a fish. When he arrived and had been introduced by his wife to her brother, he welcomed him warmly, and gave him a fish-scale, saying, "If you are in danger, call to me, 'Come and help me, King of the Fishes,' and everything will go well with you."

The young man thanked him and took his leave, and when he was outside the gates he told the boots to take him to the place where his youngest sister lived. The boots carried him to a dark cavern, with steps of iron leading up to it. Inside she sat, weeping and sobbing, and as she had done nothing else the whole time she had been there, the poor girl had grown very thin. When she saw a man standing before her, she sprang to her feet and exclaimed, "Oh, whoever you are, save me and take me from this horrible place!" Then he told her who he was, and how he had seen her sisters, whose happiness was spoilt by the spell under which both their husbands lay, and she, in turn, related her story. She had been carried off in the water-meadow by a horrible monster, who wanted to make her marry him by force, and had kept her a prisoner all these years because she would not submit to his will. Every day he came to beg her to consent to his wishes, and to remind her that there was no hope of her being set free, as he was the most constant man in the world, and besides that he could never die. At these words the youth remembered his two enchanted brothers-in-law, and he advised his sister to promise to marry the old man, if he would tell her why he could never die. Suddenly everything began to tremble, as if it was shaken by a whirlwind, and the old man entered, and flinging himself at the feet of the girl, he said: "Are you still determined never to marry me? If so you will have to sit there weeping till the end of the world, for I shall always be faithful to my wish to marry you!" "Well, I will marry you," she said, "if you will tell me why it is that you can never die."

Then the old man burst into peals of laughter. "Ah, ah, ah! You are thinking how you would be able to kill me? Well, to do that, you would have to find an iron casket which lies at the bottom of the sea, and has a white dove inside, and then you would have to find the egg which the dove laid, and bring it here, and dash it against my head." And he laughed again in his certainty that no one had ever got down to the bottom of the sea, and that if they did, they would never find the casket, or be able to open it. When he could speak once more, he said, "Now you will be obliged to marry me, as you know my secret." But she begged so hard that the wedding might be put off for three days, that he consented, and went away rejoicing at his victory. When he had disappeared, the brother took off the cap which had kept him invisible all this time, and told his sister not to lose heart as he hoped in three days she would be free. Then he drew on his boots, and wished himself at the seashore and there he was directly. Drawing out the fish-scale, he cried, "Come and help me, King of the Fishes!" and his brother-in-law swam up, and asked what he could do. The young man related the story, and when he had finished his listener summoned all the fishes to his presence. The last to arrive was a little sardine, who apologised for being so late, but said she had hurt herself by knocking her head against an iron casket that lay in the bottom of the sea. The king ordered several of the largest and strongest of his subjects to take the little sardine as a guide, and bring him the iron casket. They soon returned with the box placed across their backs and laid it down before him. Then the youth produced the key and said "Key, open that box!" and the key opened it, and though they were all crowding round, ready to catch it, the white dove within flew away.

It was useless to go after it, and for a moment the young man's heart sank. The next minute, however, he remembered that he had still his feather, and drew it out crying, "Come to me, King of the Birds!" and a rushing noise was heard, and the King of the Birds perched on his shoulder, and asked what he could do to help him. His brother-in-law told him the whole story, and when he had finished the King of the Birds commanded all his subjects to hasten to his presence. In an instant the air was dark with birds of all sizes, and at the very last came the white dove, apologising for being so late by saying that an old friend had arrived at his nest, and he had been obliged to give him some dinner. The King of the Birds ordered some of them to show the young man the white dove's nest, and when they reached it, there lay the egg which was to break the spell and set them all free. When it was safely in his pocket, he told the boots to carry him straight to the cavern where his youngest sister sat awaiting him.

Now it was already far on into the third day, which the old man had fixed for the wedding, and when the youth reached the cavern with his cap on his head, he found the monster there, urging the girl to keep her word and let the marriage take place at once. At a sign from her brother she sat down and invited the old monster to lay his head on her lap. He did so with delight, and her brother standing behind her back passed her the egg unseen. She took it, and dashed it straight at the horrible head, and the monster started, and with a groan that people took for the rumblings of an earthquake, he turned over and died.

As the breath went out of his body the husbands of the two eldest daughters resumed their proper shapes, and, sending for their mother-in-law, whose sorrow was so unexpectedly turned into joy, they had a great feast, and the youngest sister was rich to the end of her days with the treasures she found in the cave, collected by the monster.

—*The Grey Fairy Book* (1900)

Why the Sea Is Salt

NORSE

———◆◆◆———

Once upon a time, long, long ago, there were two brothers, the one rich and the other poor. When Christmas Eve came, the poor one had not a bite in the house, either of meat or bread; so he went to his brother, and begged him, in God's name, to give him something for Christmas Day. It was by no means the first time that the brother had been forced to give something to him, and he was not better pleased at being asked now than he generally was.

"If you will do what I ask you, you shall have a whole ham," said he. The poor one immediately thanked him, and promised this.

"Well, here is the ham, and now you must go straight to Dead Man's Hall," said the rich brother, throwing the ham to him.

"Well, I will do what I have promised," said the other, and he took the ham and set off. He went on and on for the livelong day, and at nightfall he came to a place where there was a bright light.

"I have no doubt this is the place," thought the man with the ham.

An old man with a long white beard was standing in the outhouse, chopping Yule logs.

"Good-evening," said the man with the ham.

"Good-evening to you. Where are you going at this late hour?" said the man.

"I am going to Dead Man's Hall, if only I am in the right track," answered the poor man.

"Oh! yes, you are right enough, for it is here," said the old man. "When you get inside they will all want to buy your ham, for they don't get much meat to eat there: but you must not sell it unless you can get the hand-mill which stands behind the door for it. When you come out again I will teach you how to stop the hand-mill, which is useful for almost everything."

So the man with the ham thanked the other for his good advice, and rapped at the door.

When he got in, everything happened just as the old man had said it would: all the people, great and small, came round him like ants on an ant-hill, and each tried to outbid the other for the ham.

"By rights my old woman and I ought to have it for our Christmas dinner, but, since you have set your hearts upon it, I must just give it up to you," said the man. "But, if I sell it, I will have the hand-mill which is standing there behind the door."

At first they would not hear of this, and haggled and bargained with the man, but he stuck to what he had said, and the people were forced to give him the hand-mill. When the man came out again into the yard, he asked the old wood-cutter how he was to stop the hand-mill, and when he had learnt that he thanked him and set off home with all the speed he could, but did not get there until after the clock had struck twelve on Christmas Eve.

"But where in the world have you been?" said the old woman. "Here I have sat waiting hour after hour, and have not even two sticks to lay across each other under the Christmas porridge-pot."

"Oh! I could not come before; I had something of importance to see about, and a long way to go, too; but now you shall just see!" said the man, and then he set the hand-mill on the table, and bade it first grind light,

then a table-cloth, and then meat, and beer, and everything else that was good for a Christmas Eve's supper;
and the mill ground all that he ordered. "Bless me!"
said the old woman as one thing after another appeared;
and she wanted to know where her husband had got the
mill from, but he would not tell her that.

"Never mind where I got it; you can see that it is a
good one, and the water that turns it will never freeze,"
said the man. So he ground meat and drink, and all
kinds of good things, to last all Christmas-tide, and on
the third day he invited all his friends to come to a
feast.

Now when the rich brother saw all that there was at
the banquet and in the house, he was both vexed and
angry, for he grudged everything his brother had. "On
Christmas Eve he was so poor that he came to me and
begged for a trifle, for God's sake, and now he gives a
feast as if he were both a count and a king!" thought he.
"But, for heaven's sake, tell me where you got your
riches from," said he to his brother.

"From behind the door," said he who owned the
mill, for he did not choose to satisfy his brother on that
point; but later in the evening, when he had taken a
drop too much, he could not refrain from telling how he
had come by the hand-mill. "There you see what has
brought me all my wealth!" said he, and brought out
the mill, and made it grind first one thing and then
another. When the brother saw that he insisted on
having the mill, and after a great deal of persuasion got
it; but he had to give three hundred dollars for it, and
the poor brother was to keep it till the haymaking was
over, for he thought: "If I keep it as long as that, I can
make it grind meat and drink that will last many a long
year." During that time you may imgine that the mill
did not grow rusty, and when hay-harvest came the rich
brother got it, but the other had taken good care not to
teach him how to stop it. It was evening when the rich
man got the mill home, and in the morning he bade the
old woman go out and spread the hay after the mowers,

and he would attend to the house himself that day, he
said.

So, when dinner-time drew near, he set the mill on
the kitchen-table, and said: "Grind herrings and milk
pottage, and do it both quickly and well."

So the mill began to grind herrings and milk pottage,
and first all the dishes and tubs were filled, and then it
came out all over the kitchen-floor. The man twisted
and turned it, and did all he could to make the mill
stop, but, howsoever he turned it and screwed it, the
mill went on grinding, and in a short time the pottage
rose so high that the man was like to be drowned. So he
threw open the parlour-door, but it was not long before
the mill had ground the parlour full too, and it was with
difficulty and danger that the man could go through the
stream of pottage and get hold of the doorlatch. When
he got the door open, he did not stay long in the room,
but ran out, and the herrings and pottage came after
him, and it streamed out over both farm and field. Now
the old woman, who was out spreading the hay, began
to think dinner was long in coming, and said to the
women and the mowers: "Though the master does not
call us home, we may as well go. It may be that he finds
he is not good at making pottage, and I should do well
to help him." So they began to straggle homewards, but
when they had got a little way up the hill they met the
herrings and pottage and bread, all pouring forth and
winding about one over the other, and the man himself
in front of the flood. "Would to heaven that each of you
had a hundred stomachs! Take care that you are not
drowned in the pottage!" he cried as he went by them
as if Mischief were at his heels, down to where his
brother dwelt. Then he begged him, for God's sake, to
take the mill back again, and that in an instant, for, said
he: "If it grind one hour more the whole district will be
destroyed by herrings and pottage." But the brother
would not take it until the other paid him three hundred dollars, and that he was obliged to do. Now the
poor brother had both the money and the mill again. So

it was not long before he had a farmhouse much finer than that in which his brother lived, but the mill ground him so much money that he covered it with plates of gold; and the farmhouse lay close by the sea-shore, so it shone and glittered far out to sea. Everyone who sailed by there now had to put in to visit the rich man in the gold farmhouse, and everyone wanted to see the wonderful mill, for the report of it spread far and wide, and there was no one who had not heard tell of it.

After a long, long time came also a skipper who wished to see the mill. He asked if it could make salt. "Yes, it could make salt," said he who owned it, and when the skipper heard that he wished with all his might and main to have the mill, let it cost what it might, for, he thought, if he had it, he would get off having to sail far away over the perilous sea for freights of salt. At first the man would not hear of parting with it, but the skipper begged and prayed, and at last the man sold it to him, and got many, many thousand dollars for it. When the skipper had got the mill on his back he did not long stay there, for he was so afraid that the man should change his mind, and he had no time to ask how he was to stop it grinding, but got on board his ship as fast as he could.

When he had gone a little way out to sea he took the mill on deck. "Grind salt, and grind both quickly and well," said the skipper. So the mill began to grind salt, till it spouted out like water, and when the skipper had got the ship filled he wanted to stop the mill, but, whichsoever way he turned it, and how much soever he tried, it went on grinding, and the heap of salt grew higher and higher, until at last the ship sank. There lies the mill at the bottom of the sea, and still, day by day, it grinds on: and that is why the sea is salt.

—*The Blue Fairy Book* (1889)

The Witch and Her Servants

RUSSIAN

A LONG time ago there lived a King who had three sons; the eldest was called Szabo, the second Warza, and the youngest Iwanich.

One beautiful spring morning the King was walking through his gardens with these three sons, gazing with admiration at the various fruit-trees, some of which were a mass of blossom, whilst others were bowed to the ground laden with rich fruit. During their wanderings they came unperceived on a piece of waste land where three splendid trees grew. The King looked on them for a moment, and then, shaking his head sadly, he passed on in silence.

The sons, who could not understand why he did this, asked him the reason of his dejection, and the King told them as follows:

"These three trees, which I cannot see without sorrow, were planted by me on this spot when I was a youth of twenty. A celebrated magician, who had given the seed to my father, promised him that they would grow into the three finest trees the world had ever seen. My father did not live to see his words come true; but on his death-bed he bade me transplant them here, and to look after them with the greatest care, which I accordingly did. At last, after the lapse of five long

460

years, I noticed some blossoms on the branches, and a few days later the most exquisite fruit my eyes had ever seen.

"I gave my head-gardener the strictest orders to watch the trees carefully, for the magician had warned my father that if one unripe fruit were plucked from the tree, all the rest would become rotten at once. When it was quite ripe the fruit would become a golden yellow.

"Every day I gazed on the lovely fruit, which became gradually more and more tempting-looking, and it was all I could do not to break the magician's commands.

"That night I dreamt that the fruit was perfectly ripe; I ate and tasted it, and it was more delicious than anything I had ever tasted in real life. As soon as I awoke I sent for the gardener and asked him if the fruit on the three trees had not ripened in the night to perfection.

"But instead of replying, the gardener threw himself at my feet and swore that he was innocent. He said that he had watched by the trees all night, but in spite of it, and as if by magic, the beautiful trees had been robbed of all their fruit.

"Grieved as I was over the theft, I did not punish the gardener, of whose fidelity I was well assured, but I determined to pluck off all the fruit in the following year before it was ripe, as I had not much belief in the magician's warning.

"I carried out my intention, and had all the fruit picked off the tree, but when I tasted one of the apples it was bitter and unpleasant, and the next morning the rest of the fruit had all rotted away.

"After this I had the beautiful fruit of these trees carefully guarded by my most faithful servants; but every year, on this very night, the fruit was plucked and stolen by an invisible hand, and next morning not a single apple remained on the trees. For some time past I have given up even having the trees watched."

When the King had finished his story, Szabo, his eldest son, said to him: "Forgive me, father, if I say I think you are mistaken. I am sure there are many men in your kingdom who could protect these trees from the cunning arts of a thieving magician; I myself, who as your eldest son claim the first right to do so, will mount guard over the fruit this very night."

The King consented, and as soon as evening drew on Szabo climbed up on to one of the trees, determined to protect the fruit even if it cost him his life. So he kept watch half the night; but a little after midnight he was overcome by an irresistible drowsiness, and fell fast asleep. He did not awake till it was bright daylight, and all the fruit on the trees had vanished.

The following year Warza, the second brother, tried his luck, but with the same result. Then it came to the turn of the third and youngest son.

Iwanich was not the least discouraged by the failure of his elder brothers, though they were both much older and stronger than he was, and when night came climbed up the tree as they had done. The moon had risen, and with her soft light lit up the whole neighbourhood, so that the observant Prince could distinguish the smallest object distinctly.

At midnight a gentle west wind shook the tree, and at the same moment a snow-white swan-like bird sank down gently on his breast. The Prince hastily seized the bird's wings in his hands, when, lo! to his astonishment he found he was holding in his arms not a bird but the most beautiful girl he had ever seen.

"You need not fear Militza," said the beautiful girl, looking at the Prince with friendly eyes. "An evil magician has not robbed you of your fruit, but he stole the seed from my mother, and thereby caused her death. When she was dying she bade me take the fruit, which you have no right to possess, from the trees every year as soon as it was ripe. This I would have done to-night too, if you had not seized me with such force, and so broken the spell I was under."

Iwanich, who had been prepared to meet a terrible magician and not a lovely girl, fell desperately in love with her. They spent the rest of the night in pleasant

IWANICH HOLDS FAST THE SWAN

conversation, and when Militza wished to go away he begged her not to leave him.

"I would gladly stay with you longer," said Militza, "but a wicked witch once cut off a lock of my hair when I was asleep, which has put me in her power, and if morning were still to find me here she would do me some harm, and you, too, perhaps."

Having said these words, she drew a sparkling diamond ring from her finger, which she handed to the Prince, saying: "Keep this ring in memory of Militza, and think of her sometimes if you never see her again. But if your love is really true, come and find me in my own kingdom. I may not show you the way there, but this ring will guide you.

"If you have love and courage enough to undertake this journey, whenever you come to a cross-road always look at this diamond before you settle which way you are going to take. If it sparkles as brightly as ever go straight on, but if its lustre is dimmed choose another path."

Then Militza bent over the Prince and kissed him on his forehead, and before he had time to say a word she vanished through the branches of the tree in a little white cloud.

Morning broke, and the Prince, still full of the wonderful apparition, left his perch and returned to the palace like one in a dream, without even knowing if the fruit had been taken or not; for his whole mind was absorbed by thoughts of Militza and how he was to find her.

As soon as the head-gardener saw the Prince going towards the palace he ran to the trees, and when he saw them laden with ripe fruit he hastened to tell the King the joyful news. The King was beside himself for joy, and hurried at once to the garden and made the gardener pick him some of the fruit. He tasted it, and found the apple quite as luscious as it had been in his dream. He went at once to his son Iwanich, and after embracing him tenderly and heaping praises on him, he asked him how he had succeeded in protecting the costly fruit from the power of the magician.

This question placed Iwanich in a dilemma. But as he did not want the real story to be known, he said that about midnight a huge wasp had flown through the branches, and buzzed incessantly round him. He had warded it off with his sword, and at dawn, when he was becoming quite worn out, the wasp had vanished as suddenly as it had appeared.

The King, who never doubted the truth of this tale, bade his son go to rest at once and recover from the fatigues of the night; but he himself went and ordered many feasts to be held in honour of the preservation of the wonderful fruit.

The whole capital was in a stir, and everyone shared in the King's joy; the Prince alone took no part in the festivities.

While the King was at a banquet, Iwanich took some purses of gold, and mounting the quickest horse in the royal stable, he sped off like the wind without a single soul being any the wiser.

It was only on the next day that they missed him; the King was very distressed at his disappearance, and sent search-parties all over the kingdom to look for him, but in vain; and after six months they gave him up as dead, and in another six months they had forgotten all about him. But in the meantime the Prince, with the help of his ring, had had a most successful journey, and no evil had befallen him.

At the end of three months he came to the entrance of a huge forest, which looked as if it had never been trodden by human foot before, and which seemed to stretch out indefinitely. The Prince was about to enter the wood by a little path he had discovered, when he heard a voice shouting to him: "Hold, youth! Whither are you going?"

Iwanich turned round, and saw a tall, gaunt-looking man, clad in miserable rags, leaning on a crooked staff and seated at the foot of an oak tree, which was so much the same colour as himself that it was little wonder the Prince had ridden past the tree without noticing him.

"Where else should I be going," he said, "than through the wood?"

"Through the wood?" said the old man in amazement. "It's easily seen that you have heard nothing of this forest, that you rush so blindly to meet your doom. Well, listen to me before you ride any further; let me tell you that this wood hides in its depths a countless number of the fiercest tigers, hyenas, wolves, bears, and snakes, and all sorts of other monsters. If I were to cut you and your horse up into tiny morsels and throw them to the beasts, there wouldn't be one bit for each hundred of them. Take my advice, therefore, and if you wish to save your life follow some other path."

The Prince was rather taken aback by the old man's words, and considered for a minute what he should do; then looking at his ring, and perceiving that it sparkled as brightly as ever, he called out: "If this wood held even more terrible things than it does, I cannot help myself, for I must go through it."

Here he spurred his horse and rode on; but the old beggar screamed so loudly after him that the Prince turned round and rode back to the oak tree.

"I am really sorry for you," said the beggar, "but if you are quite determined to brave the dangers of the forest, let me at least give you a piece of advice which will help you against these monsters.

"Take this bagful of bread-crumbs and this live hare. I will make you a present of them both, as I am anxious to save your life; but you must leave your horse behind you, for it would stumble over the fallen trees or get entangled in the briers and thorns. When you have gone about a hundred yards into the wood the wild beasts will surround you. Then you must instantly seize your bag, and scatter the bread-crumbs among them. They will rush to eat them up greedily, and when you have scattered the last crumb you must lose no time in throwing the hare to them; as soon as the hare feels itself on the ground it will run away as quickly as possible, and the wild beasts will turn to pursue it. In this way you will be able to get through the wood unhurt."

Iwanich thanked the old man for his counsel, dismounted from his horse, and, taking the bag and the hare in his arms, he entered the forest. He had hardly lost sight of his gaunt grey friend when he heard growls and snarls in the thicket close to him, and before he had time to think he found himself surrounded by the most dreadful-looking creatures. On one side he saw the glittering eye of a cruel tiger, on the other the gleaming teeth of a great she-wolf; here a huge bear growled fiercely, and there a horrible snake coiled itself in the grass at his feet.

But Iwanich did not forget the old man's advice, and quickly put his hand into the bag and took out as many bread-crumbs as he could hold in his hand at a time. He threw them to the beasts, but soon the bag grew lighter and lighter, and the Prince began to feel a little frightened. And now the last crumb was gone, and the hungry beasts thronged round him, greedy for fresh prey. Then he seized the hare and threw it to them.

No sooner did the little creature feel itself on the ground than it lay back its ears and flew through the wood like an arrow from a bow, closely pursued by the wild beasts, and the Prince was left alone. He looked at his ring, and when he saw that it sparkled as brightly as ever he went straight on through the forest.

He hadn't gone very far when he saw a most extraordinary looking man coming towards him. He was not more than three feet high, his legs were quite crooked, and all his body was covered with prickles like a hedgehog. Two lions walked with him, fastened to his side by the two ends of his long beard.

He stopped the Prince and asked him in a harsh voice: "Are you the man who has just fed my bodyguard?"

Iwanich was so startled that he could hardly reply, but the little man continued: "I am most grateful to you for your kindness; what can I give you as a reward?"

"All I ask," replied Iwanich, "is, that I should be allowed to go through this wood in safety."

"Most certainly," answered the little man; "and for greater security I will give you one of my lions as a protector. But when you leave this wood and come near a palace which does not belong to my domain, let the lion go, in order that he may not fall into the hands of an enemy and be killed."

With these words he loosened the lion from his beard and bade the beast guard the youth carefully.

With this new protector Iwanich wandered on through the forest, and though he came upon a great many more wolves, hyenas, leopards, and other wild beasts, they always kept at a respectful distance when they saw what sort of an escort the Prince had with him.

Iwanich hurried through the wood as quickly as his legs would carry him, but, nevertheless, hour after hour went by and not a trace of a green field or a human habitation met his eyes. At length, towards evening, the mass of trees grew more transparent, and through the interlaced branches a wide plain was visible.

At the exit of the wood the lion stood still, and the Prince took leave of him, having first thanked him warmly for his kind protection. It had become quite dark, and Iwanich was forced to wait for daylight before continuing his journey.

He made himself a bed of grass and leaves, lit a fire of dry branches, and slept soundly till the next morning.

Then he got up and walked towards a beautiful white palace which he saw gleaming in the distance. In about an hour he reached the building, and opening the door he walked in.

After wandering through many marble halls, he came to a huge staircase made of porphyry, leading down to a lovely garden.

The Prince burst into a shout of joy when he suddenly perceived Militza in the centre of a group of girls who were weaving wreaths of flowers with which to deck their mistress.

As soon as Militza saw the Prince she ran up to him and embraced him tenderly; and after he had told her all his adventures, they went into the palace, where a sumptuous meal awaited them. Then the Princess called her court together, and introduced Iwanich to them as her future husband.

Preparations were at once made for the wedding, which was held soon after with great pomp and magnificence.

Three months of great happiness followed, when Militza received one day an invitation to visit her mother's sister.

Although the Princess was very unhappy at leaving her husband, she did not like to refuse the invitation, and, promising to return in seven days at the latest, she took a tender farewell of the Prince, and said: "Before I go I will hand you over all the keys of the castle. Go everywhere and do anything you like; only one thing I beg and beseech you, do not open the little iron door in the north tower, which is closed with seven locks and seven bolts; for if you do, we shall both suffer for it."

Iwanich promised what she asked, and Militza departed, repeating her promise to return in seven days.

When the Prince found himself alone he began to be tormented by pangs of curiosity as to what the room in the tower contained. For two days he resisted the temptation to go and look, but on the third he could stand it no longer, and taking a torch in his hand he hurried to the tower, and unfastened one lock after the other of the little iron door until it burst open.

What an unexpected sight met his gaze! The Prince perceived a small room black with smoke, lit up feebly by a fire from which issued long blue flames. Over the fire hung a huge cauldron full of boiling pitch, and fastened into the cauldron by iron chains stood a wretched man screaming with agony.

Iwanich was much horrified at the sight before him, and asked the man what terrible crime he had committed to be punished in this dreadful fashion.

"I will tell you everything," said the man in the cauldron; "but first relieve my torments a little, I implore you."

"And how can I do that?" asked the Prince.

"With a little water," replied the man; "only sprinkle a few drops over me and I shall feel better."

The Prince, moved by pity, without thinking what he was doing, ran to the courtyard of the castle, and filled a jug with water, which he poured over the man in the cauldron.

In a moment a most fearful crash was heard, as if all the pillars of the palace were giving way, and the palace itself, with towers and doors, windows and the cauldron, whirled round the bewildered Prince's head. This continued for a few minutes, and then everything vanished into thin air, and Iwanich found himself suddenly alone upon a desolate heath covered with rocks and stones.

The Prince who now realised what his heedlessness had done, cursed too late his spirit of curiosity. In his despair he wandered on over the heath, never looking where he put his feet, and full of sorrowful thoughts. At last he saw a light in the distance, which came from a miserable-looking little hut.

The owner of it was none other than the kind-hearted gaunt grey beggar who had given the Prince the bag of bread-crumbs and the hare. Without recognising Iwanich, he opened the door when he knocked and gave him shelter for the night.

On the following morning the Prince asked his host if he could get him any work to do, as he was quite unknown in the neighbourhood, and had not enough money to take him home.

"My son," replied the old man, "all this country round here is uninhabited; I myself have to wander to distant villages for my living, and even then I do not very often find enough to satisfy my hunger. But if you would like to take service with the old witch Corva, go straight up the little stream which flows below my hut for about three hours, and you will come to a sand-hill on the left-hand side; that is where she lives."

Iwanich thanked the gaunt grey beggar for his information, and went on his way.

After walking for about three hours the Prince came upon a dreary-looking grey stone wall; this was the back of the building and did not attract him; but when he came upon the front of the house he found it even less inviting, for the old witch had surrounded her dwelling with a fence of spikes, on every one of which a man's skull was stuck. In this horrible enclosure stood a small black house, which had only two grated windows, all covered with cobwebs, and a battered iron door.

The Prince knocked, and a rasping woman's voice told him to enter.

Iwanich opened the door, and found himself in a smoke-begrimed kitchen, in the presence of a hideous old woman who was warming her skinny hands at a fire. The Prince offered to become her servant, and the old hag told him she was badly in want of one, and he seemed to be just the person to suit her.

When Iwanich asked what his work, and how much his wages would be, the witch bade him follow her, and led the way through a narrow damp passage into a vault, which served as a stable. Here he perceived two pitch-black horses in a stall.

"You see before you," said the old woman, "a mare and her foal; you have nothing to do but to lead them out to the fields every day, and to see that neither of them runs away from you. If you look after them both for a whole year I will give you anything you like to ask; but if, on the other hand, you let either of the animals escape you, your last hour is come, and your head shall be stuck on the last spike of my fence. The other spikes, as you see, are already adorned, and the skulls are all those of different servants I have had who have failed to do what I demanded."

Iwanich, who thought he could not be much worse off than he was already, agreed to the witch's proposal.

At daybreak next morning he drove his horses to the field, and brought them back in the evening without their ever having attempted to break away from him. The witch stood at her door and received him kindly, and set a good meal before him.

So it continued for some time, and all went well with the Prince. Early every morning he led the horses out to the fields, and brought them home safe and sound in the evening.

One day, while he was watching the horses, he came to the banks of a river, and saw a big fish, which through some mischance had been cast on the land, struggling hard to get back into the water.

Iwanich, who felt sorry for the poor creature, seized it in his arms and flung it into the stream. But no sooner did the fish find itself in the water again, than, to the Prince's amazement, it swam up to the bank and said:

"My kind benefactor, how can I reward you for your goodness?"

"I desire nothing," answered the Prince. "I am quite content to have been able to be of some service to you."

"You must do me the favour," replied the fish, "to take a scale from my body, and keep it carefully. If you should ever need my help, throw it into the river, and I will come to your aid at once."

Iwanich bowed, loosened a scale from the body of the grateful beast, put it carefully away, and returned home.

A short time after this, when he was going early one morning to the usual grazing place with his horses, he noticed a flock of birds assembled together making a great noise and flying wildly backwards and forwards.

Full of curiosity, Iwanich hurried up to the spot, and saw that a large number of ravens had attacked an eagle, and although the eagle was big and powerful and was making a brave fight, it was overpowered at last by numbers, and had to give in.

But the Prince, who was sorry for the poor bird, seized the branch of a tree and hit out at the ravens with it; terrified at this unexpected onslaught they flew away, leaving many of their number dead or wounded on the battlefield.

As soon as the eagle saw itself free from its tormentors it plucked a feather from its wing, and, handing it to the Prince, said: "Here, my kind benefactor, take this feather as a proof of my gratitude; should you ever be in need of my help blow this feather into the air, and I will help you as much as is in my power."

Iwanich thanked the bird, and placing the feather beside the scale he drove the horses home.

Another day he had wandered farther than usual, and came close to a farmyard; the place pleased the Prince, and as there was plenty of good grass for the horses he determined to spend the day there. Just as he was sitting down under a tree he heard a cry close to him, and saw a fox which had been caught in a trap placed there by the farmer.

In vain did the poor beast try to free itself; then the good-natured Prince came once more to the rescue, and let the fox out of the trap.

The fox thanked him heartily, tore two hairs out of his bushy tail, and said: "Should you ever stand in need of my help throw these two hairs into the fire, and in a moment I shall be at your side ready to obey you."

Iwanich put the fox's hairs with the scale and the feather, and as it was getting dark he hastened home with his horses.

In the meantime his service was drawing near to an end, and in three more days the year was up, and he would be able to get his reward and leave the witch.

On the first evening of these last three days, when he came home and was eating his supper, he noticed the old woman stealing into the stables.

The Prince followed her secretly to see what she was going to do. He crouched down in the doorway and heard the wicked witch telling the horses to wait next morning till Iwanich was asleep, and then to go and hide themselves in the river, and to stay there till she told them to return; and if they didn't do as she told them the old woman threatened to beat them till they bled.

When Iwanich heard all this he went back to his room, determined that nothing should induce him to fall asleep next day. On the following morning he led the mare and foal to the fields as usual, but bound a cord round them both which he kept in his hand.

But after a few hours, by the magic arts of the old witch, he was overpowered by sleep, and the mare and foal escaped and did as they had been told to do. The Prince did not awake till late in the evening; and when he did, he found, to his horror, that the horses had disappeared. Filled with despair, he cursed the moment when he had entered the service of the cruel witch, and already he saw his head sticking up on the sharp spike beside the others.

Then he suddenly remembered the fish's scale, which, with the eagle's feather and the fox's hairs, he always carried about with him. He drew the scale from his pocket, and hurrying to the river he threw it in. In a minute the grateful fish swam towards the bank on which Iwanich was standing, and said: "What do you command, my friend and benefactor?"

The Prince replied: "I had to look after a mare and foal, and they have run away from me and have hidden themselves in the river; if you wish to save my life drive them back to the land."

"Wait a moment," answered the fish, "and I and my friends will soon drive them out of the water." With these words the creature disappeared into the depths of the stream.

Almost immediately a rushing hissing sound was heard in the waters, the waves dashed against the banks, the foam was tossed into the air, and the two horses leapt suddenly on to the dry land, trembling and shaking with fear.

Iwanich sprang at once on to the mare's back, seized the foal by its bridle, and hastened home in the highest spirits.

When the witch saw the Prince bringing the horses home she could hardly conceal her wrath, and as soon as she had placed Iwanich's supper before him she stole away again to the stables. The Prince followed her, and heard her scolding the beasts harshly for not having hidden themselves better. She bade them wait next morning till Iwanich was asleep and then to hide themselves in the clouds, and to remain there till she called. If they did not do as she told them she would beat them till they bled.

The next morning, after Iwanich had led his horses to the fields, he fell once more into a magic sleep. The horses at once ran away and hid themselves in the clouds, which hung down from the mountains in soft billowy masses.

When the Prince awoke and found that both the mare and the foal had disappeared, he bethought him at once of the eagle, and taking the feather out of his pocket he blew it into the air.

In a moment the bird swooped down beside him and asked: "What do you wish me to do?"

"My mare and foal," replied the Prince, "have run away from me, and have hidden themselves in the clouds; if you wish to save my life, restore both animals to me."

"Wait a minute," answered the eagle; "with the help of my friends I will soon drive them back to you."

With these words the bird flew up into the air and disappeared among the clouds.

Almost directly Iwanich saw his two horses being driven towards him by a host of eagles of all sizes. He caught the mare and foal, and having thanked the eagle he drove them cheerfully home again.

The old witch was more disgusted than ever when she saw him appearing, and having set his supper before him she stole into the stables, and Iwanich heard her abusing the horses for not having hidden themselves better in the clouds. Then she bade them hide themselves next morning, as soon as Iwanich was asleep, in the King's hen-house, which stood on a lonely part of the heath, and to remain there till she called. If they failed to do as she told them she would certainly beat them this time till they bled.

On the following morning the Prince drove his horses as usual to the fields. After he had been overpowered by sleep, as on the former days, the mare and foal ran away and hid themselves in the royal hen house.

When the Prince awoke and found the horses gone he determined to appeal to the fox; so, lighting a fire, he threw the two hairs into it, and in a few moments the fox stood beside him and asked: "In what way can I serve you?"

"I wish to know," replied Iwanich, "where the King's hen-house is."

"Hardly an hour's walk from here," answered the fox, and offered to show the Prince the way to it.

While they were walking along the fox asked him what he wanted to do at the royal hen-house. The Prince told him of the misfortune that had befallen him, and of the necessity of recovering the mare and foal.

"That is no easy matter," replied the fox. "But wait a moment. I have an idea. Stand at the door of the hen-house, and wait there for your horses. In the meantime I will slip in among the hens through a hole in the wall and give them a good chase, so that the noise they make will arouse the royal henwives, and they will come to see what is the matter. When they see the horses they will at once imagine them to be the cause of the disturbance, and will drive them out. Then you must lay hands on the mare and foal and catch them."

All turned out exactly as the sly fox had foreseen. The

Prince swung himself on the mare, seized the foal by its bridle, and hurried home.

While he was riding over the heath in the highest of spirits the mare suddenly said to her rider: "You are the first person who has ever succeeded in outwitting the old witch Corva, and now you may ask what reward you like for your service. If you promise never to betray me I will give you a piece of advice which you will do well to follow."

The Prince promised never to betray her confidence, and the mare continued: "Ask nothing else as a reward than my foal, for it has not its like in the world, and is not to be bought for love or money; for it can go from one end of the earth to another in a few minutes. Of course the cunning Corva will do her best to dissuade you from taking the foal, and will tell you that it is both idle and sickly; but do not believe her, and stick to your point."

Iwanich longed to possess such an animal, and promised the mare to follow her advice.

This time Corva received him in the most friendly manner, and set a sumptuous repast before him. As soon as he had finished she asked him what reward he demanded for his year's service.

"Nothing more nor less," replied the Prince, "than the foal of your mare."

The witch pretended to be much astonished at his request, and said that he deserved something much better than the foal, for the beast was lazy and nervous, blind in one eye, and, in short, was quite worthless.

But the Prince knew what he wanted, and when the old witch saw that he had made up his mind to have the foal, she said, "I am obliged to keep my promise and to hand you over the foal; and as I know who you are and what you want, I will tell you in what way the animal will be useful to you. The man in the cauldron of boiling pitch, whom you set free, is a mighty magician; through your curiosity and thoughtlessness Militza came into his power, and he has transported her and her castle and belongings into a distant country.

"You are the only person who can kill him; and in consequence he fears you to such an extent that he has set spies to watch you, and they report your movements to him daily.

"When you have reached him, beware of speaking a single word to him, or you will fall into the power of his friends. Seize him at once by the beard and dash him to the ground."

Iwanich thanked the old witch, mounted his foal, put spurs to its sides, and they flew like lightning through the air.

Already it was growing dark, when Iwanich perceived some figures in the distance; they soon came up to them, and then the Prince saw that it was the magician and his friends who were driving through the air in a carriage drawn by owls.

When the magician found himself face to face with Iwanich, without hope of escape, he turned to him with false friendliness and said: "Thrice my kind benefactor!"

But the Prince, without saying a word, seized him at once by his beard and dashed him to the ground. At the same moment the foal sprang on the top of the magician and kicked and stamped on him with his hoofs till he died.

Then Iwanich found himself once more in the palace of his bride, and Militza herself flew into his arms.

From this time forward they lived in undisturbed peace and happiness till the end of their lives.

—The Yellow Fairy Book (1894)

The Witch in the Stone Boat

ICELANDIC

———◆◆———

THERE were once a King and a Queen, and they had a son called Sigurd, who was very strong and active, and good-looking. When the King came to be bowed down with the weight of years he spoke to his son, and said that now it was time for him to look out for a fitting match for himself, for he did not know how long he might last now, and he would like to see him married before he died.

Sigurd was not averse to this, and asked his father where he thought it best to look for a wife. The King answered that in a certain country there was a King who had a beautiful daughter, and he thought it would be most desirable if Sigurd could get her. So the two parted, and Sigurd prepared for the journey, and went to where his father had directed him.

He came to the King and asked his daughter's hand, which he readily granted him, but only on the condition that he should remain there as long as he could, for the King himself was not strong and not very able to govern his kingdom. Sigurd accepted this condition, but added that he would have to get leave to go home again to his own country when he heard news of his father's death. After that Sigurd married the Princess, and helped his father in-law to govern the kingdom. He

The Witch comes On board

and the Princess loved each other dearly, and after a year a son came to them, who was two years old when word came to Sigurd that his father was dead. Sigurd now prepared to return home with his wife and child, and went on board ship to go by sea.

They had sailed for several days, when the breeze suddenly fell, and there came a dead calm, at a time when they needed only one day's voyage to reach home. Sigurd and his Queen were one day on deck, when most of the others on the ship had fallen asleep. There they sat and talked for a while, and had their little son along with them. After a time Sigurd became so heavy with sleep that he could no longer keep awake, so he went below and lay down, leaving the Queen alone on the deck, playing with her son.

A good while after Sigurd had gone below the Queen saw something black on the sea, which seemed to be coming nearer. As it approached she could make out that it was a boat, and could see the figure of some one sitting in it and rowing it. At last the boat came alongside the ship, and now the Queen saw that it was a stone boat, out of which there came up on board the ship a fearfully ugly Witch. The Queen was more frightened than words can describe, and could neither speak a word nor move from the place so as to awaken the King or the sailors. The Witch came right up to the Queen, took the child from her and laid it on the deck; then she took the Queen, and stripped her of all her fine clothes, which she proceeded to put on herself, and looked then like a human being. Last of all she took the Queen, put her into the boat, and said—

"This spell I lay upon you, that you slacken not your course until you come to my brother in the Underworld."

The Queen sat stunned and motionless, but the boat at once shot away from the ship with her, and before long she was out of sight.

When the boat could no longer be seen the child began to cry, and though the Witch tried to quiet it she could not manage it; so she went below to where the

King was sleeping with the child on her arm, and awakened him, scolding him for leaving them alone on deck, while he and all the crew were asleep. It was great carelessness of him, she said, to leave no one to watch the ship with her.

Sigurd was greatly surprised to hear his Queen scold him so much, for she had never said an angry word to him before; but he thought it was quite excusable in this case, and tried to quiet the child along with her, but it was no use. Then he went and wakened the sailors, and bade them hoist the sails, for a breeze had sprung up and was blowing straight towards the harbour.

They soon reached the land which Sigurd was to rule over, and found all the people sorrowful for the old King's death, but they became glad when they got Sigurd back to the Court, and made him King over them.

The King's son, however, hardly ever stopped crying from the time he had been taken from his mother on the deck of the ship, although he had always been such a good child before, so that at last the King had to get a nurse for him—one of the maids of the Court. As soon as the child got into her charge he stopped crying, and behaved well as before.

After the sea-voyage it seemed to the King that the Queen had altered very much in many ways, and not for the better. He thought her much more haughty and stubborn and difficult to deal with than she used to be. Before long others began to notice this as well as the King. In the Court there were two young fellows, one of eighteen years old, the other of nineteen, who were very fond of playing chess, and often sat long inside playing at it. Their room was next the Queen's, and often during the day they heard the Queen talking.

One day they paid more attention than usual when they heard her talk, and put their ears close to a crack in the wall between the rooms, and heard the Queen say quite plainly, "When I yawn a little, then I am a nice little maiden; when I yawn half-way, then I am half a troll; and when I yawn fully, then I am a troll altogether."

As she said this she yawned tremendously, and in a moment had put on the appearance of a fearfully ugly troll. Then there came up through the floor of the room a three-headed Giant with a trough full of meat, who saluted her as his sister and set down the trough before her. She began to eat out of it, and never stopped till she had finished it. The young fellows saw all this going on, but did not hear the two of them say anything to each other. They were astonished though at how greedily the Queen devoured the meat, and how much she ate of it, and were no longer surprised that she took so little when she sat at table with the King. As soon as she had finished it the Giant disappeared with the trough by the same way as he had come, and the Queen returned to her human shape.

Now we must go back to the King's son after he had been put in charge of the nurse. One evening, after she had lit a candle and was holding the child, several planks sprang up in the floor of the room, and out at the opening came a beautiful woman dressed in white, with an iron belt round her waist, to which was fastened an iron chain that went down into the ground. The woman came up to the nurse, took the child from her, and pressed it to her breast; then she gave it back to the nurse and returned by the same way as she had come, and the floor closed over her again. Although the woman had not spoken a single word to her, the nurse was very much frightened, but told no one about it.

Next evening the same thing happened again, just as before, but as the woman was going away she said in a sad tone, "Two are gone, and one only is left," and then disappeared as before. The nurse was still more frightened when she heard the woman say this, and thought that perhaps some danger was hanging over the child, though she had no ill-opinion of the unknown woman, who, indeed, had behaved towards the child as if it were her own. The most mysterious thing was the

woman saying "and only one is left," but the nurse
guessed that this must mean that only one day was left,
since she had come for two days already.

At last the nurse made up her mind to go to the
King, and told him the whole story, and asked him to
be present in person next day about the time when the
woman usually came. The King promised to do so, and
came to the nurse's room a little before the time, and
sat down on a chair with his drawn sword in his hand.
Soon after the planks in the floor sprang up as before,
and the woman came up, dressed in white, with the
iron belt and chain. The King saw at once that it was his
own Queen, and immediately hewed asunder the iron
chain that was fastened to the belt. This was followed
by such noises and crashings down in the earth that all
the King's Palace shook, so that no one expected anything else than to see every bit of it shaken to pieces.
At last, however, the noises and shaking stopped, and
they began to come to themselves again.

The King and Queen embraced each other, and she
told him the whole story—how the Witch came to the
ship when they were all asleep and sent her off in the
boat. After she had gone so far that she could not see
the ship, she sailed on through darkness until she landed
beside a three-headed Giant. The Giant wished her to
marry him, but she refused; whereupon he shut her up
by herself, and told her she would never get free until
she consented. After a time she began to plan how to
get her freedom, and at last told him that she would
consent if he would allow her to visit her son on earth
three days on end. This he agreed to, but put on her
this iron belt and chain, the other end of which he
fastened round his own waist, and the great noises that
were heard when the King cut the chain must have
been caused by the Giant's falling down the underground passage when the chain gave way so suddenly.
The Giant's dwelling, indeed, was right under the Palace, and the terrible shakings must have been caused
by him in his death-throes.

The King now understood how the Queen he had had for some time past had been so ill-tempered. He at once had a sack drawn over her head and made her be stoned to death, and after that torn in pieces by untamed horses. The two young fellows also told now what they had heard and seen in the Queen's room, for before this they had been afraid to say anything about it, on account of the Queen's power.

The real Queen was now restored to all her dignity, and was beloved by all. The nurse was married to a nobleman, and the King and Queen gave her splendid presents.

—*The Yellow Fairy Book* (1894)

Afterword

———◆◆———

And half I envy him who now
   Clothed in her Court's enchanted green,
By moonlit loch or mountain's brow
   Is Chaplain to the Fairy Queen.
                —Andrew Lang,
                  "The Fairy Minister,"
                1893

1.

"I do not write the stories out of my own head," Andrew Lang insisted in his preface to the last of his famous fairy books, *The Lilac Fairy Book* (1910). He never claimed anything else. From the first, *The Blue Fairy Book* (1889), to the twelfth and final volume in the series, he tried to give proper credit where it was due. At times he turned to the literary fairy tales, or *kunstmärchen*, of Charles Perrault, Hans Christian Andersen, Madame D'Aulnoy, even Anatole France and Zacharius Topelius; but the bulk of his fairy books reprinted in English countless little known *volksmärchen*. "The stories," he explained, "are taken from those told by grannies to grandchildren in many countries and in many languages—French, Italian, Spanish, Catalan, Gaelic, Icelandic, Cherokee, African, Indian, Austra-

486

lian, Slavonic, Eskimo, and what not." Lang was a prominent member of the Folk Lore Society in London, but except for two in *The Brown Fairy Book* (1904), told to him by an Indian, he did not seek his selections directly from oral tradition. Instead he gleaned them from many other collections in several languages, all of which he tried to fully acknowledge in the fairy books. He did not even translate them himself. That was begun by several women friends including his wife, who eventually took over these labors entirely herself. He finally confessed, "The fairy books have been wholly the work of Mrs. Lang, who has translated and adapted them from the French, German, Portuguese, Italian, Spanish, Catalan, and other languages."* What Andrew Lang *did* do in these books is similar to what Walt Disney contributed to his animated cartoons. Just as Lang was not the "author" of the fairy books, Disney did not draw Mickey Mouse. Lang and Disney merely supervised others. "I find where the stories are," Lang modestly acknowledged, "and advise, and, in short, superintend." His "sense of literary honesty" compelled him to repeat from book to book that "he *is* the Editor, and not the author of the Fairy Tales, just as a distinguished man of science is only the Editor, not the Author of *Nature*." But it was all to no avail. Mothers and children still asked him "how he can invent so many stories—more than Shakespeare, Dumas, and Charles Dickens could have invented in a century." This misconception persists: even today, whenever something is lifted from one of the fairy books for an anthology or a picture book, the selection is always said to be "*by* Andrew Lang."

This accomplished man of letters came to believe

---

*In a letter of October 12, 1912, written only a few months after her husband's death (now in the Osborne Collection of Early Children's Books, Toronto Public Library), Mrs. Lang stated that she "wrote the *bulk* of all the Fairy Books after the first four, and edited (and often re-wrote) those contributed by other people. . . . My husband never *saw* the stories till they were ready for Press, when he read them through and wrote the Preface."

himself "rather an imposter, because so many children seem to think that he made up these books out of his own head." He was nevertheless an enormously prolific writer; his bibliography lists one hundred and fifty titles. He once remarked that save for his fairy books, he had written "almost everything else, except hymns, sermons, and dramatic works." Only two selections in the twelve volumes are actually his work, and neither is really a fairy tale. "The Terrible Head" in *The Blue Fairy Book* is just a retelling of Jason and the Argonauts, taken from classical sources but revamped in *conte de fées* clichés; "The Story of Sigurd" in *The Red Fairy Book* (1890) is merely an adaptation of William Morris's prose version of the Volsunga Saga. J. R. R. Tolkien found nothing to admire in this "turning mythology into fairy-story." Of course Nathaniel Hawthorne did much the same thing in *The Wonder Book* (1852) and *Tanglewood Tales* (1853), but no matter how skilled the reteller, these watered-down versions are debasements of the great legends. Lang, however, believed that fairy tales hovered somewhere between primitive superstitions and the great Western myths. He argued that one can find in Homer's epics "the witch who turns men into swine, and the man who bores out the big foolish giant's eye, and the cap of darkness, and the shoes of swiftness, that were worn later by Jack the Giant-Killer." However, while incidents, plots, and characters may be common to both traditions, myth differs from fairy tale in intention. As Tolkien replied, "It is precisely the colouring, the atmosphere, the unclassifiable individual details of a story, and above all the general purport that informs with life the undissected bones of plot, that really count."

Andrew Lang lacked the gift of invention. He did write several original fairy tales that were entirely his own. The first of these, *The Princess Nobody* (1884), was composed under the most uninspired circumstances. The publisher asked him to write a new text to accompany an old suite of colored wood engravings from

Richard Doyle's *In Fairyland* (1870). The result was a tiresome little narrative about what Tolkien called "that long line of flower-fairies and fluttering sprites with antennae that I so disliked as a child, and which my children in their turn detested." The principal ones Lang published—*The Gold of Fairnilee* (1888), *Prince Ricardo* (1889), and *Prince Ricardo of Pantouflia* (1893)— are not much better than *The Princess Nobody*. The last two, the chronicles of Pantouflia, have had their modern defenders but without much justification or conviction. They fail in much the same manner as do other original fairy tales such as those Lang himself so soundly trounced. "They think that to write a new fairy tale is easy work," he complained of their authors in *The Lilac Fairy Book*. "They are mistaken: the thing is impossible. Nobody can write a *new* fairy tale; you can only mix up and dress up the old, old stories, and put the characters into new dresses." That was all that Lang did in his efforts, picking up incidents, plots, and characters from the *kunst* and *volksmärchen* he knew so well. "They are rich in romantic adventure," he claimed, "and the Princes always marry the right Princesses and live happy ever afterwards; while the wicked witches, stepmothers, tutors and governesses are *never* cruelly punished, but retire to the country on ample pensions. I hate cruelty: I never put a wicked stepmother in a barrel and send her tobogganing down a hill. It is true the Prince Ricardo *did* kill the Yellow Dwarf; but that was in fair fight, sword in hand, and the dwarf, peace to his ashes! *died in harness*." (Evidently Lang was correcting an old wrong, for the evil Yellow Dwarf triumphs in Mme. D'Aulnoy's French tale by slaying the King of the Gold Mines.)

Another model for Lang's Pantouflia tales was William Thackeray's *The Rose and the Ring* (1855). In his preface to *The Yellow Fairy Book* (1894), Lang announced that this modern fairy story was "quite indispensable in every child's library, and parents should be urged to purchase it at the first opportunity, as without

it no education is complete." Consequently, Lang's efforts are likewise facetious, updated fairy pantomimes,
lacking in true belief and seriousness of purpose. These
fairies, like those of his contemporaries which he so
hated, "try to be funny, and fail; or they try to preach
and succeed. Real fairies never preach or talk slang." On
the other hand, Lang himself admitted, the old stories
"unobtrusively teach the true lessons of our wayfaring
in a world of perplexities and obstructions." They do
not get bogged down in allegory or excessive descrip-
tion as did the recent examples. "We want *story*, and
human beings, and human interest," he demanded of
fairy tales. Fortunately, while not to be found in his
own vain attempts at the form, these qualities are in
evidence everywhere in the fairy books which he edited.

Lang was intellectually a dilettante. Struggling to
make his living solely by his pen, Lang wrote on a vast
variety of topics. Once when a friend asked if he was
working on any new book at the time, the writer bitterly snapped that he was *always* working on a new
book. The work he did champion was that of Robert
Louis Stevenson, Rudyard Kipling, Arthur Conan Doyle,
H. Rider Haggard, J. M. Barrie. He was proud of his
seemingly wide erudition on a wealth of subjects. "A
French gentleman, too, an educationist and expert in
portraits of Queen Mary, once sent me a newspaper
article in which he had written that I was exclusively
devoted to the composition of fairy books, and nothing
else. He then came to England, visited me, and found,"
Lang boasted, "I knew rather more about portraits of
Queen Mary than he did." He also liked cats, loved
cricket and fishing.

Perhaps the most devastating portrait of Lang was
that given after his death by Edmund Gosse, a friend
for over thirty-five years. This other critic found Lang's
"character, intellectual and moral, was full of so many
apparent inconsistencies, so many pitfalls for rash asser-
tion, so many queer caprices of impulse." Lang's appre-
ciation of literature was severely limited. Gosse thought

there was "something maidenly about his mind, and he glossed over ugly matters, sordid and dull conditions, so they made no impression whatever upon him." Lang preferred Dumas to Dostoyevski; he was shaky about William Blake but stalwart on Kipling. "Lang's only misfortune," Gosse concluded, "was not to be completely in touch with life." Perhaps Gosse was overstating his friend's aesthetic limitations; after all, Gosse was equally angry toward his own father's romantic delusions. Still there must have been more than an ounce of truth in these criticisms. Max Beerbohm did not like Lang. He could not find one spark of imagination in the man. Somewhat foppish, sporting an unmounted monocle, Lang could be suddenly caustic with others without any apparent reason for the outburst; as a result of this habit, he had few intimates among his colleagues. Even Rider Haggard, who called his friend "one of the sweetest-natured and highest-minded men," had to admit that Lang also possessed "a certain obtrusive honesty" and "an indifferent off-handedness of manner." Still he got on handsomely with children.

Andrew Lang was clearly a man outside of his own period. His wife noted that he had to be convinced to get into an automobile, refused to ride in an airplane, had no interest in owning a telephone. When he learned of one little boy who had said he liked old things better than new, Lang commented, "I wish I knew that little boy." Gosse noticed that Lang throughout their long association never changed his point of view, that what he adored in youth he did so throughout his adult life. He fell in love with cricket and fishing when a boy. But nothing enthralled him more than the spell of fairy tale.

Born and raised at Selkirk, a Scottish border country, before the Industrial Revolution had scoured the land, Lang was weaned on romance. His nurse regaled him with local legends, so that, "if you believed her, there was hardly an old stone on the hillside, but had gold under it." The streams seemed "haunted by old legends, musical with old songs." In this "superstitious eeriness," he confessed, "one seemed forsaken in an enchanted world; one might see the two white fairy deer flit by, bringing to us, as to Thomas the Rhymer, the tidings that we must back to Fairyland."

All these feelings were further fueled by his youthful reading. "A boy of five is more at home in Fairyland than in his own country," he explained. "The sudden appearance of the White Cat as a queen after her head was cut off, the fiendish malice of the Yellow Dwarf, the strange cake of crocodile eggs and millet seed which the mother of the Princess Frutilla made for the Fairy of the Desert—these things, all fresh and astonishing, but certainly to be credited, are my first memories of romance." "A Midsummer Night's Dream," devoured by firelight, also proved to be epiphanal. "At that moment I think that I was happy," he recalled; "it seemed an enchanted glimpse of eternity in Paradise; nothing resembling it remains with me out of all the years." These stories naturally led him to Sir Walter Scott and Dumas and Dickens and eventually to Stevenson, Rider Haggard, Kipling, Conan Doyle, and Barrie. "Romances are only fairy tales grown up," he believed.

Perhaps his whole life may be seen as the sad struggle to recapture that happy time, when he briefly glimpsed Paradise among the flitting fays in the firelight. He joined the Folk Lore Society, where he could learn so many more old stories. He eventually became chairman of the Psychical Society, where he was embroiled in trying to prove the existence of spirits, sprites and fairies, and other supernatural phenomena. Perhaps he did believe in all that; G.K. Chesterton described him as "a spiritualist who is truly spiritual." And then perhaps not. As to the existence of fairies, he noted in *The Yellow Fairy Book* that he "never saw any himself, but he knows several people who have seen them—in the Highlands—and heard their music. If ever you are in Nether Lochaber, go to the Fairy Hill, and you may hear the music yourself, as grown-up people have done, but you must go on a fine day. . . .

The Rev. Mr. Baring-Gould saw several fairies when he was a boy, and was travelling in the land of the Troubadours. For these reasons, the Editor thinks that there are certainly fairies, but they never do anyone any harm; and, in England, they have been frightened away by smoke and schoolmasters." He may not have actually believed in them, but neither did he *disbelieve* in them. "I am not so sure that there are no fairies," he said with irony, "and I am only too well aware that the best 'history stories' are not true." At the very least, he believed in the *possibility* of fairies. "It is dangerous, in the end it is fatal," Gosse observed, "to sustain the entire structure of life and thought on the illusions of romance." And that was exactly what Lang did do: "He built his house upon the rainbow." He was finally, for Gosse, "the fairy in our midst, the wonder-working, incorporeal, and tricky fay of letters, who paid for all his wonderful gifts and charms by being not quite a man of like passions with the rest of us."

2.

Initially Lang had absolutely no intention of producing a dozen big books of fairy tales. In 1889, when he agreed apparently with some reluctance to do *The Blue Fairy Book*, he did not expect to follow it with a sequel. At the time, fairy tales had grown out of fashion, but Charles Longman, Lang's friend and publisher, believed there was a need for a new popular edition of some of the best-known stories and Lang was the obvious choice for editor. He had already edited several anthologies of prose or verse for Longman and others, and was an established expert in fairy lore. As early as May 1873, when his essay "Mythology and Fairy Tales" had appeared in *The Fortnightly*, Lang was one of the leading defenders of this discredited literature. One of his best arguments was the lengthy introduction he wrote for a facsimile of Charles Lamb's early nineteenth-century retelling in verse of *Beauty and the Beast*, reissued in 1887.

Nevertheless, despite his reputation, Lang's knowledge of fairy literature at this time was quite limited. Those tales that he did know well were primarily the ones he recalled from his boyhood. To inspire him, Longman gave him a set of *Le Cabinet des fées*, a sixty-volumed encyclopedia of *kunstmärchen* first written for the French court and published in 1786, just prior to the Revolution. "Probably," Lang noted, "their attempt to be simple charmed a society which was extremely artificial, talked about 'the simple life' and the 'state of nature,' and was on the eve of a revolution in which human nature revealed her most primitive traits in orgies of blood." But Lang seems to have only dipped into it at the time, for *The Blue Fairy Book* contains largely the tales he had loved when a child, mostly those by Perrault and Mme. D'Aulnoy, with a smattering from Grimms' and Asbjørnsen and Moe's collections and one from Galland's edition of *The Arabian Nights*. There are no surprises in his choices here. "Speaking of fairy tales," he once admitted, "one has often marvelled why they are so scarce and so dull, just like the ballads of England." Consequently he included only the obvious, "The History of Whittington" and "The History of Jack the Giant-Killer" as well as "The Black Bull of Norroway" but in a thick Scottish dialect. Some are not fairy tales at all, such as May Kendall's retelling of Swift's "A Voyage to Lilliput" and the editor's own "The Terrible Head," taken from Apollodorus, Simonides, and Pindar.

To everyone's surprise (including the editor's), *The Blue Fairy Book* was a great success and demanded another volume. *The Red Fairy Book* appeared the next year, Lang apologizing in the preface, "In a second gleaning of the fields of Fairy Land we cannot expect to find a second Perrault." Not surprisingly the second largely duplicated the first, being more from Asbjørnsen and Moe, Grimm and D'Aulnoy, and "Jack and the Beanstalk." However, to fill out the new collection, Lang looked to less obvious sources, to Russian, Hibernian and Roumanian collections as well as to Charles Marelles' little-known French variants of "Little Red Riding Hood" and "The Pied Piper of Hamelin," respectively "The True History of Little Golden-Hood" and "The Rat-catcher."

The Red Fairy Book sold almost as well as the first, and so another and another and another fairy book followed in quick succession. And in each, Lang confessed that it would most likely be the last. He just did not see how he could find still more stories to reprint. However, once he exhausted the obvious sources, he sought obscure collections of folk literature in many languages. He also relied more and more on *Le Cabinet des fées* for lesser-known French *kunstmärchen* to balance the wealth of *volksmärchen* he was now making available to English schoolchildren for the first time. In effect, what Lang achieved was the creation of a new *Cabinet des fées* but one designed for British boys and girls. Whether consciously or not, Lang reinforced the Empire and its aims in his fairy books, eventually drawing on stories from Africa, India, and Australia. While he must be praised for making available all this wonderful material finally in English, Lang also suffered from British chauvinism. He would not give them "exactly as they are told by all sorts of outlandish natives, but makes them up in the hope white people will like them, skipping the pieces which they will not like." Perhaps he can be forgiven his snobbery, for he still believed in the community of fairy tale. These stories, rather than separating peoples, reflected their similarities. "All people, black, white, brown, red, and yellow, are like each other when they tell stories," he argued in *The Brown Fairy Book* (1904); "for these are meant for children, who like the same sort of thing, whether they go to school and wear clothes, or, on the other hand, wear skins of beasts, or even nothing at all, and live on grubs and lizards and hawks and crows and serpents, like the little Australian blacks."

Lang's fairy books reflected and represented his best

defense of his theories on folklore. Lang argued with contemporary folklorists on the origin and diffusion of the same tales to all peoples of the earth, throughout all history, whether primitive or civilized nations. Was it actually conscious borrowing one from another, or the slow transmission of the same incidents, plots, and characters from culture to culture? "Why do the stories of the remotest people so closely resemble each other?" he asked in his preface to *The Orange Fairy Book* (1906). "Of course, in the immeasurable past, they have been carried about by conquering races, and learned by conquering races from vanquished peoples. Slaves carried far from home brought their stories with them into captivity. Wanderers, travellers, shipwrecked men, merchants, and wives stolen from alien tribes have diffused the stories; gipsies and Jews have passed them about; Roman soldiers of many different races, moved here and there about the Empire, have trafficked in them. From the remotest days men have been wanderers, and whenever they went their stories accompanied them." But transmission and diffusion did not fully explain why some of the same elements could be found to be universal among the remotest cultures. He was not convinced that there must be a central origin, such as the Aryan source popularized by the Grimms and their successors; Lang suggested that "the uniformity of human fancy in early societies must be the cause of many other resemblances." It was all possible, but Lang was not fully convinced. "The conclusion which one would draw as a folklorist," he admitted, "is that a certain stock of ideas, partly human and natural, partly concerned with magic and things impossible, has been common to the human race. These ideas may be found anywhere." In that way, Lang's arguments may be seen as aligned to Carl Jung's collective unconsciousness and to Claude Levi-Straus's structuralist studies.

Not surprisingly but predictably, similarities between stories appear from fairy book to fairy book. "A certain number of incidents," Lang explained in *The Grey Fairy*

Book (1900), "are shaken into many varying combinations, like the fragments of coloured glass in the kaleidoscope. Probably the possible combinations, like possible musical combinations, are not unlimited in number, but children may be less sensitive in the matter of fairies than Mr. John Stuart Mill was as regards music." Consequently "The Story of a Gazelle" is a Swahili version of the French "Puss in Boots," the rampion of "Rapunzel" becomes the parsley of "Puddocky," the Serbian "Nine Pea-Hens and the Golden Apples" begins much as does the German "The Golden Bird." But, as Tolkien warned, it is in their very differences that these tales can be most fully appreciated.

Despite Lang's dabbling in folklore, the fairy books do not constitute accurate recordings from oral tradition. These volumes were designed expressly for children. He acknowledged that Mrs. Lang often abridged and simplified, as well as further modified the stories as husband and wife thought appropriate. "The stories are not literal, or word by word translations," he warned in *The Orange Fairy Book*, "but have been altered in many ways to make them suitable for children. . . . In many tales, fairly cruel and savage deeds are done, and these have been softened down as much as possible." The little terrors of folklore may have been acceptable in other ages and to other peoples; he confessed that one narrative "has been altered, and is really much more horrid in the language of the Danes, who, as history tells us, were not a nervous or timid people." But not so the average Victorian child. "When the tales are found," Lang assured nervous mothers in *The Crimson Fairy Book* (1903), "they are adapted to the needs of British children by various hands, the Editor doing little beyond guarding the interests of propriety, and toning down to mild reproofs the tortures inflicted on wicked stepmothers, and other naughty characters." Lang certainly lamented this concession to Mrs. Grundy. He had always hoped to compile a book of the deadliest, creepiest ghost stories he could find. Before the age of twelve, he had loved these harmless tales of horror. "They were a pure joy till bedtime," he recalled in *The Lilac Fairy Book*, "but then, and later, were not wholly a source of unmixed pleasure." He never did collect his "Grey True Ghost-Story Book" because he was afraid not so much of what the children might say but what their mothers might.

Of course Lang's fairy books have had their critics, particularly among folklorists. The strongest contemporary protest came from G. Lawrence Gomme, president of the Folk Lore Society. He did not approve of the inclusion of *kunst-* and *volksmärchen* within the same covers. He did not believe the literary experiments by Andersen, D'Aulnoy, and other writers of fancy were as true as the narratives from folk tradition. But, Lang replied in *The Yellow Fairy Book*, "*we* say that all stories which are pleasant to read are quite true enough for us." He did not intend to, nor succeeded, in misleading children with his charming versions. What Lang did was popularize many tales which otherwise would not be known to modern boys and girls. As his colleague Joseph Jacobs acknowledged, Lang through his fairy books "revived the vogue of the folk-tale among English-speaking children."

Lang's collections contain such a vast, rich feast of the fairy literature of the world that it has been no simple task selecting a precious few of the best examples. Some restrictions have been followed. None of the literary fairy tales, whether by D'Aulnoy, Andersen, or any of the others, have been included; most may be found in other anthologies anyway. The same is true of the traditional tales immortalized by Perrault or the Grimm Brothers. What remains is a selection reflecting the international love for fairy tale. Here may be found princes and princesses, wicked witches and wicked stepmothers, ogres, giants, dragons, mermaids, trolls, gnomes, and fairies, who, if not for Andrew Lang, might have long faded from the collective consciousness of childhood. Here again, as Lang himself said, "are fancies brought from all quarters: we see that black, white, and yellow peoples are fond of just the same kinds of adventures. Courage, youth, beauty, kindness, have many trials, but they always win the battle; while witches, giants, unfriendly cruel people, are on the losing end. So it ought to be, and so, on the whole, it is and will be; and that is all the moral of fairy tales." In preserving these old stories in so enchanting a form, Andrew Lang has earned the eternal gratitude of children.

—*Michael Patrick Hearn*

FAIRY BOOKS BY ANDREW LANG

The Blue Fairy Book, 1889
The Red Fairy Book, 1890
The Green Fairy Book, 1892
The Yellow Fairy Book, 1894
The Pink Fairy Book, 1897
The Grey Fairy Book, 1900
The Violet Fairy Book, 1901
The Crimson Fairy Book, 1903
The Brown Fairy Book, 1904
The Orange Fairy Book, 1906
The Olive Fairy Book, 1907
The Lilac Fairy Book, 1910

BIOGRAPHY AND CRITICISM

Beerbohm, Max. "Two Glimpses of Andrew Lang," *Life and Letters*, London, 1928.

Chesterton, G. K. "Andrew Lang," *The Illustrated London News*, July 27, 1912.

Gosse, Edmund. *Portraits and Sketches*. London, 1912.

Green, Roger Lancelyn. *Andrew Lang, a Critical Biography*. Leicester, England, 1946.

Haggard, H. Rider. *The Days of My Life*. London, 1926.

Jacobs, Joseph. "Andrew Lang as a Man of Letters and Folk-Lorist," *Journal of American Folk-Lore*, 1928.

27 million Americans can't read a bedtime story to a child.

It's because 27 million adults in this country simply can't read.

Functional illiteracy has reached one out of five Americans. It robs them of even the simplest of human pleasures, like reading a fairy tale to a child.

You can change all this by joining the fight against illiteracy.

Call the Coalition for Literacy at toll-free **1-800-228-8813** and volunteer.

Volunteer Against Illiteracy.
The only degree you need is a degree of caring.